STAR TREK
THE NEXT GENERATION®

THE
CONTINUING
MISSION

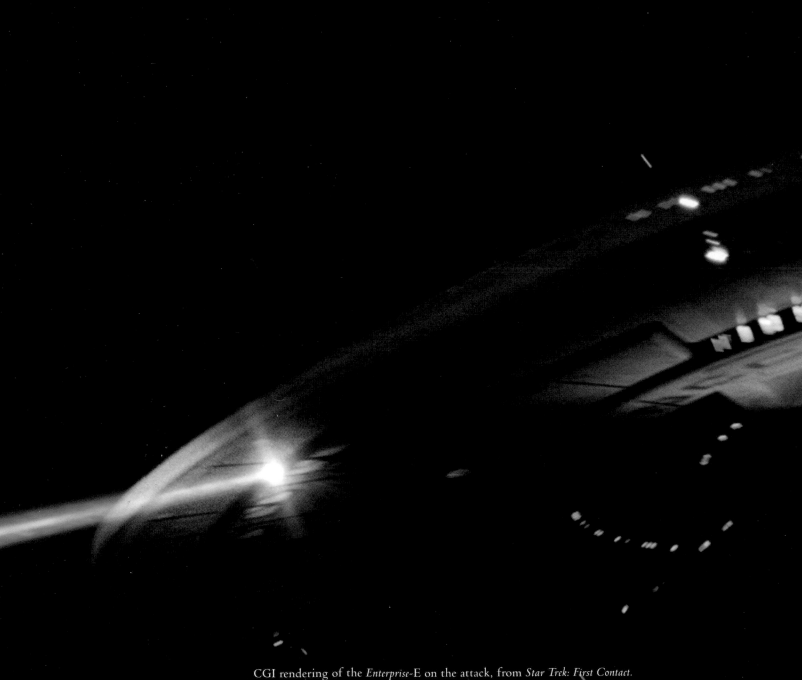

CGI rendering of the *Enterprise*-E on the attack, from *Star Trek: First Contact*.
COURTESY OF INDUSTRIAL LIGHT & MAGIC.

MISSION

A Tenth Anniversary Tribute

Judith & Garfield Reeves-Stevens

Foreword by Rick Berman
Afterword by Robert Justman

POCKET BOOKS

New York   London   Toronto   Sydney   Tokyo   Singapore

Originally developed for dimensional transport studies
at the Banzai Institute, this crucial device has since flown
on Zefram Cochrane's *Phoenix,* and appeared on several
starships and space stations in many different universes.
PHOTOGRAPH BY ROBBIE ROBINSON.

POCKET BOOKS, a division of Simon & Schuster Inc.
1230 Avenue of the Americas, New York, NY 10020

Copyright © 1997, 1998 by Paramount Pictures. All Rights Reserved.

STAR TREK is a Registered Trademark of Paramount Pictures.

ISBN: 0-671-02559-7

First Pocket Books trade paperback printing November 1998

10   9   8   7   6   5   4   3   2   1

POCKET and colophon are registered trademarks of Simon & Schuster Inc.

Book design by Richard Oriolo

Printed in the U.S.A.

Patrick Stewart prepares for the ultimate pullback sequence which opens *First Contact*. ELLIOTT MARKS.

Two ten-year anniversaries are celebrated with this book—the second is our own first contact with Pocket Books in December, 1987, when we suggested we might write a *Star Trek* novel for them. Ten years and eleven—soon to be twelve—fiction and nonfiction projects later, thanks are due the publishing team that has worked so hard and with such enthusiasm and patience to help us bring forth books that are no less a collaborative venture than a television or movie production. So, to Margaret Clark, Carol Greenberg, John Ordover, Richard Oriolo, John Pinella, Kevin Ryan, Dave Stern, and Tyya Turner at Pocket Books, to Paula Block and Harry Lang at Viacom Consumer Products, and to our agents—Laurence Dent, who started us on our *Star Trek* journey, and Richard Curtis, who kept us on course ever since—we dedicate this book with deep appreciation.

"The warning to us to keep our distance—presumably so that we wouldn't interfere with their development ..."

"Where have I heard that idea before? Of course, Frank—it goes back a thousand years—to your own time! 'The Prime Directive'! We still get lots of laughs from those old *Star Trek* programs."

—*ARTHUR C. CLARKE*, 3001: The Final Odyssey

CONTENTS

From *Star Trek: First Contact*, the *Starship Enterprise* blazes
into a temporal vortex above a Borgified Earth.
COURTESY OF INDUSTRIAL LIGHT & MAGIC.

Rick Berman.

FOREWORD

by Rick Berman

Executive Producer, *Star Trek: The Next Generation*

ONE DAY IN early November of 1986, I received a call that I was to meet with Gene Roddenberry the following morning. I had recently been promoted to Vice-President, Longform and Special Projects for Paramount's Television division. I guess somebody figured that a new television series based on *Star Trek* should be categorized as a "special project."

It seemed that Mr. Roddenberry had some points of disagreement regarding a proposed new series and that he wanted to air them at this meeting. I had never met Gene, but he had been pointed out to me during one of his many strolls around the studio. As far as I was concerned, it was just another routine meeting about yet another proposed television series.

When I arrived at the meeting, Gene's office was filled with a number of high-ranking studio executives. Gene didn't want to do whatever they were proposing. Gene pounded the desk and the executives pounded back. Gene raised his voice and the executives raised theirs even louder. In the midst of all this pounding and shouting, I sat with my mouth shut.

It wasn't that I had chosen this as a tactic, it was simply that I had no idea what they were talking about. But I clearly remember that on at least two occasions during that meeting, Gene's eyes locked on to mine for an instant and I responded with a slightly mischievous smile. Later, Gene Roddenberry would tell me how that smile was filled with subtext ... that I was really saying, "Can you believe what assholes these guys are?" While this interpretation of my facial expression put me in good standing with my soon-to-be employer and mentor, I actually believe it was nothing more than a slightly mischievous smile. Nevertheless, this occasion turned out to be anything but another routine meeting about yet another proposed television series.

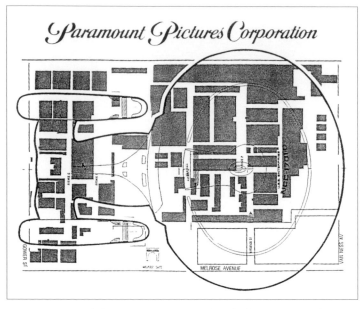

Exact size of the *Enterprise* compared with the Paramount lot.

The next morning I received a call asking me to join Gene for lunch. We sat in the commissary and spoke of everything *but Star Trek,* which was fine with me because I knew very little about it. Instead, Gene spoke of his travels, his days in the army, and his days as an airline pilot. He was fascinated that I had spent most of the seventies traveling the world as a documentary filmmaker. In a playfully challenging moment, he asked me, "What's the capital of Upper Volta?" I politely corrected him, explaining that the country in question was now called Burkina Faso and that the capital was still Ouagadougou. I also pointed out that I had actually been there once. Now it was my chance to see a mischievous twinkle in *his* eye. It was love at second sight and we both knew it.

The next day, I received a call from Gene's attorney and close friend, Leonard Maizlish, asking me to join *him* for lunch. I already had a lunch date, but something told me to cancel it. Sitting at the same table in the Paramount commissary, Leonard informed me that Gene wanted me to resign from my position with the studio and join him and his team as a producer on the new series. As I walked back to my office I clearly remember saying to myself, 'This is crazy. The project has three strikes against it already. 1. It's science fiction and nobody is doing science fiction. 2. It's a sequel and sequels never work. 3. Instead of putting it on a network, they wanted to syndicate it ... and who ever heard of a successful syndicated television drama?" With all that said (or thought), I reached my office and immediately called my wife, Elizabeth, to tell her I was quitting my job and taking the plunge back into production, where I had happily been for all but the previous two years of my career. The job offered far less security, but it was where I belonged and we both knew it.

Now, nearly eleven years later, I look back and smile, realizing how little I knew at the time about the adventures and responsibilities I was about to undertake.

In Hollywood, "numbers" is the name of the game. Box-office gross, adjusted net, households using television, ratings, shares ... bigger is better. More is merrier. But while numbers serve a purpose, they are rarely what they appear to be. *Star Trek: The Next Generation, Deep Space Nine,* or *Voyager* may not garner as large an audience as *Seinfeld* or *Friends,* and *First Contact* may never reach the worldwide grosses of *Space Jam* or *Independence Day,* but *Star Trek* very often has a far greater impact on its viewers than these blockbusters. As a result, the satisfaction level for me and my colleagues is immeasurable.

There are many kinds of satisfaction that I get from my job. The joy of being involved with a remarkably talented group of people ... the sense of completion that comes with having a hand in each facet of a project, from the story stage through to the scoring stage ... the sheer pleasure of turning out quality television and motion pictures. But none of these match the wonder I experience each time I hear how *Star Trek* makes people think! I continually receive letters from viewers who have been stimulated and provoked by an episode; or from families who find that watching and discussing *Star Trek* is often the only chance they get to really be together. Even more satisfying are the letters that speak of people who have begun to overcome different kinds of adversities as the result of a specific theme or metaphor they drew from a particular episode.

With this sense of satisfaction comes a deep-rooted sense of responsibility. When people watch a television show not only to be entertained, but to be provoked into thinking about the world around them, it becomes my responsibility, as well as my colleagues', to think long and hard about just what ideas we should present. When the audience looks toward our shows for a hopeful, uplifting sense of what's to come, it becomes a serious job to decide what that future will hold. So when it comes to ratings vs. content, I'll take the latter every time. Quality over quantity ... a cornerstone of Gene Roddenberry's legacy that I've never ignored.

Soon after those early meetings with Gene, I found that the strongest bond forming between us was our shared sense of wonder. I may not have known a lot about *Star Trek,* but I had spent fifteen years as a documentary filmmaker working in over ninety countries. Gene, too, was fascinated by faraway places with strange-sounding names. But as I was soon to learn, his concept of exploration was far more complex than mine. His sense of wonder wasn't limited to the past and present, as mine was. He saw the future as a vast empty canvas upon which he could create images of hope. Luckily, he was able to see broader possibilities within *my* Earthbound imagination. Within the first year of working with Gene, I began to understand the limitless possibilities humanity might have in store. It was his job (and eventually mine and many others') to hypothesize about what *might* be. To create a twenty-fourth century that could spark the imagination of tens of millions of viewers around the world. A vision of possibilities and hope.

Gene Roddenberry saw humanity as an evolving species that was going to keep getting better and better. He believed that the future was something to look forward to and that the exploration of space and the development of a better quality of life were goals humanity was going to pursue. His vision of tolerance and cooperation among all beings gave a further sense of hope to a lot of people. It also did a good job of entertaining them.

After nearly eleven years, I realize I've learned a new language. It's not really surprising when you think about it. If you drop someone in the middle of Madrid, sooner or later they're going to learn Spanish. I was dropped in the middle of *Star Trek* and had to learn its vocabulary, its meaning, and its rules. As we approach our four hundredth episode, I'm often asked how we can continue to follow Gene's rules and still keep the shows fresh. The answer is somewhat of a paradox. *We must change it while keeping it the same.* In the world of *Star Trek,* rules were *not* made to be broken. But they *were* made to be bent. Gene would be the first to agree. So my job also includes monitoring the "degree of bend" ... letting the shows and the films evolve, but keeping Gene's vision true to course. I'm not quite fluent yet, but I'm getting there.

When *Star Trek: The Next Generation* first aired, in 1987, with the episode "Encounter at Farpoint," it was the beginning of a journey of exploration ... for Picard and his crew, and also for me. My life was about to change in remarkable ways. I would soon undertake a progression of steps ... a process of learning about *Star Trek,* but, more important, a process of learning how to open my mind and my imagination to the limitless possibilities of Gene Roddenberry's vision. At this tenth anniversary of *The Next Generation,* I'm confident that *Star Trek* will continue to positively affect tens of millions of people, and that there will be many more decade marks to be celebrated.

Rick Berman
Los Angeles, CA

BRIDGE 9.

MONITORS —
WOULD LAY FLUSH WITH
THE TABLE TOP UNTIL NEEDED —

A preliminary bridge concept for the *Starship Enterprise*, dated December 4, 1986,
reflecting the idea that the starship's computer is so advanced that everything is run
by voice control, requiring no operational crew. This approach was considered too
advanced for the 24th century, at least, by 20th-century standards.
COURTESY OF THE ARTIST.

INTRODUCTION

100 Years of Star Trek

LESS THAN SEVEN decades from now, on September 8, 2066, *Star Trek* will celebrate its hundredth anniversary. On that day, on whatever communications system has supplanted twentieth-century television as a medium of entertainment, the images of Captains Kirk, Picard, Sisko, and Janeway will flicker once more, no doubt accompanied by other characters not yet created, perhaps brought to life by actors not yet born.

Some in the audience of that day will smile at the primitive nature of the visual effects, even those of the currently unmade ninth and tenth films, which will usher *Star Trek* into the twenty-first century. Some in the audience will shake their heads in wonder at how many obvious aspects of future technology the series failed to anticipate. Perhaps others will be surprised by how close the series came to predicting other advances. And some will altogether reject watching two-dimensional video images, and instead will prefer to don neural inputs to experience those episodes converted into three-dimensional virtual reality, ignoring the indignant objections recorded by long-dead directors who claimed the episodes were never intended to be viewed that way.

Whatever the technology and the audience of that future, we are confident that *Star Trek* will survive in some form, as curious footnote or ongoing franchise, and will be celebrated on that day. We are also confident that some of the people in that audience will be watching the *Star Trek* hundredth-anniversary specials in habitats orbiting the Earth, perhaps even in outposts on the moon or Mars. And we hope those people realize that they are, in a way, the children of *Star Trek*. Just as the first flights to the moon were conceived and realized by scientists and engineers inspired by the science fiction of an earlier age,

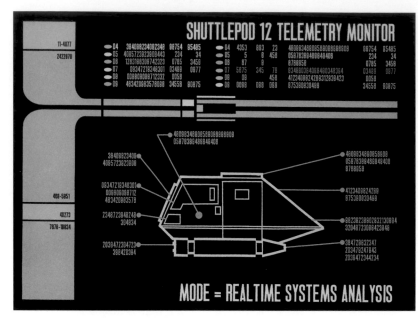

Before actual computer monitor screens were incorporated into some of *The Next Generation*'s sets, most computer displays were created by back-lighting pieces of negative film to which transparent colored gels were attached. This display screen shows the status of the second-season shuttlepod from "Time Squared."

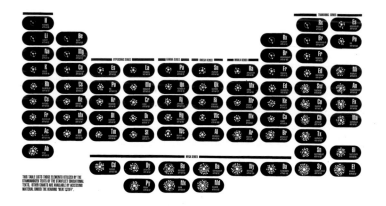

An idiosyncratic 24th-century periodic table, glimpsed in the sixth-season episode "Rascals."

From the beginning, Gene Roddenberry sought to make the *Star Trek* universe a believable and self-consistent reality. Throughout the production of *The Next Generation*, Michael Okuda and a dedicated art department helped fulfill Roddenberry's goal by creating literally tens of thousands of meticulously crafted images to establish an indelible, instantly recognizable vision of the information-rich environment of the 24th century. These images, some of which are featured throughout this book, came to be known as Okudagrams.

COURTESY OF PARAMOUNT.

the space missions and technology of the next seven decades will arise from generations who have grown up inspired by *Star Trek*.

Even now, barely thirty years on, that influence is already apparent, in everything from Motorola's cellular flip-phones to space-shuttle mission specialist Mae Jemison. The first person to walk on Mars is already alive and growing up in a world where *Star Trek* is no longer a mere entertainment franchise, but a cultural icon. When that person takes her or his first footsteps on Mars, the story of *Star Trek* will be mentioned as often as the works of Ray Bradbury, Robert Heinlein, and Edgar Rice Burroughs, as one of the sources of inspiration that helped impel humanity to travel to another world.

But the audiences of 2066 will not be watching their *Star Trek* specials simply to be amused by their ancestors' primitive under-takings, nor to feel nostalgic for what they will no doubt see as the innocence and sim-plicity of life in the late, uncomplicated twen-tieth-century. And unlike today's *Star Trek* audience, they will not be watching to learn about their future. With history as our guide, there is no doubt the challenges of the late twenty-first century will include some that none of us can even imagine here at the close of the twentieth.

Instead, our descendants, of flesh and blood, perhaps even of circuitry, will watch *Star Trek* to learn of their *past*. Because, no mat-ter how far in the future it's projected, no matter what alien vistas serve as its setting, the best science fiction is always about the people, events, and beliefs of the time in which it is written.

Star Trek is no exception.

For the audience of 2066, the episodes and specials and "best-of" clip shows they'll watch will show them *us*, in *our* world, *today*, perhaps not as we are, but—far more impor-tant—as we aspire to be.

In episodes, *Star Trek: The Original Series* will show them the dreams of the 1960s and, in films, the dreams of the seventies and early eighties. Then, *Star Trek: The Next Generation* will show them how those dreams matured and were re-formed to direct us into the next century, accompanied, for now, by that series' own children—*Star Trek: Deep Space Nine* and *Star Trek: Voyager.*

It is for that unborn audience, almost seventy years from now, that we write this book. It will be only one of many available to them, because unquestionably others will come after this. As we have found from our own investigations of other, earlier versions of *Star Trek,* as time passes for the participants, the need for political correctness and masking platitudes becomes diminished, memories become sharper, and the need to set the record straight intensifies. Those books to come, some no doubt to be written by the actors, producers, writers, artists, and crew who appear in these pages, will clarify uncertainties we have not noticed or can only mention in passing, correct any inaccuracies that might have built up in *Star Trek* folklore, and look back at the past with clearer eyes and more insight than any writer could have at this time, so close to the source.

But until enough years have passed so that those other books can be written, on the occasion of *Star Trek: The Next Generation*'s tenth anniversary, we hope this work will stand as a way station in the series' history, one stage in the continuing mission to a twentieth, thirtieth, even centennial anniversary of the series' own.

This book, then, is not an analysis of starship technology or Klingon sociology, but the story of the people who came together in 1986, who took from *The Original Series* the core elements that make *Star Trek* such a powerful, compelling, and timeless metaphor for our dreams, and launched, to coin a phrase, a bold new enterprise of their own. And it is the story of all the others who have come aboard since then, each contributing in ways small and large, to keep *Star Trek: The Next Generation* a constantly evolving reflection of the changing aspirations of their era.

It is a fond memory of what was, a celebration of what is, and a time capsule for what is still to come. And with that note of optimism—that core *Star Trek* belief that there *is* more to come which will be better than today—we start this story by returning to where it all began.

To *Star Trek*'s first and original creator, Gene Roddenberry.

ONE

RODDENBERRY'S REVENGE

The First Twenty Years

To KNOW HIM was to be passionate about him, either for or against. As is the case for many creative, driven, visionary people, there was little room for middle ground in how Gene Roddenberry was perceived. That such a dichotomy exists is no surprise in Hollywood. It is a truism that producers are never anyone's friend when they're producers. They become, instead, a driven machine that *has* to get a show on the air, no matter the casualties left by the side of the road. In the high-pressure environment of television and movie production, a producer's personal relationships with those who work with him almost inevitably become strained, especially when decisions regarding money, creative input, and credit must be made, often strictly for reasons of business and personal career management. In the course of his life, like any other producer, Roddenberry made his share of tough decisions, and in true Hollywood fashion, some friendships were strengthened by them, and some crumbled.

Tellingly, though, whether their relationship with him was one of love or hate, what almost everyone agrees with is that Roddenberry was indeed a man of vision.

As *Star Trek* scripter, television writer, and novelist David Gerrold describes him, "Gene's first strength was that he could inspire people. He could get people to do what needed to be done. His second great skill was that he could 'speak' a vision of what the show should be. He'd get writers in there and he'd say, 'I want you to tell me a story that no one else will let you tell, that thing that sticks in your craw, and you just have to say it.' Writers would get so inspired by hearing that speech that they would come in and write stories that were better than they were capable of. And his best skill of all, and he never knew what a skill it was, was he could pick brilliant people."

What Gerrold has described is the perfect portrait of the skills a successful producer must have, and a successful producer is exactly what Gene Roddenberry was. But before he was a producer, Roddenberry had begun his Hollywood career as a writer, and in the tradition of the great writers of television's Golden Era, writing was not Roddenberry's first job.

He had been a bomber pilot in World War II, and a pilot for Pan Am in the years following. Writing was a dream he had always nurtured, along with his love of science fiction. But it was not until 1948, at the age of twenty-seven, that Roddenberry came to Los Angeles to pursue a career as a television writer.

Again, as for most writers, success did not come immediately, and within six months of arriving in LA, Roddenberry sought a more secure job by joining the Los Angeles Police Department. However, he held himself to a self-imposed schedule of writing, including composing articles for the LAPD's own internal magazine, and his police experience later became his first entree into the field of television writing when he began selling stories to Jack Webb's production company to be used as the basis for episodes of *Dragnet*.

Fortunately, Roddenberry did not keep his writing aspirations hidden from his friends on the force. In 1953, when his captain was contacted about the LAPD providing a technical consultant for the series *Mr. District Attorney*, Roddenberry was given the assignment. Ever ready to recognize an opportunity, after studying the show he quickly made his first script sale to the producer.

More sales followed, and just over two years later, Roddenberry made the momentous decision to resign from the LAPD and become a full-time writer.

Sales continued to a variety of series—*I Led Three Lives, Highway Patrol, The West Side Story, Bat Masterson,* and twenty-four episodes of *Have Gun Will Travel,* of which one, "Helen of Abajinian," won the prestigious Writers' Guild Award for 1957.

By 1960, Roddenberry had what's called a development deal at Screen Gems to create pilots for new series. In September 1963, his first "created by" credit appeared, on the NBC series *The Lieutenant.* Then, in September 1966, barely ten years after his decision to pursue writing full-time, the first episode of the series destined to earn a permanent place in the culture of the twentieth century—and of grossing more than $2 billion according to *Entertainment Weekly*[4]—aired on the same network.

Star Trek was born.

Three years later it was dead.

In television terms, a failure.

But, as the Klingons say, *bortaS blr jablu'Dl'reH QaQqu' nay'*. Revenge is a dish which is best served cold. Roddenberry's ultimate revenge, decades later, would be positively subarctic.

Star Trek folklore maintains that the year after NBC canceled the series, the networks changed their system of measuring ratings from one in which the total number of viewers mattered, to one in which the *composition* of the audience was assessed. In analyzing the data which showed that *Star Trek* had enjoyed a strong following among young males, one of the advertising industry's most avidly sought group of consumers, an NBC executive is reported to have said that if the network had based its decisions on demographics one year earlier, *Star Trek* would never have been canceled.

But *Star Trek's* appeal to a young and growing market did not remain hidden. What had been deemed a failure on network television became a sensation in the syndication market. Airing on independent stations, or in non-prime-time hours, the series that had been ahead of its time had a second chance to find its audience. And that audience grew larger and more appreciative each season.

In the years that followed *Star Trek's* cancellation, Roddenberry worked hard to develop new series, especially in the realm of science fiction. Two-hour television movies, produced as "backdoor pilots," were made for *The Questor Tapes* and *Spectre*. As was done for the original *Star Trek,* two different television movie/pilot episodes were made from the same starting premise—as *Genesis II* and *Planet Earth.* But success in television can be fickle, and none of these new series was picked up.

Roddenberry himself recalled the 1970s as lean years. He often told the story that, at one point in that period, he could have purchased all rights to *Star Trek* for only $100,000—at the time a sum he could not come close to raising. But during those lean seventies, Roddenberry found he could augment his income by making appearances at a rapidly growing phenomenon—*Star Trek* conventions.

These gatherings of devoted fans of the series had spun off from science-fiction conventions and, in the years following the series' cancellation, they acquired a life of their own. It was in these conventions that the seeds of *Star Trek's* rebirth were sown.

Paramount Pictures is the studio that acquired the rights to *Star Trek* when it purchased Desilu, the company that had produced *The Original Series.* Paramount executives, inspired by the turnout of fans at *Star Trek* conventions, and by the stellar syndication ratings, knew that the property had market appeal. Over many years, several attempts were made to bring the series back. In 1972, an animated series continuing the adventures of Kirk's *Starship Enterprise* was produced in conjunction with Filmation, with Roddenberry as executive consultant. Though the twenty-two episodes do not hold up to today's animation standards, they were critically acclaimed at the time.

After the animated series, several attempts to produce a *Star Trek* movie proved little more than false starts. Paramount provided Roddenberry with an office on the lot, yet rejected not only his movie scripts, but those of other writers as well.

Finally, in 1977, a business decision by Paramount Chairman and CEO Barry Diller led to *Star Trek's* near-revival on television. As the main offering of what would have been a fourth television network—PTS, the Paramount Television Service—Paramount announced that it would produce *Star Trek: Phase II,* a one-hour, live-action series that would reunite all the original cast, except for Leonard Nimoy as Spock, to present the stories of Kirk's *second* five-year mission on the *U.S.S. Enterprise.*

With Roddenberry as producer, along with new producers Harold Livingston and *The X-Files'* Robert Goodwin, a technical crew was assembled, writers hired, sets designed, and construction of a new *Enterprise* model begun.

But within six weeks of Paramount's PTS announcement, it was clear that Barry Diller, who would later create the Fox Broadcasting Network, was, like *Star Trek,* ahead of his time. In 1977, the available advertising revenue would not support another network. PTS folded before it had begun. If Paramount did make *Phase II,* it would have nowhere to show it.

Michael Eisner, Paramount's president and chief operating officer, destined to achieve fame as the Disney Company's acclaimed CEO, is credited with making the decision to salvage the project—and

Star Trek—by changing *Phase II*'s two-hour pilot episode, "In Thy Image," from a television production to a film.

Two years later, *Star Trek: The Motion Picture* opened to mixed reviews and phenomenal success. Though the unique burdens of its troubled production added to its overall budget and prevented it from becoming a highly profitable film, it was a solid hit with the public.

Thus, like any business responsible to its shareholders, Paramount was determined to duplicate that success, but without revisiting any of the expensive lessons it had learned in the movie's production. The studio's first task was to insure that those people it perceived as being responsible for *The Motion Picture*'s shortcomings would not be involved in a second film.

At this point, it is instructive to remember that the culture of Hollywood is such that when five superlative directors or writers or actors are called out of a field of hundreds or thousands by the American Motion Picture Academy of Arts and Sciences, and given the honor of being nominated for an Oscar, the media and the public invariably label the four distinguished, remarkable, and talented people who subsequently are not awarded the Oscar, 'losers.' It's as if a medical school awarded a degree only to the one student with the highest marks, and expelled everyone else.

With that example of Hollywood "think" in mind, it is easier to understand how Paramount executives could come to consider Gene Roddenberry's involvement in the production of new *Star Trek* movies as something less than an asset. The first title cards for *Star Trek: The Motion Picture* had read: *Paramount Pictures Presents ... A Gene Roddenberry Production.* A later card read: *Produced by Gene Roddenberry.* The movie had been expensive, late, and troubled during production.

Thus, when *Star Trek II: The Wrath of Khan* was released in 1982, Roddenberry's title card reflected the new role he had been forced to accept—*Executive Consultant.* He had lost control of his own creation.

To be fair, movies are different from television. Successful writer-producers are rare in either field, but it is even more unheard of for one to cross from television to movies and do equally well in both arenas. Roddenberry was not abandoned by Paramount, though technically and legally the studio had that right. Instead, he was placed in a position in which he could be privy to every detail of the ongoing production of new *Star Trek* films, and be free to offer his comments, criticism, and praise for every aspect of their production. The only catch was that Paramount was under no binding obligation to act on any of Roddenberry's comments.

Some people have speculated that Roddenberry was placed in this position by a studio that didn't want to alienate *Star Trek*'s fan base. But even in the early eighties, the number of people who were devoted *Star Trek* fans—that is, those who regularly attended conventions and purchased the memorabilia—was a small, almost statistically insignificant percentage of the total number of people who purchased a *Star Trek* movie ticket. If every devoted fan had steadfastly boycotted a new *Star Trek* film, there might have been some publicity about that decision—publicity which Paramount might wish to avoid—but box-office results would have barely reflected the fans' absence.

The real reason for Paramount's concern about keeping Roddenberry tied to each *Star Trek* film was that every executive involved with the productions shared the maddening knowledge that no one had the slightest idea why *Star Trek* was a success ... except Gene Roddenberry. Without his input, there was always the chance that the next movie wouldn't capture whatever it was that made *Star Trek* so enticing.

Thus, with each new movie Roddenberry dispensed his opinions about the script. Sometimes he liked what was proposed, sometimes he was critical. Sometimes his suggestions and notes were incorporated into the final draft, sometimes they were not. Although Paramount clearly felt that Roddenberry's opinions, insights, and experience were useful for *Star Trek,* Roddenberry's ongoing role in his creation had been severely diminished. Then came 1986, *Star Trek*'s twentieth-anniversary year.

After two decades, it was obvious to everyone that *Star Trek* was more than just an entertainment property with market appeal. It was a phenomenon. As always, Paramount sought to expand *Star Trek*'s success into new areas, and television once again became an area of investigation, not only because the syndicated market had grown since *The Original Series'* cancellation, but because the

stations having such success with those twenty-year-old episodes were constantly asking Paramount to produce more.

Though *Star Trek IV: The Voyage Home* was not scheduled to be released until Thanksgiving, by early 1986 Paramount executives knew they had another *Star Trek* hit on their hands and began serious discussions about how to bring the franchise back to television.

The major challenge the studio faced was that some of the principal cast members of *The Original Series* had gone on to other, lucrative careers. After receiving substantial sums to appear in a single movie once every two years, it would be unlikely that they could be lured back to the grueling world of weekly television production for a fraction of their movie paychecks.

Thus, instead of remaking or continuing *The Original Series,* the idea of making a sequel with a new crew emerged as the most promising way to proceed.

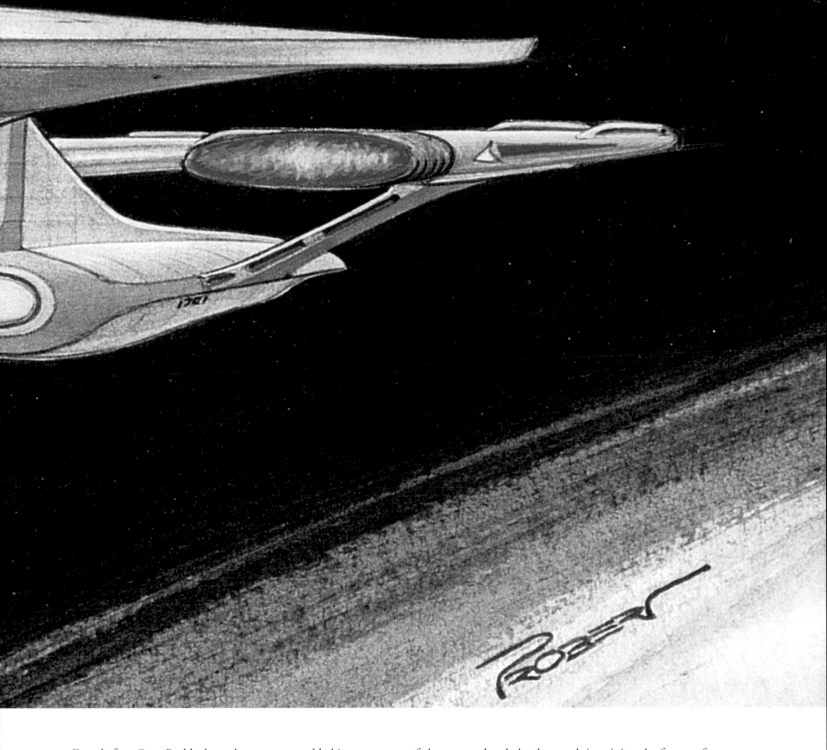

Even before Gene Roddenberry began to assemble his team, some of them were already hard at work imagining the future of *Star Trek*. Andrew Probert painted this illustration of a future starship concept for his own enjoyment, creating a preliminary visual direction for what would be his distinctive design of the *Enterprise*-D. Another early sketch by Probert (shown on pages 8 and 9), was on the wall in his office at Paramount. Writer David Gerrold saw the sketch and took it to Roddenberry who approved it as the starting point. COURTESY OF THE ARTIST.

The question then became, To which broadcaster would Paramount sell the new series? Each network, and there were four now, was interested—why wouldn't they be? But it was with Fox that Paramount actually began preliminary negotiations in the summer of '86.

Paramount knew how valuable *Star Trek* was, if only as a movie series, and the studio executives wanted to protect any new version of the show as much as possible. Thus they had set as their initial conditions that any broadcaster wanting the new show must commit to a full season's order of twenty-six episodes, with a guarantee that either the episodes would never be preempted or that the broadcaster would run a major promotional campaign to support the series. In return, the broadcaster would receive half-interest in the series, which was projected to have the same success in syndication that *The Original Series* had.

But Fox executives had to be just as responsible to their shareholders as the Paramount executives were to theirs. What if the revival, without Kirk, Spock, and McCoy, wasn't successful? Without the ability to cancel the new series, Fox was facing a full year of advertising losses, to say nothing of the per-episode license fee it would pay Paramount to produce the show.

On August 6, *USA Today* reported that Fox executives could not bring themselves to commit to Paramount's requested guarantees. As Mel Harris, president of Paramount Television Group, later said in an interview in the *New York Times,* on November 2, 1986, "We realized that nobody else was going to care as much about *Star Trek* as we did."

So Paramount made a cautious, though reasonable business decision. The studio would produce the new series by itself, then syndicate the new episodes to the same stations currently running *The Original Series* episodes. The risk they faced was that there was no broadcaster to cover part of the production cost with a license fee. But the potential payoff was that if the series was successful, Paramount would have no partner with which it would have to share any potential profits.

The heart of Paramount's gamble was what's termed "deficit financing." Simply put, it generally costs more to produce an hour-long episode of a television series than a network will pay to run it. Thus, the production company, Paramount, for example, covers the shortfall out of its own funds, hoping to recoup that money—and much more—when the series is eventually sold for syndication. And Paramount had a good idea what an episode of a *Star Trek* series was worth in syndication.

The Original Series' episodes, which in the mid-sixties had cost, on average, from almost $200,000[1] each to make in the first season, to just under $180,000[1] in the third, had earned back more than $1 million each in syndication fees[2], despite being two decades old. New episodes, which hadn't been rerun uncountable times, would be considerably more valuable, even with a projected 1986 budget of, on average, $1.2 million per episode[2].

But though Paramount was willing to make up the deficit between that $1.2 million per episode and the $400,000 to $500,000 a network might pay as a licensing fee, a half-season order of thirteen episodes, which is what Fox wanted to commit to, wasn't large enough. To be successful in later syndication, a series generally needs sixty-five episodes available, which allows stations to "strip" a series—that is, show a different episode each weekday for thirteen weeks.

A sixty-five-episode commitment—which at $1.2 million per episode came to $78 million—was something not even Paramount was willing to make. So, with the studio's decision to make the series on its own, a two-part strategy was mapped out.

First of all, to make the new and unproven series as attractive as possible to individual stations, Paramount would not charge any up-front cash payments to show the episodes. Instead, Paramount would offer the series on an "all-barter" basis. That is, in exchange for receiving the right to run the series for free, stations would allow Paramount to control seven minutes of commercial time in each episode. Paramount would make its money by selling those commercial slots to national advertisers. Each station would make its money by selling the remaining five minutes to local advertisers. The only party that could lose in such a situation was Paramount, which, at $1.2 million per episode, was committing more than $30 million of shareholder money with the realistic expectation of earning back just over half that amount from advertising sales[2]. Even factoring in the expected 6.5-million-dollar earnings from foreign and home-video rights[2], the total deficit in the first season of the new series was projected to be $7 million. Studio executives have been known to lose their jobs over much smaller losses. As Rick Berman later said, at the time, in financial terms, the series represented "a considerable risk" to the studio.

However, Paramount, with its extensive *Star Trek* experience, had a unique safety net to protect itself from that potential financial loss. If after thirteen episodes had been made it was clear that the series was not viable, the studio was prepared to cut its losses and stop production. Then, even though thirteen episodes were not nearly enough to guarantee success in the syndication market, they would be packaged with the seventy-nine *Original Series* episodes that were always in constant demand. In other words, if a station wanted to syndicate the original *Star Trek,* it would have to purchase the rights to the new *Star Trek* as well—they wouldn't be able to buy one without the other.

The bottom line was that, in terms of responsible financial planning, the failure of a new *Star Trek* series might be embarrassing, but at least it wouldn't be disastrous. With the studio's projected investment protected, the purely business decision was made to proceed. By August, 1986, a new *Star Trek* series was, unofficially at least, a "go."

Paramount executives were enthusiastic enough about the return of *Star Trek* to television that they originally planned to announce the new series to the two thousand guests who would attend the twentieth-anniversary party on September 8, 1986. Only at the last minute did someone realize that such an announcement might prove embarrassing to the *Original Series* cast members who would be present, and who would soon be expected to begin traveling the country to promote *Star Trek IV.*

One last detail remained: the prospect of Gene Roddenberry's involvement. Paramount executives had already mentioned to Roddenberry the possibility of a new series, but up to this point Roddenberry had not responded favorably, resisting any proposal that he felt might dilute the appeal of the original *Star Trek.*

However, on Friday, September 12, 1986, just four days after the party, the president of Paramount Television, John Pike, sent Roddenberry a copy of the studio's initial approach to a new *Star Trek* series, which would place the *Starship Enterprise* in the hands of a crew of Starfleet cadets.

Roddenberry replied with five pages of notes, mostly negative.

But intentionally or not, Paramount had laid down the challenge to Roddenberry by showing him that though they would prefer to have him involved with the new series, they were ready to proceed without him.

The executives were not unrealistic enough to claim that a new series was a certain success—the extent of their financial contingency plans proved the seriousness of their concerns. Indeed, they let Roddenberry know, there was a good chance that the magic of *Star Trek* could never be repeated, even with his involvement. Ironically, it was that reservation on Paramount's part, that perhaps *Star Trek*'s success could *never* be duplicated, that reportedly compelled Roddenberry to finally make his decision.

Roddenberry's initial reluctance to become involved with the new series earlier that year was understandable. Creative concerns aside, he knew firsthand the strenuous demands of television production, and he was now sixty-four, an age when most people contemplated a peaceful retirement.

But the challenge he had been offered was, in the end, impossible to refuse—an appropriate state of affairs considering it came from the studio that had made the *Godfather* films.

Roddenberry had created the original *Star Trek.* He had shepherded his creation from television into what would become a successful series of films. Then he had been relegated to a mere consultant's role.

But now he was being offered a way back, a way to regain control of the universe he had brought forth, and a way to improve on his own original concept and prove that his creation of *Star Trek* was not a once-in-a-lifetime fluke.

Leonard Nimoy later said that any attempt to recapture the success of the original *Star Trek* would be like trying to capture lightning in a bottle.

But twenty years earlier, Gene Roddenberry had already proved himself to be one of those rare creative lightning rods.

Now, drawing on what David Gerrold referred to as his greatest skill, Roddenberry readied himself to face the first task of his new endeavor: to once again call that lightning to him by assembling his team.

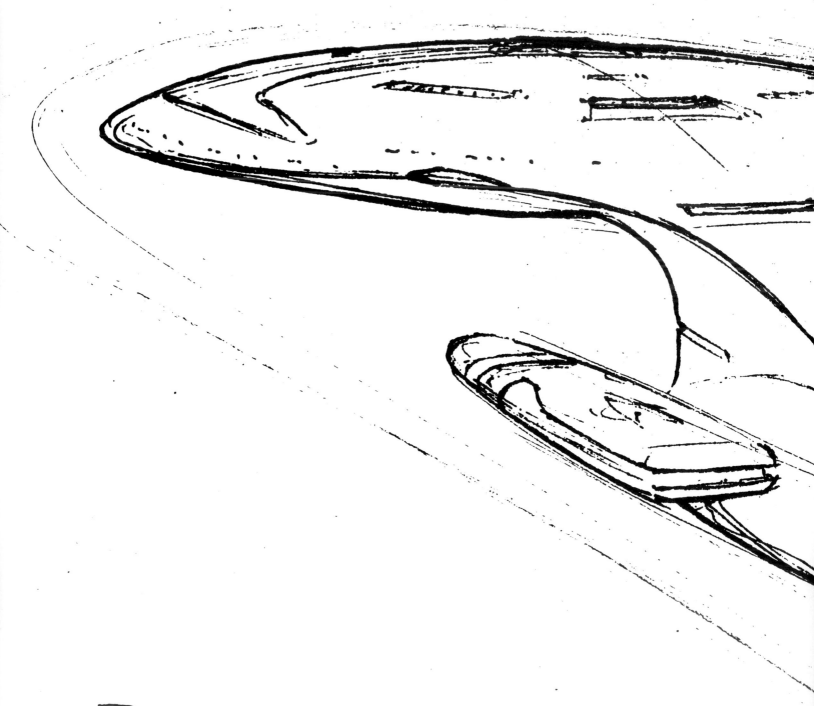

PROBERT 120186

T HE first to join Roddenberry's team were Robert H. Justman, Edward K. Milkis, and David Gerrold. Though in this instance it was more a case of *re*joining, for each of these people had played memorable roles in the production of *The Original Series*.

Bob Justman began his film career in 1950, working as a fifty-dollar-a-week "gofer" on independent films. In 1953, the same year Roddenberry had made his first television script sale, Justman moved to major films as an assistant director working for noted director Robert Aldrich on movies including *Apache,* with Burt Lancaster, *The Big Knife,* with Rod Steiger and Shelly Winters, and the 1955 production of Mickey Spillane's *Kiss Me Deadly,* an acclaimed film considered to be years ahead of its time, and which

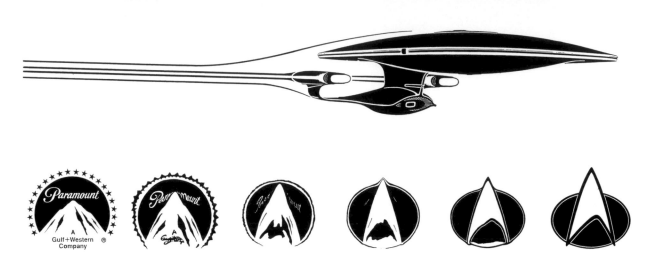

Three illustrations by Andrew Probert, prepared for *The Next Generation*'s Writers/Directors Guide, also known as the show's "bible." Though this art locked in the look of the series' logo, the section showing the Paramount logo morphing into the *Star Trek* delta was never used. COURTESY OF THE ARTIST.

exerted a strong influence on the French "New Wave" directors of the 1960s.

Justman eventually moved into the television industry, where he worked on a variety of series, including *The Adventures of Superman, The Thin Man,* and the groundbreaking science-fiction series, *The Outer Limits.*

Justman began his association with *Star Trek* as assistant director on the two pilots that were made for *The Original Series.* Then, when *Star Trek* began full production, he became the series' associate producer, and, by the third season, co-producer. Since the first series' cancellation, he had gone on to produce many other television projects, including the series, *Then Came Bronson* and *The Man from Atlantis.* He also produced *Planet Earth,* Gene Roddenberry's two-hour science-fiction pilot for Warner Bros.

By the fall of 1986, with more than thirty-five feature-film projects and five hundred television episodes, pilots, and movies to his credit, Justman, like Roddenberry, had been thinking of slowing down the pace of his work. He had gone as far as promising himself that he would never again produce a television series. But when Roddenberry called him that September to screen some science-fiction films with him, Justman found himself facing the same challenge Paramount had laid down for Roddenberry, and he had the same reaction—he wanted another crack at *Star Trek* if only to prove that a *Star Trek* television series could be a success after all.

Joining Roddenberry and Justman for those screenings was Edward K. Milkis. Milkis had also been associate producer on *The Original Series* and had gone on to produce feature films including *Silver Streak,* with Richard Pryor, *Foul Play,* with Goldie Hawn, and several hit television series including *Happy Days, Laverne and Shirley, Bosom Buddies,* and *Mork and Mindy.* In October 1986, Milkis was already under contract to Paramount as a producer, so it was a simple matter to add his expertise to the mix.

As Justman and Milkis joined Roddenberry in the screening room to watch the newest, cutting-edge science-fiction films, among them *Aliens* and *Blade Runner,* Paramount once more prepared to make the public announcement of *Star Trek*'s return to television, this time guided by Gene Roddenberry, not as a consultant, but as executive producer.

The news was officially released by the president of the Paramount Television Group, Mel Harris, on Friday, October 10, 1986. "Twenty years ago," Harris's statement began, "the genius of one man brought to television a program that has transcended the medium. We are enormously pleased that that man, Gene Roddenberry, is going to do it again. Just as public demand kept *The Original Series* on the air, this new series is also a result of grassroots support for Roddenberry and his vision."

Paramount's decision to employ Roddenberry as executive producer of the new series was not a change of direction for the studio. Roddenberry would continue to function as a consultant on future films, because his role and experience in that medium were limited. But in the area of television production, Roddenberry had long ago proven himself, and his capabilities in that medium were respected. True, he was older and, as many people have noted, his health was failing to the point where there were some concerns about his ability to keep pace with the duties of an executive producer. But with Justman and Milkis at his side as supervising producers, everyone was confident that Roddenberry would be the closest thing they could get to a guarantee that lightning would strike twice.

That October, with a financial plan in place, an official announcement made public, and producers hired, there was just one more key part of the equation to be put in place ...

What the heck was this new *Star Trek* series going to be about, anyway?

That decision—or, to be exact, that ongoing series of decisions—would ultimately be up to Gene Roddenberry. Which brings us to an important consideration—perhaps *the* most important consideration in the television industry: What does it mean to create a television series?

At one level, the act of artistic creation is simple to understand. An artist conceives of an image and paints it on canvas. She has created that work. A sculptor shapes clay with his own hands, a musician composes every note of a song, a writer sets down every word in a novel—all are clearly creators of their individual works.

But what happens when the works become larger and more complex? We all know Michelangelo as the artist who created the famed mural on the ceiling of the Sistine Chapel. But he did not apply every brushstroke. He had assistants who filled in his outlines to create his magnificent work under his direction. Yet art scholars consider the fact of others' contributions to the execution of his vision to in no way diminish Michelangelo's role as the mural's creator.

So it is with *Star Trek.*

In creating a television series, the creator does not fill in every shape and detail. The nature of television, indeed the very nature of writing for television and film, does not permit that degree of completeness. The reason becomes apparent on closer examination of the process and the product.

The end result of any television production—the finished film or tape—can involve the input of dozens of creative workers, and more than a hundred specialized technical workers, all with specific skills and talents, usually honed through years of education and on-the-job experience. Each one of these people can make significant and original contributions to that end result. Designers contribute sets, costumes, starships, props, and makeup. Science advisers contribute technology and technical dialogue. Actors contribute character detail, perhaps even lines of dialogue. Directors contribute and establish pacing, structural emphasis, and story details, and even, on occasion, dialogue. Together, all of these contributions from all of these contributors bring to life the distinctive signature, style, tone, and essence of a series.

But—and this is important—none of these contributions could be made if there were no writer's script to begin with, and that writer's script would never exist if there were no creator to set the starting premise in place within whose context that script's story could be told.

Gene Roddenberry wrote the preliminary draft of what is called the bible for *Star Trek: The Original Series*. In it, he sketched out the broad strokes of a weekly television series in which a starship traveled the galaxy. He set the tone of the series by stating that the characters would behave like real people, not the *Buck Rogers* caricatures most people had come to expect in science-fiction productions. He described the future world these real people inhabited as one in which the social problems of the twentieth century had been eradicated.

In television terms, even if Roddenberry had never written another word beyond his first bible, he would forever after be entitled to the all-important "created by" credit for every incarnation of *Star Trek* that followed.

But, of course, Roddenberry did continue to write for *Star Trek*—entire scripts of his own, as well as rewrites and polishes of other writers' work.

But there were other people responsible for various elements of the *Star Trek* mythos.

Among the contributions others made to *Star Trek* were Producer Herb Solow's suggestion to use the "Captain's Log" entries to speed up the story-telling and explain science-fiction concepts that the audience might have trouble grasping. Leonard Nimoy, who portrayed the supposedly emotionless Vulcan who can be seen smiling in the first *Star Trek* pilot, forever set the tone for all future portrayals of Vulcans when, at the suggestion of director Joseph Sargent, he reacted to the mind-boggling alien spacecraft of "The Corbomite Maneuver" with a curious "Fascinating," rather than a reaction of fear. And the beloved Klingons, named after Wilbur Clingan, an old friend of Roddenberry's from his LAPD days, originated in the first-season episode "Errand of Mercy," written by Gene L. Coon.

The United Federation of Planets, Spock's parents, the instantly recognizable basics of starship design ... all the creative inventions that constantly added to the growing mosaic of *Star Trek*'s universe came not just from Roddenberry, but from the show's producers, designers, and writers.

And in the television industry, the fact that these people all added creative elements to *Star Trek* in no way diminishes Gene Roddenberry's role as *Star Trek*'s creator.

That's because the talented individuals who expanded upon Roddenberry's creation were there at Roddenberry's invitation—they were his team, either because he or another member of his team specifically asked for them. And every element they added to *Star Trek*, no matter how small or how far-reaching, made it to the screen because Gene Roddenberry said, "Yes, that's what *Star Trek* is."

In other words, Roddenberry had two functions as executive producer. First, to be the lightning rod that gathered the creative storm of talented contributors around him. And second, to be the filter through which all their individual inventions had to pass before being incorporated into his overall vision of what his series should be.

Undeniably, those contributors brought unique characters, aliens, ongoing story situations, and important background detail to *Star Trek*, and as producers, directors, writers, artists, and technicians they deserve to be called out for adding to and strengthening the appeal of an enduring cultural icon. But for all that came to *Star Trek* through the efforts of others, as far as Hollywood is concerned it is the artist who stood beneath the chapel ceiling and directed the placement of each brushstroke in his universe who truly and rightly is *Star Trek*'s creator.

After Justman and Milkis had been brought on board the new series as supervising producers, one of the first people Roddenberry approached about the challenge before him was David Gerrold.

Gerrold, as all *Star Trek* aficionados know, is the writer whose episode, "The Trouble with Tribbles," is consistently rated as one of the most popular episodes, if not *the* most popular episode, from *The Original Series*. In 1996, it was also the basis for one of the highest-rated episodes of *Star Trek: Deep Space Nine*, "Trials and Tribble-ations," in which the *Deep Space Nine* crew go back in time to the tribble-infested space station of Kirk's era, and are seamlessly blended in with footage shot thirty years earlier.

In addition to his ongoing career as a television writer, Gerrold is also well known as the author of many acclaimed science-fiction novels, including *The Man Who Folded Himself*, the *War Against the Chtorr* series, and the classic tale of artificial intelligence *When Harlie Was One*.

"The Trouble with Tribbles" had been Gerrold's first script sale, and Roddenberry forever after viewed him as a protégé. The two had remained in touch since the first series was canceled, and when Gerrold heard the announcement of the new series, he phoned Roddenberry's assistant, Susan Sackett, and asked if the news was true. Sackett said yes, Gerrold sent Roddenberry a note of congratulations, and four days later Gerrold and Roddenberry had lunch.

Gerrold began the business part of the lunch by asking Roddenberry what his plans for the new series were. Gerrold recalls that Roddenberry's reply was a question of his own: "Well, you tell me what *you'd* like to see in the new *Star Trek.*"

Gerrold says that his first thought was that Roddenberry didn't yet know what the new series would be, but he also knew that Roddenberry was clever enough to keep any plans he did have a secret. So Gerrold wasted no time and began to outline what he saw as valid directions for a new *Star Trek.*

Gerrold wasn't just talking off the cuff, either. He had already given much thought to the exercise in his book *The World of Star Trek,* first published in 1973, then revised and reissued in 1984.

Part of that book consists of a detailed analysis of the logic underlying the *Original Series* episodes, and with affection and respect the book outlines what Gerrold saw as some of the flaws in the established structure of *Star Trek* stories.

One of Gerrold's most important conclusions from that book was printed in italics: "*A captain, whether he be the captain of a starship or an aircraft carrier, simply does not place himself in danger. Ever.*"

Gerrold proposed that since a starship captain was so important to the ship's mission, the dangers of beaming to a new world should become the responsibility of what he called the "contact team." It would be a dangerous assignment, but preferable to placing the captain in danger.

Roddenberry responded favorably to these suggestions. Indeed, the idea that the captain delegate landing missions to a subordinate officer had been incorporated, at least in the planning stages, into *Star Trek: Phase II,* the 1977 attempt to bring *Star Trek* back to television. In that series, Captain Kirk would have spent more time on the bridge of the *Enterprise* as first officer Will Decker led landing parties into danger.

After that lunch and exchange of ideas, Roddenberry asked Gerrold to join him, Justman, and Milkis for the daily viewings of science-fiction films, including, Gerrold recalls, four days in a row when they reviewed the first *Star Trek* film, followed by lunchtime discussions of the new series in the Paramount commissary's private executive dining room. Gerrold had been officially invited to join the team.

Wil Wheaton as Wesley Crusher. The chair in which he's sitting was originally built as a bridge chair for the lost series, *Star Trek: Phase II.*

Intriguingly, what became clear at these lunches was that Roddenberry was intending nothing less than "reinventing *Star Trek.*"

Think about that for a moment.

Over the previous twenty years, *Star Trek* had mushroomed into a property worth millions of dollars. Why? No one really knew. But the most prominent components of it were easy to identify—the brash captain, the logical science officer, the acerbic doctor, the Scottish engineer, and the Russian, Asian, and African officers. In other words, the *characters.*

Television drama is nothing without characters. Certainly Hollywood blockbuster movies can hold an audience's attention with explosive stunts and stunning visual effects for a mere two hours. But television series have to hold the audience for *years.* The space battle between the *Enterprise* and the *Reliant* in *Star Trek II* was exciting, but even the most devoted viewer would be hard-pressed to want to watch a variation on that scene twenty-six weeks in a row, even presuming that a television production could come close to matching the technical and visual excellence of the movie.

For *Star Trek,* as with any other series, the strength of its appeal rested with its characters, and now Roddenberry, with breathtaking audacity, was going to dispense with them.

The new *Star Trek* would not feature new actors in the familiar roles. It would not even take place in the same time period. Unlike any other remake or spinoff in television history, the new *Star Trek* was really going to be what Roddenberry said it was—new.

Bob Justman explains why that decision was so important to everyone working on the series. "We didn't want fans—or anyone else for that matter—saying that we were just ripping off our own show. There's a lot of diversity in the universe, and we wanted to have totally different people, different faces, different personalities, different kinds of characters."

The first thing to change was the title. Everyone went to work on it.

A memo from Bob Justman dated October 24, 1986, carried these suggestions, along with thirty-four others:

STAR TREK: THE MISSION CONTINUES   STAR TREK: A NEW BEGINNING
STAR TREK: THE NEW ADVENTURE   STAR TREK: THE ENTERPRISE CONTINUES
STAR TREK: FUTURE TREK   STAR TREK: THE FINAL FRONTIER
STAR TREK: A NEW GENERATION   STAR TREK: THE NEW GENERATION
STAR TREK: ENTERPRISE VII   STAR TREK: THE SECOND GENERATION

So near, yet so far.

Of course, not everything about *Star Trek* could change. It was quickly agreed that the new series would feature a *Starship Enterprise*—in this case, the NCC-1701-7, to be known as the *Enterprise Seven*. Reportedly, Roddenberry had briefly considered doing without the starship at all, by merely increasing the power of the transporter so that characters could beam from planet to planet. Fortunately, that particular suggestion didn't make it through lunch.

Bob Justman also felt strongly that the opening title sequence, though new, should feel familiar to the audience. He addressed this concern in a memo dated November 2, 1986. In it, he describes an opening shot remarkably close to the one that would eventually end up in the title sequence used for the series' first three seasons.

FADE IN as Camera rapidly pulls back from a close shot of Earth and tracks through our entire solar system, showing the Sun and its planets in their relationships to each other in a continually changing perspective. As we continue to pull away and our solar system diminishes in size, our camera executes a 180-degree turn and forges ahead faster through our galaxy. The first four shimmering notes of mysterious music seem to swim in space while shining stars, light years away, flash past us as we hurtle forward.

CAPTAIN'S VOICE

Space, the final frontier. These are the voyages of the *Starship Enterprise Seven*. Its continuing mission ... to explore strange new worlds ... to seek out new life and new civilizations ... to boldly go where no man has gone before!

No doubt about it, Bob Justman had a knack for getting close, and by his March 15, 1987, memo, the "Seven" had been dropped from the starship's name, and he had changed "no man" to the politically correct "no one."

However, as changes for the new *Star Trek* continued to be developed, everyone was also aware that some elements, like the captain's opening words, must be preserved intact—especially Gene Roddenberry's vision of the future.

As Bob Justman explains it, Roddenberry's vision included the idea "that it's a good thing to lead an ethical existence, to be moral. We should understand that other people, perhaps aliens, have as much

```
                    MEMO

TO:Gene Roddenberry          DATE: OCTOBER 17, 1986
FROM:Bob Justman             SUBJECT: STAR TREK/STORY IDEA
                                      "Soylent Green"
```

There should be a "special" area on board the Enterprise where a
crew member can go to be psychically connected with his, her, or
its home planet in an emotionally evocative connotation. People
have a deep need to "go home again" and it would be marvelous if
our future technology could afford them this opportunity.
Although in the original "Soylent Green" movie, Edward G. Robinson
experienced Earth as beautiful as it used to be while he lay
dying, we would not confine ourselves to such a situation but
would rather, instead, explore all the dramatic possibilities
inherent therein.

For instance, imagine what would happen to our heroes if one (or
some) of the most important characters aboard could not be
extricated from an "Earthwise" sojourn. How would the ship continue to function while under attack if the Captain and his/her
command staff were unavailable at this most critical time? Would
a young "acting" Science Officer be able to determine whether the
problem was in fact a mechanical dysfunction or sabotage by some
entity on board? What steps would he/she take to remedy the
situation, manage the ship's defense, solve the mechanical problem and unmask the enemy intruder?

```
cc: Jeff Hayes
    Ed Milkis
    David Gerrold
```

```
                    MEMO

TO: Gene Roddenberry         DATE: OCTOBER 18, 1986
FROM: Bob Justman            SUBJECT: STAR TREK/BIBLE
                                      Klingon Marine
```

Despite your aversion to using Klingons in the new series, I
think I've thought of something which might just change your
mind.

Would you believe a Klingon (or part Klingon) as one of our regulars? Because of his (or her) race's military skills and
prowess, this person would be well-suited for a role of this
sort. We would portray the character as loyal to the
Federation, but subject to some suspicion by certain of the
other crew members. If the Klingon were part human, he (or she)
might suffer emotionally because of this unfair prejudice.
Perhaps the audience might also wonder if there is, in fact,
something there that doesn't quite add up.

This character might possibly afford us the air of "mystery"
which always was part and parcel of Mr. Spock.

```
cc: Jeff Hayes
    Ed Milkis
    David Gerrold
```

```
                    MEMO

TO: Gene Roddenberry         DATE: OCTOBER 17, 1986
FROM: Bob Justman            SUBJECT: STAR TREK/BIBLE
                                      "Noah's Ark" Premise
```

There is one element which I always felt was lacking in our
original series. Although our ship was engaged in a "five year
mission," there were only crew members aboard. For the new
series, we are postulating travel through space which could last
for an even longer period of time. To expect people to leave
everyone and everything they hold most dear for such a long
journey is, I think, unconscionable. Why should Enterprise crew
be denied the opportunity to live a full and rewarding life?

Therefore, I propose that we have men, women, <u>and</u> children on
board throughout the whole new series. There would be births,
deaths, marriages, divorces, etc. Crew members would go "home"
to the various living quarters aboard at the end of their duty
shifts. They'd have dinner with the family, help the children
with their homework or, if unattached, pursue the opposite sex in
mankind's oldest imperative - the mating game. What we would
have then is, indeed, "Wagon Train to the Stars." The pioneers
didn't leave their families (or their desires) behind when they
migrated westwards, so why should we deny our people the same
human rights?

Most of the time we would not make a big deal out of the presence of children on board - we'd just see them in various areas
of the ship, in passing. Additionally, I propose that <u>certain
specific family members would become a part of a continuing story
thread throughout the various episodes</u> but only once in a while
would a family situation become the paramount (if you'll excuse
the expression) focus of an individual episode. This new
approach to STAR TREK would give us much the same sort of dramatic continuity that current shows like "Hill Street Blues" and
"L.A. Law" have.

```
cc: Jeff Hayes
    Ed Milkis
    David Gerrold
```

In just three memos over two days, Robert Justman laid the
groundwork for almost every holodeck story ever told, paved
the way for Worf's presence on the bridge, and set the stage
for Wesley as Dr. Crusher's son, as well as the Ishikawa-
O'Briens and all the other family storylines that would
appear over the next seven seasons.

In Season Six, Rick Berman honored Robert Justman for his
contributions to *The Original Series* and *The Next Generation* by
naming the *Enterprise*'s newest shuttle after him.
COURTESY OF ROBERT JUSTMAN.

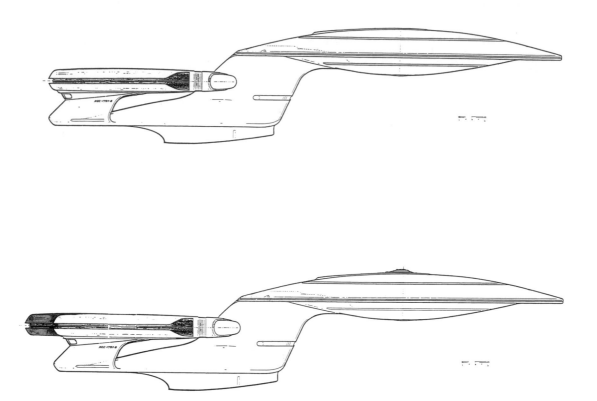

The final modification to the new *Enterprise* designed by Andrew Probert came when Gene Roddenberry asked that the warp nacelles be lengthen. DRAWING BY ANDREW PROBERT. COURTESY OF THE ARTIST.

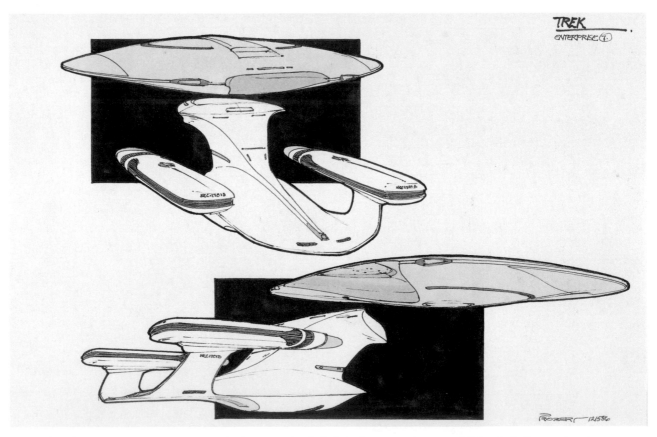

After designing the new *Enterprise* to be "an organic whole," Probert was given an additional challenge when he was informed that this *Enterprise* would be shown separating. DRAWING BY ANDREW PROBERT. COURTESY OF THE ARTIST.

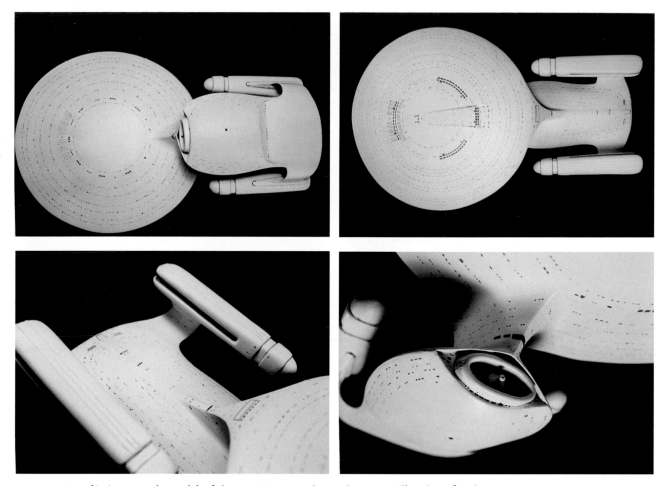

A preliminary study model of the new *Enterprise* shows the areas still to be refined.   COURTESY OF GREG JEIN.

right to pursue what is important to them as we have to pursue what is important to us. That just because someone looks different, or seems too foreign, doesn't mean that they are automatically suspect, or dangerous, or evil, or should be killed right away. That every day, we can get a little better."

As the discussions continued about the specifics of what elements to keep, what elements to change, and what the *Star Trek* universe would be like one hundred years after Kirk and Spock, the chief area of focus in the late fall of 1986, became the new characters.

Some were obvious. There had to be a captain. And following Gerrold's suggestion and what had been planned for *Star Trek: Phase II*, there would also be a younger first officer who would be in charge of landing parties, eventually to be called *away-mission teams,* and, finally, just *away teams.*

Beyond those two given characters, Roddenberry had been quite taken by the character of Vasquez, the tough, female Colonial Marine in *Aliens.* He felt she represented a vision of equality of the sexes in the future, and so the character of "Macha Hernandez" was born, destined to be the *Enterprise*'s security chief.

For his part, Justman was equally taken with Sean Young's role as the replicant Rachel in *Blade Runner,* and suggested a similar type of female character as a science officer who might be part Vulcan, related to Spock, or even to Kirk.

Though the Sean Young idea didn't fly, two of Justman's other character suggestions did. In a memo dated October 17th, Justman first proposed an android as a regular character, and he later wrote that he thought the character might fill the same role as Spock had in *The Original Series*—as an outsider

A second study model is prepared, with artboard ribs to provide the contours for clay. COURTESY OF GREG JEIN.

Greg Jein, left, and Andrew Probert study the final blueprints of the new *Enterprise*. COURTESY OF GREG JEIN.

One-to-one plans for the eight-foot model of the *Enterprise* are laid out at Industrial Light & Magic.
COURTESY OF GREG JEIN.

Just as the smaller study model was created, the final version begins with a skeleton of metal and Plexiglas to hold the clay from which it is sculpted. The clay form is then used to create a mold. COURTESY OF GREG JEIN.

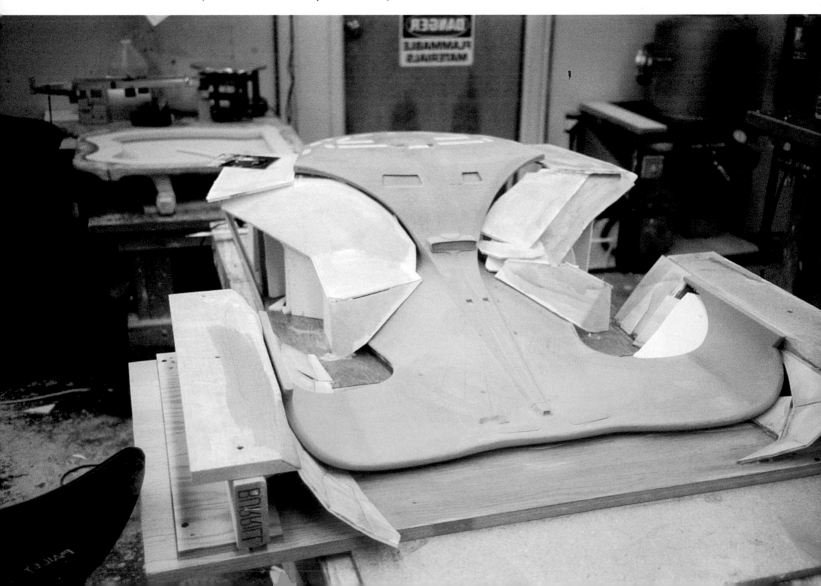

Meanwhile, the ribs of the saucer section are filled in with foam, not clay. COURTESY OF GREG JEIN.

Modelmakers carefully mask the areas of the molded-fiberglass saucer section that are to remain transparent after painting, so interior lights will show through. COURTESY OF GREG JEIN.

The interior lights of the saucer section. COURTESY OF GREG JEIN.

Not only must the final model look good, it must be engineered to remain rigid when placed on a model stand to be photographed. COURTESY OF GREG JEIN.

trying to understand humans. Roddenberry had created a similar character in his 1974 pilot *The Questor Tapes,* and the as-yet-unnamed Data joined the crew.

Justman also proposed placing a Klingon marine on the bridge of the *Enterprise*—an idea Roddenberry initially rejected because of his commitment to not having any "retread" characters. Klingons were from the old series. He wanted something new. Justman wouldn't take no for an answer though, and the question of the Klingon marine remained up in the air during the series' initial development stage.

Like the first officer, another character arose, in part, from the so-called lost series, *Star Trek: Phase II*—the ship's counselor. In *Phase II*, the ship's Deltan navigator, Ilia, had the ability to sense people's emotions. She also once had been involved in a passionate affair with first officer Will Decker. Now it was the counselor, Deanna Troi, who could sense emotions, and who had once had a passionate affair with the new *Enterprise*'s first officer, Will Ryker, later to be spelled Riker.

One of the most problematic characters to be considered was a definite first for *Star Trek*—a teenager. In one of his earliest memos, Justman had proposed a "Noah's Ark" concept for the new *Enterprise*'s mission, and the idea that Starfleet personnel on long missions would bring their families with them appealed to Roddenberry. He was unhappy with what he felt was the militaristic turn the *Star Trek* movies

An early lighting test of the impressive new *Enterprise*.
COURTESY OF GREG JEIN.

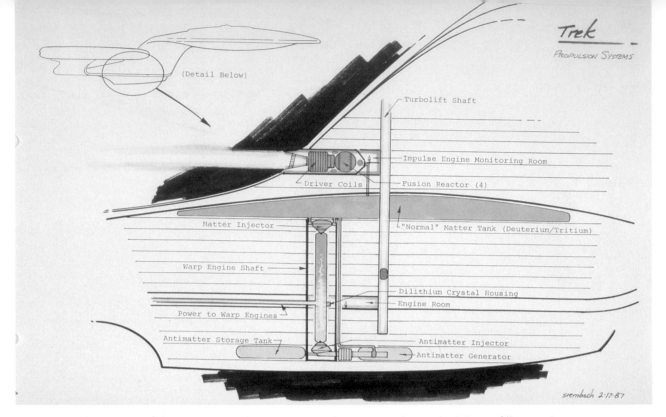

Labels on diagram:
- Trek Propulsion Systems
- (Detail Below)
- Turbolift Shaft
- Impulse Engine Monitoring Room
- Driver Coils
- Fusion Reactor (4)
- Matter Injector
- "Normal" Matter Tank (Deuterium/Tritium)
- Warp Engine Shaft
- Dilithium Crystal Housing
- Engine Room
- Power to Warp Engines
- Antimatter Storage Tank
- Antimatter Injector
- Antimatter Generator
- sternbach 2·17·87

As the exterior of the *Enterprise* was being constructed at ILM, Rick Sternbach began filling in the interior engineering details. COURTESY OF THE ARTIST.

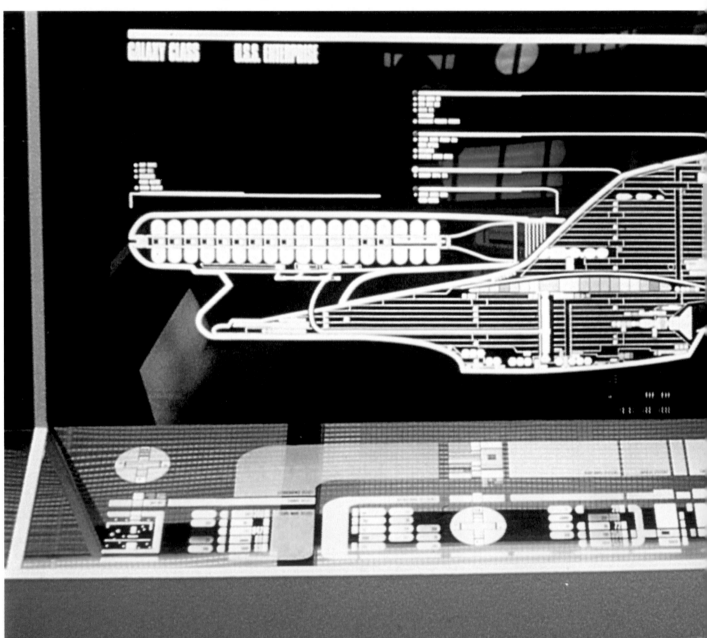

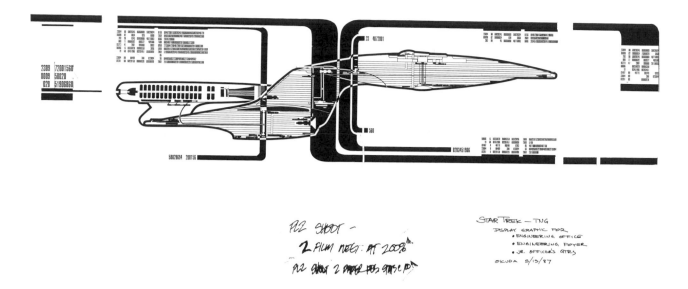

Interior engineering details were then incorporated into the hand-assembled graphic art used to produce the distinctive computerlike displays that helped define the look of the *Star Trek* universe.

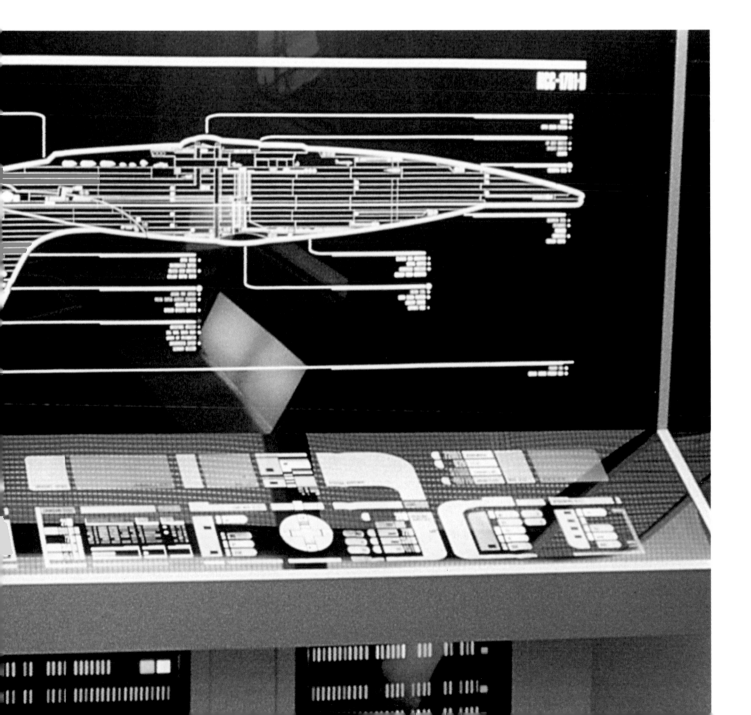

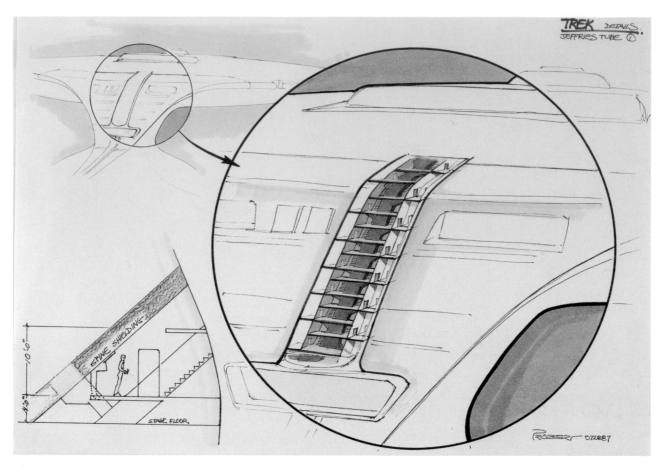

The design of the *Enterprise*'s interior was a continuing process. Here Probert illustrates a Jefferies tube service spine for the starship, named for the designer of the original *Enterprise*, Matt Jefferies. The Jefferies tubes constructed for the series were much smaller and located throughout the ship. DRAWING BY ANDREW PROBERT. COURTESY OF THE ARTIST.

appeared to be taking, and he envisioned the new *Enterprise* as less a battleship and more a comfortable base for the peaceful exploration of the galaxy. If families were going to be on board, then a young person should be part of the mix.

The teenager first appeared in memos as Wesley, Roddenberry's own middle name. But Justman pushed for a sex change for the character, on the grounds that teenage boys appeared too often in similar roles. It was time for a girl, Justman argued, in this case, Leslie. The Leslie/Wesley decision wavered back and forth so often that even when the casting call for the series went out, on December 10th, the character was described as "an appealing 15-year-old caucasian girl."

Other than Lieutenant Macha Hernandez and Leslie Crusher, the initial casting-call sheet for the new series, now officially *Star Trek: The Next Generation,* would be very familiar to the series' eventual audience. It included Captain "Julien" Picard, William Ryker, Data the android, Deanna Troi, Dr. Beverly Crusher, and Lieutenant Geordi La Forge, named after George La Forge, a well-known *Star Trek* fan who had been a quadraplegic, and who had died in 1975. Missing was the Klingon marine whose presence on the bridge was still being questioned by Roddenberry.

As the search for actors began, the behind-the-camera team grew as well. Bob Justman persuaded a junior executive in Paramount's television postproduction department to give up his steady, guaranteed position to join the fledgling series to coordinate its complex postproduction requirements. The junior executive was Peter Lauritson, who eventually earned a producer's title on the series and the two—for now—*Next Generation* movies.

Other key people brought to the series by Justman included production designer Herman Zimmerman and scenic artist Michael Okuda.

In television, Herman Zimmerman explains that the production designer "is responsible for everything you see on the screen—except for the acting." This responsibility requires an intensive meshing of technical knowledge about everything from film stock and camera lenses to visual effects, wardrobe, set, and prop design, all combined with the eye of an artist.

Like so many others who work in the film and television industries, Zimmerman didn't set out to be a production designer. His original goal was to become an actor and singer, for which he studied at Northwestern University. However, when he graduated, the only way he could qualify for the assistantship position he needed in order to earn his master's degree was to switch his major from acting and directing to scene design. That was the inadvertent beginning of his career.

Zimmerman came to Los Angeles in 1965 and was hired as the assistant art director for the pilot of the new NBC soap opera *Days of Our Lives*. When the series went into production, Zimmerman's job became an intense learning experience. Each

Every devoted *Star Trek* follower knows the *Enterprise* wasn't built at Industrial Light & Magic. It was built in orbit of Mars.

day's episode required from five to seven sets, and there were five episodes each week. After three months, the original art director moved to another show and Zimmerman was promoted to replace him. He recalls sneaking into the NBC art department after hours to check out the work of other designers—not to steal their ideas, but to try and figure out exactly what he was supposed to be doing.

Michael Okuda, a television graphic artist in Honolulu, had designed control panels and set signage for *Star Trek IV: The Voyage Home*. Like David Gerrold, as soon as Okuda had heard the news about the new *Star Trek* series he had written to Gene Roddenberry to inquire about working for the show. Roddenberry replied in less than a week, saying how much he liked Okuda's work in the film and promising to recommend him.

Over the next few months, Okuda met with Roddenberry, Milkis, and Justman, and in February 1987 he was offered a job by Herman Zimmerman to work on the main sets—an assignment that was supposed to take somewhere between one and four weeks. However, like Peter Lauritson, after ten years Okuda is still contributing to *Star Trek*'s distinctive visual style, from *The Next Generation, Deep Space Nine*, and *Voyager* to every movie since *Star Trek IV*.

By the time Okuda reported for his "four-week" assignment, two other key contributors to *Star Trek*'s look were already at work—Rick Sternbach and Andrew Probert.

Sternbach, a Hugo Award-winning science fiction artist who has won two Emmy Awards, including one for his work on the landmark PBS series *Cosmos*, had begun his association with *Star Trek* as a designer working on *Star Trek: The Motion Picture*. He didn't write to Roddenberry when he heard the new series announcement—he pulled off the road at the nearest phone booth and called within minutes. He has been designing the technology of the twenty-fourth century—and myriad alien cultures—ever since.

Andrew Probert had also worked on *The Motion Picture*, most notably as the key designer of the refitted *Starship Enterprise*. The *Enterprise*'s original designer, Matt Jefferies, had created an intermediate, updated design for the starship for the *Phase II* television series. When production switched from television to film, Probert worked from Jefferies' intermediate designs to create the striking *Enterprise* that appeared in all six *Original Series* movies. It was Probert who was given the all-important task of designing the new *Starship Enterprise* from scratch.

Some of the technical and design crew joining *The Next Generation* had connections to *Star Trek* which predated even the movies. William Ware Theiss, who had been the imaginative costume designer for all three seasons of *The Original Series*, returned to fill the same role on *The Next Generation*.

Also returning from *The Original Series* were set decorator John Dwyer, special-effects coordinator Dick Brownfield, and composer Fred Steiner.

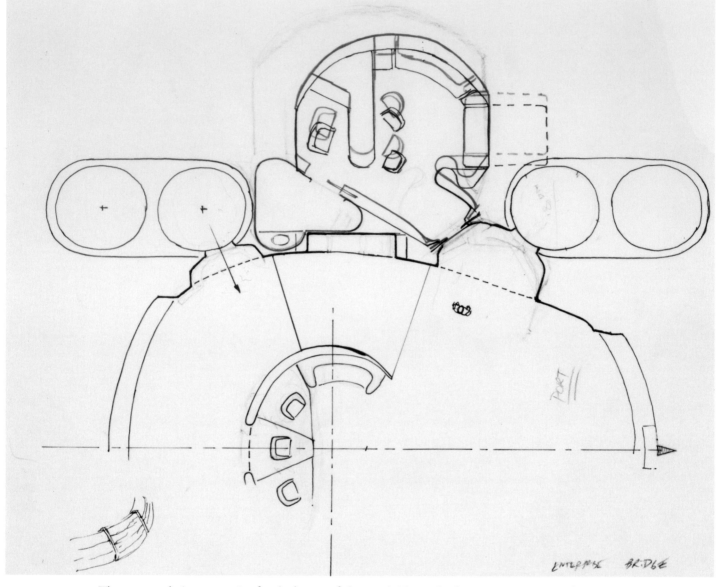

The greatest design constraint for the layout of the new bridge and other *Enterprise* sets was that, to save money, their floorplan had to match the lighting already in place for the sets of the movie *Enterprise*.

But one of the most notable people from *The Original Series* who came to join the new one, again at Justman's suggestion, was D. C. Fontana. During *The Original Series,* she had started as Gene Roddenberry's secretary, but beginning with her teleplay for "Charlie X" (from a story by Gene Roddenberry), Justman hails her as "one of the most valuable and dependable writers ever to work on *Star Trek.*" Among her many other writing credits for *The Original Series* are two of its most popular episodes: "The *Enterprise* Incident," and "Journey to Babel," the episode that introduced Spock's parents, Sarek and Amanda.

As the deadline approached for beginning preproduction on *The Next Generation*'s pilot episode, it was Dorothy Fontana who was given the initial assignment. She ran into trouble almost immediately. Not because of anything Fontana did, but because no one seemed quite certain exactly what it was she should do.

At the time—December 1986—Paramount had still not decided whether *The Next Generation* pilot episode should be one hour in length, ninety minutes, or two hours.

Fontana completed her assignment in mid-March by turning in a revised draft of a ninety-minute

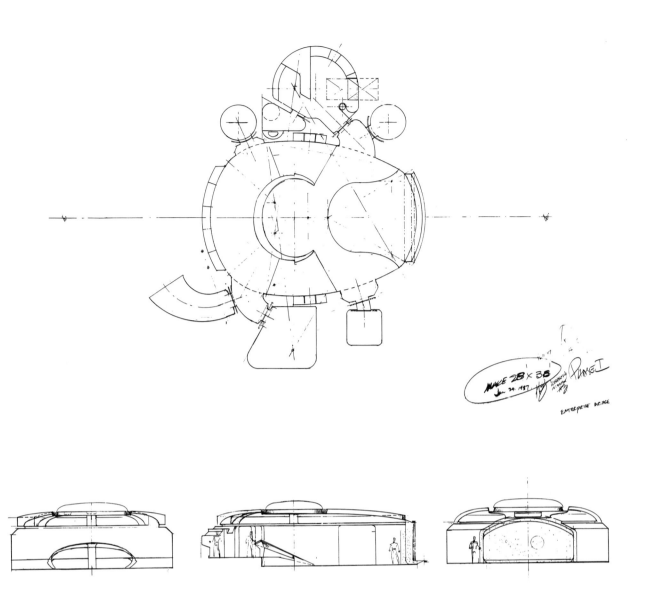

An early Andrew Probert concept for the *Enterprise*'s secondary battle bridge, incorporating some of the components of the existing movie sets. COURTESY OF THE ARTIST.

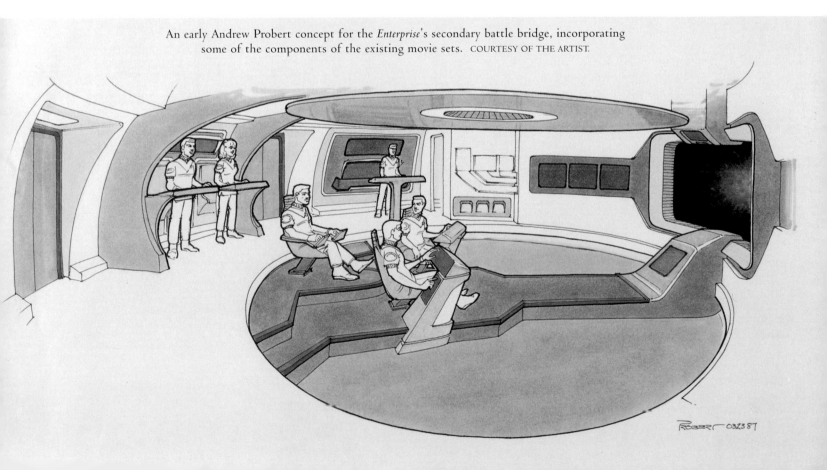

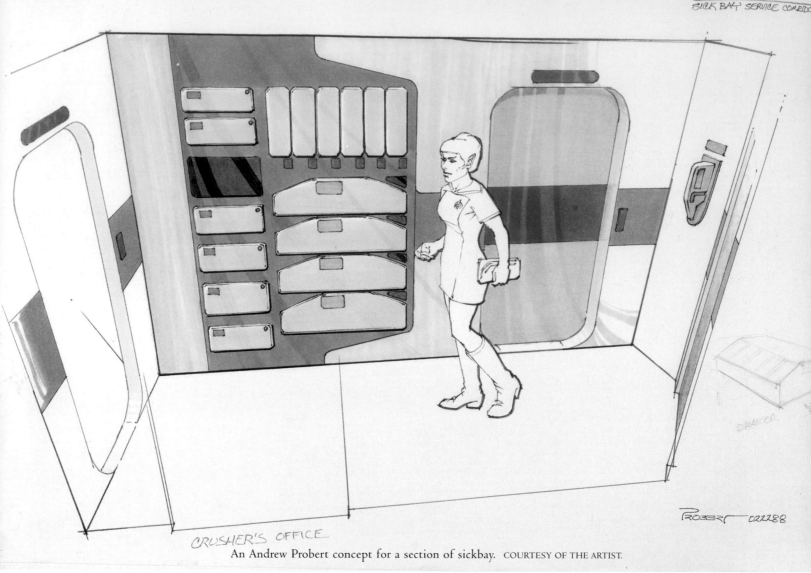

CRUSHER'S OFFICE

Probert 022288

DRAWER

An Andrew Probert concept for a section of sickbay. COURTESY OF THE ARTIST.

The floor lenses from *The Original Series'* transporter room became the ceiling lenses in *The Next Generation's.* In keeping with tradition, they are currently being used in the transporter room of the *Starship Voyager.*

Though budget constraints meant that not every new set could be designed and built from scratch, the long history of *Star Trek* productions meant there was a large store of existing material to draw from. This wall section, for instance, was originally built as part of the transporter room for the "lost series," *Star Trek: Phase II*. When that project was changed to *Star Trek: The Motion Picture*, the wall became part of the movie-set *Enterprise*'s sickbay, and for *The Next Generation*, it was put back into service as part of the transporter room once more.

Original Series costume designer William Ware Theiss returned to create the distinctive new look for Starfleet uniforms, which has served as the basis for all the modifications over the past ten years.

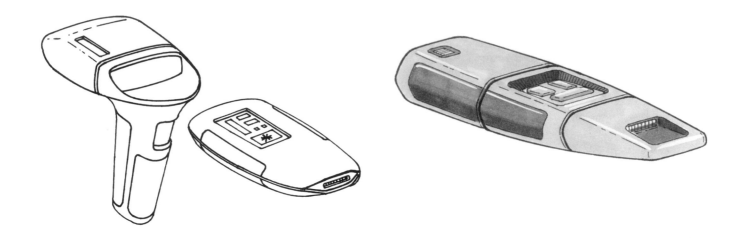

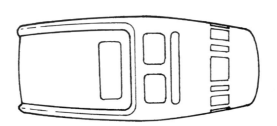

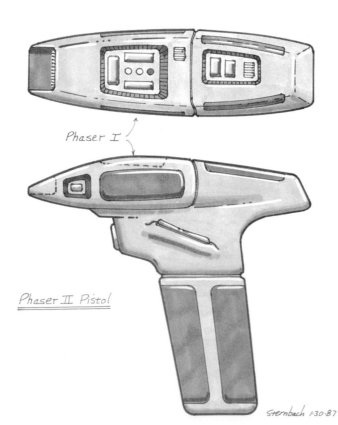

Phaser I

Phaser II Pistol

Though phasers were a necessary part of a starship's mission, Gene Roddenberry was determined to downplay the more military aspects of Starfleet in *The Next Generation*. Thus, the new phaser designs were intended to make the devices look less like weapons, and more like tools.

ALL ILLUSTRATIONS BY RICK STERNBACH.
COURTESY OF THE ARTIST.

Sternbach 1·30·87

Gene Roddenberry's intent to reduce the visual impact of weapons reached its extreme with this first-season phaser, nicknamed "the cricket." Though it fit with Roddenberry's vision of the future's immensely powerful technology, it was so small it was almost impossible to see on a television screen when an actor held it. It was only used a few times, then retired. ROBBIE ROBINSON.

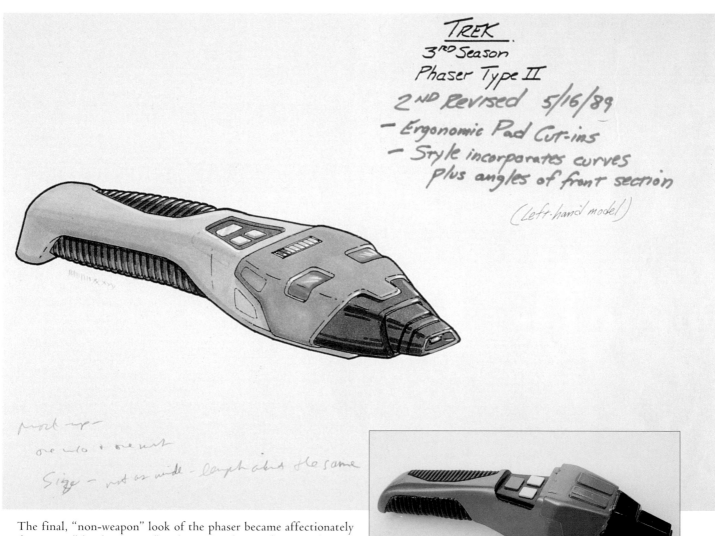

TREK.
3ʳᵈ Season
Phaser Type II
2ᴺᴰ Revised 5/16/89
— Ergonomic Pad Cut-ins
— Style incorporates curves
plus angles of front section

(left-hand model)

The final, "non-weapon" look of the phaser became affectionately known as "the dustbuster," and continued to evolve over the run of the series. ILLUSTRATION BY RICK STERNBACH. COURTESY OF THE ARTIST. PHOTOGRAPH BY ROBBIE ROBINSON.

The Original Series tricorder, designed by Wah Chang.

Tricorder

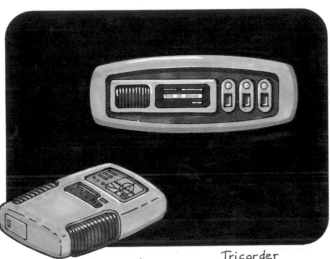

Tricorder

Star Trek:

Like the phaser, the tricorder was an indispensable piece of *Star Trek* technology which had to be updated for the 24th century. These concepts by Rick Sternbach show how the device evolved into the small, handheld unit that flipped open much like the original communicators.

ALL SKETCHES COURTESY OF THE ARTIST.

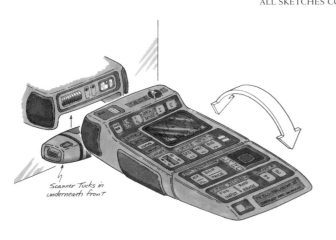

Scanner Tucks in underneath front

Star Trek:
The Next Generatio
PERSONNEL GEAR

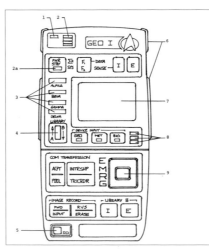

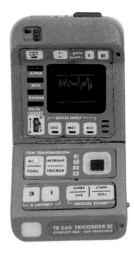

The first-season tricorder.
PHOTOGRAPH BY ROBBIE
ROBINSON.

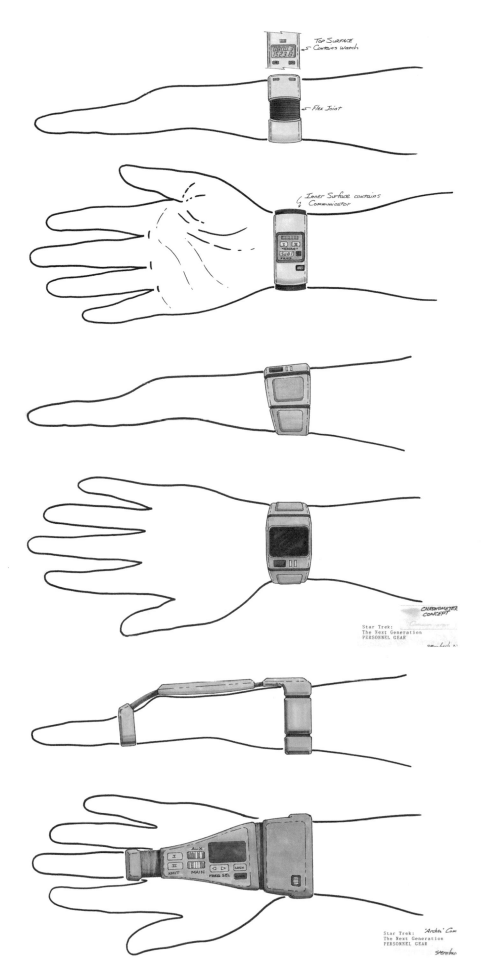

Top Surface
Contains Watch

Flex Joint

Inner Surface contains
Communicator

Communicator
(Inner)

Watch Section (Outer)

CHRONOMETER
CONCEPT

Star Trek:
The Next Generation
PERSONNEL GEAR

Of the three key pieces of *Star Trek* technology—phasers, tricorders, and communicators—it was the latter that underwent the greatest design change from *The Original Series* to *The Next Generation*. As these drawings show, initially, the design team went back to the wrist-communicator concept that had been used in *Star Trek: The Motion Picture*. ILLUSTRATIONS BY RICK STERNBACH. COURTESY OF THE ARTIST.

AUX
I
II
XMIT   MAIN   FREQ. SEL   LOCK

Star Trek: 'Archer' Com
The Next Generation
PERSONNEL GEAR
                     Sternbach

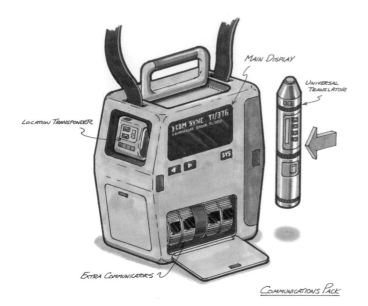

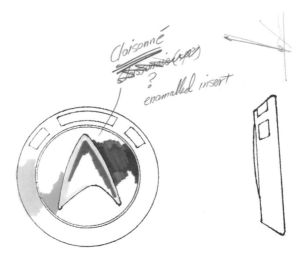

In a brief detour from the ultra-miniaturization approach to 24th-century technology, this "communications pack" was proposed, perhaps more with an eye toward potential toy spin-offs for the series than for usefulness on an away-team mission. ILLUSTRATION BY RICK STERNBACH. COURTESY OF THE ARTIST.

The great conceptual breakthrough of combining the communicator with the Starfleet emblem is illustrated in this early sketch, in which actual control surfaces are shown for communicator functions. ILLUSTRATION BY RICK STERNBACH. COURTESY OF THE ARTIST.

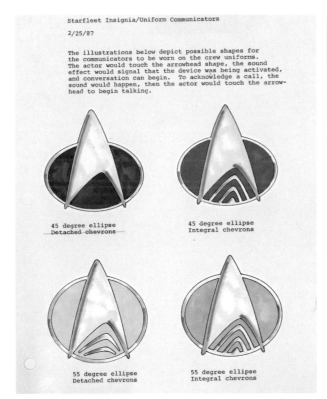

An illustrated memo in which the new communicator design is close to being finalized. ILLUSTRATIONS BY RICK STERNBACH. COURTESY OF THE ARTIST.

version of "Encounter at Farpoint." When the decision was finally made to make the pilot two hours in length, Roddenberry took Fontana's story and added to it the story of Q—the omnipotent alien portrayed by John de Lancie who puts Picard and his crew on trial for the sins of humanity.

By the time Fontana had turned in that first script, *The Next Generation* was moving toward full production in fits and starts. And though the present sometimes seemed confused and complicated, the future, as befits *Star Trek,* looked bright.

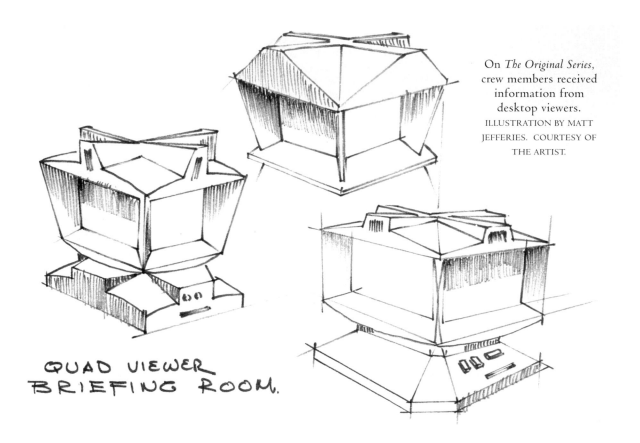

QUAD VIEWER
BRIEFING ROOM.

On *The Original Series*,
crew members received
information from
desktop viewers.
ILLUSTRATION BY MATT
JEFFERIES. COURTESY OF
THE ARTIST.

Industrial Light & Magic, the leading visual-effects house founded by George Lucas, which had contributed spectacular sequences to the last three *Star Trek* films, had been contracted to provide visual effects for the series.

To save money, Paramount had investigated shooting the series in Vancouver, Canada. However, when the executives added the time-intensive complications of travel to and from Vancouver to the expected demands of what was promising to be a complex series, they decided to keep production at their own studio.

Every role except for the troublesome Klingon marine had been cast, though not as originally expected. At first, dark-haired Marina Sirtis had read for the part of Macha Hernandez, and blond Denise Crosby had read for the part of Deanna Troi. The Greek-English Sirtis, though, was seen as a perfect choice for the exotic, half-alien counselor. But since one important aspect of casting a series is to make each of the main characters visually distinct, the presence of a dark-haired, olive-skinned woman as the counselor precluded the original idea of having a Hispanic chief of security. Thus, Macha Hernandez became Tasha Yar, and Denise Crosby swapped roles with Marina Sirtis.

In other areas of the production, costumes had been designed. Sets were under construction. The first draft

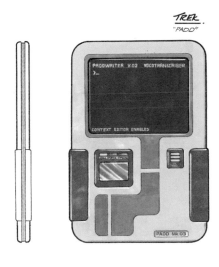

On *The Next Generation*, padds became the
preferred means of imparting information.
They are also the design direction being taken
by real-world handheld personal computers,
such as the Apple Newton. ILLUSTRATIONS BY
RICK STERNBACH. COURTESY OF THE ARTIST.

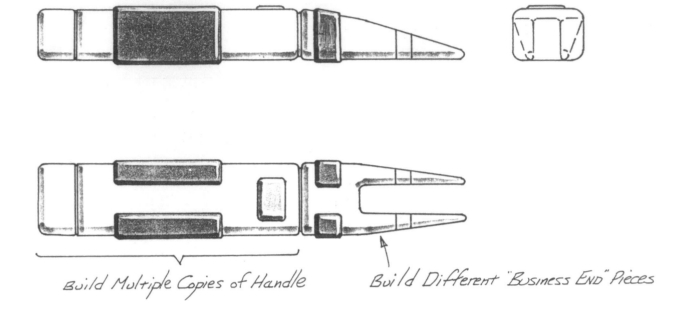

Build Multiple Copies of Handle   Build Different "Business End" Pieces

Medical equipment.   ILLUSTRATIONS BY RICK STERNBACH.   COURTESY OF THE ARTIST.

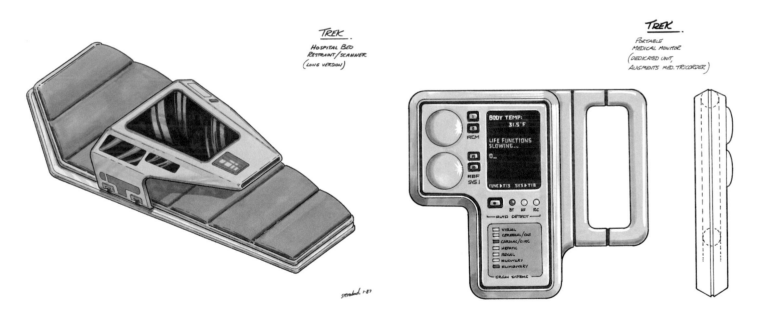

TREK.
HOSPITAL BED
RESTRAINT/SCANNER
(LONG VERSION)

TREK.
PORTABLE
MEDICAL MONITOR
(DEDICATED UNIT,
AUGMENTS MED. TRICORDER)

of the series bible and the first group of *Next Generation* writers was already being put to work. Though, as additional foreshadowing of troubles to come, Gerrold was not among them.

Then, finally, there was no more time left for preproduction.

Eighteen years after the last episode of *The Original Series* had wrapped production on the Paramount lot, it was time to roll the camera—and the dice—again, remembering all the while that millions of dollars were riding on the outcome, along with a number of careers.

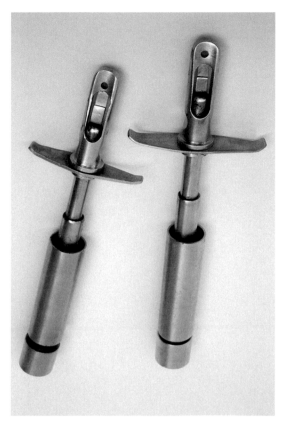

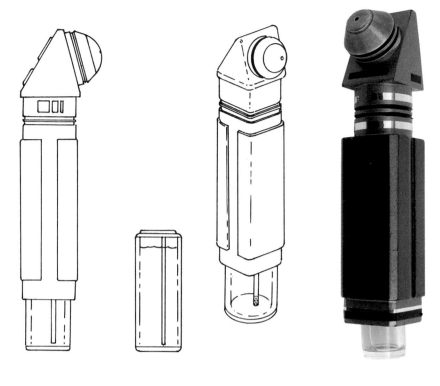

Original Series hyposprays.
PHOTOGRAPH BY ROBBIE ROBINSON.

Next Generation hypospray designed by Rick Sternbach. ILLUSTRATION COURTESY OF THE ARTIST.
PHOTOGRAPH BY ROBBIE ROBINSON.

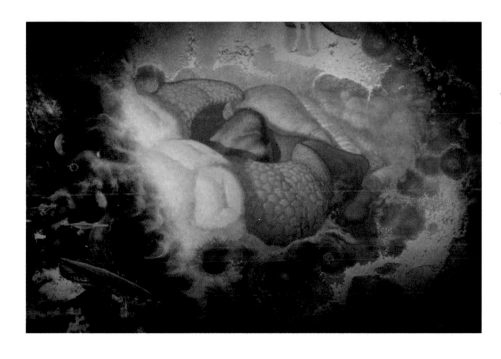

This unique—and
unfinished—painting by
Andrew Probert incorporates
internal organs and various
Enterprises in an unusual wall
decoration that hung in the
waiting area outside Dr.
Crusher's office in sickbay
throughout the series.
COURTESY OF THE ARTIST.

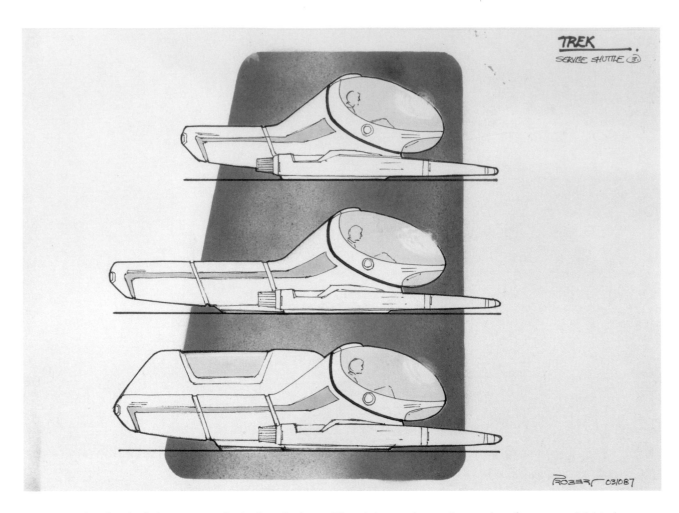

Service-shuttle design concepts by Andrew Probert. Though impressive, such curved surfaces are prohibitively expensive to incorporate in full-scale models built for television. COURTESY OF THE ARTIST.

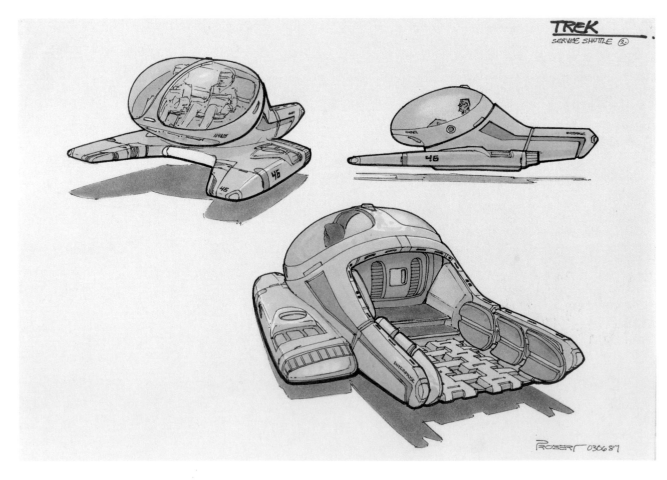

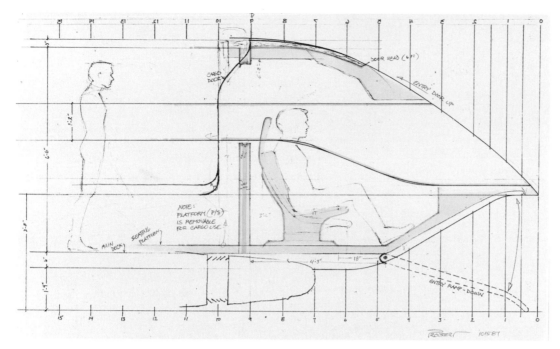

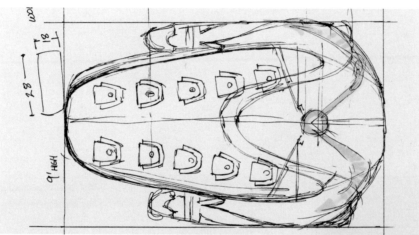

Andrew Probert's design for the first *Next Generation* shuttle takes form. COURTESY OF THE ARTIST.

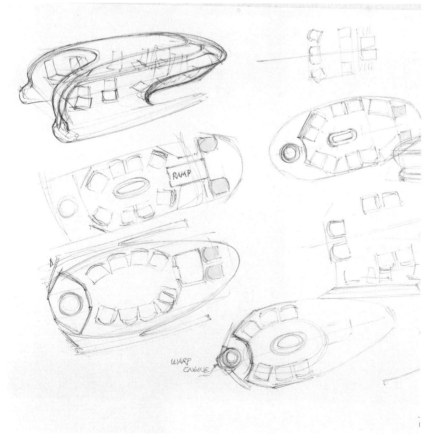

A study model of Probert's shuttle design under construction at Greg Jein's modelshop.
COURTESY OF GREG JEIN.

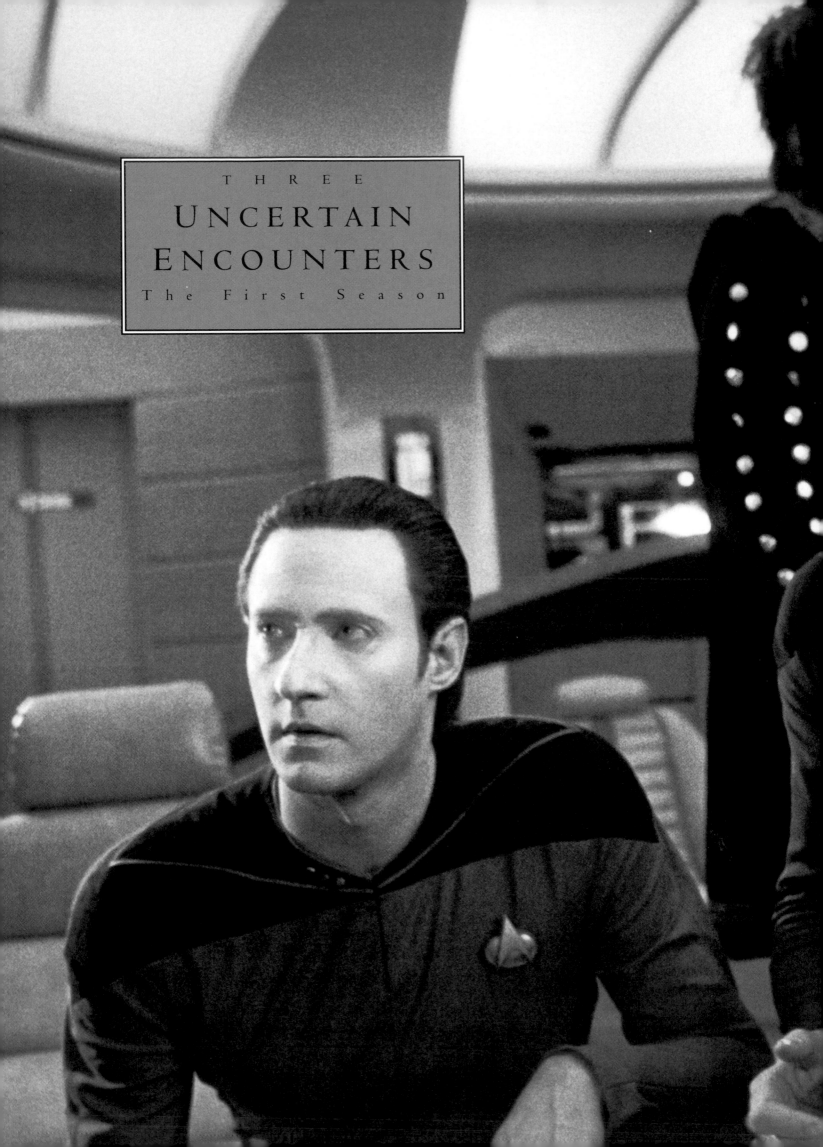

THREE

UNCERTAIN
ENCOUNTERS

The First Season

T ELEVISION pro-
duction, at least in
hindsight, used to be a more
leisurely process.

Consider the original
Star Trek series. The first
episode of its first season premiered in September 1966.
The pilot episode that had
convinced NBC to order the
series had begun principal
photography more than a year
earlier, in July 1965. The
original pilot, with Jeffrey
Hunter as Captain Christopher
Pike, which had tantalized
NBC with the notion that a
serious science-fiction series
might succeed, had been
filmed almost *two* years earlier, beginning in November
1964.

That extensive develop-
ment process had afforded the
production team the time to
try out and review almost
every creative decision that
led to the first *Star Trek* series.

The world's first glimpse of the *U.S.S. Enterprise* NCC-1701-D, from the opening frames of "Encounter at Farpoint."

Old characters were eliminated, new ones added. Sets, props, and costumes were redesigned, special visual effects were modified, and scripts were written with months available for revisions.

But this extended period of development was one part of *Star Trek*'s history that was not repeated for *The Next Generation.*

When the two-hour pilot, "Encounter at Farpoint," began principal photography on May 29, 1987, two months later than originally planned in the November 1986 schedule, the series' September premiere, only four months away, had already been tentatively scheduled. "Farpoint" wrapped filming on June 25th, and only eight working days later, on July 6th, principal photography began on the first regular episode, "The Naked Now." The production team, cast, and crew of *The Next Generation* had approximately five weeks to cover the same ground *The Original Series* had explored over twenty-two months.

It was true that this accelerated schedule was typical of television production then and now. And since these high-pressure situations deprive producers of an opportunity to work out different options for the production of a series, approaches to tone, appearance, and content must be selected and then, only if necessary, altered on the fly.

In the case of *The Next Generation,* the producers were at even more of a disadvantage because the initial order for the series was based solely on the *premise* of an updated *Star Trek* with new characters. Who those characters were, how they would interact, and what their relationship to the original characters would be was still to be refined.

In addition to those development pressures common to any series entering its first year without benefit of a pilot, *The Next Generation* faced the additional burden of requiring virtually *everything* on the screen to be conceived, designed, and built from scratch. In seasons to come—if there *were* any seasons to come—a storehouse of graphics, props, costumes, and sets could be assembled, with the potential to ease the staggering visual needs of the series. But in

TREK.
PRELIM. CONCEPT
FARPOINT EXTERIOR
(MINIATURE)

Sternbach 3-4-87

Farpoint Station takes
shape by the Bandi village.
CONCEPT ART BY RICK
STERNBACH. COURTESY OF
THE ARTIST.

The Bandi village under
construction.
PHOTOGRAPHS COURTESY
OF GREG JEIN.

ENCOUNTER AT FARPOINT
*Written by D. C. Fontana and
Gene Roddenberry
Directed by Corey Allen*

The first mission of the new *U.S.S.
Enterprise* is to travel to Deneb IV to
investigate the mysterious Farpoint
Station, which the Federation is considering using as a new base. The base
seems too technologically advanced
to have been built by its alien owners
and operators—the Bandi. But the
mission is complicated when Picard's
command crew is taken captive, tried,
and sentenced to death by a member
of "the Q," a self-described omni-
scient race unconvinced of humanity's right to survive. Picard asks Q
to delay execution of his judgment
until he monitors how Picard and his
crew complete their mission. Picard
wins his crew's freedom when, in
spite of the Q's urging, he refuses to
destroy what appears to be an alien
ship as it attacks the Bandi city. The
"ship" is actually an enormous creature that has come to rescue its mate—
held captive by the Bandi to form
Farpoint Station. Picard and his
crew free the trapped creature from
its Bandi captors, and Q decides that
though humanity passed this test, it
will be tested again in the future.

SEASON ONE: EPISODE 3
THE NAKED NOW
*Teleplay by J. Michael Bingham
Story by John D. F. Black and
J. Michael Bingham
Directed by Paul Lynch*

After investigating the derelict
research ship *Tsiolkovsky,* near a col-
lapsed star, most of the crew of the
Enterprise is infected with a mentally
debilitating virus that causes symptoms of intoxication and lowered
inhibitions. Under the virus's influence, Wesley Crusher compromises
the ship's computers, placing the
Enterprise in danger from the collaps-
ing star. The ship is saved when
Data and Chief Engineer MacDougal
fight the virus's effects until they
can repair the computer's memory
and bring the ship back on line,
allowing time for a cure to be found.

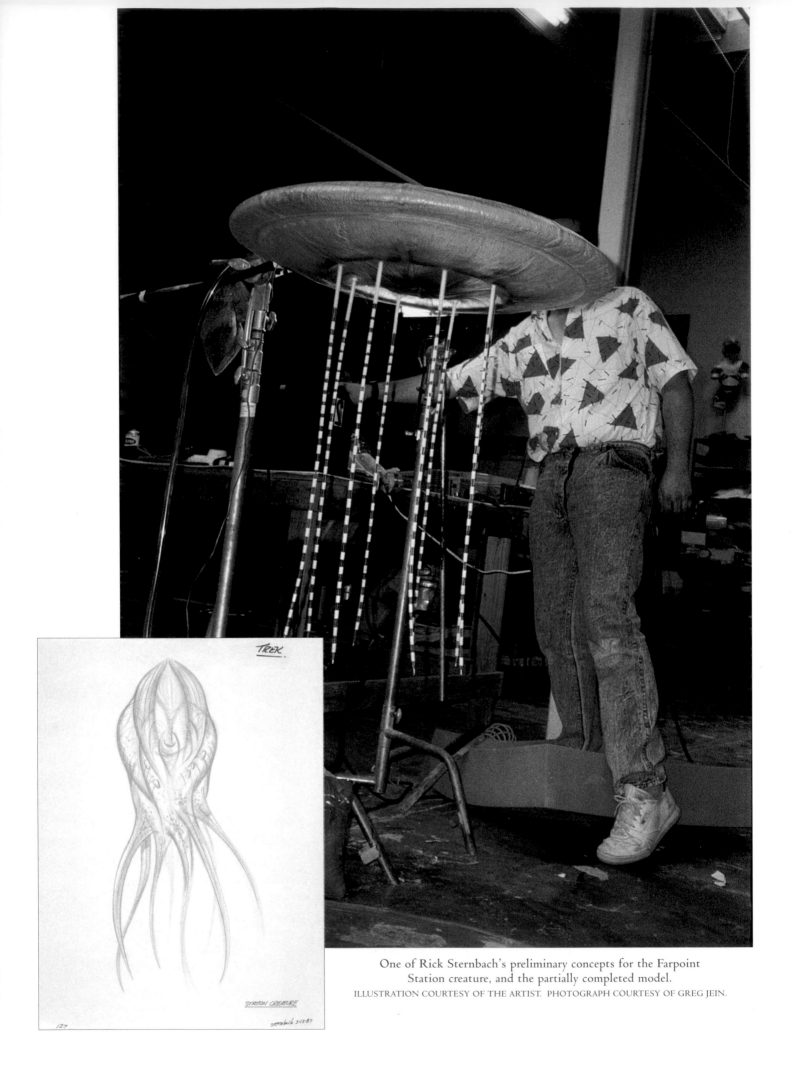

One of Rick Sternbach's preliminary concepts for the Farpoint
Station creature, and the partially completed model.
ILLUSTRATION COURTESY OF THE ARTIST. PHOTOGRAPH COURTESY OF GREG JEIN.

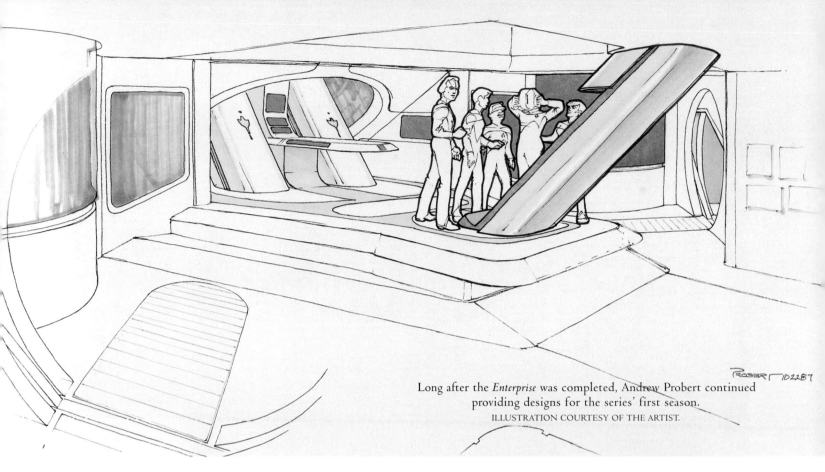

Long after the *Enterprise* was completed, Andrew Probert continued providing designs for the series' first season.
ILLUSTRATION COURTESY OF THE ARTIST.

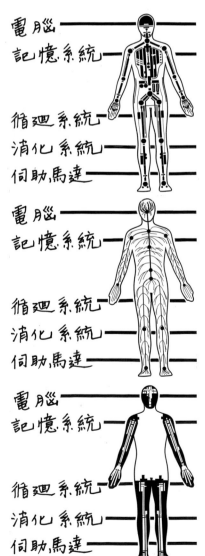

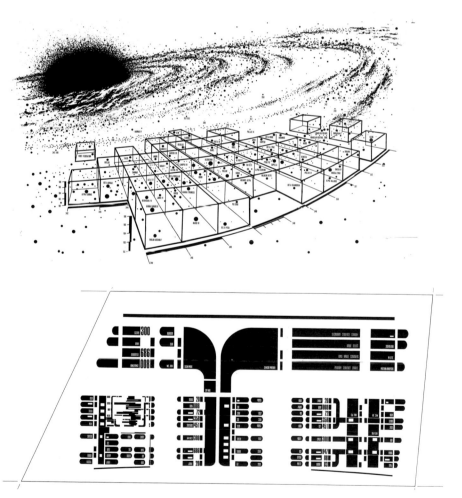

Creating the visual environment of humanity's 24th century, as well as those of alien worlds, required an incredible weekly output of graphic art, from the plans for Data's construction, to galactic maps, and the control console of the *Enterprise*.

Deanna Troi being comforted
by her mother, Lwaxana, played
by Majel Barrett Roddenberry.

Starfleet ID labels; brown for duty decks, lavendar for residential.

that first year, the production team was literally creating a new world, episode by episode, and set by set.

Admittedly, the producers, Roddenberry, Justman, and Milkis, weren't starting from scratch. They had already produced *The Original Series* and knew the pitfalls and shortcuts peculiar to *Star Trek* that lay ahead. Key members of the design team, Andrew Probert, Michael Okuda, and Rick Sternbach, had also been through the process of bringing *Star Trek* to the movie screen, and the initial principal supplier of visual effects, Industrial Light & Magic, was no stranger to *Star Trek* or to science fiction.

Though the fledgling series did face the challenges of an accelerated and design-heavy production schedule, the producers were confident they had assembled a team with the experience, ability, and drive to meet it—and now, from a vantage point of ten years later, it's apparent that the producers were right.

However, in addition to the general demands of television production, and the specific demands of a *Star Trek* project, *The Next Generation* faced one additional complication, unique to itself—the turmoil that existed within the writing staff.

At the time *The Next Generation* went into production, the Hollywood writing community buzzed with rumors about the apparent disarray in some areas of the series' production. Looking back, Rick Berman confirms that writing staff came and went in that first season as if through a revolving door. But in that first season, few members of the production team commented on the rumors, and rightly so. Almost every television production must withstand a shaky start-up, and efforts were under way almost from the beginning to correct any problems that might interfere with a smooth production.

Eventually, though, in seasons to come, the pas-

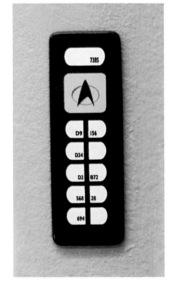

A 24th-century door-
knob, also known as an
entry keypad.

sage of time helped people look back at what was, for some, a trying experience, and the details of that initial unsettled period were discussed openly. Today, the mere fact that there *is* something to look back upon—ten years of *The Next Generation*'s solid success—implies that whatever the problems of that first season, they were faced, dealt with, and ultimately became atypical footnotes in the history of a consistently well-run production.

With that approach in mind, it is interesting and illuminating to take a brief look back at what was transpiring in some of the production offices in that first season.

As earlier described, Gene Roddenberry is the person who created *Star Trek*. Drawing inspiration from decades of science-fiction and adventure tales in print and film, he brought into being a unique structure for the presentation of compelling stories both new and familiar. Students of science fiction can find in *Star Trek* echoes of A. E. Van Vogt's *Voyage of the Space Beagle* and MGM's classic 1956 movie *Forbidden Planet*. There's the communicator from *Tom Corbett: Space Cadet,* the matter transmitter from the 1958, 20th Century Fox film, *The Fly,* and even the distinctive circular bridge and viewscreen from the 1960 East German production of Stanislaw Lem's *First Spaceship on Venus*.

But *Star Trek* was and is much more than the sum of its parts. The true creative spark that Gene Roddenberry brought to his assemblage of traditional science-fiction elements was the hallmark tone and content of what millions of people have come to recognize as a *Star Trek* story—one that examines the human condition against the backdrop of a positive, optimistic future.

Actor Eric Menyuk came close to being cast as Data, but made his way to *The Next Generation* as the Traveler in "Where No One Has Gone Before," and two subsequent episodes.

Noted science-fiction writer Damon Knight once offered a solution to the age-old debate over how to define science fiction by stating, "Science fiction is whatever I'm pointing to when I say: 'This is science fiction.'" In his role as a filter for the contributions of his team, Gene Roddenberry's definition of what is and isn't *Star Trek* was much the same. The fact that tens of millions of fans around the world maintained an ongoing and passionate interest in his definition proved that he was doing his job well.

That proven ability to define *Star Trek* was what made Roddenberry's participation so critical to Paramount's plans for *The Next Generation*. It is also the situation that helped fuel some of

A Rick Sternbach concept for the Klingon pet "targ" which appeared in "Where No One Has Gone Before." The part was played by a wild boar named Emmy Lou, in a costume designed by William Ware Theiss. ILLUSTRATION COURTESY OF THE ARTIST.

SEASON ONE: EPISODE 6
WHERE NO ONE
HAS GONE BEFORE
Written by Diane Duane & Michael Reaves
Directed by Rob Bowman

A test of the new propulsion system throws the *Enterprise* into a bizarre dimension that causes the crew to perceive dangerously disorienting alternate realities while at the same time endangering the life of the mysterious Traveler—an alien with the ability to move through time and other dimensions. The friendship that develops between the Traveler and Wesley saves both the alien's life and the *Enterprise*. The alien's private revelation of Wesley's potential leads Picard to promote Wesley to acting ensign.

SEASON ONE: EPISODE 7
THE LAST OUTPOST
Teleplay by Herbert Wright
Story by Richard Krzemien
Directed by Richard Colla

The Federation and the Ferengi meet for the first time when the *Enterprise* and a Ferengi ship lose power above an outpost of the fallen Tkon Empire. This less than auspicious first meeting worsens when, instead of investigating the outpost together as agreed by both sides, the Ferengi double-cross Riker's away team. Riker's professionalism and the Federation's beliefs and practices, in contrast to the Ferengi's pettiness, convince the outpost's simulated guardian to allow both ships to proceed on their way.

LONELY AMONG US

Teleplay by D. C. Fontana
Story by Michael Halperin
Directed by Cliff Bole

While ferrying the representatives of two antagonistic races, the *Enterprise* is boarded by an energy creature that causes both equipment and people to behave erratically. Data takes on the persona of Sherlock Holmes to investigate the mystery, but is too late to prevent the creature from taking over Picard's body. Though the creature succeeds in hijacking Picard's body by transforming it into energy, the crew is able to use the transporter to restore his physical form and escape.

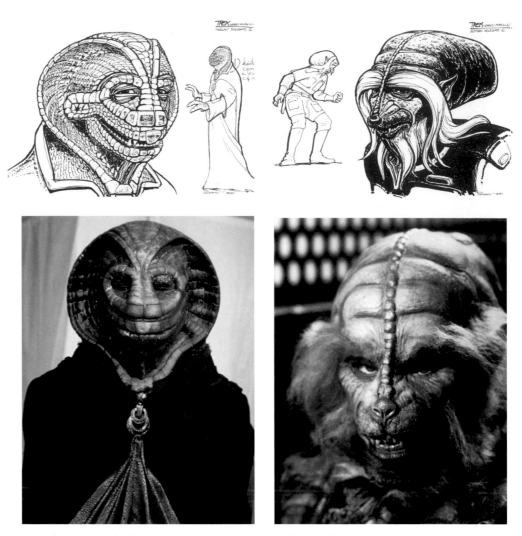

Andrew Probert's designs were not limited to starships and sets. Here he created the look for the antagonistic Selay and Antican species in "Lonely Among Us."
ILLUSTRATION COURTESY OF THE ARTIST.

the confusion which developed in the quest for new stories to tell. For though Gene Roddenberry was indispensable to the production of *The Next Generation*, he was no longer the young man who had produced *The Original Series*. After more than twenty years, Roddenberry had been given a second chance to prove that *Star Trek* was a valid television series, and the irony was that his health was such that he was no longer capable of taking on the lion's share of the immense workload that second chance would require.

The reason is complex, personal, and without question connected to Roddenberry's diabetes and the inevitable decline of age. In addition, the complications of diabetes, typically more severe in older patients, were further exacerbated by Roddenberry's headstrong insistence on ignoring his doctor's advice concerning medication and diet. Thus, as *The Next Generation* moved closer to production and the demands on Roddenberry's time and talent increased, he could not keep up.

Because there were no textbooks on the future, the new series needed a visionary authority to say what the Ferengi and twenty-fourth-century shuttlecraft would look like. The designers needed direction on instrumentation, vehi-

At the time of *The Original Series*, costume designer William Ware Theiss was known for the "Theiss Theory of Titillation," which stated that the degree to which a costume is considered sexy is directly proportional to how likely it seems it will fall off. Though his newer designs for *The Next Generation* were more subdued than his earlier *Star Trek* work, in "Justice," the Edo's preoccupation with health and sex gave Theiss a good story reason to return to his signature style of precariously draped costumes.

SEASON ONE: EPISODE 9
JUSTICE
Teleplay by Worley Thorne
Story by Ralph Wills and Worley Thorne
Directed by James L. Conway

Wesley's life is forfeit when he accidentally breaks local law by entering a "forbidden zone" during an "R and R" stop on Rubicun III, home of the pleasure-loving Edo. Despite misgivings about going against the Prime Directive, Picard uses force to rescue Wesley from the Edo, whose machinelike "god" now orbits the planet and keeps Picard and his team from beaming back to the *Enterprise*. The Edo's "god" relents when Picard makes the case that true justice allows for merciful interpretation of laws.

SEASON ONE: EPISODE 10
THE BATTLE
Teleplay by Herbert Wright
Story by Larry Forrester
Directed by Rob Bowman

DaiMon Bok of the Ferengi returns Picard's old ship, the *Stargazer*, which Picard lost in the Battle of Maxia. Bok's son was the Ferengi captain who died in that encounter with Picard, and Bok has rigged the *Stargazer* with a mind-control device that forces Picard to relive the battle—only now the *Enterprise* is the enemy. As Picard replays history with a repeat of the famous Picard Maneuver, Data counters Picard's strategy, giving Riker a chance to contact the captain, who then locates and destroys the mind-controller.

cles, and costumes. The writers needed to know the capabilities and limits of technology, and the directions for character development. The producers needed guidance on casting, story arcs, and, most important, a pilot script. In a situation where even a younger producer could be overwhelmed by the demands on his time, it was clear that Roddenberry needed to delegate some of his responsibilities in order to continue to do what he did best—create the future.

Roddenberry chose to delegate some responsibilities. When Ed Milkis left the series after he had completed his duties on the pilot episode, in a decision which would have a profound and long-lasting influence on the future of all *Star Trek* projects, Roddenberry accepted Rick Berman aboard as a *Next Generation* producer.

Berman had come to Paramount in 1984, as Director of Current Programming. His responsibilities included overseeing the hit Paramount sitcoms *Cheers, Family Ties,* and *Webster.* Within his first year at the studio, he had been upped to Executive Director of Dramatic Programming, overseeing the

John de Lancie returns as Q, tempting Riker with an offer of superhuman powers.

SEASON ONE: EPISODE 11

HIDE AND Q

Teleplay by C. J. Holland and Gene Roddenberry
Story by C. J. Holland
Directed by Cliff Bole

Q returns to tempt Riker by offering him Q-like powers after Worf and Wesley are killed in a Q-induced "test." Riker uses the power to bring Worf and Wesley back to life, and, with Picard's permission, to let La Forge see, to give Worf a Klingon mate, to let Data become human, and to make Wesley an adult. However, as Picard had predicted, all refuse Riker's gifts because of the gift's origins. Q is recalled by his own kind for failing to win a bet based on Riker's actions, and all effects of Riker's temporary powers vanish—except for the restoration of Worf and Wesley.

SEASON ONE: EPISODE 12

TOO SHORT A SEASON

Teleplay by Michael Michaelian and D. C. Fontana
Story by Michael Michaelian
Directed by Rob Bowman

Forty years earlier, Starfleet Admiral Mark Jameson ended a hostage situation on Mordan IV by secretly exchanging arms for the hostages' freedom—an illegal act which prolonged a vicious civil war. Now the governor of Mordan IV has engineered a trap for Jameson, to gain revenge. But when Jameson arrives on the *Enterprise*, the governor doesn't recognize him—the admiral has been rejuvenated by an alien de-aging compound. However, as Jameson's illegal actions are revealed, the compound begins to fail, and even the governor knows the time for revenge has passed as Jameson finally dies.

production of the ABC miniseries *Space, Wallenberg: A Hero's Story,* and the top-rated, one-hour dramatic adventure series *MacGyver.*

In May 1986, Berman's responsibilities increased again when he became Vice-President, Longform and Special Projects. Longform is an industry term meaning television projects longer than one hour, which includes made-for-television movies and miniseries. It was also an area of television production that Paramount coincidentally decided to abandon just as Berman took on his new position. If it hadn't been for that extra phrase, "Special Projects," in his title, Berman might have left Paramount along with television movies.

However, there was one special project that promised to come to fruition, and when the new *Star Trek* series was announced, Berman was, as he puts it, assigned to be "the studio guy" on the project. His job would be to oversee the expenditure of almost $30 million of Paramount shareholders' money.

As Milkis's replacement, Berman became an avid student of *Star Trek,* even making unexpected, though appreciated, visits to members of the crew with long *Star Trek* experience in order to be brought up to date on the science and technology of the twenty-fourth century. His education paid off. As Berman recalls, "over the first three-month period, I went from producer, to supervising producer, to co-executive producer, and by the middle of the first season, I was running the show with Gene." Though none could know it at the time, Gene Roddenberry had taken the first step in preparing to pass the torch of *Star Trek*'s stewardship.

Some of Roddenberry's other responsibilities were taken over by people on his staff. But what might have begun as an effort to help Roddenberry with the immense burden of producing resulted, according to former staffers, in a great deal of miscommunication. The one area that seemed the most affected was the writing staff. On a show like *The Next Generation* where the writing is so essential, this resulted in frustration and frayed nerves, and the end result was that many of the writers chose to leave.

Looking back on the quality of the stories told in the first season, it's clear that script consistency was an elusive goal, hampered by a larger than usual turnover in the writing staff. But what is intriguing is that, because of the

One of the more unusual aliens encountered by the crew of the *Enterprise,* courtesy of Q in "Hide and Q."

strength of the production team Roddenberry had helped assemble, the confusion in the writing offices did not spread beyond their walls. As Jonathan Frakes recalls, "I think in spite of the chaos that may have been going on in the writers' building, Rick Berman maintained the quality of the show throughout all those changes. So there was never a time when we had scripts that were in total disarray."

Twice in that first season, however, production was shut down for a few days because scripts were not ready—once in November, for "Angel One," and again in January for "The Arsenal of Freedom." But given the breakneck schedule the cast and crew had been keeping, those shutdowns were gratefully accepted as welcome holidays for some, and catch-up days for others.

Like the future Gene Roddenberry had charted for humanity, the production of *The Next Generation* proceeded with the optimism of all who remained with the show, and from that passion came one of the many reasons for its success.

Beginning with the first day of principal photography for "Encounter at Farpoint" in May, the producers, cast, and crew of *The Next Generation* worked for six months in a type of limbo. With no episodes scheduled to air until September, there was no feedback for their work. There would not even be a completed version of "Farpoint" for them to view until a week before the series' broadcast premiere. And studio executives are notoriously tight-lipped when it comes to commenting on future plans.

In fact, though Paramount was, on paper at least, committed to delivering twenty-six hours of *Next Generation* programming to the stations it had contracted with, even the show's stars were not aware of that minimal level of job security. Because, strictly speaking, it wasn't guaranteed.

Jonathan Frakes recalls that it was an uncertain time, though typical in an actor's experience. "We worked on the pilot before we heard that we got the first thirteen. Then, in the middle of the next thirteen, we heard that we were picked up for the full season. And then, in the middle of the back thirteen, we got picked up for the second year." Only in the third contract covering the second set of thirteen episodes did a full-fledged, long-term option finally come into play, covering the actors' participation in the series for a standard period of five years recalls Frakes.

Because of this characteristic lack of hard information for those involved in any television production, cast and crew members alike generally become keen observers of telling details—noticing anything that might give a hint as to their future.

In the case of *The Next Generation*, one of the first unequivocal signs to the rank-and-file that Paramount felt it had a hit series in the making was the appearance of phone lines coming out of the actors' trailers. That was the type of extra expense which money-conscious studios are loath to approve for short-term projects, but which can be justified for the long-term.

The fact that the phone lines made their appearance in the weeks before the pilot episode's airdate was universally considered a sign that the actors were expected to be occupying their trailers for a long time to come.

Michael Dorn, especially, got a welcome indication of his ongoing role as Worf in the series when the opening-title sequence was revised at the last minute to include his credit as one of the regular characters. Bob Justman had finally won the battle of the Klingon marine.

Confirming Paramount's prediction, the pilot's premiere lived up to its promise. On one hand, the show was hailed as the highest-rated syndicated one-hour drama on television, with the caveat that it was also the *only* syndicated one-hour drama on television. But jokes aside, the 98 independent stations and 112 network affiliates that ran "Encounter at Farpoint" set a record with their ratings. In Dallas, Denver, Los Angeles, Miami, and Seattle, *The Next Generation* stations actually beat the four networks in prime time.

But executives involved in television production are also realists. Like the cast and crew, they knew the premiere ratings of *The Next Generation* might only be the onetime product of curiosity. Two million copies of the home-video ver-

Captain Picard in his hard-boiled Dixon Hill persona, introduced in the first hour-long dramatic television episode ever to win a George Foster Peabody Award.

SEASON ONE: EPISODE 13
THE BIG GOODBYE
Written by Tracy Tormé
Directed by Joseph L. Scanlan

In a break from preparations for contact with the Jaradan, an insectoid race obsessed with protocol, Picard demonstrates his Dixon Hill holodeck program for Data, Dr. Crusher, and Whalen, a literary historian. However, when the Jaradan make a long-distance scan of the *Enterprise*, the program is lethally altered. Whalen is killed by real bullets before Wesley and La Forge can open the holodeck. Some of the fictional characters then try to escape into the *Enterprise*, but immediately dematerialize, unable to exist beyond the holodeck. Still dressed as Dixon Hill, Picard successfully greets the Jaradan.

SEASON ONE: EPISODE 14
DATALORE
Teleplay by Robert Lewin and Gene Roddenberry
Story by Robert Lewin and Maurice Hurley
Directed by Rob Bowman

On Omicron Theta, Data discovers the lab of his creator—Dr. Noonien Soong—and his own "twin": Lore, Dr. Soong's first attempt to create an android. The proverbial evil twin, Lore replaces Data, then summons the Crystalline Entity responsible for killing the planet's colonists, to have it attack the *Enterprise*. Wesley alone realizes that Data is actually Lore, and convinces his mother to reactivate the real Data. Data and Lore fight in a cargo bay until Lore is beamed into space on wide dispersal.

SEASON ONE: EPISODE 15
ANGEL ONE
Written by Patrick Barry
Directed by Michael Rhodes

While searching for survivors from a long-missing freighter, Riker and his away team are taken captive by the matriarchal rulers of Angel One. As a male, and therefore a second-class citizen, Riker has no status, and Troi and Yar must conduct the negotiations for their freedom. Meanwhile, the survivors are found to have formed a community with the planet's dissidents and face death. Any attempt to save the survivors, the dissidents, and his away team will result in Picard's breaking the Prime Directive, so Riker convinces the planet's ruler that a compromise is possible, allowing the survivors and dissidents to relocate to a more distant part of the planet.

Instead of remaining a background character, Worf became an integral member of the crew.

sion of *Star Trek IV,* the *Star Trek* film with the highest domestic box-office earnings, had reached the stores in the week before the premiere, and each one carried a commercial for the new series, insuring that the fan base had been primed for *Star Trek*'s next incarnation. But it remained possible that fans of *The Original Series* might decide that Picard and his crew were not as interesting as Kirk and his. True to his word, Roddenberry hadn't produced a retread series; *The Next Generation* was indeed something new. And if there's one thing television executives know, it's that they know nothing about how the audience will respond to something new.

But the ratings held.

To be sure, reviews were mixed. Martha Bayles of the *Wall Street Journal* called the first episode a "cross between *Masterpiece Theatre* and an action cartoon—in other words, full-blown kitsch." John Carman of the *San Francisco Chronicle* was not impressed, though he stated that the series "has the potential to become a gem in the scruffy realm of first-run syndication," and allowed that *The Next Generation* did share its theme with *The Original Series:* "the primacy of traditional human virtues."

Meanwhile, Monica Collins of *USA Today* was much more enthusiastic. She said "Farpoint" was "a fabulous meshing of story, character, and special effects," which "succeeds brilliantly." *The Next Generation* shows "how good sci-fi on TV can still be, while following in the footsteps of a legend but creating a mood, a feeling, a being all its own." Paula Dietz of the *New York Times* also praised the show, stating that it had "the power to make us see ourselves in a new way." And Don Merrill, reviewing "Farpoint" in *TV Guide,* praised the show for what it maintained from *The Original Series:* stories and themes that "carry a message of hope, a belief that mankind is growing—and maturing." He concluded by calling *The Next Generation* "a worthy successor to the original."

Overall, after the first regular episodes had been aired, the stations showing them reaped a whopping eighty-seven-percent ratings increase over the previous year.

Divining the future from the appearance of telephone wires was no longer necessary. On November 19, 1987, less than eight weeks after *The Next Generation*'s premiere, Paramount officially announced that the series had been renewed for a second season. Jonathan Frakes says this was when "it became clear that *The Next Generation* was something that was going to last for a while. And I was thrilled."

The first bridge shot from "Encounter at Farpoint."

But, despite Frakes's confidence, security for the show did not necessarily translate into security for the actors.

One effect of the constant parade of writers was that the main characters were still in a state of flux. Knowing the importance of defining characters, Roddenberry had shrewdly decided to reuse a premise from an *Original Series* episode, "The Naked Time," as a way to reveal the new characters to the audience. In the *Original Series* episode, Kirk and his crew are exposed to a disease that creates symptoms similar to intoxication, leading to a lowering of inhibitions. That episode unforgettably revealed Sulu as a swashbuckling swordsman, showed the emotional pain Spock hid from the world, let Nurse Chapel state her love for Spock, and exposed Kirk's divided passion for his ship.

By exposing Picard's crew to a similar threat, Roddenberry hoped to offer viewers a glimpse of the new characters' innermost qualities. Indeed, Tasha Yar's implied seduction of the "fully functional" Lieutenant Commander Data is as memorable a moment to *The Next Generation* viewers as was Sulu's swordsmanship in *The Original Series*.

When he assigned this episode to D. C. Fontana, Roddenberry knew he was taking a calculated risk. Despite his stated intention that the new show would not be a retread of the past, he could be accused of simply recycling *The Original Series*. Indeed, that was the reaction of many fans to this story. Not only did the episode make reference to the first ship to encounter the disease—the *U.S.S. Enterprise* under Captain James Kirk—but the writer of that original episode, John D. F. Black, received co-story credit. Subsequent rewrites on the *Next Generation* version led D. C. Fontana to conclude that it had changed

Bynars, a race of computer specialists, face death on the bridge of the *Enterprise* when their plan to "borrow" the ship's computer fails.

SEASON ONE: EPISODE 16
1 1 0 0 1 0 0 1
Written by Maurice Hurley and Robert Lewin
Directed by Paul Lynch

Riker is entranced by Minuet, a very realistic holographic character in a New Orleans jazz bar holodeck program, but he finds that her creation is linked to a hijacking attempt by computer-dependent aliens called Bynars. To foil the Bynars' plan, Picard and Riker program the *Enterprise* to self-destruct, but halt the program when they find that their hijackers are dying. The Bynars had hoped to borrow *Enterprise*'s memory core to offset the effects of a nova-induced eletromagnetic pulse on their world's master computer. But it's too late—the pulse has hit. Picard and Riker use the ship's computer to rejuvenate the Bynars, but Riker discovers that Minuet no longer exists, and never will again.

SEASON ONE: EPISODE 17
HOME SOIL
Teleplay by Robert Sabaroff
Story by Karl Guers & Ralph Sanchez and Robert Sabaroff
Directed by Corey Allen

On a routine mission to report on the status of a terraforming station on Velara III, the crew of the *Enterprise* find themselves at war with an alien life-form—a microbrain, native to the planet, whose race and ecosphere is threatened by the terraformers' efforts to desalinate the subsurface groundwater. In compliance with the wishes of the indigenous Velarans, Picard declares the planet off limits to Federation contact for 300 years.

significantly from her original intent and she asked for her credit to be withdrawn.

But after "The Naked Now," character development faltered, especially when compared with the deeply personal stories that would be explored in later seasons. And unfortunately, despite Gene Roddenberry's desire to portray the future as an environment in which women and men were fully equal, the female characters suffered most of all. In fact, Counselor Troi, with her vaguely defined power to sense the emotions of others, became such an enigma to new writers that she was not included in the drafts of several episodes, and by November rumors spread that Marina Sirtis might be cut from the cast.

Sirtis recalls that time as one in which she felt she was "hanging on by a thread. The writers really didn't know what to do with the character, so Troi started getting written out of episodes, and I was very nervous. I was terrified that I was going to be fired.

"I knew it wasn't because they thought I was a bad actress, but because the character was psychic: if she was on the bridge when the alien came on the viewscreen, she could read his mind and that was the end of the story. It would be time to go to a forty-minute commercial."

While the rumors of Sirtis's departure proved to be unfounded, a month later similar rumors began concerning Denise Crosby's role as Tasha Yar. In this case, the rumors were true. Crosby was disappointed with her character's

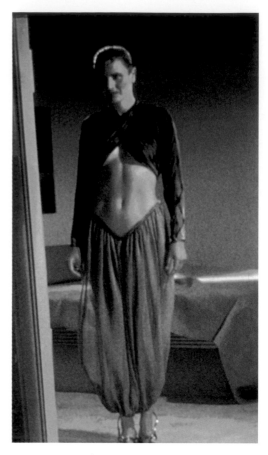

Tasha Yar greets Data in "The Naked Now."

The computer-dependent Bynars were cast as women, just as Gene Roddenberry had cast women to play the Keepers in the first *Star Trek* pilot, "Menagerie," more than twenty years earlier.

Mark McChesney being suited up for his role as Armus—the malevolent alien who killed Tasha Yar in "Skin of Evil."

lack of development, and requested that she be released from the series. The producers agreed, and Tasha's death was written into Episode 22, "Skin of Evil." At Roddenberry's insistence, the death was to be senseless—an act of random violence that was part of the daily risk a security officer faced. Though the episode was scripted that way, without a dramatic purpose Tasha's demise was oddly emotionless, though the moving final scene in which her friends gather in the holodeck to listen to her last message tape more than made up for it.

Crosby later mused that if more scripts had presented parts for her that were as strong as her part in "Skin of Evil," she would never have asked to be released.

A death of another sort also occurred in that first season. Since Roddenberry was adamant that *The Next Generation* not reuse the villains of the past, a new race of threatening aliens was conceived—the Ferengi.

The Ferengi were to be horrendous creatures driven solely by their quest for profit, however achieved. The first mention of them came in "Encounter at Farpoint" when Riker made a veiled reference to the Ferengi practice of eating their business partners.

Unfortunately, by the time the Ferengi made their first appearance in Episode 7, "The Last Outpost," a confluence of events guaranteed that despite everyone's best intentions, they would be no substitute for Klingons.

In the words of Armin Shimerman, who portrayed one of the first Ferengi in that episode, the actors were directed to "jump up and down like crazed ger-

The Andrew Probert concept drawing that set the style for the Ferengi.
COURTESY OF THE ARTIST.

CREW
MEMBERS

LETEK

SALESMAN, THIRD CLASS

TAAR

SALESMAN, SECOND CLASS

(FUTURE
TATLOOS)

SALESMAN, FIRST CLASS
(ASSISTANT MANAGER)

STAR TREK - TNG
• IDEAS FOR FERENGI
RANK TATOOS
—OKUDA 8/13/87

In keeping with the mercantile preoccupation of the Ferengi, Michael Okuda suggested this breakdown of Ferengi rank tattoos.
COURTESY OF MICHAEL WESTMORE.

bils." Rick Berman confirms that memory, and states that the Ferengi's "silliness quotient" ruled them out as major *Star Trek* adversaries.

Six years later, though, Shimerman was given the chance to repair some of the damage to the Ferengi's character when he was cast as Quark on *Star Trek: Deep Space Nine*. In that series, he has brought a complex character to life, helping to redefine Ferengi as more than mere comic foils.

But for every episode that did not work out as the production team had hoped, there were successes, perhaps none so notable as Episode 13, "The Big Goodbye." Not only did it win one of *The Next Generation*'s first Emmy Awards, for Best Achievement in Costuming, but it became the first hour-long drama to win a Peabody Award for excellence in television production.

"The Big Goodbye" introduced the recurring plot element of a "holonovel," in this case a holodeck reconstruction of a series of pulp detective novels from the mid-twentieth century, featuring the hardboiled detective Dixon Hill. It was also one of only four episodes in that first season for which a writer received sole credit. In this case, the writer was Tracy Tormé, whose credits

The fearsome Ferengi Whip appeared only in "The Last Outpost."
ILLUSTRATIONS BY RICK STERNBACH. COURTESY OF THE ARTIST.

Andrew Probert also designed the Ferengi starship, taking his inspiration from a horseshoe crab. ILLUSTRATIONS COURTESY OF THE ARTIST.

Armin Shimerman in a partial makeup test for his role as one of the first Ferengi to appear on *Star Trek* in "The Last Outpost." Shimerman went on to rehabilitate the Ferengi as Quark, in *Star Trek: Deep Space Nine*.

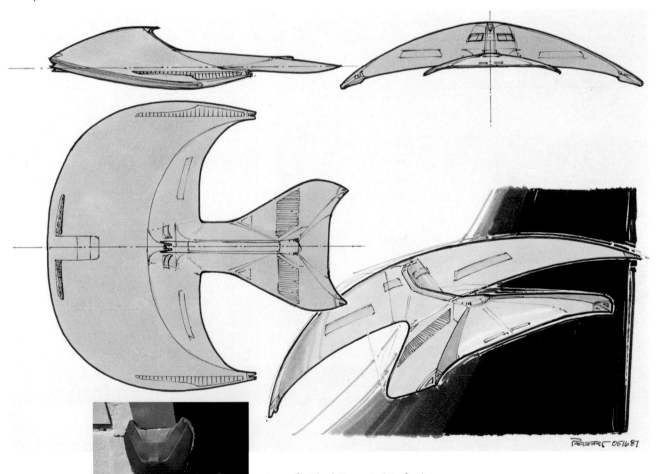

An unfinished Ferengi ship, fresh from the mold. PHOTOGRAPH COURTESY OF GREG JEIN.

SEASON ONE: EPISODE 18
WHEN THE BOUGH BREAKS
Written by Hannah Louise Shearer
Directed by Kim Manners

Wesley and six other children are kidnapped by the inhabitants of the planet Aldea to perpetuate their race in the face of apparent planet-wide sterility. But Dr. Crusher discovers that the Aldeans are both sterile and dying because of an ozone leak in the planet's protective shield. When Wesley leads a hunger strike among the captured children, the Aldeans request Crusher's and Picard's help, giving Riker and Data the opportunity to beam down undetected. The crew is then able to alert the Aldeans to their true dilemma, offer the Federation's assistance in solving their problems, and retrieve the children.

SEASON ONE: EPISODE 19
COMING OF AGE
Written by Sandy Fries
Directed by Michael Vejar

Both Wesley and Picard are tested when Wesley competes for a single opening in Starfleet Academy. Picard's loyalty is questioned by Admiral Quinn, an old friend who suspects a conspiracy is forming within Starfleet. Wesley fails to beat his competition and remains on the *Enterprise*, while Picard passes Quinn's test and is offered the position of commandant of the Academy. Picard declines, and the nature of the suspected conspiracy is unresolved.

The real view out the observation lounge windows.

John Putch as the Benzite, Mordock, in "Coming of Age."

Old Klingons meet the new in "Heart of Glory."

included writing stints on both *Saturday Night Live* and *SCTV,* and who would go on to create the successful Fox science-fiction series *Sliders.*

Tormé's first script credit on *The Next Generation* was on Episode 5, "Haven." By Episode 20, "Heart of Glory," he was an executive story editor. And at the end of the first season, he was one of the few writers who was invit-ed back for the second season. Joining him were Maurice Hurley, and the team of Richard Manning and Hans Beimler.

Among those not invited back was Gates McFadden, who portrayed Dr. Beverly Crusher. Like Marina Sirtis and Denise Crosby, she had also felt that her character's development needed strengthening, and she had been persistent in asking for expanded parts and rewritten dialogue. Though the producers were split on the decision to continue the character of Dr. Crusher, in the end McFadden was told that Paramount would not be exercising its option on her services for the second season. McFadden admits that initially she was surprised

Tasha Yar, moments before her
senseless death.

SEASON ONE: EPISODE 22
SKIN OF EVIL
*Teleplay by Joseph Stefano & Hannah
Louise Shearer
Story by Joseph Stefano
Directed by Joseph L. Scanlan*

An away team sent to rescue
Counselor Troi from a shuttle crash
encounters Armus, a malevolent alien
life-form whose only purpose is to
torment others. In the course of his
first encounter with the away team,
an indifferent Armus kills Security
Chief Tasha Yar. When Worf and
Wesley realize Armus loses his powers when enraged, Picard provokes
the creature, distracting him long
enough for the away team to escape.
The episode ends with a moving
holodeck wake in which Tasha's final
message to her friends is played.

and upset by the producers' decision, but was happy for having had the experience and soon felt ready to move on to more demanding roles. A year later, one
of those more demanding roles would be a new and improved Beverly Crusher.

Then there were some members of the production who declined to come
back.

Supervising Producer Bob Justman had, like Gene Roddenberry, proved his
point: *Star Trek* was, once more, a success. He had made it work once, at a time
when the ratings system was not sophisticated enough to recognize the series'
value, and now, twenty years later, he had helped make it work again. He felt
vindicated, and was ready to take life at a slower pace, just as he had promised
himself before Roddenberry had called almost two years earlier. Taking over
some of Justman's duties was David Livingston, the young man he had hired as
unit production manager for the pilot, and who would later become a director
of some of *Star Trek*'s most visually striking episodes in all three series.

Production designer Herman Zimmerman left the series, but not *Star Trek*.
He went to work for director William Shatner on *Star Trek V: The Final Frontier*,
and brought a new, more welcoming look to that movie's *Enterprise*-A, creating
a transition between the battleship sterility of *The Original Series'* starship and
the hotel-like opulence of *The Next Generation*'s. Zimmerman would return to
Star Trek as production designer on *Star Trek VI: The Undiscovered Country*, and
again for *Star Trek: Deep Space Nine* and the *Next Generation* feature films.

Despite the varying consistency of the first-season episodes, and the rapid
turnover of staff, one aspect of *The Next Generation* was unchanged from *The
Original Series*—many stories addressed the issues of the day.

Three episodes specifically dealt with disease, reflecting the growing
impact of the AIDS epidemic. The Iran-Contra affair inspired the arms-for-
hostages story element in "Too Short a Season," and was even the starting
point for Tracy Tormé's initial thoughts on the nature of the conspiracy within Starfleet in Episode 25.

As LeVar Burton explains, "Gene always knew that the important issues of
today are best presented in terms of the future or the past, where they are at a
safe distance for the audience to consider."

For all that was new about *The Next Generation*, at its heart it was still the
Star Trek millions of people had come to appreciate, enjoy, and love.

Ten months after the cameras had first rolled on "Encounter at Farpoint,"
production wrapped on "The Neutral Zone," and Season One. The confidence
displayed in that last episode was unmistakable.

Secure in the knowledge that the audience had accepted Picard's crew as a
new version of *Star Trek,* and not retreads, Roddenberry felt comfortable in
bringing back a favorite alien race—the Romulans. The incidents that brought
them back into Starfleet's scrutiny was the mysterious disappearance of several of their outposts in the Neutral Zone—an ominous story point that was
deliberately inserted to set up the appearance of a new alien threat for the second season.

But the most telling element of that episode was the Romulan commander's final line to Captain Picard.

"We are back."

That wasn't just the Romulans talking.

That was Gene Roddenberry and the entire *Star Trek* family.

Lightning had been caught for an unprecedented second time, and now, in the best tradition of science fiction, it was time to see what the future would bring.

Merritt Butrick as T'Jon in "Symbiosis." Butrick had earlier played Captain Kirk's son, David, in *Star Trek II: The Wrath of Khan*, and *Star Trek III: The Search for Spock*.

Cafe des Artistes

Le menu

Croissants D'ilithium
Avec le frommage creme et les tomats fraiche

Tribbles dans les Blankettes
Trois petit jeune tribbles saute avec les beurre chaud serve dans les pains tubulaire

Targ Klingon a la Mode
Un petite targ fait avec glace vanilla serve sur un plat de jour et poisson. Serve avec les bynar frittes et parslais.

Cheveaux avec Sauce Brun
Un piece grande de cheveaux de trente-huit ans fait avec un sauce brilliante et brun, avec un plat petit de pierre.

Jean Cougar Mellencamp
Le flancs d'un cougar capture par dix aquanautes avec cafe fraiche. Serve sans le fleures violete ou le bateaux jaune.

•••••••••

Les Desserts Formidable

*L'antimatter flambe
Posesse le gateaux et le mange aussi
Le terrapin suprise*

•••••••••

Le management reserve le droit a expulse le personnes qui ne comprend pas ce menu. Si vous require le prix, vous n'affordez pas a mange dans cette restaurant. Ne pas de chemise, ne pas de service. Cinquant million Français n'es pas wrong. Gauling, isn't it?

The menu from the small Parisian restaurant in "We'll Always Have Paris." Clearly the strain of producing hundreds of graphics for each episode was beginning to take its toll on the art department.

Michelle Phillips, from the singing group The Mamas and the Papas, as Jenice Manheim in "We'll Always Have Paris."

SEASON ONE: EPISODE 23
SYMBIOSIS
*Teleplay by Robert Lewin and Richard Manning and Hans Beimler
Story by Robert Lewin
Directed by Win Phelps*

Picard faces another Prime Directive dilemma when the *Enterprise* comes to the rescue of a crippled freighter, picking up four passengers and their mysterious cargo. Two passengers are from the world of Onara, two from Brekka. The cargo is a drug called felicium, available only on Brekka, and needed to fight a plague on Onara. However, Crusher discovers that felicium is really a narcotic, and that the Brekkans have knowingly addicted the Onarans. Unable to take action against the oppressive relationship between the two worlds, Picard does the next best thing—he refuses to repair the freighters that carry the felicium, bringing the drug trade to an end.

SEASON ONE: EPISODE 24
WE'LL ALWAYS HAVE PARIS
*Written by Deborah Dean Davis and Hannah Louise Shearer
Directed by Robert Becker*

The *Enterprise* encounters strange temporal distortions caused by the experiments of Dr. Paul Manheim, whose wife, Jenice, was once romantically involved with Picard. Twenty-two years earlier, Picard had not kept a date with her at a restaurant in Paris in order to take on a Starfleet assignment. Manheim's team has died as a result of his experiments, and Manheim himself is dying. Data beams into the scientist's lab, and despite finding himself existing simultaneously in three different time streams, manages to seal the dimensional rift created there. Manheim recovers, and on the holodeck, Picard re-creates the Parisian restaurant in order to properly say his farewell to Jenice.

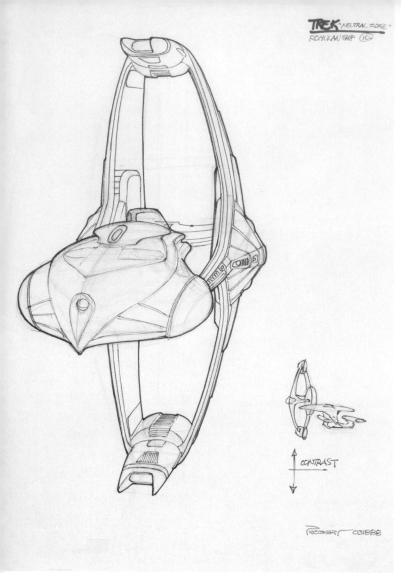

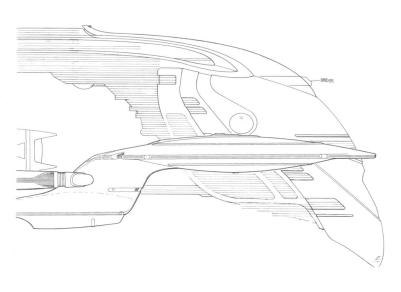

Andrew Probert's last design contribution to
The Next Generation was the ominous, double-hulled
Romulan Warbird.
ILLUSTRATIONS COURTESY OF THE ARTIST.

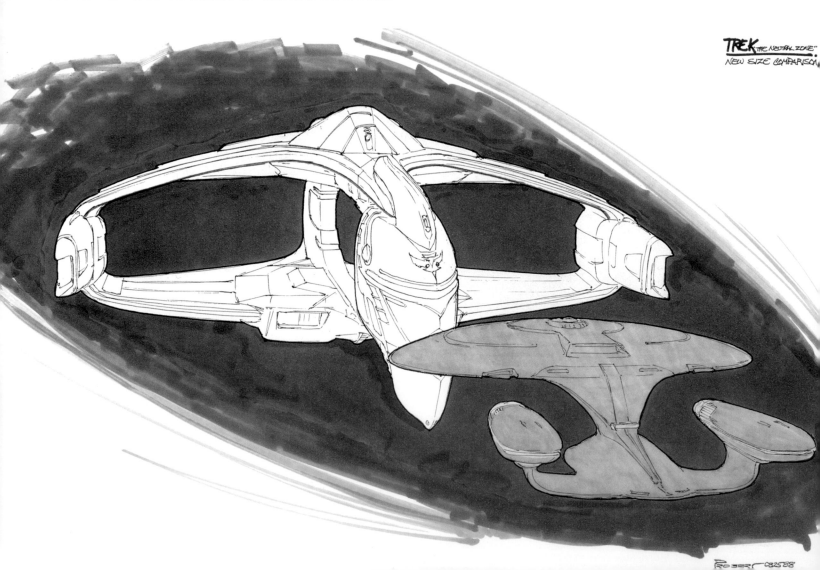

Two early steps in the creation of a Warbird—a master carving in foam, and the first molds taken from the carving.
PHOTOGRAPHS COURTESY OF GREG JEIN.

The symbol of the Romulan Star Empire designed by Monte Thrasher. Look closely and you'll see a bird of prey clutching the twin worlds of Romulus and Remus, one in each claw.

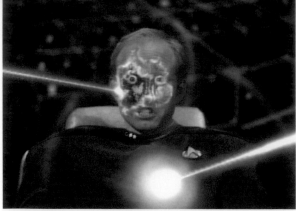

SEASON ONE: EPISODE 25
CONSPIRACY
Teleplay by Tracy Tormé
Story by Robert Sabaroff
Directed by Cliff Bole

Following a clandestine meeting with three other officers and the mysterious death of an old friend, Picard concludes that the possible conspiracy within Starfleet, first mentioned in Episode 19, "Coming of Age," might be real. He takes the *Enterprise* to Earth to investigate his suspicions and discovers that key Starfleet personnel have been taken over by alien parasites. Picard and Riker identify the officer whose body contains the mother creature and destroy him, ending the threat, though leaving open the possibility of the parasites' return.

"We are back."

SEASON ONE: EPISODE 26
THE NEUTRAL ZONE
Television story and teleplay by Maurice Hurley
From a story by Deborah McIntyre & Mona Glee
Directed by James L. Conway

The *Enterprise* discovers a drifting space capsule that contains three humans from Earth's twentieth century, frozen in cryonic suspension. They are brought aboard, treated for their terminal diseases, and introduced to life in the twenty-fourth century, causing complications for the ship's crew. At the same time, Picard must deal with the renewed threat of Romulan activity in the Neutral Zone, though the Romulans claim merely to be investigating the mysterious disappearances of their outposts ... a plot thread to be picked up in Season Two.

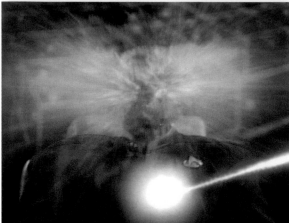

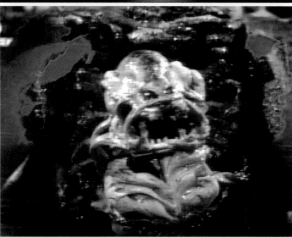

One of the most controversial episodes of *The Next Generation*'s first season was "Conspiracy," in which small parasites infested Starfleet personnel. Its gruesomeness went considerably beyond what was expected for *Star Trek* television at the time. The most notorious sequence involved Picard and Riker confronting Starfleet inspector, Dexter Remmick, who was host to the "mother" creature. At first, Remmick's throat is seen to bulge ominously. The effect was courtesy of air bladders, placed under a false neck, being inflated by makeup supervisor Michael Westmore, who was hiding behind Remmick's chair. This particular sequence took many shots to complete because, Westmore claims, the director, Cliff Bole, was determined to make his old school-friend Westmore hyperventilate.

The exploding head was created by packing an old mold of actor Paul Newman's face with raw meat, then blowing it up. Viewing the completed effect, Rick Berman and Peter Lauritson were worried that they might have produced something too horrific for a family audience, so a representative test viewer was recruited—special-effects supervisor Dan Curry's six-year-old son. After watching the episode on a large screen, Berman and Lauritson asked Curry's son what he thought of it. The boy said, "I really liked the part where that guy's head blew up! You know, you could make a Remmick action figure where if you pressed the button, his head blows up!" Berman made the decision to air the episode as is. It remains the only episode of the series to have been banned by the BBC.

Concept drawing by Andrew Probert. COURTESY OF THE ARTIST.

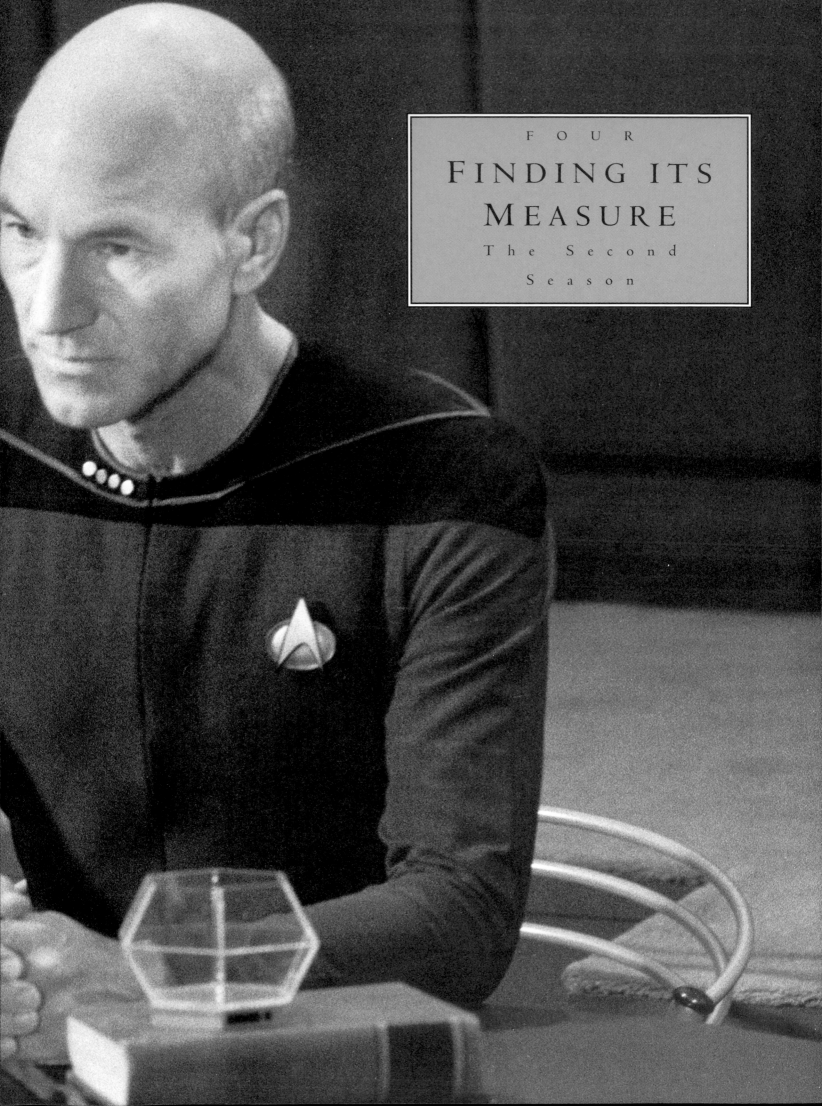

DURING the first season, a sign had appeared on Patrick Stewart's trailer—"Beware of Unknown Shakespearean Actor." As production of the second season began, the good news was that that sign was no longer necessary. Tens of millions of viewers, not just in the United States but around the world, now knew his name. After its first season, *The Next Generation* was a solid hit. Not only in syndicated ratings, but in international video sales[2].

The not-so-good news was that no one really knew why.

To the people working on the show, *The Next Generation* had yet to live up to its promise of matching and exceeding the best episodes of *The Original Series*. But

Just like the fledgling *The Next Generation*, the world of 1988-1989 was a world in transition, reflecting both continued tradition and groundbreaking change. In the United States, George Bush defeated Michael Dukakis to become the forty-first President of the United States. In Pakistan, Benazir Bhutto was elected Prime Minister, becoming the first woman to head a Muslim state.

In the world of television, Ted Turner founded Turner Network Television, adding another source of competition for the established networks' quest for television viewers. Continuing scandals among television evangelists further fueled growing cynicism in the medium.

In Washington, D.C., NASA scientists for the first time reported to the Senate Committee on Energy and Natural Resources that global warming, most likely caused by emissions from industrial sources, did constitute a growing threat to humanity.

In Seoul, Korea, the Soviet Union—*Star Trek*'s model for the Klingon Empire—enjoyed its last gasp at an Olympics Game, winning 132 gold medals to the United States' 94.

In popular culture, Salman Rushdie's *Satanic Verses* incensed many Muslim readers; movie audiences made a hit of director Penny Marshall's *Big*, with Tom Hanks, and director Barry Levinson's *Rain Man*, with Dustin Hoffman and Tom Cruise; while visual effects entered a new era of integrated live action and animation with director Roger Zemeckis's *Who Framed Roger Rabbit?*, with Bob Hoskins.

From this volatile mix, the unsettled second season of *The Next Generation* arose.

The *Original Series* meets *The Next Generation* in Season Two—at least, behind the scenes, as *Star Trek V: The Final Frontier* goes into production during *The Next Generation*'s second season. DeForest Kelly was the first of three original cast members to appear on the new series, in a touching scene as the 137-year-old Admiral McCoy in the pilot episode, "Encounter at Farpoint."

the hunger of the audience for more *Star Trek* in any form had given *The Next Generation* the ratings push it needed to bypass the studio's potential thirteen-episode cutoff and set the production team's sights on three full seasons. What would happen next, when the series had the sixty-five episodes it needed to be stripped in syndication, was a decision that lay in the unknowable future. The task at hand was to move beyond satisfying the needs of a forgiving group of diehard fans to producing consistently good television that would hold the interest of general viewers.

To that end, Paramount increased the average per-show budget. For example, episodes that required extensive visual effects, or more than the usual number of alien extras, were permitted to have the cost of their production go over the usual amount spent in those areas, on the understanding that other episodes would spend proportionately less. In practice, this strategy could lead to the final few episodes of a season being left with minimal funds for production—a situation that had a direct bearing on the final episode of the second season.

Daniel Davis as Sherlock Holmes's—and Captain Picard's—nemesis, Professor Moriarty, a holodeck character who achieves awareness in "Elementary, Dear Data." Moriarty returned in the sixth-season episode, "Ship in a Bottle."

With La Forge's second-season promotion to chief engineer came a new bridge station.

The design work of *The Next Generation* was never-ending. In Season Two, Andrew Probert had moved on to work for Disney Imagineering, leaving Rick Sternbach as the principal illustrator under new production designer Richard James. ALL ILLUSTRATIONS BY RICK STERNBACH. COURTESY OF THE ARTIST.

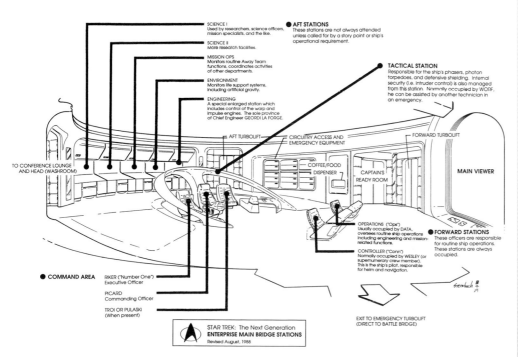

The updated, second-season bridge. Drawings such as this were prepared for the Writers/Directors Guide.

But as that season began, to Rick Berman the greatest challenge the show faced was "to take the seven or eight characters we developed in the first year, and find ways to make them interact in more entertaining fashions."

Notice the lack of specificity? "Seven *or* eight characters"? That was indicative of the changes afoot.

Unlike several other *Star Trek* characters in the past, the late Tasha Yar remained dead and Denise Crosby would not be returning to the series ... at least, not for the second season. But Gates McFadden was also gone. Dr. Beverly Crusher was said to have taken a new position as the head of Starfleet Medical, improbably leaving her young son, Wesley, to fend for himself on the *Enterprise.*

Both women had left the series, in part, because of disappointment over the way their characters had failed to develop, though in hindsight there was very little character development for anyone in the first season. However, Gene Roddenberry graciously acknowledged that, by merely changing Dr. Crusher's posting instead of killing her, it was always the producers' intention to leave the door open for McFadden's return to the show.

Replacing Dr. Crusher was Dr. Kate Pulaski, played by another veteran of *The Original Series,* Diana Muldaur. Not only had she played Dr. Ann Mulhall in "Return to Tomorrow" and Dr. Miranda Jones in "Is There in Truth No Beauty?," but Roddenberry had also earlier cast her in one of his unsold pilot episodes, *Planet Earth,* produced by Bob Justman.

The introduction of the new doctor was an attempt to skirt around the Roddenberry dictum that Starfleet professionals in the twenty-fourth century did not engage in interpersonal conflict. Since television writers are taught that compelling drama is based in conflict, this need to avoid it was seen as an obstacle to storytelling by many writers, at least until Michael Piller joined the show in the third season. However, for the second season, the producers did feel somewhat justified in reaching back into *Star Trek* history and coming up with a character who evinced more than a little of Dr. McCoy's brusqueness and irascibility.

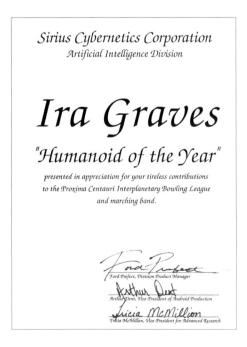

Sirius Cybernetics Corporation
Artificial Intelligence Division

Ira Graves

"Humanoid of the Year"

presented in appreciation for your tireless contributions
to the Proxima Centauri Interplanetary Bowling League
and marching band.

Ford Prefect, Division Product Manager

Arthur Dent, Vice President of Android Production

Tricia McMillan, Vice President for Advanced Research

RECOGNIZING SIGNIFICANT CONTRIBUTIONS TO SCIENCE

ZEE MAGNEES

INSTITUTE FOR THEORETICAL RESEARCH HONORS

IRA GRAVES

FOR OUTSTANDING WORK IN THE FIELD OF
CYBERNETICS AND ARTIFICIAL INTELLIGENCE
IN THE DEVELOPMENT OF THE POSITRONIC
NEURAL PROCESSING NETWORK.

Background visual detail for "The Schizoid Man."

The new CMO
takes over.

SEASON TWO: EPISODE 33

UNNATURAL SELECTION
Written by John Mason & Mike Gray
Directed by Paul Lynch

The *Enterprise* encounters a supply ship whose crew died of old age. Checking the ship's last stopover, the Darwin genetics lab, they are told of a group of artificially created "super-children." The Darwin geneticists assure the crew that they are uninfected by the hyperaging virus and are in need of rescue. By the time Data and Dr. Pulaski discover that this claim is false, Pulaski is infected as well, and Picard has her quarantined at the lab to work on a cure. The engineered children will have to live out their lives in isolation.

Diana Muldaur as *The Next Generation*'s Dr. Kate Pulaski ...

... and as *The Original Series*' Dr. Miranda Jones.

SEASON TWO: EPISODE 34

A MATTER OF HONOR
Teleplay by Burton Armus
Story by Wanda M. Haight & Gregory Amos and Burton Armus
Directed by Rob Bowman

Riker serves on the Klingon vessel *Pagh* as part of an officer-exchange program. At the same time, a young Benzite officer, Mendon, joins Picard's crew. When hull-eating bacteria attack both ships, Mendon delays reporting the threat. In the meantime, the *Pagh*'s captain, believing that the damage to his ship is not accidental, denounces Riker as a traitor and orders an attack on the *Enterprise*. Riker has the Klingon captain beamed to the *Enterprise*, making Riker the commander of the vessel. Riker then demands that Picard surrender to the *Pagh*, thus preserving Klingon honor. When Mendon helps discover a solution to the bacterial threat, both ships are saved.

A unique publicity photograph from "Unnatural Selection," showing *The Next Generation*'s makeup supervisor, Michael Westmore, and Diana Muldaur as Dr. Pulaski, before and after the episode's aging effects. PHOTOGRAPH COURTESY OF MICHAEL WESTMORE.

The *U.S.S. Lantree* model from "Unnatural Selection," on the motion-control stand at Image G. The model was originally the *U.S.S. Reliant* from *Star Trek II: The Wrath of Khan*, and would appear as many other starships, including Benjamin Sisko's *Saratoga* in the pilot episode of *Deep Space Nine*. COURTESY OF GREG JEIN.

Riker demonstrates that Data
can be considered nothing more
than a machine.

SEASON TWO: EPISODE 35
THE MEASURE
OF A MAN
Written by Melinda M. Snodgrass
Directed by Robert Scheerer

Data attempts to resign from
Starfleet to foil a Starfleet cyberneti-
cist's plan to disassemble and duplicate him, with no guarantee of successful reassembly. The scientist
cites a 300-year-old Starfleet law in
support of Data's being regarded as
Starfleet property. In the ensuing
court battle, Riker must take the case
against Data before a judge with
unhappy personal ties to Picard.
Though Riker successfully demonstrates that Data is a machine by
removing one of his arms and turning him off, Guinan convinces Picard
that the true issue is one of slavery
of sentient beings, organic or otherwise. Picard argues successfully in
defense of Data's right to self-
determination.

Where Beverly Crusher was a widow and devoted single mother, Pulaski
had three children by three different husbands. Like McCoy, she had a distinct
aversion to using the transporter, and, Starfleet professionalism be damned, to
her Data would never be more than just a lump of inhuman machinery—an
opinion that she often delighted in sharing with him.

In talking about her character, Muldaur confirmed the direction in which
the new doctor would go. "I think Kate Pulaski's closer to our old crusty
McCoy from the early days. She's very opinionated, so hopefully we'll stir up
some hornets' nests along the way and get people upset with her. It should be
fun." Muldaur also believed that the intent to involve Pulaski in an ongoing
argumentative relationship with Data was deliberately based on the popular
feud that had developed between Spock and McCoy.

The other newcomer to the *Enterprise*'s crew had not been crafted with such
calculation. Instead, the impetus came from the actor herself, a self-proclaimed
"Trekkie from way back," Whoopi Goldberg.

A prominent actor and comedian who would go on to win an Academy
Award in 1991 for her role in *Ghost,* Goldberg had always had an interest in
being part of *The Next Generation.* But when she learned that Denise Crosby had
decided to leave the show, she felt the door had been opened for a new female
character and pursued that interest with determination. At first by passing
messages along through her friend, LeVar Burton, and then by placing direct
phone calls to the production office, Goldberg kept putting herself forward for
that as yet nonexistent role.

Initially, there was a good
reason why no one in the production office ever returned
her calls or acknowledged her
interest. They just didn't take
her offer seriously. Why
would a movie star want to
become involved in an ongoing role in a television series?
After all, part of the reason
The Next Generation had come
to be at all was because the
movie careers of some of the
stars of *The Original Series* had
made them too expensive to
return to television.

But the reason for
Goldberg's interest was even
better—it was yet another
legacy of Gene Roddenberry's
earlier work.

As a child, like so many
others, Goldberg had been
touched by *Star Trek*'s vision of
the future, and for her the
series would forever be more

Soon to be an Academy Award winner for her role
in *Ghost*, Whoopi Goldberg as Guinan.

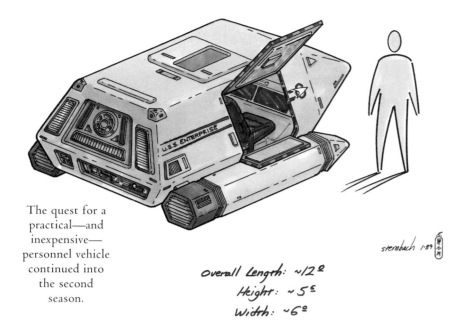

The quest for a practical—and inexpensive—personnel vehicle continued into the second season.

sternbach 1·89

Overall Length: ~12ᵉ
Height: ~5ᵉ
Width: ~6ᵉ

Wesley contemplates his first romance.

SEASON TWO: EPISODE 36
THE DAUPHIN
Written by Scott Rubenstein &
Leonard Mlodinow
Directed by Rob Bowman

When the *Enterprise* carries a princess and her zealously attentive guardian to their homeworld, Wesley's attraction to the princess provokes the overprotective guardian to reveal that she is actually a shapechanger who can take on violent forms. Contrary to Picard's orders, Wesley continues to meet with the princess, provoking the wrath of her guardian. When the princess faces down the transformed guardian with a frightening transformation of her own, Wesley is shocked to discover his first love is not human. He eventually overcomes his anger at the deception and makes peace with the princess.

than just another television show. In the round of publicity that attended her joining the show, she recalled that in her childhood the only time an audience ever saw black people in the future was on *Star Trek*. Goldberg remembered tuning in to *The Original Series* on Thursday nights and thinking it was "like heaven." In particular, Goldberg credits Nichelle Nichols as being a key source of childhood inspiration.

Indeed, Goldberg's enthusiasm for this aspect of *The Original Series* is one of the chief reasons that explain the power of Gene Roddenberry's creation. LeVar Burton also speaks eloquently of how *Star Trek* inspired him, and not just as a lifelong fan of the science-fiction genre.

"I'd read an awful lot of science fiction," Burton says, "and had seen a lot of science-fiction films. But *Star Trek* was my first experience of encountering a vision of the future where people of color were actually represented."

Burton had come to national prominence as an actor for his portrayal of the young Kunta Kinte in the phenomenal 1977 miniseries *Roots*. He had later appeared in the television movie *Emergency Room*, a two-hour backdoor pilot produced by Bob Justman. When the casting call for *The Next Generation* went out, Burton was also the host of the hit PBS children's series *Reading Rainbow*, and he was excited by Justman's suggestion that he come to the studio to read for the part of Geordi La Forge.

"I did not have any sort of objective, analytical approach to this job at all," Burton says. "It was purely emotional. Driving to Paramount that first day, for that first meeting, I remember thinking to myself: 'You know what? If I get this job, great. But if I don't get this job, at least I will have had an opportunity to meet and shake the hand of the man who put Lieutenant Uhura, Nichelle Nichols, on the bridge of the *Enterprise*.'" Describing the context for his excitement at meeting Roddenberry, and his respect for the man, Burton explains, "I can trace in my lifetime the evolution of people of color, black people in particular, in the popular culture, specifically on television—from the time Diahann Carroll had her own series, called *Julia* [1968-1971], to the present, where black faces in the media and popular cultures are a matter of course.

Both Data and the *Enterprise* are affected by an alien computer virus.

SEASON TWO: EPISODE 37
CONTAGION
Written by Steve Gerber & Beth Woods
Directed by Joseph L. Scanlon

Entering the Neutral Zone to respond to the U.S.S. *Yamato*'s distress call, the *Enterprise* arrives just in time to see the ship self-destruct owing to widespread computer malfunctions caused by a virus. When La Forge downloads the *Yamato*'s logs, the *Enterprise*'s computers also become infected, leaving the ship vulnerable to a Romulan attack. Picard tracks the source of the virus to the long-dead Iconian civilization, and during an away mission Data also becomes infected by the virus. Fortunately, his self-correcting subroutines eliminate the contagion, and La Forge is able to use the same technique to restore the *Enterprise*'s computers.

SEASON TWO: EPISODE 38
THE ROYALE
Written by Keith Mills
Directed by Cliff Bole

After finding part of a twenty-first-century Earth spacecraft near an uninhabited planet, Worf, Data, and Riker become trapped in an artificial environment based on an old mystery novel—*The Hotel Royale*. The environment was constructed by the aliens who found the twenty-first-century astronaut, in order to provide a familiar setting in which he could live out his days. The astronaut has since died, but the novel's resort casino world lives on. Data makes use of the novel's ending to break the casino's bank and allow the *Enterprise* crew to make their getaway.

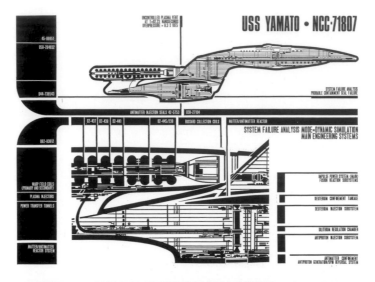

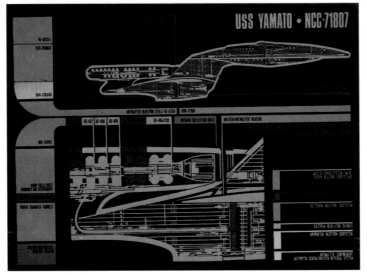

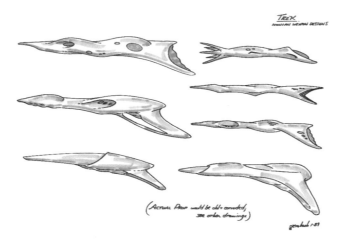

Iconian weapon concepts for "Contagion."
ILLUSTRATION BY RICK STERNBACH. COURTESY OF THE ARTIST.

To create a computer image showing an analysis of the *U.S.S. Yamato*'s destruction in "Contagion," Michael Okuda and his scenic designers first assembled black-and-white graphic art, based on existing *Enterprise* illustrations, modified with text specific to the episode's script. The art was shot onto negative line film, then colored transparent plastic—called "gel"—was attached to the back of the negative to add color. The final negative was then installed in a "display screen" on the set, and backlit to give the impression of a computer display. In other instances, such as when computer images had to be seen changing, the final negative could be shot separately, then composited into the live-action film in which actors were filmed watching an empty screen.

It's an everyday occurrence now, but it wasn't when I was growing up. And for me being this kid who devoured science-fiction novels at the rate of one a week, never having encountered heroes of color in the pages of those books, to finally in the late sixties see a representation of the future—a science-fiction series that had a black woman on the bridge—it was a big deal! Huge!"

Burton agrees that one of the reasons why *The Original Series* remains popular after thirty years is because the inclusive nature of the crew Roddenberry

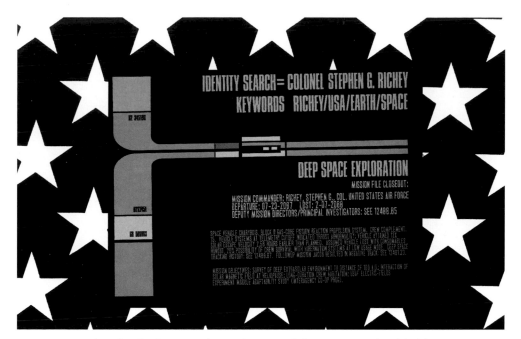

IDENTITY SEARCH = COLONEL STEPHEN G. RICHEY
KEYWORDS RICHEY/USA/EARTH/SPACE

DEEP SPACE EXPLORATION

MISSION FILE CLOSEOUT:
MISSION COMMANDER: RICHEY, STEPHEN G., COL. UNITED STATES AIR FORCE
DEPARTURE: 07-23-2037 LOST: 2-07-2038
DEPUTY MISSION DIRECTORS/PRINCIPAL INVESTIGATORS: SEE 12488.B5

As a template for the future, and an indication of the intriguing detail hidden in every frame of *The Next Generation,* the American flag dating from 2037 in "The Royale," was seen to have 52 stars for 52 states. Overlapping is an Okudagram showing the mission details of Colonel Stephen Richey's ill-fated spaceflight from "The Royale."

In "The Icarus Factor," Worf's friends help him reenact a Klingon ritual on the holodeck. The menacing Klingon second from the left is composer and *Star Trek* fan John Tesh.

had assembled keeps it looking current. "It was one of the first shows that actually represented this world that we live in," Burton says. "It was art that represented life the way it is. And, just in terms of the racial and gender makeup of that group of people, it was representative of the world as it truly is."

When Rick Berman finally met with Whoopi Goldberg, the timing for her arrival was perfect, and fit in perfectly with Roddenberry's inclusive future *and* a new component of the series. In order to create an additional setting in which the crew of the *Enterprise* could interact, plans had already been made for the

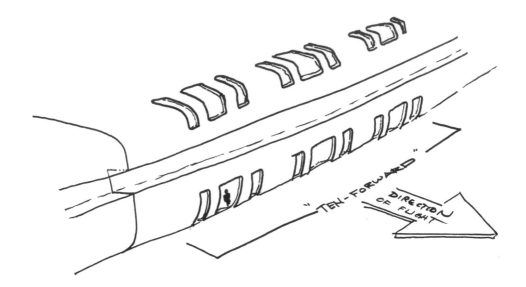

WINDOW CONFIGURATION
OF 10-FWD LOUNGE ON
SHIP MODEL
—OKUDA 10/7/88

The location of the new lounge had to be exactly determined to insure that the full-size windows built into the set matched an existing configuration on the already-completed model of the *Enterprise*. ILLUSTRATION BY MICHAEL OKUDA. COURTESY OF THE ARTIST.

"Terrace"—a 20th-century game which appeared as a 24th-century prop in Ten-Forward.

The new set lit for actual filming, and as it appeared behind the scenes. Note the wires for the table lights running up through the floor in the photo above.

Data and Riker make first
contact with the Borg.

SEASON TWO: EPISODE 42
Q WHO
Written by Maurice Hurley
Directed by Rob Bowman

Refused a crew position by Picard,
the superbeing Q throws the
Enterprise into uncharted space, where
it encounters and is engaged in a
battle with a previously unknown
race, the Borg. Picard's ship loses
shields and warp drive, and is boarded by Borg who seize information
from the *Enterprise*'s computer. Riker
boards the damaged cube-shaped
Borg ship and learns the ship is
regenerating itself—meaning the
Borg are seemingly invincible. Q
returns the *Enterprise* to its previous
location only when Picard admits he
needs his help. Nevertheless, Picard
knows it will be only a matter of
time until the Federation must face
the approaching Borg on their own.

SEASON TWO: EPISODE 43
SAMARITAN SNARE
Written by Robert L. McCullough
Directed by Les Landau

Accompanied by Wesley, who is facing more Academy tests, Picard travels by shuttlecraft to Starbase 515 to
have his defective artificial heart
repaired. Meanwhile, Riker places
the *Enterprise* in danger when he
underestimates the motives of a less-
advanced race, the Pakleds, who take
La Forge hostage. Riker and his crew
ultimately outwit the Pakleds and
rescue La Forge in time for Dr.
Pulaski to save Picard, whose surgery
has not gone as planned.

construction of Ten-Forward, a combination lounge and bar. The name came
from its location on the *Enterprise,* in the forward section of deck ten.

Ten-Forward was the last set designed by departing production designer
Herman Zimmerman, and he remembers it as his favorite. "Gene wanted a place
where the crew could socialize with each other," Zimmerman recalls, "without
having to do it in a very intimate setting in their living quarters, or in a very
formal setting in the observation lounge or on the bridge. So Ten-Forward
became the place where ordinary crew and the officers could co-mingle, and
where aliens who were not allowed on the bridge could interact with other crew
members. It was a very important set for the telling of stories."

Indeed, Roddenberry was always aware of the need for every aspect of production design to facilitate story-telling. During the initial design stages for
the new bridge, for instance, conceptual artist Andrew Probert had made the
suggestion of including a transporter pad on the bridge. Roddenberry understood the logic of Probert's idea, but acting as *Star Trek*'s filter, he decided that
the action of a walk—or run—from the bridge to the transporter room would
give future scriptwriters a perfect place to add explanatory dialogue to a script.
A transporter was not incorporated into the bridge.

As a place for socializing, Ten-Forward would need a bartender, though not
in every episode, and Whoopi Goldberg, who wasn't available for every episode,
was a perfect choice for the role. Thus, the character of Guinan was created to
appear in six episodes of the new season.

The character's name was taken from the legendary Prohibition-era nightclub hostess Mary Louise Cecilia "Texas" Guinan, who was introduced each
night to her patrons with what would become a popular catchphrase: "Give the
little girl a great big hand."

Fortunately, very little else of Texas Guinan made the transition to Ten-
Forward. Where the original was known for greeting her customers with the
cynical cry of "Hello, sucker!," the *Enterprise*'s Guinan was a five-hundred-year-
old El-Aurian, a member of an alien race known for their abilities as "listen-
ers." Goldberg thought of Guinan as old and wise, similar to the *Star Wars* character Yoda.

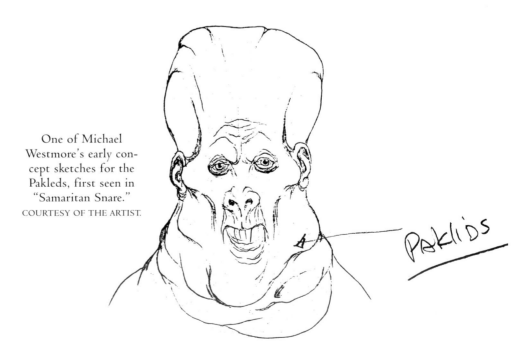

One of Michael
Westmore's early con-
cept sketches for the
Pakleds, first seen in
"Samaritan Snare."
COURTESY OF THE ARTIST.

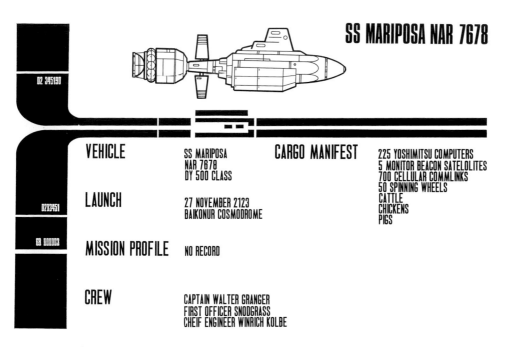

SS MARIPOSA NAR 7678

02 345190

0203451

68 1000013

VEHICLE	SS MARIPOSA NAR 7678 DY 500 CLASS	CARGO MANIFEST	225 YOSHIMITSU COMPUTERS 5 MONITOR BEACON SATELOLITES 700 CELLULAR COMMLINKS 50 SPINNING WHEELS CATTLE CHICKENS PIGS
LAUNCH	27 NOVEMBER 2123 BAIKONUR COSMODROME		
MISSION PROFILE	NO RECORD		
CREW	CAPTAIN WALTER GRANGER FIRST OFFICER SNODGRASS CHEIF ENGINEER WINRICH KOLBE		

In a tip of the hat to *Star Trek* history, Michael Okuda based the design of an old colony ship on Khan's sleeper ship from *The Original Series* episode, "Space Seed."

Unlike the departures of other cast and crew members after the first season, Herman Zimmerman's departure was in no way the result of any disappointment on his part or on the part of the producers. Indeed, his work on shepherding the design of the new *Starship Enterprise* had impressed both Harve Bennett and William Shatner, who were the producer and director, respectively, of the inevitable fifth *Star Trek* movie.

With Paramount's support, Zimmerman had taken a temporary leave of absence from *The Next Generation* in order to become production designer for *Star Trek V: The Final Frontier*. *Star Trek IV* had ended with Kirk and company being assigned to the brand-new *Enterprise*-A, and it was Zimmerman's job to oversee the redesign of that vessel's interiors, as well as to tackle the demands of creating the script's new alien worlds.

To fill in for him on *The Next Generation*, Zimmerman recommended his friend Richard James. James was no stranger to science fiction, having been art

Another long-time *Star Trek* fan guest-starred as an alien in "Manhunt." The Antidean on the right is Mick Fleetwood. Or is it the Antidean on the left ... ?

SEASON TWO: EPISODE 46
THE EMISSARY
*Television story and teleplay by Richard
Manning & Hans Beimler
Based on an unpublished story by
Thomas H. Calder
Directed by Cliff Bole*

The discovery of a Klingon sleeper
ship with the potential to threaten
Federation outposts reunites Worf
with K'Ehleyr, a half-Klingon, half-
human former lover. K'Ehleyr advises Picard to destroy the sleeper ship,
but, instead, Picard has Worf and
K'Ehleyr pretend to be the commanders of the *Enterprise* to trick the
newly awakened Klingons. Though
Worf and she renew their intimacy,
K'Ehleyr refuses Worf's offer of
marriage and takes command of
the sleeper ship.

Roy Brocksmith, as the
Zakdorn strategist, Kolrami,
helps Starfleet develop strategies for dealing with the
coming Borg threat.

SEASON TWO: EPISODE 47
PEAK
PERFORMANCE
*Written by David Kemper
Directed by Robert Scheerer*

In a battle simulation, Riker and
Picard go one-on-one as they practice to meet the Borg. Riker commands a refitted derelict, the U.S.S.
Hathaway, and Picard the *Enterprise*.
Wesley helps Riker to successfully
project an incoming Romulan
Warbird, but Picard then mistakes
reality for illusion and ignores an
attacking Ferengi vessel, which ren-
ders the *Enterprise* defenseless. The
Ferengi demand whatever new
"weapon" Riker has, but Riker fakes
his ship's destruction as it jumps to
warp, and the confused Ferengi
withdraw.

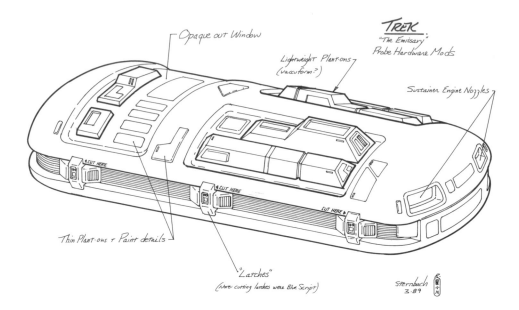

As a cost-cutting technique, props originally created for the *Star Trek* movies were
often recycled as props for *The Next Generation*. In "The Emissary," Spock's photon-torpedo
coffin became K'Ehleyr's transport probe.
ILLUSTRATIONS BY RICK STERNBACH. COURTESY OF THE ARTIST.

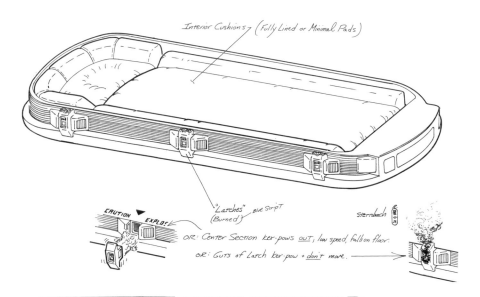

A holodeck menu
from "The Emissary,"
including references
to past episodes, *Star
Trek* lore, and a
favorite animé film.

HOLODECK PROGRAMMING

SIMULATION IN PROGRESS

AL CON	
MI WES	
MA RID	

02-734 SCUBA DIVING - HANAUMA BAY, EARTH
02-838 KLINGON RITE OF ASCENSION CHAMBER
03-298 CALISTHENICS - LT. WORF
03-348 SHI-KAHR DESERT SURVIVAL, VULCAN
03-480 DAMOCLES TOWER RECONSTRUCTION
03-624 CARNIVAL CELEBRATION, RIO DE JANIRO, EARTH
03-752 RACETRACK, LONGCHAMPS, FRANCE, EARTH
04-238 DIXON HILL IN "THE LONG DARK TUNNEL"
04-582 WINGS OF HONNEAMISE FLIGHT EXERCISE

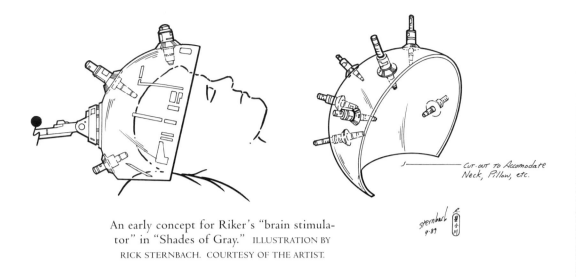

An early concept for Riker's "brain stimulator" in "Shades of Gray." ILLUSTRATION BY RICK STERNBACH. COURTESY OF THE ARTIST.

Riker is wounded by a thorn on a routine planetary survey, allowing an organism to invade his central nervous system, plunging him into a coma. After the organism reaches Riker's brain, Pulaski draws on Troi's powers to help stimulate his brain electronically. The doctor discovers that recollection of positive emotions encourages the microbe's growth, and negative ones impede it. She then provokes dangerously primitive emotions in Riker to conquer and eradicate the microbe.

```
SCENE 58:  Riker unconsious.  Enter brain-gizmo.
SCENE 59:  Pulaski:  "Let's Proceed".
SCENE 60:  Gizmo slides into place around Riker's brain.
SCENE 61:  Pulaski starts to operate gizmo.
SCENE 62:  As needles pierce Riker's skin.
SCENE 63:  Pulaski makes fine adjustments to gizmo.
SCENE 65:  More probes poke Riker (ouch!)
SCENE 66:  More adjustments
SCENE 67:  More probes.
```

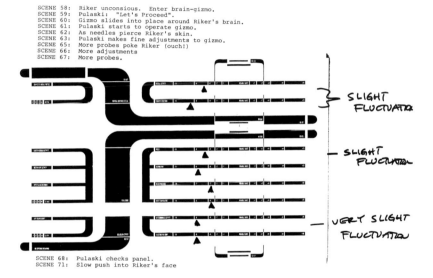

```
SCENE 68:  Pulaski checks panel.
SCENE 71:  Slow push into Riker's face
```

Even an inexpensive episode like "Shades of Gray" required careful planning of all the *Star Trek* background details viewers had come to expect. This is one of ten pages describing the animation required for Riker's medical monitor.

director on *Battlestar Galactica*. His credits also included the feature films *Silkwood* and *Local Hero*.

However, James's new position was destined to become not so temporary. After finishing his duties on *Star Trek V*, Zimmerman was offered the opportunity to serve as production designer on Ridley Scott's new film, *Black Rain*. Scott, the director of the groundbreaking science-fiction film *Blade Runner*, is known for the visual richness of his films, and Zimmerman eagerly accepted the assignment, taking a calculated gamble that by formally giving up his position on *The Next Generation*, he would be able to pursue a feature-film career. Long after the fact, Zimmerman recalls with a rueful smile that after completing *Black Rain*, he didn't work for six months, though his feature career eventually did prosper. In the meantime, he kept up his *Star Trek* connection by serving as production designer on *Star Trek VI*, the last film to feature the full cast of *The Original Series*. He was then invited back to take up the challenge of creating an all-new version of Gene Roddenberry's future by becoming production designer for *Star Trek: Deep Space Nine*—a position that in 1997 earned him the first prestigious Award of Excellence in Television from the Art Directors' Guild.

Meanwhile, Richard James's "temporary" position on *The Next Generation* lasted for the next six seasons, during which he and his designers created more science-fiction settings, alien worlds, and technology than any other team in television and movies combined, as well as earning four Emmy nominations and an Emmy Award for Art Direction. Beginning in 1994, James then applied his expertise to another new version of Gene Roddenberry's future as production designer for *Star Trek: Voyager*.

But despite the ease with which Whoopi Goldberg and Diana Muldaur were added to the cast, and with which Herman Zimmerman was followed by Richard James, as *The Next Generation* entered its second season, unease remained in the production office, and especially among the writers.

Perhaps the most well-known loss to the writing staff was David Gerrold, the first writer Gene Roddenberry had approached when the series had begun development.

In the world of scriptwriting, perhaps no other quality is sought by producers and studios more than passion. Gerrold had nothing but passion for his chance to be involved in *Star Trek*'s rebirth.

However, by its very nature, passion makes its possessor vulnerable in Hollywood. Thus, as is common in the start-up of almost any new series, because of their enthusiasm, some of the people who began working on the series at the very beginning, did so without their final deals having been negotiated. Gerrold was one of those people. He recalls, in the early development stage, that several conversations had led him to expect to become Roddenberry's own creative consultant, or an executive story editor, or even a producer on the series. However, when Gerrold's deal was finalized, his credit on the pilot episode was simply given as creative consultant.

But the terms of Gerrold's employment were not the sole reason for his decision to leave the series in the midst of first-season production. Instead, it was a three-way collision between passion, personalities, and business practicalities—a telling example of the difference between what people aspire to do and what real-world circumstances sometimes force them to accept.

The Original Series had a reputation for addressing the serious issues of the day, and *The Next Generation* was intended to follow in those footsteps. Gerrold recalls an early memo from Rick Berman that inspired the production staff, even before Berman had joined the series as a producer. The memo stated that *Star Trek* had always been an issues-based show, and that that had been one of its great strengths. Now *The Next Generation* had to continue to address those issues. The memo included a two-page list of areas Berman thought deserved to be tackled, including euthanasia, drugs, and AIDS. Gerrold remembers thinking at the time, "If we could do half of these, we would do the best series on television."

Roddenberry concurred with Berman's call to action. Gerrold remembers Roddenberry saying, "We have the power to do what we want." Referring to *The Original Series*' near-legendary run-ins with NBC censors in the 1960s, and the fact that this new *Star Trek* was being syndicated to individual stations, Roddenberry went on to say, "We don't have a network breathing down our necks, and the studio has endorsed us to do whatever we want."

With that mandate in mind, Gerrold accompanied Roddenberry to a *Star Trek* convention, where he recalls that a group of gay *Star Trek* fans asked Roddenberry if a gay character would turn up on the new series, in keeping with *Star Trek*'s theme of inclusivity. Roddenberry replied that the fans were right, and he would try to work a gay character into the series.

Roddenberry subsequently brought up that idea in a development meeting. Initially, there was some resistance to the concept, but Roddenberry told his team, "Times have changed and we have got to be aware of it."

With Roddenberry so clearly behind the idea of a *Next Generation* episode with a gay character, Gerrold pitched a story called "Blood and Fire," as an AIDS allegory, which included two members of the *Enterprise* crew who were gay. He was given the go-ahead to proceed to script and turned in a first draft that was positively received by everyone on staff. Roddenberry himself sent a telegram to Gerrold at a *Star Trek* convention aboard a ship: "Everybody loves your script. Have a great cruise. Love, Gene."

As a writer, and as someone who believed in the inspirational power of *Star Trek*'s vision of the future, Gerrold was elated. But when he returned to the production offices after the cruise, he found that his script was in disfavor. The idealism of Roddenberry's initial intentions to push the limits of television story-telling had hit the wall of business concerns. Much of the change in perception of the script resulted from Paramount's concern that because the series was syndicated, in some markets it might air in the afternoon when younger viewers would be part of the audience. Thus the studio had to weigh the mandate to produce provocative, issues-oriented episodes against the possible reaction of parents who might not want their children to see issues they felt were more suited to adult programming hours.

Though Gerrold fought for his script and it was slated for production, he also understood his responsibilities as a professional writer under contract to the series. Thus, he followed the producers' notes to revise the script by dropping the gay characters.

Though the revised script was not as powerful as the first, more and more revisions followed. While in television it is not unusual to have ten or more rounds of revisions on a script, eventually Gerrold's script was dropped from the production schedule.

Disappointed with the way he and his work had been treated, Gerrold subsequently asked Roddenberry not to renew his contract so that he could accept a development deal at Columbia.

But the turmoil that had troubled the writing and producing staff in private for almost a year did not end with Gerrold's departure and that of several other writers, some whom had been brought on for one or two scripts, subsequently declined other assignments, others were staff writers and story editors who opted for lesser roles and responsibilities as they waited for their contracts to expire.

But writer unrest was not the only reason *The Next Generation*'s second season faced upheaval. Just

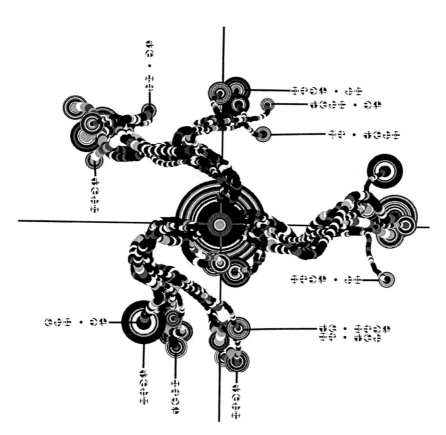

Part of the distinctive look of the *Star Trek* universe comes from the unique visual style Michael Okuda and his scenic designers create for each alien culture's means of communication and identification. This is one of the first graphic displays created for the Borg.

as the first season was ending production, the Writers Guild had gone on strike, and every series ready to begin production for the 1988-1989 television season was unable to commission scripts. Indeed, the strike delayed the start of the 1988 television season for all broadcasters.

Because of the lead time required to go from story pitch to production script, one strategy the *Next Generation* producers used to be prepared to start production the moment the strike ended was to evaluate scripts that had been purchased for *Star Trek: Phase II* but never produced. One of those scripts, "The Child," written by Jon Povill and Jaron Summers, was selected to be the first episode of the new season.

In the original script, it was the Deltan navigator, Ilia, who became pregnant with an alien life-form. As rewritten by producer Maurice Hurley, it was Ilia's *The Next Generation* counterpart, Counselor Troi, who gave birth.

Interestingly, Marina Sirtis recalls that it was in the second season that her character came into her own, specifically because of episodes like "The Child." In the first season, Sirtis had felt that Troi was in danger of being dropped from the series because the writers weren't certain how to handle the character. But with the departure of Gates McFadden and Denise Crosby in the second season, Sirtis says, "I was the young woman on the show, and I got all those 'young-woman' storylines. I felt the second season was when Troi leapt up the totem pole, and then in the third season it all just seemed to gel for everybody. I think that's when the show really took off. For me, it was the second, but, I think, for the company, it was the third."

Another positive element that came from the writers' strike was the discovery of Melinda Snodgrass's spec script, "The Measure of a Man." A spec script is one that is written on the writer's own initiative—on speculation. For beginning writers, spec scripts are considered essential samples which show producers and story editors the writer's talent. *Star Trek*'s most devoted fans share a desire to add their voices to Roddenberry's universe, and the various *Star Trek* shows traditionally receive the highest number of spec-script submissions of any series on television.

"The Measure of a Man," which concerned an attempt to have Data legally defined as a piece of equipment owned by Starfleet, is considered to be one of the series' best episodes. It was also nominated for a Writers' Guild award, an even greater honor for Snodgrass considering it was her first produced television script. Though she is now a science-fiction novelist, her first career had been as an attorney. The episode also has the distinction of having introduced the weekly poker game played by the *Enterprise*'s officers throughout the rest of the series.

On the strength of that script, Snodgrass was hired as a story editor, and continued working on the series until the third season.

A second-season episode that would exert a major influence on the future of *The Next Generation* was "Q Who?," which was written by Maurice Hurley and marked the third appearance of the popular Q, played by John de Lancie. The episode also had the distinction of introducing *Star Trek*'s nastiest villains—the Borg.

The Borg, whose name is derived from "cyborg," meaning cybernetic organism, were intended to provide the series with what the Ferengi had failed to deliver—a deadly, remorseless enemy that could not be reasoned with or defeated. The Borg's presence had been hinted at in the final episode of the first season, "The Neutral Zone," as later revelations in the series suggested that they were responsible for the disappearance of Romulan outposts mentioned in that episode.

Budget restraints kept the Borg from being depicted as insectoids as Hurley had originally intended, though the hive concept survived to become the overwhelming group mind known as the Borg Collective. In addition, the Borg's unique, cube-shaped ship, and their eerie appearance—reminiscent of both the biomechanism designs of H. Giger and the cybernetic, laser-eyed Lord Dread from the 1987 syndicated series *Captain Power and the Soldiers of the Future*—all contributed to the Borg ascending to the heights of *Star Trek* villainy, exactly as intended. Though they would appear in only five more episodes throughout the run of the series, just as Khan returned to battle Kirk in the second *Star Trek* movie, the Borg would also make the transition to the big screen in the second *The Next Generation* film.

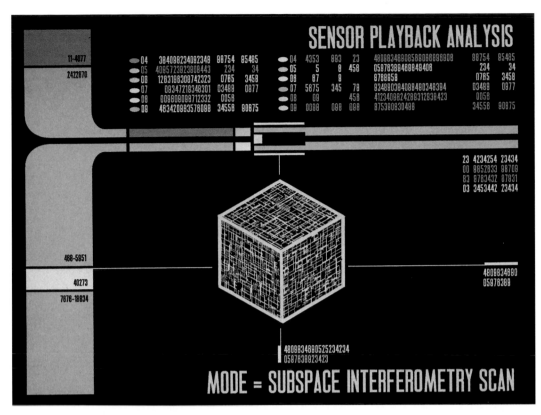

SENSOR PLAYBACK ANALYSIS

MODE = SUBSPACE INTERFEROMETRY SCAN

The ominous Borg cubeship as seen by the *Enterprise*'s sensors ...

... and as it appears onstage at Image G, the visual-effects house that took over the task of filming *The Next Generation*'s miniatures from Industrial Light & Magic. PHOTOGRAPH COURTESY OF IMAGE G.

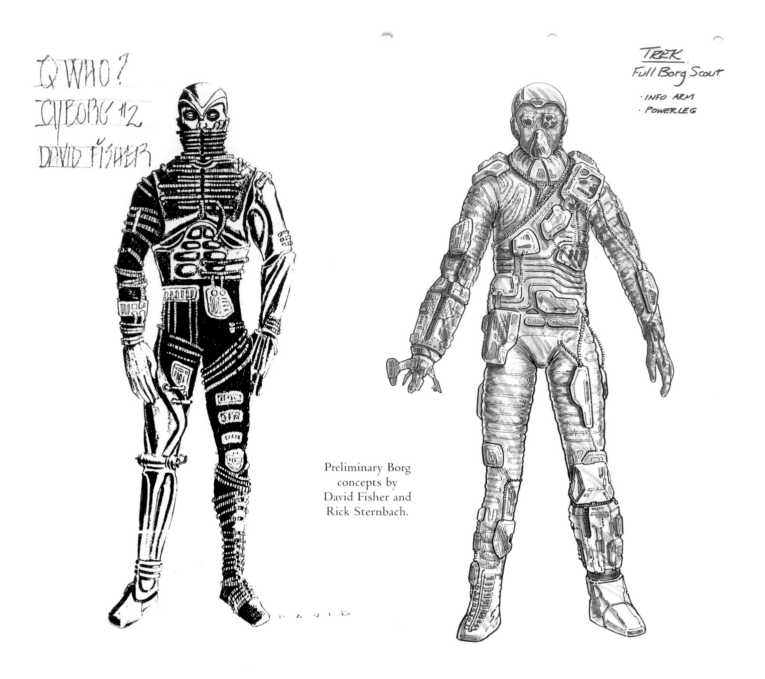

Q WHO?
CYBORG #2
DAVID FISHER

TREK
Full Borg Scout
· INFO ARM
· POWER LEG

Preliminary Borg
concepts by
David Fisher and
Rick Sternbach.

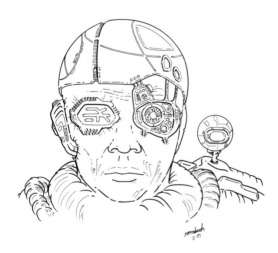

Another story element introduced in this season that would continue to play a part in the series was Suzie Plakson's role as the half-human, half-Klingon K'Ehleyr, introduced in "The Emissary." K'Ehleyr is the woman in Worf's past; in fact, in Season Four she would be revealed as the mother of the son Worf never knew he had.

It was in the second-season episode "Contagion" that Captain Picard first ordered "Earl Grey, hot."

Issues of the day that were tackled in the second season included the acceptance of sign language for the deaf as a legitimate language in "Loud as a Whisper," and the abortion debate, touched upon briefly in "The Child" and then obliquely presented in a story about cloning in "Up the Long Ladder."

By everyone's consensus, the final episode of the season, "Shades of Gray," stands as one of the weakest episodes of any of the *Star Trek* series. With the production budget almost

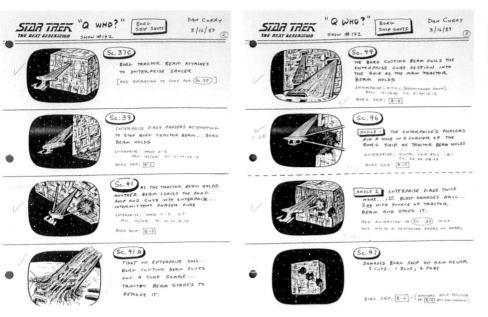

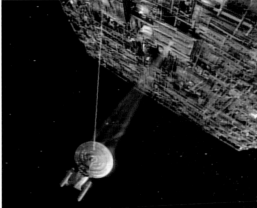

The complexity and cost of *The Next Generation*'s visual-effects sequences demand detailed planning before a single frame is shot. As the visual-effects supervisor for the first episode to feature the Borg, Dan Curry created these storyboards as a blueprint of the *Enterprise*'s first engagement with a Borg cubeship. The frames from the completed episode show how closely the visual-effects team follow the storyboards.
ARTWORK COURTESY OF DAN CURRY.

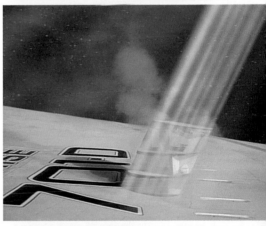

exhausted, the producers decided to fall back on a cost-saving television gimmick —a combined clip and bottle show. "Clip," because a sizable part of the episode would consist of clips from previous episodes, and "bottle," because it would be shot on already existing sets.

Two decades earlier, Gene Roddenberry had bought some time in *The Original Series'* first-season production schedule, and won science-fiction fandom's Hugo Award for Best Dramatic Presentation, with a two-part clip show, "The Menagerie," which used footage from the unaired first *Star Trek* pilot. But the producers of *The Next Generation*'s second season didn't have the luxury of unaired footage to draw from. Instead, as Riker lies in a coma in sickbay, the audience watches as he reexperiences events from seventeen other episodes. The sparse new footage for the episode was shot in only three days, compared with the usual schedule of from six to seven.

Finally, as the second season came to an end, so did much of the turmoil surrounding the series' production.

In addition to David Gerrold, other departures in the second season included producers Maurice Hurley and Robert Lewin, associate producer D. C. Fontana, writer Tracy Tormé, co-producers John Mason and Mike Gray, and story editors Leonard Mlodinow and Scott Rubenstein. Story editor Hannah Louise Shearer also left her staff position, though she would continue to write for the series in seasons to come.

But through all the behind-the-scenes turmoil, somehow the *Star Trek* magic continued to reach the screen. Even with "Shades of Gray," *The Next Generation* ended the season with more stations and higher ratings than it had at the beginning.

If the series could reach that level of success under troubled conditions, then the promise of what it could achieve under a stable production and writing team promised to be truly remarkable.

Fortunately, the wait for that ideal situation would not be long.

BY the time the third season began, the chaotic forces of evolution could at last be seen shaping *The Next Generation*'s production team into a stronger and more stable entity.

True, many producers and writers had left, but those who remained did so for a reason—they worked together efficiently and cooperatively. Tellingly, the core group of producers who began that season—Rick Berman, Peter Lauritson, and, though not quite a producer at the time, David Livingston—continued as key members of the *Star Trek* team for the duration of *The Next Generation*'s run.

Continuing in his role as executive producer, Gene Roddenberry was pleased to serve as a passionate guide to

Around the world, the trend toward reduced tensions between superpowers continued, even as regional conflicts intensified. Against this backdrop of contrasts, two events electrified the Western world—the horror of the government-orchestrated massacre of protesting students in Tiananmen Square in June 1989, and the joyful celebration that accompanied the demolition of the Berlin Wall the following November.

One month later, the United States invaded Panama in an attempt to capture General Noriega to face trial on drug charges. As if the Prime Directive were in effect, the U.N. General Assembly denounced the invasion as a violation of international law.

Showing the barriers to cultural understanding that still exist in our day, the Ayatollah Khomeini offered $3 million for the death of author Salman Rushdie, for his publication of the previous year's *Satanic Verses*.

In popular culture, Amy Tan's *The Joy Luck Club* hit the bestseller lists, Milli Vanilli hit the record charts with the ironically titled album, *Girl, You Know It's True*, and the only science-fiction competition for *The Next Generation* on television was Fox's *Alien Nation* series, which regrettably lasted only one season.

Hit movies of the year included *Glory*, with Denzel Washington, *Born on the Fourth of July*, with Tom Cruise, *Driving Miss Daisy*, with Jessica Tandy and Morgan Freeman, and Disney's *The Little Mermaid*.

Also at the movies, audiences were treated to impressive advances in visual effects in James Cameron's *The Abyss*. Other films from the science-fiction genre included *Back to the Future II*, *Batman*, *Honey, I Shrunk the Kids*, *Tremors*, and, of course, *Star Trek V: The Final Frontier*.

As Paramount had hoped when *The Next Generation* had begun production two years earlier, the voyages of both the original and new *Enterprises* now continued together.

the twenty-fourth century, with his advice and direction sought after and appreciated by all levels of the production team. With the lessening of the turmoil of the first two seasons, the new talent attracted to the series found a nurturing and dynamic home. The result would be the strongest season of *The Next Generation* yet, one which would see the production of many solid episodes, including two destined to be voted by fans as among the five best episodes ever made. One episode in particular would stand out as a real sign of growth when it presented something that Roddenberry had initially intended to avoid—a direct link to *The Original Series*.

There were changes in front of the camera as well, most notably the return of Gates McFadden in the role of Dr. Beverly Crusher. Though she had been disappointed when her contract had not been renewed after the first season, McFadden had been sought after for a number of roles, including that of Jack Ryan's wife in the blockbuster Paramount film *The Hunt for Red October*.

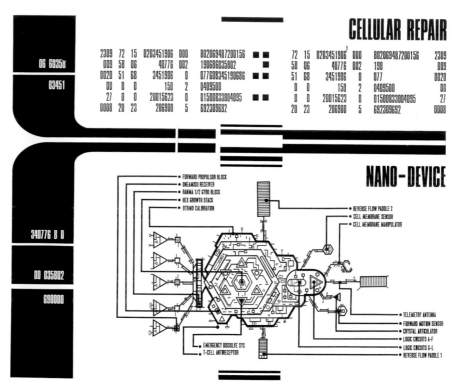

A nanite from "Evolution." As always, the level of detail provided by Michael Okuda and the *Next Generation* art department was astounding, and contributed to the series' impressive verisimilitude.

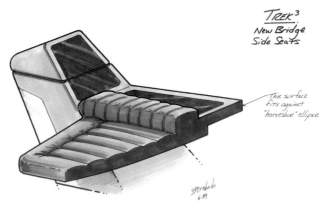

ILLUSTRATION BY RICK STERNBACH. COURTESY OF THE ARTIST.

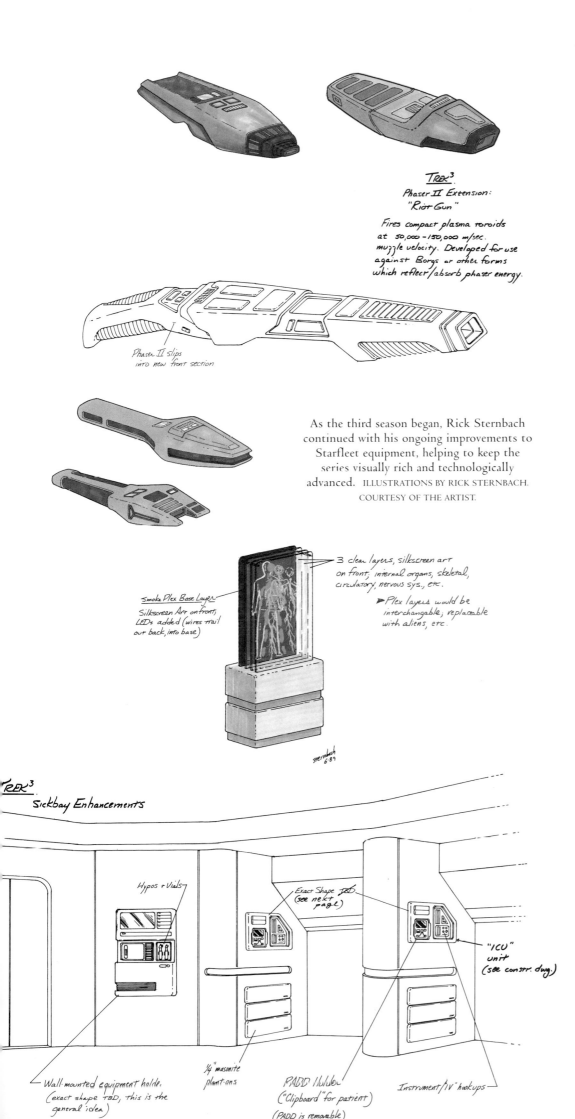

TREK³
Phaser II Extension:
"Riot Gun"

Fires compact plasma toroids
at 50,000 - 150,000 m/sec.
muzzle velocity. Developed for use
against Borgs or other forms
which reflect/absorb phaser energy.

Phaser II slips
into new front section

3 clean layers, silkscreen art
on front; internal organs, skeletal,
circulatory, nervous sys., etc.

► Plex layers would be
interchangable; replaceable
with aliens, etc.

Smoke Plex Base Layer—
Silkscreen Art on front;
LEDs added (wires trail
out back, into base)

sternbach
6-89

As the third season began, Rick Sternbach
continued with his ongoing improvements to
Starfleet equipment, helping to keep the
series visually rich and technologically
advanced. ILLUSTRATIONS BY RICK STERNBACH.
COURTESY OF THE ARTIST.

TREK³
Sickbay Enhancements

Hypos + Vials

Exact Shape TBD
(see next
page)

"ICU"
unit
(see constr. dwg.)

Wall-mounted equipment holder
(exact shape TBD, this is the
general idea)

¼" masonite
plant-ons

PADD Holder
("Clipboard" for patient)
(PADD is removable)

Instrument/IV hookups

SEASON THREE: EPISODE 49
THE ENSIGNS OF
COMMAND
Written by Melinda M. Snodgrass
Directed by Cliff Bole

Tau Cygna V, a lethally irradiated
planet, is the home of a group of
determined human colonists who
have adapted to the radiation and
who refuse to leave, even though a
treaty between the equally determined Sheliak Corporate and the
Federation demands that they evacuate their settlement. Data persuades
the colonists to leave by providing a
convincing demonstration of force,
and Picard succeeds in wielding the
Sheliak's own treaty in such a way as
to compel the Sheliak Corporate to
allow the colonists enough time
to leave peacefully.

SEASON THREE: EPISODE 50
EVOLUTION
Teleplay by Michael Piller
Story by Michael Piller & Michael Wagner
Directed by Winrich Kolbe

The launch of a scientist's probe to
study a rare stellar explosion is
threatened when Wesley's science
project, involving microscopic robots
called nanites, causes the *Enterprise*'s
computers to malfunction. When
the scientist destroys some nanites
with gamma radiation, the remainder
respond by taking the ship's life-sup-
port systems off-line. Convinced of
their sentience, Data contacts the
nanites, who ask only to be settled
on a planet of their own. They then
repair the ship's computers so that
the scientist's probe can be launched.

Riker and Worf on Delta
Rana IV.

THE SURVIVORS
Written by Michael Wagner
Directed by Les Landau

The *Enterprise* responds to a distress call from Delta Rana IV, and discovers that 11,000 colonists have been killed in an alien attack which left only two survivors—a married team of botanists. When the alien ship returns to renew the attack, Picard destroys it and beams the couple to safety aboard the *Enterprise*. There, Picard learns that the husband is really a Douwd, an immortal alien, and that his human wife is only an illusion—she also died in the first attack. The Douwd confesses that in his rage at that attack, he used his powers to wipe out all 50 billion members of the attacking race—a crime which shames him, and for which Picard knows there can be no penalty except that meted out by the alien's own conscience.

In the third season, new tricorders were introduced. The basic unit is on the left, the medical version with detachable sensor is to the right. These props, complete with working display screens and blinking lights, were built by modelmaker Ed Miarecki, who was later part of the team that built the *Enterprise*-E at Industrial Light & Magic.
ROBBIE ROBINSON.

Marking another change from what had gone before, a new opening title sequence was produced, replacing Bob Justman's flight out of the solar system with an approach toward a galaxy. A new model of the *Enterprise* was built, only four feet long in order to make it easier to be photographed. And, perhaps of greatest initial importance to the company of actors who faced another ten-month stretch of long production hours, the confining, restrictive Starfleet uniforms were finally reconceived by new costume designer, Robert Blackman.

When *The Next Generation* had been in preproduction for its first season, Gene Roddenberry had asked *Original Series* costume designer William Ware Theiss to join his team. Though known for his imaginative, 1960s flair on the first *Star Trek,* in which he used everything from silver lamé bikinis to psychedelic chiffons and rug fringes, Theiss was more than ready to work with a more restrained look for the 1980s.

His starting task was to redesign Starfleet uniforms as sleek jumpsuits for the twenty-fourth century, and his first decision was—with Roddenberry's approval—to change the traditional color scheme of gold for command, red for engineering, and blue for sciences. Theiss felt costumes that were primarily those colors weren't necessarily the most universally becoming choices. Instead, he now relegated color to a distinctive block on the chest and on the sleeves, and used black on the shoulders to set off the actors' faces, and black on their hips and legs to help smooth out their figures. The actors needed all the help they could get in that regard, for although they were all trim and fit, the fabric that was used for the first two seasons was spandex—tight, stretchy, and unforgiving of the slightest deviation from physical perfection.

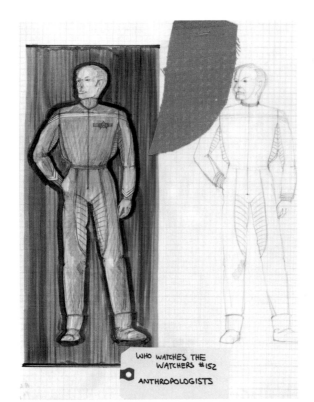

Starfleet anthropologist uniform by Robert Blackman.
COURTESY OF THE ARTIST.

WHO WATCHES THE
WATCHERS #152
ANTHROPOLOGISTS

Behind the scenes on location for
"Who Watches the Watchers?"
The number of support and technical personnel required for a *Next
Generation* episode was the key reason that schedules were so critical—it could cost upward of
$50,000 an hour to have the crew
wait and do nothing if a particular
prop wasn't ready on time, or if an
actor was late for makeup.

Just as he had for *The Original Series*, Theiss still had to keep in mind
Roddenberry's vision of the clothing technology of the future—no buttons or
zippers, so that twentieth-century audiences would not be able to see how the
clothes were fastened. Pockets were not permitted either.

Theiss's *Next Generation* Starfleet designs were so distinctive and attractive
that they set the stage for the next ten years' worth of variations. His other
first-season costume designs included an outfit for a wild boar named Emmy
Lou, who appeared as a Klingon targ in "Where No One Has Gone Before,"
and the precariously minimal outfits worn by the Edo in "Justice." His work
in evoking the hardboiled 1930s look of Picard's Dixon Hill holodeck envi-

On Mintaka III, Picard says
farewell to Oji, played by
Pamela Segall.

SEASON THREE: EPISODE 52
WHO WATCHES THE
WATCHERS?
*Written by Richard Manning &
Hans Beimler
Directed by Robert Wiemer*

Dr. Crusher violates the Prime
Directive by beaming aboard Liko, a
native of Mintaka II, who is injured
in an accident when he witnesses the
beam-up of two members of a
Federation observation team after
malfunctioning equipment exposes
their observation "blind." Seeing
the captain, Liko becomes convinced
that Picard is a legendary Mintaka
god, and when Troi beams down to
retrieve a missing observer he takes
her captive. Before Troi can be sacrificed, Picard convinces the Mintaka
leader that he is as mortal as they
are, and that they should continue to
follow the rational path, and forgo
old superstitions.

SEASON THREE: EPISODE 53
THE BONDING
*Written by Ronald D. Moore
Directed by Winrich Kolbe*

Worf and Wesley draw on their own
early loss of a parent to comfort
Jeremy, a 12-year-old boy whose
archaeologist mother has been killed
by a bomb from an ancient war while
on an away mission. When the boy's
mother mysteriously "reappears,"
Data discovers "she" is really an
energy being from the planet
Jeremy's mother was investigating.
The alien wishes to create a nurturing environment for the boy on the
planet to make up for the tragic loss
of his mother. But the crew convince
the energy being that the boy needs a
real environment with all its atten-
dant joy and pain.

SEASON THREE: EPISODE 54
BOOBY TRAP
*Teleplay by Ron Roman and Michael Piller
& Richard Danus
Story by Michael Wagner and Ron Roman
Directed by Gabrielle Beaumont*

While exploring an ancient, intact Promellian battle cruiser at the site of the destruction of the Promellian race by the Menthars, the *Enterprise* is caught by the same device that sapped the energy of the Promellian ships. La Forge calls up a holodeck re-creation of Dr. Leah Brahms, one of the original designers of the *Galaxy*-class *Enterprise,* to help him release the ship from the trap. In the end, Picard pilots the *Enterprise* in a tricky maneuver that frees the ship and enables him to destroy the Menthar device.

SEASON THREE: EPISODE 55
THE ENEMY
*Written by David Kemper and
Michael Piller
Directed by David Carson*

La Forge is stranded on a border world after an away team beams aboard an injured survivor from the crash of a small Romulan ship. Threatened by magnetic fields, La Forge is captured by an unrevealed second Romulan survivor whom the engineer convinces to be his ally to save both their lives. On board the *Enterprise,* Worf refuses to donate blood to the injured Romulan, who dies before a Romulan Warbird, defying Picard's warning not to enter Federation space, can retrieve him. The rescue of La Forge and the second Romulan prevents a direct confrontation with the Romulans, and the Warbird is escorted back to the Neutral Zone.

ronment, in "The Big Goodbye," also earned him an Emmy Award for costume design.

Theiss left the series after the first season and was replaced by Durinda Rice Wood in the second. Also a talented designer, Wood created the first of Whoopi Goldberg's memorable Guinan outfits and helped develop the look of the Borg. Her work on another episode featuring a holodeck fantasy—"Elementary, Dear Data"—earned her her own Emmy nomination for costume design.

But Wood also decided to leave the series after a single season, and just as Herman Zimmerman had suggested a friend as his replacement as production designer, so did Wood suggest her friend Robert Blackman as costume designer. Though no one knew it at the time, *Star Trek*'s design legacy was about to welcome one of its most influential contributors.

Blackman had done his graduate work at the Yale School of Drama, at the time one of the most competitive programs in the country. Blackman was one of only eighteen students to be invited to take part, and only one of six to graduate three years later. It was his design excellence and his subsequent theater experience that would make him so valuable to the ongoing *Star Trek* productions over the next eight years. Nevertheless, when Blackman took his first interview for the position of *The Next Generation*'s costume designer he had no intention of accepting the job. In fact, he recalls that he only went to the interview with David Livingston as a favor to Paramount's head of television production, Mel Harris.

But at some point in that interview, Blackman was struck by Livingston's description of the series and the challenges it presented, and thought, 'Well, okay, I could do it for a season.' The rest, as they say, is future history.

The first task Blackman was given was the same as the one William Theiss had faced—the Starfleet uniforms. Blackman says, "I was brought in early that season to redesign new uniforms, and it was really hard to do. They wanted things that didn't stretch, didn't hurt their shoulders, and breathed, but still looked like spandex. So we kept trying to make these sleek, wool outfits."

Blackman admits that his first attempts weren't fully successful. "If you watch the first six or seven episodes, you'll see the actors look like they're in spandex outfits, but they're made of wool and the actors can't move, they can't raise their arms, they can't do anything."

Eventually, though, Blackman refined the cut of the new uniforms so there was an acceptable compromise between the producers' desire to maintain the sleek, formfitting look of the original costumes, and the ease of movement the actors required to feel comfortable. For the men, comfort was easier to come by because their costumes were changed from jumpsuits to two-piece outfits. One minor offshoot of this successful redesign was the so-called Picard Maneuver, a tongue-in-cheek phrase used to describe the distinctive downward tug Patrick Stewart gave to his tunic after changing position.

But McFadden and Sirtis remained in tight jumpsuits, and as a result faced ongoing pressure to maintain their ideal weights without variation. Though the twenty-fourth century was supposedly one of equality between the sexes, on the television stage of the twentieth century women were held to a different standard from men. To be fair, this double standard was not just in place on *The Next Generation,* but exists on virtually all television series.

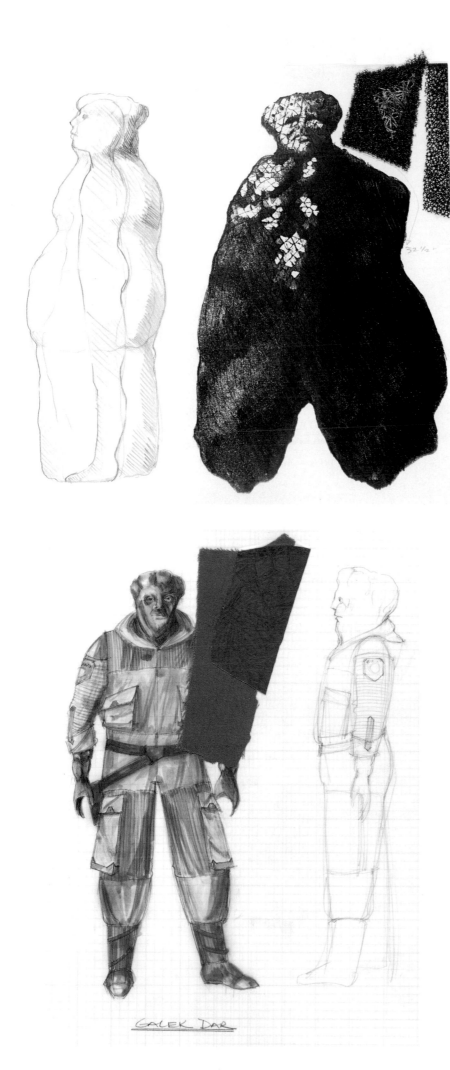

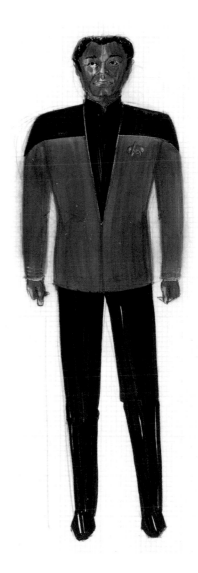

GALEK DAR

Three of Robert Blackman's distinctive costume designs for the third season: a new admiral's uniform from "The Defector," a Sheliak from "The Ensigns of Command," and Galek Sar from "Booby Trap." ILLUSTRATIONS BY ROBERT BLACKMAN. COURTESY OF THE ARTIST.

Riker and Devinoni Ral, played by
Matt McCoy, in Ten-Forward.

A seemingly stable wormhole near
Barzan II prompts a fierce bidding
war on board the *Enterprise*, which is
disrupted by unethical Ferengi representatives and a human negotiator
who hides his half-Betazoid ancestry
in order to use his empathic powers
to his advantage. Troi reveals the
negotiator's unethical edge to the
Barzan after they accept his bid, but
Data and Geordi, just barely escaping
the wormhole's collapse, report that
the wormhole is unstable and
worthless.

When Picard discovers that raids on
a Federation science post are the
work of the Gatherers, a rebel group
that split off from the rest of Acamar
III's inhabitants more than 100 years
ago, he decides the rift must be
mended to stop the raids. While
Picard acts to bring both sides
together, Riker is attracted to Yuta, a
food-taster for Acamar's leader.
Unfortunately, Yuta is an assassin
plotting revenge against an opposing
faction. When Yuta tries to kill the
rebel chief, Riker is forced to shoot
her, adding a tragic note to the
successful peace talks.

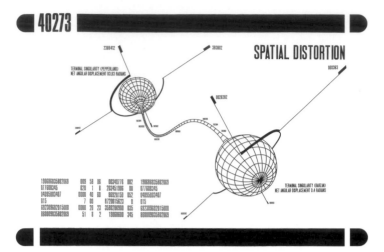

40273

SPATIAL DISTORTION

"The Price"
marked the first
appearance in the
Star Trek saga of a
wormhole suitable
for passage—a con-
cept which would
become a key factor
in *Star Trek: Deep
Space Nine.*

40273

PROPOSAL BY THE UNITED FEDERATION OF PLANETS

- **KEY PROVISIONS**
  - LUMP SUM PAYMENT OF 1,500,000 FEDERATION CREDITS TO BE MADE UPON CONCLUSION OF AGREEMENT, 100,000 CREDITS PER BARZANIAN YEAR THEREAFTER
  - COST OF ORBITAL FACILITIES TO BE BORNE BY THE UNITED FEDERATION OF PLANETS
  - COST OF DEVELOPMENT OF WORMHOLE YURI VECTOR FIELD CONTROL TECHNOLOGY AND RELATED SYSTEMS TO BE BORNE BY UNITED FEDERATION OF PLANETS
  - BARZANIAN PLANETARY REPUBLIC TO BE EQUAL PARTNER IN PROCEEDS OF OPERATIONAL REVENUES OF VENTURE
  - BARZANIAN PLANETARY REPUBLIC TO SERVE AS PRINCIPAL SUPPLIER OF RAW MATERIAL AND CARBON COMPOSITE STRUCTURAL ELEMENTS FOR ORBITAL FACILITY
  - BARZANIAN PERSONNEL TO BE EMPLOYED AS PRINCIPAL OPERATING STAFF OF GROUND-BASED SUPPORT FACILITY
  - LONG-TERM ECONOMIC, TECHNICAL, AND EDUCATIONAL ASSISTANCE TO BE PROVIDED BY UNITED FEDERATION OF PLANETS
  - TERM OF AGREEMENT: EXPIRES STARDATE 53000, UFP TO HAVE FIRST REFUSAL ON ANY RENEGOTIATED AGREEMENT

- **BENEFITS TO THE PEOPLE OF THE BARZANIAN PLANETARY REPUBLIC**
  - IMMEDIATE INFLUX OF CAPITAL INTO LOCAL PLANETARY ECONOMY
  - LONG-TERM ECONOMIC INCOME DUE TO ANNUAL USAGE PAYMENTS AND PERCENTAGE USAGE FEES FOR WORMHOLE TRAFFIC
  - LONG-TERM DEVELOPMENT OF PLANETARY INDUSTRIAL BASE DUE TO USE OF LOCAL INDUSTRIES AND MATERIAL FOR GROUND-BASED AND ORBITAL FACILITY
  - GUARANTEED BARZANIAN ACCESS TO WORMHOLE FOR INTERSTELLAR TRADE AND RESEARCH
  - INCREASED PLANETARY SECURITY DUE TO PROTECTION BY FEDERATION STARFLEET

The fine print of
the Federation's
offer in "The
Price."

Starfleet uniforms were just the beginning of Blackman's impressive contributions to the unique visual identity of *Star Trek*. In that third season, he was
able to draw upon the work of his old friend Robert Fletcher, costume designer for *Star Trek: The Motion Picture*, to create fresh variations on Klingon costumes
in "Sins of the Fathers," and variations on Vulcan costumes in "Sarek." Like
Theiss and Wood before him, he also had fun with a holodeck period fantasy
in "Hollow Pursuits," dressing Picard, Data, and La Forge as the Three
Musketeers, Wesley as Gainesborough's Blue Boy, and Troi as a "goddess of
empathy" in a flowing gown.

But for Blackman, assignments as clear-cut as Klingons, Vulcans, and the
Three Musketeers were few and far between. "The hardest part of the job," he
says, "and at the same time a great moment of creativity, is when there is no
description. There are some days you just wish they would give you a descrip-
tive paragraph so you could just do the job, but it never is that way, really."
Blackman says the guidelines he would most often receive would be a line in
the script which read: " 'The alien enters. His name is Berkoff. He speaks.' And
that's about as far as it gets."

Blackman's approach to creating costume designs from such minimal
information is to "try and put myself into the story as much as possible. That's

from my training in theater arts. Script analysis was something we all had to learn, and that was how we were taught to approach design. I started off as a scene designer, moving into costume design at the same time, doing scenery and costumes for many productions. That technique does not change because we're in the future and outer space."

It is from script analysis that Blackman derives the detail he needs to arrive at his designs. And some detail is always necessary.

"If they just said, 'We need four aliens, so sit in a corner and come up with them,' three years later you'd see me still struggling with a pencil. That whole notion that you can design something because you have the whole world to pull from—that's not how it works. You talk to any artist, and the tighter the parameters, the greater the creativity. Because the smaller the box, the more you want to elbow every corner, and you find ways to turn that box over in directions that no one has ever seen before. That's what I do."

From his analysis of a script, Blackman determines the writer's intent, but not necessarily in detail. "Sometimes," he says, "because it's television and only forty-four minutes, it's more like Magic Marker strokes—a very broad kind of stroke."

But once Blackman has determined the writer's intent, he has to decide on his own approach. And sometimes he chooses to go against type. "Sometimes a character will be written as 'the lethal killer.' But do we really want to see them in black with a black hat? Do we need to know that they are the villain the first time we see them, or is that something that unfolds a little bit in the script?"

From the beginning, Blackman's authority on the subject of costume design was executive producer Rick Berman. The only blanket instruction he ever received was to avoid "O.S.T."—that is, any designs that resembled something that might have appeared on "Old *Star Trek*," especially anything that remotely resembled togas! Beyond that directive, every design Blackman sketched for the series came under the close scrutiny of Rick Berman.

Echoing a sentiment with which every member of *The Next Generation* staff and crew agrees, Blackman says, "Rick Berman has an eye for detail that is unlike anyone I've ever seen. I mean, it is amazing to watch him watch dailies, and stop, and go back frame by frame by frame, to notice an extra, three people deep, and say to me, 'What's going on with that neckline?' "

Like the rest of the team, Blackman appreciates Berman's close attention to detail. "You respect that. I have learned that there is no getting away with murder here. You cannot backslide at all. You can't even relax, which is good. I mean, as an artist, it's good to know that there's always going to be a challenge."

Thus Blackman joined *The Next Generation* design team of production designer Richard James, makeup supervisor Michael Westmore, set decorator Jim Mees, senior illustrator Rick Sternbach, and scenic artist supervisor Michael Okuda, all of whom would continue to define the look of *Star Trek* productions for years to come.

But the appearance of the *Star Trek* universe is only part of its appeal. The nature of its characters and the content of its stories provide the core of what ultimately attracts and holds its audience, and in that regard perhaps one of the most pivotal people to join the series in its third year was Michael Piller.

Piller had always been drawn to becoming a writer, and with that goal in

SEASON THREE: EPISODE 58
THE DEFECTOR
Written by Ronald D. Moore
Directed by Robert Scheerer

When a Romulan admiral defects and convinces Picard that a Romulan invasion is imminent, the *Enterprise* is lured into the Neutral Zone and set upon by Romulan Warbirds, whose commanders demand Picard's surrender. Only the sudden appearance of three Klingon warships causes the Romulans to depart. But the admiral, realizing he was manipulated by his own command to create an incident, commits suicide, leaving a letter for Picard to deliver to his home when peace exists between the Romulan Empire and the Federation.

SEASON THREE: EPISODE 59
THE HUNTED
Written by Robin Bernheim
Directed by Cliff Bole

Angosia III, a new applicant for Federation membership, is revealed to have an ugly skeleton in its closet when Picard discovers the existence of a lunar prison colony filled with Argosian veterans. The prisoners are supersoldiers who were altered for war through biochemical and mind control; the war over, they have been judged incapable of reentry into civilian life. When one of the prisoners—a former "patriot"—escapes and frees his fellow inmates, the planet's leaders appeal to Picard for help. But he withdraws, telling both sides that Federation membership will now depend on the outcome of their internal "debate."

Dr. Crusher assessing the
results of a terrorist attack on
Angosia III.

SEASON THREE: EPISODE 60
THE HIGH GROUND
Written by Melinda M. Snodgrass
Directed by Gabrielle Beaumont

Ansata terrorists from war-torn, non-
aligned Rutia IV capture Dr. Crusher
on the planet's surface and then
Picard on the *Enterprise,* in an attempt
to prevent the ship from supplying
more medical aid to the Rutian victims of the Ansata's attacks. After
Wesley locates the terrorists' underground base, the Rutian police chief
kills the terrorist leader as he is
about to kill Picard. The *Enterprise*
leaves, with her crew somberly realizing that peace will remain elusive on
this world for a long time to come.

SEASON THREE: EPISODE 61
DEJA Q
Written by Richard Danus
Directed by Les Landau

In the middle of an operation to prevent its moon from crashing into
Bre'el IV, Q appears on the *Enterprise,*
telling Picard the Q Continuum has
revoked his powers for past trans-
gressions. Although the crew doubts
Q's claims, Data discovers that
they're true when he's damaged pro-
tecting Q from a revenge-seeking
gaseous life-form, a Calamarain.
Moved by Data's sacrifice, Q steals a
shuttlecraft to draw off the
Calamarain who is preventing the
Enterprise from completing its moon-
deflecting mission. Impressed by the
selfless act, another Q arrives to
restore Q's powers, at least
temporarily, as a reward for his
improved behavior.

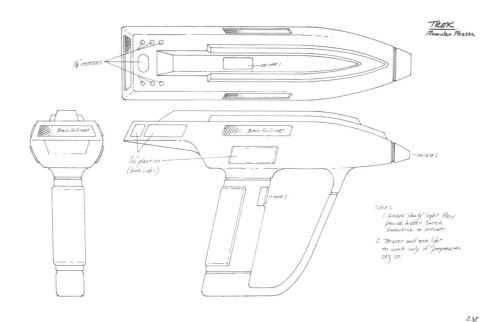

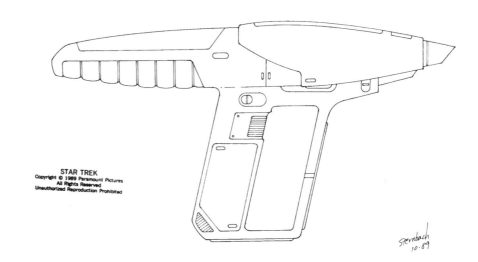

Rick Sternbach's initial
and final design for a
Romulan phaser to be used
in "The High Ground."
ILLUSTRATIONS COURTESY OF
THE ARTIST. PHOTOGRAPHY
BY ROBBIE ROBINSON.

Once again, Dan Curry's storyboarding skills helped create a memorable scene by giving the director an exact composition for a shot.
ILLUSTRATION COURTESY OF THE ARTIST.

SEASON THREE: EPISODE 62
A MATTER OF
PERSPECTIVE
Written by Ed Zuckerman
Directed by Cliff Bole

When a scientist who was working on developing a new, wave-based energy source is killed seconds after Riker beams up from the science station, evidence points to him as the murderer. However, Riker is eventually exonerated by Picard's holodeck re-creation of the event, and by the crew's discovery of the scientist's still-operational wave generator. The scientist had created a weapon that he planned to sell. Fearing Riker had discovered his scheme, the scientist had attempted to kill Riker with his generator—and ended up killing himself instead.

Picard in an alternate timeline where the Federation is at war with the Klingon Empire.

SEASON THREE: EPISODE 63
YESTERDAY'S
ENTERPRISE
Teleplay by Ira Steven Behr & Richard Manning & Hans Beimler & Ronald D. Moore
From a story by Trent Christopher Ganino & Eric A. Stillwell
Directed by David Carson

An alternate timeline in which the Federation and the Klingon Empire are at war—and Tasha Yar still lives—is created when Picard and the *Enterprise*-D encounter their ship's predecessor, the long-destroyed *Enterprise*-C. Only Guinan knows that history has been changed and she advises Picard that to set things right, he must send the *Enterprise*-C back to its fate through the temporal time rift from which it has emerged. Learning that she has died in the "real" timeline, Tasha chooses to go back with the crew of the C, to see if she can make a difference in the historic battle they must fight, whose outcome will ultimately bring peace between the Klingons and the Federation.

mind, he enrolled in a creative-writing course when he was in college. As he remembers it, "I had a very, very bad experience.

"The creative-writing teacher was a fairly renowned writer, at least at that time, and he opened his class by telling all the students, 'There are enough bad writers out there, and if I think you can't write, I'm going to do everything in my power to discourage you.' I happened to be one of those people whom he decided should not be a writer."

Piller recalls that the teacher would read his work in class, tear it apart, and the class would laugh. "It was horrible. By the time it was over, I couldn't go near a typewriter. I didn't want to write anymore." Piller decided he would, by default, go into journalism. That way he could still put words on paper, but it would be different from creative writing. He didn't write another word of fiction for five years.

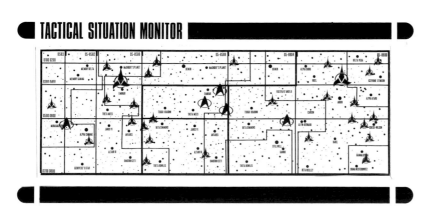

TACTICAL SITUATION MONITOR

The Federation's precarious position, surrounded by Klingon forces in the alternate timeline of "Yesterday's *Enterprise*."

THE OFFSPRING
Written by René Echevarria
Directed by Jonathan Frakes

To Picard's dismay and the interest
of Starfleet Research, Data creates a
"daughter" by duplicating his neural
nets in a new android body. His
creation exceeds her programming
and independently begins developing
emotions. But unfortunately, her
systems degrade and, though Data
has no emotions of his own, he
experiences one of the most tragic of
human events: the death of a child.

Picard, Worf, and Worf's brother
Kurn, played by Tony Todd, on the
Klingon Homeworld.

SINS OF THE FATHER
Teleplay by Ronald D. Moore &
W. Reed Morgan
Based on a teleplay by Drew Deighan
Directed by Les Landau

Worf's newfound brother, Kurn, a
Klingon exchange officer who has
come to serve on board the *Enterprise,*
alerts Worf to a charge of treason at
Khitomer against their late father,
Mogh. Picard travels to *Qo'noS* to
help the brothers defend their family
honor, and ends up as Worf's advocate in a life-or-death trial before the
Klingon High Council. Picard and
Worf uncover the real traitor: the
father of Worf's accuser. But Worf
lets the stain on his family honor
stand, to avoid causing a civil
war for his people.

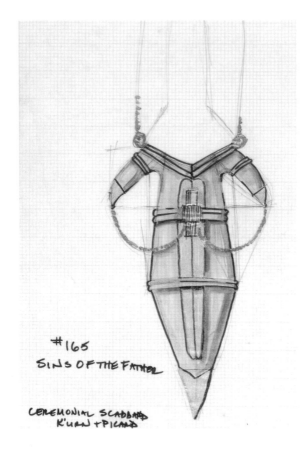

#165
SINS OF THE FATHER

CEREMONIAL SCABBARD
K'URN + PICARD

In the world of television
production, knives are the
design responsibility of the art
department, and scabbards—
which are worn—are the
design responsibility of the
costume department.
ILLUSTRATION BY ROBERT
BLACKMAN. COURTESY OF
THE ARTIST.

A Klingon display from "Sins of
the Father," utilizing graphic
elements originally created for
Star Trek IV, Michael Okuda's
first *Star Trek* feature.

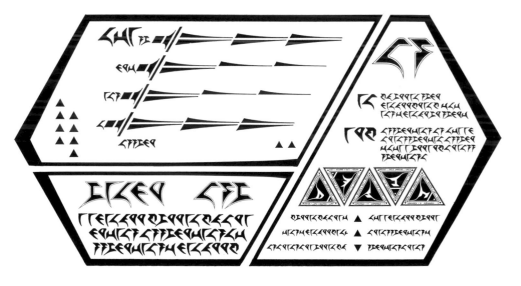

"Then one night in New York, I went to see a very early performance of *A
Chorus Line,*" Piller explains. "One of the kids in the chorus tells the story of
the acting teacher who has the students in his class pretend to go down a hill
on a toboggan. And he basically says if you don't have talent, you won't feel the
snow and the wind in your face. And if you don't start feeling the wind in your
face, you're going to get transferred and you're never going to make it. In the
song the kid in the chorus sings, she confesses that she feels, 'Nothing.'

"Now, I'm sitting on the edge of my seat saying, This is my story! I know
this teacher. And the kid in the chorus goes to her church and prays to Santa

ALLEGIANCE
Written by Richard Manning &
Hans Beimler
Directed by Winrich Kolbe

Alien energy beings kidnap Picard and replace him with a double to test the reactions of the crew of the *Enterprise* to authority. The experiment ends when Picard, being held captive with three others in a strange holding cell, discovers that one of his cellmates, ostensibly a Starfleet cadet, knows something only known to Picard's crew. On his return to command, Picard traps the aliens in an energy field and, before releasing them, admonishes them on the ethics of responsible "research."

Make-up supervisor, Michael Westmore, strikes again with this impressive Chalnoth from "Allegiance."

Patrick Stewart got what he wished for when he asked the writing staff to provide Captain Picard with more "sex and shooting." Jennifer Hetrick would return as the archaeologist, Vash, in Season Four's, "Qpid," and the *Deep Space Nine* episode, "Q-Less." ILLUSTRATION BY ROBERT BLACKMAN. COURTESY OF THE ARTIST. PHOTOGRAPHY ROBBIE ROBINSON.

VASH #167

CAPTAIN'S HOLIDAY
Written by Ira Steven Behr
Directed by Chip Chalmers

While reluctantly vacationing, Picard is swept up into a romantic adventure in which he and an archaeologist named Vash become involved in tracking down the Tox Uthat. Although two time-traveling Vorgons tell Picard he is destined to locate the super-weapon, Picard suspects their motives and has the *Enterprise* destroy the weapon in transporter transit.

Maria for guidance. And I'm saying to myself, What's the answer to this?, because I never could find the answer. And, of course, the voice of Santa Maria comes down and tells her, 'This class is *nothing.* This man is *nothing.* Go out and find a better class.' And I said: Why didn't I think of that?

"So," Piller says with a laugh, "I had a very religious experience watching *A Chorus Line.* It was a big night for me, and I started writing again from that time on."

TIN MAN

Written by Dennis Putnam Bailey &
David Bischoff
Directed by Robert Scheerer

Near a star about to go supernova, a powerful Betazoid telepath traveling on board the *Enterprise* establishes contact with a suicidal, spacecraft-like alien life-form code-named Tin Man. Two Romulan Warbirds are also interested in Tin Man, and when a Warbird attacks it and the *Enterprise,* the telepath pushes the alien to destroy the Warbird with a shock wave. Just before the star goes nova, Data boards the alien with the telepath, and as the second Warbird attacks, the alien's shock-wave reaction saves both the Warbird and the *Enterprise.* Data returns to the *Enterprise,* but the lonely alien and the troubled telepath decide to remain together.

HOLLOW PURSUITS

Written by Sally Caves
Directed by Cliff Bole

Reg Barclay, an ineffectual engineering officer, takes refuge in heroic holodeck scenarios in which he seduces Troi and defeats Picard, La Forge, and Data in swordplay. When a real-life scenario develops that requires engineering ingenuity, Barclay surprises himself by solving a runaway-acceleration problem that has eluded La Forge and had threatened to destroy the *Enterprise.* Filled with new confidence, Barclay decides to give up his holographic retreats from reality, except for the mysterious "program 9."

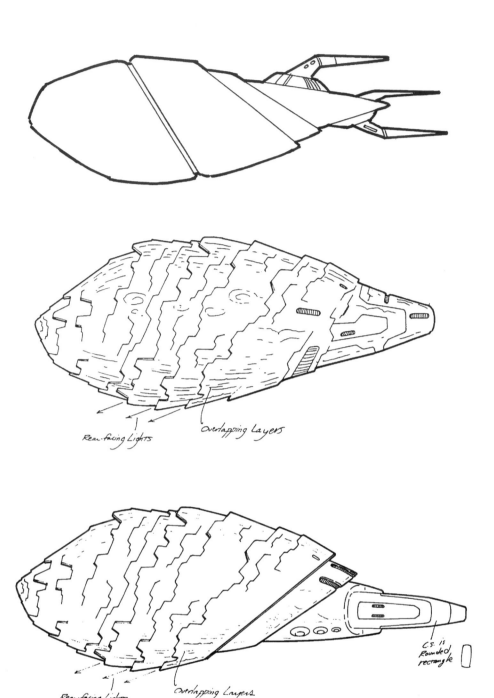

Rick Sternbach's designs for the living spaceship of "Tin Man" are translated into a clay sculpture in Greg Jein's model shop. ILLUSTRATIONS COURTESY OF THE ARTIST. PHOTOGRAPH COURTESY OF GREG JEIN.

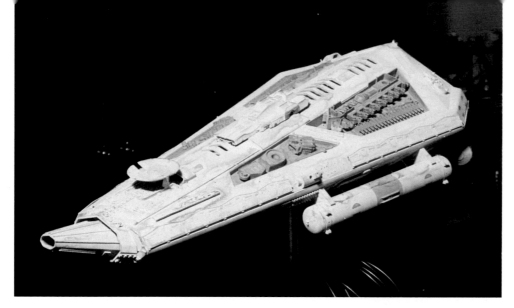

Another starship is born in Tony Meininger's shop. This one belongs to Kivas Fajo from "The Most Toys." PHOTOGRAPH COURTESY OF GREG JEIN.

SEASON THREE: EPISODE 70
THE MOST TOYS
Written by Shari Goodhartz
Directed by Timothy Bond

When his shuttlecraft explodes, Data is presumed lost by his crewmates. But he has actually become the latest addition to a collection of unique items, owned by a trader called Kivas Fajo. Data agrees to behave as the collector demands only when Fajo threatens the life of his own assistant. But when the assistant is killed by Fajo as she tries to help Data escape, the android takes Fajo prisoner with his own weapon. Taunted by the collector, who knows of Data's prohibition against killing for no reason, Data fires the weapon, as he is transported back aboard the *Enterprise*. Fajo is arrested, unharmed, and Data does not reveal any details about his decision to use the weapon.

#170 THE MOST TOYS
FAJO
SAUL RUBINEK

In "The Most Toys," the role of Kivas Fajo was originally played by David Rappaport, a little person well known for his frequent film and television appearances. When Rappaport was hospitalized following a suicide attempt, the producers were forced to recast the role with Saul Rubinek. Tragically, David Rappaport later died when a second suicide attempt was successful. ILLUSTRATIONS BY ROBERT BLACKMAN. COURTESY OF THE ARTIST.

From "The Most Toys," a Rick Sternbach design with a decidedly non-technobabble title.
COURTESY OF THE ARTIST.

Mark Lenard reprises his role as Spock's father, Ambassador Sarek. ROBBIE ROBINSON.

SEASON THREE: EPISODE 71
SAREK
Written by Peter S. Beagle
Story by Marc Cushman and Jake Jacobs
Directed by Les Landau

Ambassador Sarek of Vulcan, Spock's father, comes on board the *Enterprise* to establish a landmark treaty between the Federation and aliens called the Legaran. However, when emotional turmoil spreads through the ship, it is revealed that Sarek suffers from Bendii syndrome, which results in loss of emotional control and is projected onto others by Vulcan telepathy. Since Sarek is the only acceptable negotiator to the Legaran, Picard offers to mind-meld with Sarek in order to help him achieve sufficient emotional control to complete his mission. Although Picard briefly suffers the full weight of Sarek's emotional pain, the mission is a success.

Walter Koenig visits with Mark Lenard behind the scenes, during the filming of "Sarek." Lenard, who died in 1996, brought great dignity to the *Star Trek* universe, and helped bind the generations together with his powerful portrayal of Spock's father in *The Original Series*, the feature films, and *The Next Generation*. ROBBIE ROBINSON.

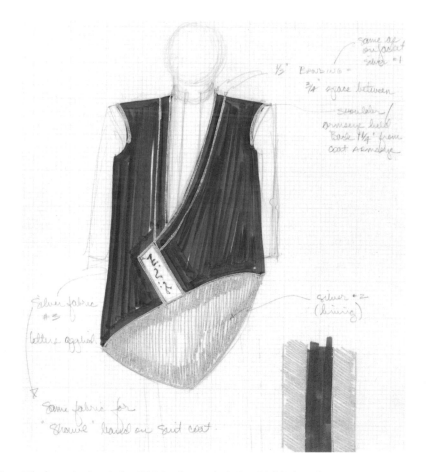

Robert Blackman's sketch for Ki Mendrossen's jacket highlights the ongoing pressures of design requirements for a series in which virtually no costumes or props can be purchased off the shelf—everything must be custom made according to the well-established principles of the 24th century. ILLUSTRATION COURTESY OF THE ARTIST.

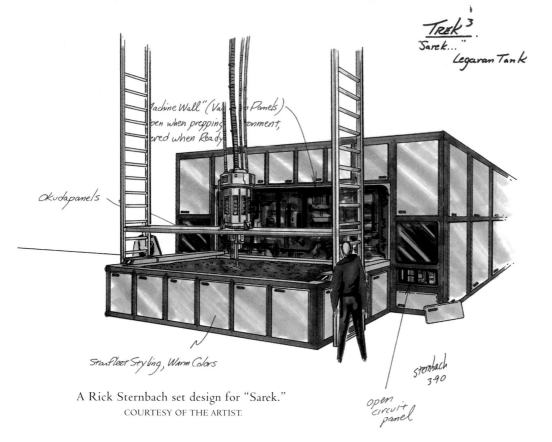

Trek³
"Sarek..."
Legaran Tank

"Machine Wall" (Va... Panels)
... open when prepping ... onment,
...ered when Ready

Okuda panels

Starfleet Styling, Warm Colors

sternbach
3·90

open
circuit
panel

A Rick Sternbach set design for "Sarek."
COURTESY OF THE ARTIST.

130

#172 MENAGE A TR...
LWAXANA
NEGLIGEE

Robert Blackman costume designs for
mother and daughter, as Lwaxana returns to
the *Enterprise* in "Menage à Troi."
COURTESY OF THE ARTIST.

SEASON THREE: EPISODE 72
MÉNAGE À TROI
Written by Fred Bronson & Susan Sackett
Directed by Robert Legato

Following a trade conference on
Betazed, the planet where Riker and
Troi met and fell in love, the couple
are kidnapped along with Troi's
mother, Lwaxana, by a Ferengi who
plans to make profitable use of
Lwaxana's telepathic skills. Lwaxana
convinces her captor to release her
daughter and Riker, who have secretly signaled the *Enterprise* for help, and
Picard saves the day by masquerading
as Lwaxana's spurned lover to fright-
en off her Ferengi suitor.

SEASON THREE: EPISODE 73
TRANSFIGURA-
TIONS
Written by René Echevarria
Directed by Tom Benko

The *Enterprise* rescues a severely
injured amnesiac humanoid with
strange healing powers. Dubbed
"John Doe," the alien suffers from
pain that drives him to attempt to
leave the ship in a stolen shuttlecraft, fearing that his presence is
dangerous to the crew. An alien ship
arrives and threatens the *Enterprise* if
Picard will not surrender John, but
the humanoid recovers his memory
and helps the crew. John explains
that he is evolving into a being of
pure energy, and his world's government has been attempting to destroy
him and his kind. But he has
advanced to a point where they can
no longer interfere. He completes
his transformation and prepares to
return to his people to help them
with their own evolution.

But Piller had not wasted the years in which he had not written fiction.
True to his revised goals, he began his career writing local news for CBS in New
York. That led to positions as managing editor of the WBTV-TV News in
Charlotte, North Carolina, and senior news producer at WBBM-TV, the CBS
affiliate in Chicago. While at WBBM-TV, Piller became the senior producer on
the 5 and 10 o'clock news, and produced two Emmy-winning news specials.

Worf and Lieutenant Commander Shelby, played by Elizabeth Dennehy, hunt for Picard on a Borg vessel.
JULIE DENNIS.

SEASON THREE: EPISODE 74
THE BEST OF BOTH WORLDS, PART I
Written by Michael Piller
Directed by Cliff Bole

Suspecting that the Borg have finally reached Federation space, Starfleet sends tactician Lieutenant Commander Shelby to the *Enterprise,* where Riker and Shelby immediately clash. When the Borg attack and damage the *Enterprise,* Shelby finds a place to hide the ship while La Forge works on a weapon to defeat the Borg. But before it's finished, the Borg capture Picard and transform him into Locutus, the "speaker" who will assist in the assimilation of Earth. The episode ends as the *Enterprise* engages the Borg, with Riker giving the command to fire on his own captain.

But his desire to be a creative writer led him to abandon newswriting and accept a position at CBS in Los Angeles as part of the network's department of broadcast standards and practices, specializing in docudramas—a good use of his background in news. What the industry refers to as "BS&P" is known to the public as "the censors." But for Piller, the position was an important educational experience.

"As a censor, I was reading a script every day, so I started reading some very good scripts, and I also read some very bad scripts. And I found myself saying, 'I can do this.' And I started writing.

"Frankly, the first couple of scripts were not great. It took me two years of writing to write a good script. By that time, I'd been promoted to the Entertainment Division of CBS and was working on prime-time shows, and I started writing speculative material."

With speculative material in hand, Piller eventually received two writing assignments, which he says were given to him as favors. One was an episode of *Cagney & Lacey,* the other an episode of *Simon & Simon.* Both scripts were produced, and Piller was hired to a staff position on *Simon & Simon,* and after three years became a producer.

Other shows followed, until he worked on a short-lived science-fiction series for Disney—*Hard Time on Planet Earth*—just as *The Next Generation* was finishing its second season. It was then that Piller had his first unexpected contact with *Star Trek* by calling Maurice Hurley, with whom he had worked on *Simon & Simon.* "I called to ask him about a writer we were considering, who had worked for *Star Trek.* I wanted to know what he thought of that writer and, during the course of our conversation, I told Maurice how much I enjoyed *The Next Generation.* I had been watching it with my family for two years and I thought it was a wonderful show.

"Then he said, 'Hey, if you're interested in the show, I'm leaving. You should meet Roddenberry.' So he set me up with a lunch with Rick Berman, Gene Roddenberry, and himself, to just get acquainted. We had a very nice lunch at Le Chardonnay, and the week before, I believe, 'Measure of a Man' had been on for the first time, and I told them what a remarkable show I thought that was. We got along quite well."

Since Hurley's decision to leave the show had been made before the lunch, it was no surprise that a replacement had already been found—Michael Wagner, who had been a story editor on the acclaimed *Hill Street Blues.*

"As so often happens in this town," Piller says, "Michael and I were old friends. He had been co-creator of a show called *Probe* [with Isaac Asimov], and I had been one of the producers on the show. So I said, 'Maybe I can do an episode for you,' and a few weeks later, after Michael came on board, he called me up and said, 'I've got an idea [for a script]. Would you like to come in and do it? I said, 'Sure.'

"But then I called my agent and told him I wanted to write a freelance script for *Star Trek: The Next Generation.* He said, 'Don't do it! You will be pigeon-holed as a freelance writer. You'll never work on staff again!' "

Fortunately, Piller didn't take his agent's advice. The script he wrote, from a story credited to himself and Wagner, was titled "Evolution" and brought Dr. Crusher back to the *Enterprise.* It was also a script everyone on the production team liked so much that when Wagner left the series Piller was the unanimous choice to replace him. And when Piller arrived, the final piece of *Star Trek*'s new foundation was firmly in place.

To begin with, though, Piller had no intention of serving as a foundation for anything. Like Robert Blackman, he did not plan to stay with the series longer than a season. "I was one of those guys who said, 'I'm just going to take the money I earn here this year and go off to Mexico and write my screenplay.' "

Piller also had no illusions about his abilities as a writer of science fiction. "I had been writing television for four or five years at that point, and had become fairly entrenched in what I felt made good television shows. I didn't know yet if it was going to work on *Star Trek*, but when I came to the show I told Gene and Rick what my strengths and weaknesses were. I did not have a pocketful of *Star Trek* ideas. I didn't really feel I knew science fiction all that well. But I said, 'I understand character. I can help your characters grow.' "

That was the mandate Piller laid out for the writing staff, and himself. "Every show is going to be about a character's growth. And every show has got to be *about* something." Piller hastens to add that after stating those lofty ideals, the realities of television meant, "especially in that third season, that you had to come up with anything to fill an hour just so the show won't be dark next week. But, at the same time, you need to look at every idea that comes in and ask, 'All right, how will this meet those needs?' "

Piller feels it was important to ask that question, especially on *Star Trek*, because the series was "smart television," and the people who watched it were "smart viewers. They don't put *Star Trek* on to act as a background and then leave the room or read the paper. They're paying attention so there have to be scenes that we explore. Our characters must change as a result."

The rationale for Piller's view of the series is easy to explain. "It seems to me that Gene's vision, and one I quickly adopted, is that *Star Trek: The Next Generation* was a show about a group of people who

Captain Picard is assimilated by the Borg—a story point that would have important repercussions in both the pilot episode of *Deep Space Nine,* and the second *Next Generation* motion picture. JULIE DENNIS.

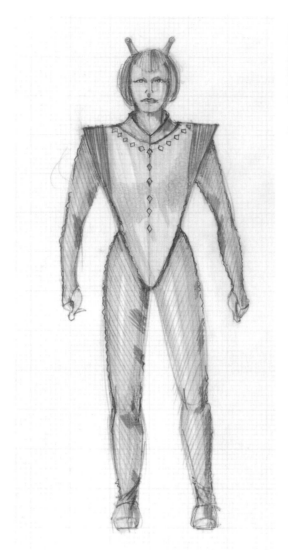

In "The Offspring," Data's "daughter" tries out different appearances, leading to the first appearance of an Andorian in *The Next Generation*. ILLUSTRATION BY ROBERT BLACKMAN. COURTESY OF THE ARTIST.

are learning about themselves from their interaction with strange aliens and phenomena. So if somebody came in with a story and it was about a phenomenon or a strange alien, I'd say, 'Fine, but whose story is it?' "

As an example of what he means, Piller refers to the third-season episode "The Offspring." It was a spec script written by René Echevarria, a writer whom Piller praises for his ongoing contributions to *Star Trek,* and who is another of the team who became involved with *The Next Generation* in that season, and who has continued working in *Star Trek* up to the tenth anniversary, most recently as a producer on *Star Trek: Deep Space Nine.*

" 'The Offspring,' " Piller says, "was a great spec script, except it was, at first, barely about our people. It was really about a very brand-new, exciting female android that Data created out of his own image, and it was all about her. And I said, 'That's great. But it can't be about the guest star. It's got to be about one of our people. It's got to be about Data. It's not about Data's child as much as it is about how Data deals with being a parent. Everybody will be able to relate to that and empathize with the problems he has as a parent of a new child. Especially when that child is threatened by all sorts of outside forces.'

"So those were the kinds of things that I was doing. There had to be themes that people could talk

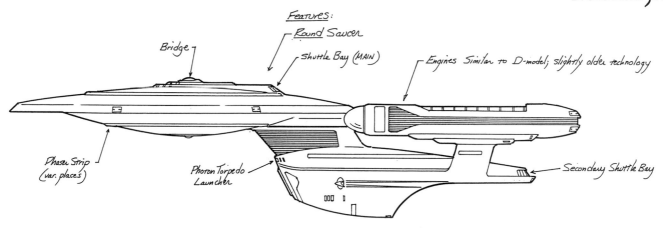

FEATURES:
- Round Saucer

Bridge

Shuttle Bay (MAIN)

Engines Similar to D-model; slightly older technology

Phaser Strip
(var. places)

Photon Torpedo
Launcher

Secondary Shuttle Bay

Basic Side Elevation

Rick Sternbach's original sketch for the new, *Ambassador*-
class *Enterprise*-C from "Yesterday's *Enterprise*."
COURTESY OF THE ARTIST.

about with their families at breakfast the next morning. I was looking for a depth that only genuine character exploration can bring to a television show."

Looking back on the third season, it's easy to see that Piller's intentions were ably translated to the screen. Though that process was not as easy as the quality of the episodes might suggest, Piller recalls that when he joined the show, "There was no pleasure in what was going on there."

"There was so much energy being expended on moves and counter-moves, and so much anger, that there was no energy left for writing. We had no stories in development. We had no scripts in development." Thus, Piller remembers that the first thing he did was to say, "I want to see all the material that's been abandoned. I want to see all the stories that haven't been made into pictures, to see if any of them can be fixed."

In addition to discovering René Echevarria, Piller's decision to sift through the wide range of spec scripts also brought one of *Star Trek*'s most influential writers to light—Ronald D. Moore. His first script sale was the third-season episode "The Bonding." Piller then commissioned Moore to write "The Defector," and shortly after offered him a staff job.

With Brannon Braga as his writing partner, Moore later went on to co-write both *Next Generation* features, and by the time of *The Next Generation*'s tenth anniversary he was a producer of *Star Trek: Deep Space Nine*.

Another influential writer who joined *The Next Generation* that season was Ira Steven Behr, whom Piller calls "my saving grace. When he came on board in the middle of the season, he knew what we needed to do, and helped me on half the last dozen or fifteen shows. After that, we had to

Denise Crosby made a surprise return to *The Next Generation* in "Yesterday's *Enterprise*," where she reprised her role as Tasha Yar in an alternate timeline in which she hadn't been killed two years earlier.

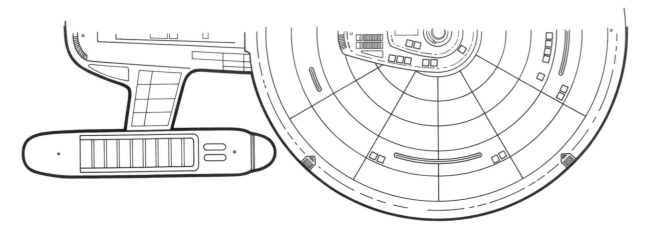

Because the *Enterprise*-C was from 22 years in the past, "Yesterday's *Enterprise*" required a complete new set of computer displays to distinguish the C from the D, as it would be unlikely that the same style of display would have been used by Starfleet over that length of time. The first step in preparing the art for the new displays was to create a technical illustration of the ship. Because the ship is symmetrical, only half of it had to be drawn. The other half was added by flipping a photostat and placing it beside the original art.

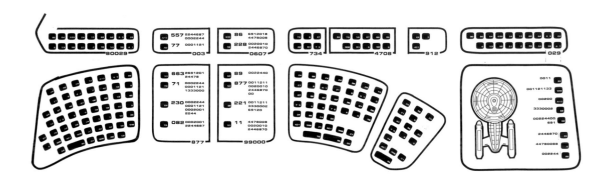

look at each other, exhausted, numb from writing and storybreaking, and say, 'Man, we are riding on the rims. There's no rubber left on the tires.'

"It was the most nightmarish and the most rewarding experience of my life. At the end of it, you sort of feel like John Wayne at the end of one of those movies where you're walking away victorious over all the odds, and you know that nothing's going to beat you, because it'll never get that bad again.

"If you can do it," Piller says, "if you can survive in that circumstance where every day you had to write the words that were going to be in the actor's mouth the next day, and it was coming out okay, basically, you know you can survive anything."

Surprisingly, one of the best episodes of that or any other season, according to numerous fan polls, was written under the worst of the conditions Piller describes. "Yesterday's *Enterprise*" had its beginnings in one of the rejected stories Piller came across which had been pitched the previous year. Piller made some suggestions, and the "storybreaking" session—a group meeting in which the story is broken into dramatic beats by the writing staff—continued over a withering eight days.

The final script, which is credited to six credited writers, was ultimately turned out by having each act written by a different member of the staff, in order to finish it within three days so that Guinan's crucial scenes could be filmed during Whoopi Goldberg's limited window of availability. The episode also marked the first return of Denise Crosby to the series, reprising her role as Tasha Yar in an alternate timeline in which she did not die as shown in the first-season episode "Skin of Evil."

But if "Yesterday's *Enterprise*" had brought forth the most concentrated effort from the writing staff, it was "Sarek" which caused the most internal debate—most of it involving not the prominent guest star, but the inclusion of a single word ... "Spock."

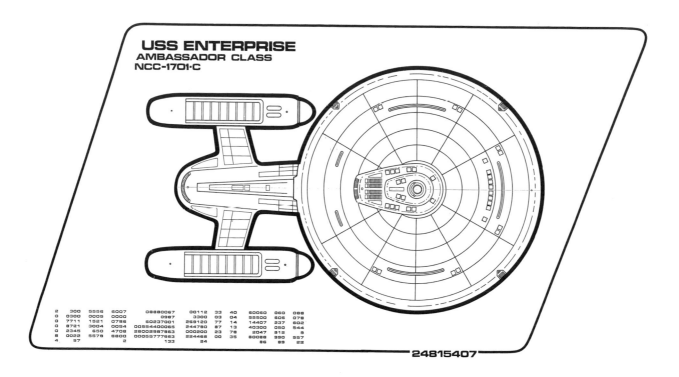

USS ENTERPRISE
AMBASSADOR CLASS
NCC-1701·C

24815407

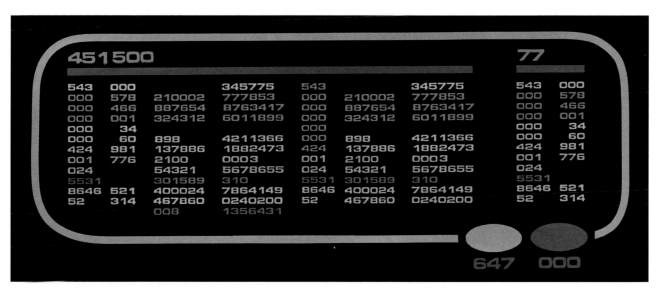

For the new control panel surfaces and displays of the *Enterprise*-C Michael Okuda deliberately incorporated the style and color palette that had been established for the *Enterprise*-A in the *Star Trek* features, representing the design continuity that people would expect to see in a real Starfleet.

In the beginning, Gene Roddenberry had wanted *The Next Generation* to stand on its own, and for two and a half seasons he and Rick Berman had steadfastly resisted any mention of *The Original Series*, with the single exception of Captain Kirk's name being read out in "The Naked Now."

Piller says that that decision was "very, very smart. It's what you had to do to sustain this series on its own.

"What it really came down to is that anything that was easy was taken away from you. The kind of conflicts that would make it easy to write ensemble drama were taken away from you. The kind of traditional storytelling where you go back and play out scenarios that had begun in the past, that was taken away from you. So we were forced to be original. We were forced to come up with new solutions. And after we had proven to ourselves, and to, I hope, the world, that we were our own show, and could stand

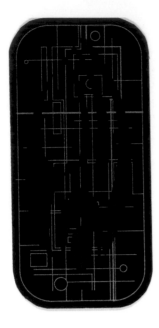

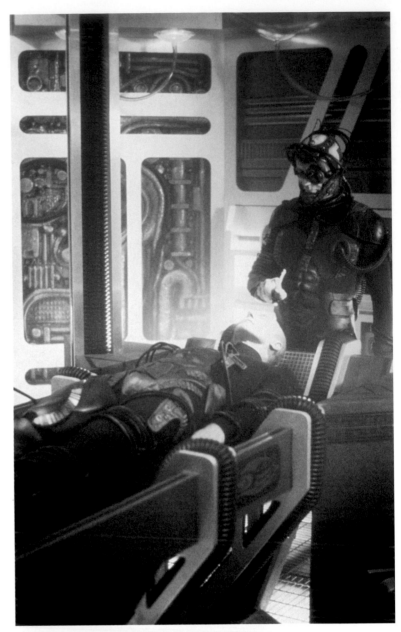

In "The Best of Both Worlds, Part I," considered to be one of the best episodes of the entire seven-season run, the set designs of Rick Sternbach and graphic embellishments of Michael Okuda came together to create the ominous interior of the Borg cubeship that kidnapped Captain Picard. ILLUSTRATION COURTESY OF THE ARTIST. PHOTOGRAPHY BY JULIE DENNIS.

up to any criticism, that was when Rick started allowing a little bit more to happen within the context of those rules."

By halfway through the third season, *The Next Generation* was well on its way to accomplishing what Roddenberry had hoped—building a reputation of its own. So, together with the decision to base an episode on the character of Spock's father, Sarek, came an important question: Was it now time to open the doors to *Star Trek* history, and tie the two generations together?

What it came down to was this—in the episode's climactic scene, in which Picard is overwhelmed by the emotional turmoil he has mentally absorbed from Sarek, should he call out the name of Sarek's son?

The final decision was yes. And, as Michael Piller remembers, "The mention of Spock was the breakthrough that allowed us to open the doors, that allowed us to begin to embrace our past."

But there was more going on in that episode than just the linking of the two generations. Piller further recalls, "What I remember most about that episode, however, is that in a very real way it reflected what was going on with the show at the time we wrote it.

"Gene was beginning to go into decline. Not that he was completely uncommunicative, but it was clear that he was not the same man that he had been. We all respected him so much, and he had been such an important, strong leader of the franchise and everything it stood for. But

ROBBIE ROBINSON

here is this great man—and I've only known him for less than a year at this point—here is this great man going into decline, and I immediately felt a very strong connection to the premise of 'Sarek,' because I could see that it really was about the universe that we lived in on a daily basis.

"If you go back and look at 'Sarek' closely, what that character is, is Gene Roddenberry."

The last episode of the third season is consistently called out as one of the series' finest—"The Best of Both Worlds, Part I." In it, Captain Picard is captured by the Borg, and assimilated by the Collective to become Locutus. The power of that character would return in pivotal roles in both the pilot episode of *Deep Space Nine* and the second *Next Generation* film, *Star Trek: First Contact*.

Intriguingly, that episode was a season-ending cliffhanger, and its unsettled ending also reflected what was going on in the real world.

Michael Piller wrote it without knowing how the story would be resolved, without even knowing if he would be back the next season to complete it.

Of course, he did return, and like so much else in *Star Trek*, one of the people responsible was Gene Roddenberry himself.

"At the end of the year," Piller recalls fondly, "Gene walked into my office and he said, 'Look, this show's just beginning to come around. It needs one more year and it's going to be on top of the world. Please come back next year. This show is really going to make it next year.'

"And," Piller concludes, "as usual, Gene was right."

THERE was a reason why Michael Piller's approach worked so well within the *Star Trek* universe.

As he said, he wanted to tell stories that were *about* something—stories that families could discuss over breakfast. And since fully eleven of the first thirteen episodes of the new season were concerned with families and family issues, his influence was definitely being felt.

Which is exactly what Gene Roddenberry had had in mind in the first place.

"That was Roddenberry's approach," Jonathan Frakes explains. "That's why he called the first *Star Trek* 'Wagon Train in space.' He wanted to do a family show, but the family just happened to be on a spaceship."

That sense of family is also what continues to help nourish the sometimes star-

Two months before the fourth season of *The Next Generation* premiered, Iraqi forces invaded Kuwait, and for the next six months America's television viewing habits changed as news broadcasts and CNN rose to prominence.

Meanwhile, the legacy of Communism continued to crumble. Perhaps signalling a future in which the ideal of a united Earth might be achieved, the long-divided German nation reunited, helping to inspire a record-setting, two-part *The Next Generation* episode for the fifth season.

Another hopeful sign for a more peaceful future was the triumphant release of Nelson Mandela from a South African prison. The United States took a step closer to achieving the ideals of inclusivity espoused by Gene Roddenberry when President Bush signed the Americans with Disabilities Act, which prohibits discrimination against forty-three million disabled Americans. And in a still-controversial decision, another of Earth's many threatened life-forms was put on the Endangered Species List— the Northern spotted owl.

Popular films included *Ghost,* for which Whoopi Goldberg won an Oscar for Best Actress in a Supporting Role, and *Dances with Wolves,* directed by and starring Kevin Costner.

On television, Fox's cancellation of *Alien Nation* was so unexpected that fans were left with a season-ending cliffhanger that had been planned for resolution in the second season. Irate fans took a page out of *Star Trek* history to protest the unpopular decision, and in 1994 the cliffhanger was resolved when the first of a successful series of *Alien Nation* television movies was aired on Fox.

But as the 1990 broadcast season began, despite the growing success of *The Next Generation,* science fiction remained noticeably absent from the networks' lineups. The only exceptions were the comic-book-inspired *The Flash* on CBS, and, on ABC, the borderline genre series *Twin Peaks.*

tling phenomenon of *Star Trek* fandom. Often depicted as comical eccentrics with an unhealthy obsession for the minutiae of the *Star Trek* universe, the devoted, hardcore fans of the many *Star Trek* series are, in fact, truly misunderstood by those who don't make the effort to see where the fans' devotion comes from.

Any popular form of entertainment has its group of dedicated followers who might appear unusual to outsiders. Football fans have been known to paint their bodies with their team's colors. Baseball fans can recite statistics from sixty-year-old games. There are even those dedicated souls who can sing every part of every opera ever written. But the appeal of *Star Trek,* some might argue, is deeper in its connection to its followers' lives and aspirations than almost any other form of entertainment.

The most devoted of *Star Trek*'s fans feel a very close connection between their lives and the ideal future depicted in *Star Trek* episodes and movies. Indeed, that is the appeal of the *Star Trek* universe. Gene Roddenberry created a future in which all are welcome. He built that future around stories focused on what are clearly extended families. By simple extension, the audience is also part of that family, so it's no wonder they want to join in.

"That's absolutely it," Frakes says. "The people that stay with the show every week, either consciously or unconsciously, want to be on that ship and serve under Captain Picard, on the bridge, in Ten-Forward, sickbay, or whatever.

"That was an atmosphere I think we captured quite well. It was a good place to work. It was a good job to have. And one of the things Roddenberry always said was that the people who make it through Starfleet Academy are the cream of the crop. Intelligent human beings—or aliens or androids—who have risen to the top of their class and were fortunate enough to be assigned to the flagship."

That sentiment is shared by costume designer Robert Blackman, who is always interested to see how his designs have been interpreted and reproduced

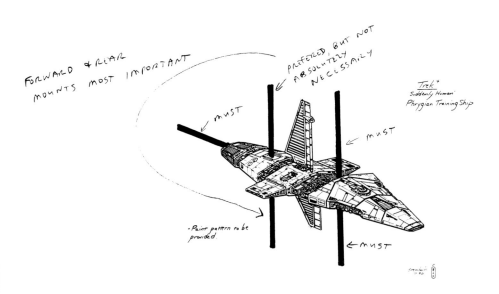

Rick Sternbach's design for a Phrygian training ship in "Suddenly Human," which demonstrates an understanding of 24th-century technology, as well as the 20th-century techniques used to film models by mounting them on rods in front of cameras.
COURTESY OF THE ARTIST.

Preliminary Design

STAR TREK
the next generation

New Shuttlecraft Proposal
(to replace difficult 1st
Season shuttlecraft)

Design Features:

• Flat Surfaces for Simpler Construction
  (similar to Hyundai Shuttlepod)
  <u>NO</u> Compound Curves
• Does Not Dwarf Existing Shuttlebay Set
• Radius Edges Consistant with Starfleet Style
• Easy Moving on Rubber Wheels
  (again similar to Shuttlepod, more easily
  moved than existing large shuttle)
• Removable Warp Engines
• Sliding Entry Door
• Flip-Open Rear Hatch
• Design Allows for Wildable Side Panels for Filming
• 6-8 Crew Capacity
• Side and Rear Entry using same
  4-step portable stairway
• Interior Design Can Be 'Palletized' for
  Different Missions

sternbach #90

Front 3/4 View

STAR TREK
the next generation

New Shuttlecraft Proposal
(to replace difficult 1st
Season shuttlecraft)

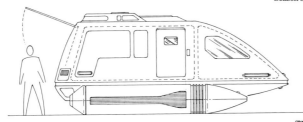

sternbach #90

Starboard Elevation

Season Four continued the
series' quest for the perfect
shuttlecraft. ILLUSTRATIONS
BY RICK STERNBACH.
COURTESY OF THE ARTIST.

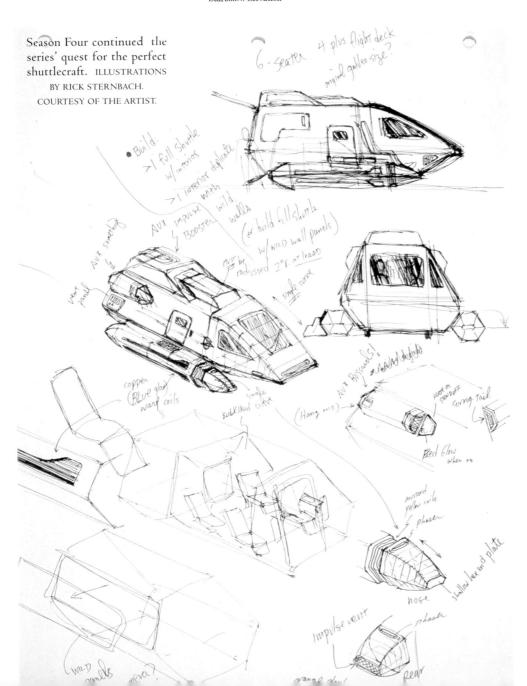

SEASON FOUR: EPISODE 75

THE BEST OF BOTH WORLDS, PART II

Written by Michael Piller
Directed by Cliff Bole

Continuing from "The Best of Both
Worlds, Part I," Riker and
Lieutenant Commander Shelby discover that La Forge's deflector-dish
weapon will not stop the Borg.
Riker decides to retrieve Picard with
the hopes that the Borgified captain
will serve as a conduit Data can use
to influence the Borg collective.
Still in his assimilated form, Picard
fights his programming to supply
Data with the key command: Sleep.
Vulnerable because of their group
mind, all the Borg obey and their
ship is destroyed by a power feedback. Picard begins his long recov-
ery. The Borg threat is ended ...
for now.

SEASON FOUR: EPISODE 76

SUDDENLY HUMAN

Teleplay by John Whelpley & Jeri Taylor
Story by Ralph Phillips
Directed by Gabrielle Beaumont

The retrieval of a drifting Talarian
ship containing a human teenager
pulls Picard into a difficult decision
that could cause war: should he
return the boy, named Jono, to his
closest human relative, a Starfleet
admiral, or surrender him to the
Talarian who took him in after the
boy's family was killed in a Talarian
raid on a colony ten years' earlier?
Picard and the boy's adoptive father
agree to let Jono decide, but he is
unable to choose. Jono tries to kill
Picard, hoping that he will be put to
death for the crime, thus removing
the need to choose. Picard under-
stands, and makes the choice,
returning Jono to his grateful
adoptive family.

Brent Spiner as Data's creator,
Dr. Noonien Soong.
JULIE DENNIS

SEASON FOUR: EPISODE 77
BROTHERS
Written by Rick Berman
Directed by Rob Bowman

En route to a nearby starbase to deliver a child made seriously ill by his brother's prank, Data unexpectedly takes control of the *Enterprise*, diverting the ship from its emergency mission. The android has been summoned "home" by his creator, Dr. Noonien Soong, for the installation of a chip that Soong hopes will give him emotions. But Data's predecessor, the evil Lore, also arrives at the doctor's lab and steals the chip for himself, leaving Soong with fatal injuries. Soong insists that the *Enterprise* get the stricken child to medical help, even if it means leaving him behind to die. Data reflects on the loss of Soong and his gift, and on his relationship with his "brother."

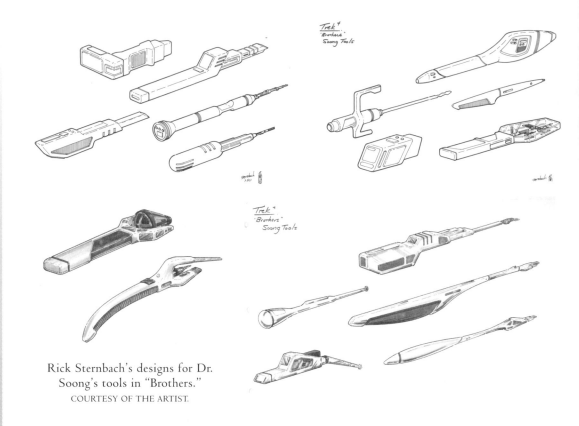

Rick Sternbach's designs for Dr. Soong's tools in "Brothers."
COURTESY OF THE ARTIST.

by fans who create their own *Star Trek* costumes to wear at conventions. "*Star Trek* is so inclusive," he says, "all-inclusive, in fact. You have a world, and that's my favorite part about it. I really do think that it is the best part. No one is excluded.

"You know you can become an avid follower and rattle off the information that interests you, and you will find an ear somewhere. Whether it's on the Internet, [or] at a convention, you will find a group that you can be with. And it doesn't matter if you are seven feet, eight inches and weigh a hundred and ten

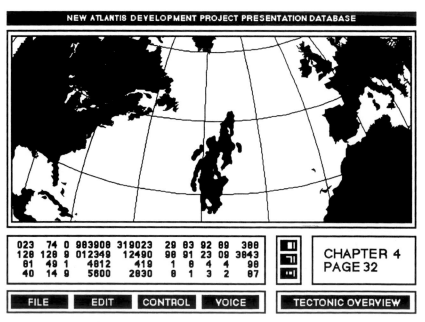

Though Atlantis did not exist in the past, according to this Okudagram from "Family," it will in the future.

Picard with his nephew, René, played by David Tristen Birkin, in his family's vineyard in France. FRED SABINE.

SEASON FOUR: EPISODE 78
FAMILY
Written by Ronald D. Moore
Directed by Les Landau

This atypical episode begins with the *Enterprise* in dry-dock for repairs following the Borg attack. Given shore leave with the rest of the crew, Picard visits his brother's family in France after a twenty-year absence, and considers accepting a new job outside Starfleet. Meanwhile, Worf's adoptive, human parents offer their support for him following his recent "discommendation" by the Klingon High Council. And Wesley Crusher learns more about his late father, Jack, when his mother gives him a holotape made after Wesley's birth. Heeding his brother's advice to come to terms with the guilt and self-doubt he feels in the wake of his assimilation by the Borg, Picard decides to remain with Starfleet, and returns to the ship.

Samantha Eggar, Patrick Stewart, David Tristen Birkin, and Jeremy Kemp enjoying a Picard family reunion behind the scenes of "Family." FRED SABINE

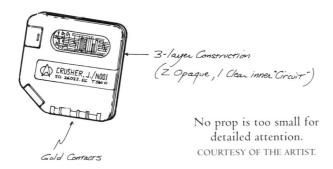

3-layer Construction
(2 Opaque, 1 Clean inner "Circuit")

CRUSHER, J./N001

Gold Contacts

No prop is too small for detailed attention.
COURTESY OF THE ARTIST.

pounds, or you're four-nine and weigh three hundred pounds, or you're in a wheelchair, or blind, or black, yellow, green, purple, or blue—it doesn't matter. This is Gene's greatest legacy to all of us—inclusion for the world."

Not surprisingly, it is that sense of inclusion, that desire to be part of the family, that resulted in so many fans trying to get jobs on *The Next Generation*. As writers, several were successful with spec-script sales, especially Ron Moore, who returned for the fourth season as Executive Story Editor. Fans also found their way into the show through visual effects. As a child, Greg Jein contributed fanciful spaceship drawings to the first mimeographed *Star Trek Concordance*, produced by well-known fan Bjo Trimble in 1967. Today, Jein is one of the leading suppliers of model spacecraft to all the *Star Trek* series, with film credits that stretch all the way from *Close Encounters of the Third Kind* to *Starship Troopers*.

Like Whoopi Goldberg, many actors threw their hats in the ring as well, expressing their interest in taking a role in an episode, no matter how small,

SEASON FOUR: EPISODE 79

REMEMBER ME

Written by Lee Sheldon
Directed by Cliff Bole

While thinking about the loss of
friends and loved ones, Dr. Crusher
is accidentally transferred to an alternate universe as the result of a warp
experiment conducted by Wesley.
Unaware of the switch, Crusher is
alarmed when the inhabitants of her
universe begin to disappear. In the
real world, Wesley learns about his
mother's disappearance from the
alien known as the Traveler. Aided
by the Traveler, Wesley, La Forge, and
Data create a swirling vortex to
retrieve Crusher but the doctor
avoids it. But when the last person
disappears and the alternate universe
itself begins to follow, she realizes
what has happened and rushes
through the vortex into her
own world.

SEASON FOUR: EPISODE 80

LEGACY

Written by Joe Menosky
Directed by Robert Scheerer

The *Enterprise* travels to Tasha Yar's
home planet on a rescue mission to
locate two Federation engineers.
Picard discovers that the Alliance—
one of two warring factions—has
captured the engineers, and accepts
the help of a guide from the other
faction, the Coalition. The guide is
Tasha Yar's sister, Ishara, who
believes Tasha ran away from her
people and their cause. Ishara
betrays Picard's crew, and Data, in
particular, when she uses their
friendship to try to defeat the
perimeter detectors that have been
shielding the two factions from each
other. Riker arrives just in time to
stop Ishara from killing Data.

Varied and distinctive
fabric textures are
important to the final
appearance of *Star Trek*
costumes on the small
television screen. All
of Robert Blackman's
final costume designs
include representative
fabric swatches. These
designs are for
"Legacy." COURTESY OF
THE ARTIST.

*Trek 4 "Reunion"
New Klingon Main Ship*

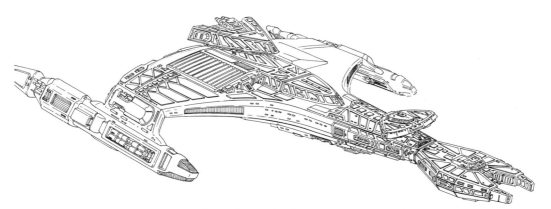

Rick Sternbach's new design for a Klingon battle cruiser incorporated elements from the first Klingon vessel designed by Matt Jefferies for *The Original Series*. The model was built by Greg Jein. ILLUSTRATION COURTESY OF THE ARTIST. DETAIL PHOTOGRAPHY COURTESY OF GREG JEIN.

Rick Sternbach 9.90

Worf instructs his son, Alexander, in the art of the *bat'leth*.
ROBBIE ROBINSON.

SEASON FOUR: EPISODE 81
REUNION
Teleplay by Thomas Perry & Jo Perry and Ronald D. Moore & Brannon Braga
Story by Drew Deighan & Thomas Perry & Jo Perry
Directed by Jonathan Frakes

K'Ehleyr, Worf's half-human, half-Klingon lover, informs him he has a son, Alexander. She also reveals that the Klingon leader, K'mpec, has been poisoned. K'mpec asks Picard to help select his successor, and to discover which of the two contenders, Gowron and Duras, has murdered him. When K'Ehleyr learns that Duras is the poisoner, Duras kills her. Although Duras could clear the name of Worf's father, falsely accused of treason at Khitomer, Worf kills him in revenge for K'Ehleyr. Gowron succeeds K'mpec and Worf sends Alexander to Earth, away from his father's shame, to live with the human foster parents who raised Worf.

SEASON FOUR: EPISODE 82
FUTURE IMPERFECT
Written by J. Larry Carroll & David Bennett Carren
Directed by Les Landau

Riker loses consciousness on a mission to Alpha Onias III and regains it sixteen years in the future, where he finds he is the widowed captain of the *Enterprise*. More surprises follow: Dr. Crusher says a sleeper virus has destroyed his memory of the intervening years; Admiral Picard and an old Romulan enemy are aboard and about to sign a peace treaty between the Federation and the Romulan Empire; a married Troi is Picard's adviser; and Riker has a son. When Riker discovers flaws in the scenario, he discovers his "son" is Barash, a lonely alien who wished only for company in exile. Riker extends an invitation to visit the *Enterprise*.

just so they could be part of the *Star Trek* family. John Tesh, Mick Fleetwood, astronaut Mae Jemison, and even renowned physicist Stephen Hawking joined the list of celebrities who turned up in episodes, all becoming part of the family they had enjoyed for so long.

Many of the behind-the-scenes staff on the show were also what special effects producer Dan Curry calls "closet fans." That is, they were already followers of *Star Trek* when they came to work on the series, and they could be counted on to provide extra effort for reasons other than just their paychecks. Intriguingly, though, many staff members on *The Next Generation* were reticent about openly discussing their knowledge and enthusiasm for *Star Trek*.

"It's just not done," Curry says. "There's a level of 'fanness' that's good, because that keeps us all employed. But sometimes a fan attitude can take the

FINAL MISSION
Written by Kacey Arnold-Ince and Jeri Taylor
Story by Kacey Arnold-Ince
Directed by Corey Allen

Assigned to one last mission before he leaves for Starfleet Academy, Wesley accompanies Picard and a pilot in a less-than-reliable shuttlecraft that crash-lands on a desert moon. A search for water leads the three to a fountain, guarded by an energy sentry. Picard is injured in a landslide caused by the pilot, who later goads Wesley into attacking the sentry. The pilot dies in the attack and Wesley figures out how to defeat the sentry to keep his captain alive until the *Enterprise* can locate and rescue them.

Troi and Riker in Ten-Forward.
MICHEL LESHNOV.

THE LOSS
Teleplay by Hilary J. Bader and Alan J. Adler & Vanessa Greene
Story by Hilary J. Bader
Directed by Chip Chalmers

Troi loses her empathic abilities when the path of the *Enterprise* coincides with that of powerful two-dimensional beings headed toward a cosmic string that will destroy the *Enterprise*. Racked with self-doubt, she resigns as ship's counselor, and tries to help Picard alert the beings to their danger. However, Troi soon realizes that the beings are deliberately seeking the string, and Data manages to distract the creatures with a decoy "string" that allows the *Enterprise* to break free from them. After the beings escape, Troi's abilities return.

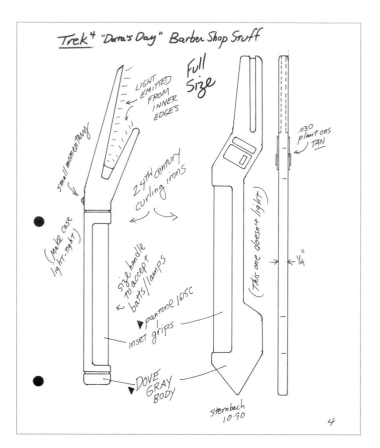

"Data's Day" revealed parts of the *Enterprise* viewers had never seen before, including the ship's barbershop. ILLUSTRATIONS BY RICK STERNBACH. COURTESY OF THE ARTIST.

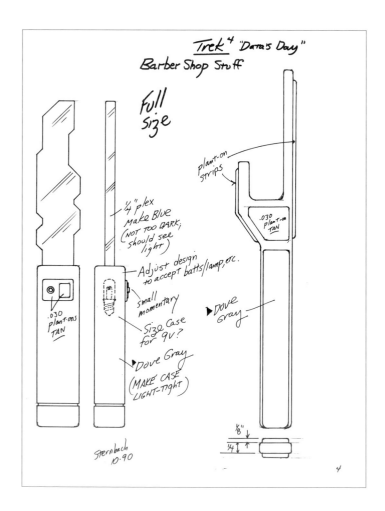

SEASON FOUR: EPISODE 85
DATA'S DAY
Teleplay by Harold Apter and Ronald D. Moore
Story by Harold Apter
Directed by Robert Wiemer

Against an unusual "day-in-the-life" backdrop of Data's preparations for Keiko and O'Brien's on-again, off-again, on-again wedding, Data turns to his Sherlock Holmes persona to solve a diplomatic homicide. The Vulcan ambassador T'Pel is seemingly murdered just after Data denies her request for access to security information. However, Data discovers that T'Pel did not die; she was a spy for the Romulans, seeking an edge in the upcoming Vulcan-Romulan treaty talks in the Neutral Zone.

Starship models have many lives. The *Ambassador*-class *Enterprise-C* was renamed the *U.S.S. Zhukov*, as mentioned in "Data's Day." PHOTOGRAPHY COURTESY OF GREG JEIN.

Robert Blackman's costume design for the false Vulcan ambassador, T'Pel, in "Data's Day." COURTESY OF THE ARTIST.

seriousness out of what you're doing. So when we're on the lot, we're here to work as professionals. Then, when you're a fan, you're a fan somewhere else."

Curry recalls that in a few instances, dedicated fans who came to work on the series didn't perform satisfactorily. "They were so into that fan aspect of being around *Star Trek* that other aspects of their work suffered. I think that's an interesting sociological phenomenon."

Of course, not everyone who came to work on the series was a fan of *Star Trek*. Some, in fact, had absolutely no familiarity with the *Star Trek* universe at all. That wasn't necessarily a negative situation, either. From that infusion of fresh and unfiltered viewpoints came many people who went on to become important contributors to the ongoing *Star Trek* saga. And in the fourth season, one of the most important new contributors was Jeri Taylor.

Taylor was an experienced television writer, who had worked as a producer on police and detective series, including *Quincy, Magnum P.I., Jake and the Fatman*, and *In the Heat of the Night*. Like Michael Piller, her strengths as a writer were, as

U.S.S. PHOENIX

**NEBULA CLASS • STARFLEET REGISTRY NCC-65420
40 ERIDANI-A STARFLEET CONSTRUCTION YARDS • YOYODYNE DIV.
COMMISSIONED STARDATE 40250.5
UNITED FEDERATION OF PLANETS**

STARFLEET COMMAND, SOL SECTOR

CHIEF OF STAFF, STARFLEET: Adm. Gene Roddenberry	FLEET YARDS OPERATIONS: Capt. Chip Chalmers
FLEET OPERATIONS: Adm. Rick Berman	ADVANCED TECHNOLOGIES DIV: Capt. Richard James
EXPLORATORY DIVISION: Adm Michael Piller	STELLAR IMAGING DIV: Capt. Marvin Rush
FLEET ADMINISTRATION: V Adm David Livingston	ORBITAL OPERATIONS: Capt. Doug Dean
TACTICAL COMMAND: V Adm Jeri Taylor	STARFLEET ACADEMY: Capt. Adele Simmons
MISSION OPERATIONS: V Adm Peter Lauritson	RESEARCH & DEVELOPMENT: Capt. Dan Curry

"No matter where you go, there you are."

The *Starship Phoenix*'s commissioning plaque from "The Wounded" salutes many members of the series' team, as well as the movie *Buckaroo Banzai.*

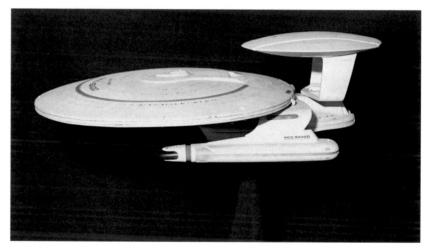

The *U.S.S. Phoenix* from "The Wounded" illustrates Starfleet's modular approach to starship design, based on using existing parts of various *Enterprise* models. COURTESY OF GREG JEIN.

she describes them, "long on character and personal relationships, and very short on sci-fi."

She was recommended to *The Next Generation* by Lee Sheldon, who wrote the episode "Remember Me" and served as producer on the series for only a short time. But during Sheldon's brief association, there was one script that was proving troublesome and that led to Jeri Taylor's invitation into the world of *Star Trek.*

Taylor recalls: "Lee Sheldon and I had known each other for a number of years, and I think he simply respected my work as a writer. There was a script that needed to be rewritten, and he remembered 'people-writing' was my stock in trade. So, he called and asked me to do that, and because it was a script that played into my strengths, I did a credible job on it and was offered a job on

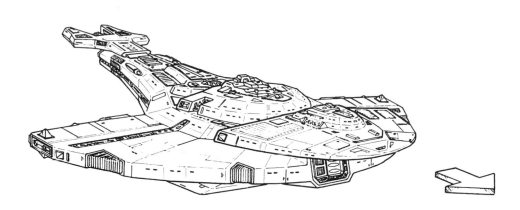

CLUES
*Teleplay by Bruce D. Arthurs and
Joe Menosky
Directed by Les Landau*

En route to an uncharted planet, the crew of the *Enterprise*, except for Data, loses consciousness. But while Data insists only 30 seconds elapsed, increasing evidence points to a much greater lapse—twenty-four hours. Picard orders the ship to continue to the planet, over Data's objections. Ultimately the truth is revealed when a Paxan, an alien being, takes over Troi's body. The Paxans wish no visitors to their planet, and deflect starships after stunning their crews. But Data's presence foiled their plan, and the Paxans were prepared to destroy the *Enterprise* until Picard suggested a short-term memory wipe for the crew. Unfortunately, the wipe did not take care of all details, but Picard promises the Paxans the second try will be perfect.

The impressive *Galor*-class Cardassian ship made its debut in "The Wounded."
ILLUSTRATION BY RICK STERNBACH. COURTESY OF THE ARTIST. PHOTOGRAPH BY GARY HUTZEL.

staff on that basis." With a laugh, Taylor adds, "Then I realized what I was getting into. It was quite a shock when I saw that it was an entire universe of which I knew nothing, that I had to learn about."

Unlike fans who had come to work on *The Next Generation* with full knowledge of everything that had gone before, Taylor had to take what she calls "a crash course."

"I started watching tapes," she explains. "I watched all the *Next Generation* tapes, which at the time numbered just under the total episodes of *The Original Series*. Then I went back and watched all *The Original Series*. And this is while I had the job all day long. So I was taking four or five tapes home at night, and after dinner my husband would say, 'Goodbye,' and I would go and watch until my eyes were little pinwheels. I just started absorbing it all.

"I read the technical manuals, the writers' guide, all the things that had been put out. I read about *The Original Series*. I read *The Making of Star Trek* [by

Riker "undercover" as a
Malcorian. ROBBIE ROBINSON

SEASON FOUR: EPISODE 89
FIRST CONTACT
Teleplay by Dennis Russell Bailey &
David Bischoff and Joe Menosky &
Ronald D. Moore and Michael Piller
Story by Marc Scott Zicree
Directed by Cliff Bole

Riker is captured while on an undercover mission to a planet not yet
aware of the existence of the
Federation, but poised on the brink
of its first warp flight. Picard and
Troi beam down to contain the damage, and the panic that is likely to
follow, meeting with the planet's reasonable leader and his science minister. But a security officer, wishing to
discredit the alien visitors, unsuccessfully tortures Riker for more
information; he then stages his own
death, implicating Riker, hoping to
convince the populace of the danger
of the aliens. While the leader does
not believe the Federation intent is
hostile, he ultimately decides his
planet is not yet ready for the knowledge that it is not alone. He puts
the planet's space program on hold,
but allows the disappointed science
minister to leave with the *Enterprise*.

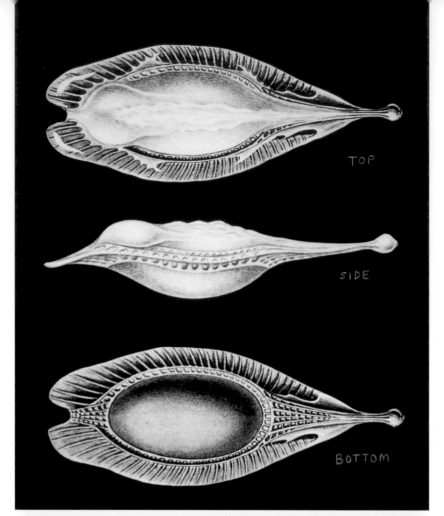

Visual-effects producer Dan Curry's design for a space-dwelling creature was
translated exactly to the screen for "Galaxy's Child."
ILLUSTRATION COURTESY OF THE ARTIST.

Stephen Whitfield]. I read biographies of Gene. I just immersed myself in *Star
Trek* and it was sort of like an endless finals week, where you're not sleeping and
you're drinking coffee and you're cramming information in.

"At the same time, I was trying to write my second script, which was long
on sci-fi and short on character! And it wasn't going well at all."

In fact, Taylor admits that she was convinced the producers were not going
to pick up her option to continue on the series.

Fortunately, however, her initial concerns about the script were not shared
by the other producers, and might only have been a result of her trying to take
in all the accumulated *Star Trek* lore at once.

For "Night Terrors," the old *Reliant* model was once again given back its "roll bar" and reused, this time as the *Brattain*. COURTESY OF GREG JEIN.

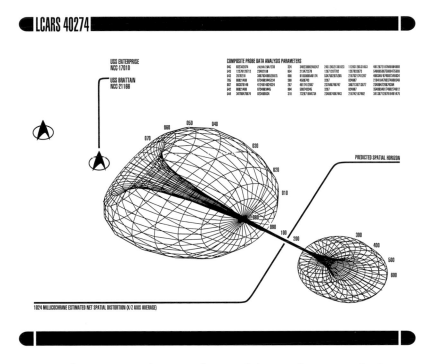

LCARS 40274

USS ENTERPRISE
NCC-17010

USS BRATTAIN
NCC-21166

COMPOSITE PROBE DATA ANALYSIS PARAMETERS

PREDICTED SPATIAL HORIZON

1024 MILLICOCHRANE ESTIMATED NET SPATIAL DISTORTION (X/Z AXIS AVERAGE)

By the fourth season, elements of many of the series' computer displays were in fact being created on the art department's own computers. This display is from "Night Terrors."

Taylor had prepared for her first script, "Suddenly Human," by watching only two episodes and reading two other scripts. "It was all about the relationship between Picard and this adolescent boy, and so, having had adolescent boys, I had that down pretty well. Then I just filled in past that. I actually lifted a whole section of tech from one of the scripts they had given me and just copied that. So that part came out sounding very good."

Though Taylor wasn't knowledgeable about *Star Trek,* it is almost impossible to think of anyone raised in North America not having at least an idea of what it is about. And Taylor did have an idea.

"I perceived it as a children's show. Something like a 1950s, B-movie,

SEASON FOUR: EPISODE 90
GALAXY'S CHILD
Teleplay by Maurice Hurley
Story by Thomas Kartozian
Directed by Winrich Kolbe

La Forge discovers that his holodeck "dream woman," Dr. Leah Brahms, one of the original designers of the *Galaxy*-class warp engines, is in real life married, and a sharp critic of his changes to her designs. Nevertheless, the two put aside their differences to work together and save the *Enterprise* from an energy-draining alien baby that mistakes the starship for its mother. The baby had been "born" when Dr. Crusher and Worf performed a phasered caesarian on a pregnant life-form that had inadvertently been killed. As the ship loses power, La Forge and Brahms separate the baby from the ship's exterior, allowing it to join life-forms of its species.

SEASON FOUR: EPISODE 91
NIGHT TERRORS
Teleplay by Pamela Douglas and
Jeri Taylor
Story by Shari Goodhartz
Directed by Les Landau

The *Enterprise* locates the *Brattain,* a derelict ship whose crew is dead, except for their Betazoid counselor, who is beset by nightmares. When the *Enterprise* attempts to leave the area, its engines fail, Troi begins having nightmares, and the crew's sanity is threatened by dream deprivation. Data reasons that a nearby space rift is draining energy from the ship. Troi intuits that her dream images are a message from a third ship trapped on the other side of the rift. The *Brattain* did not decode the message in time to save its crew, but Troi manages to contact the other ship in a dream, letting it know that they are taking the action suggested. By venting the ship's stored hydrogen, the *Enterprise* triggers an explosion that frees both ships.

La Forge and Lieutenant
Commander Susanna Lietjen,
played by Maryann Plunkett.
ROBBIE ROBINSON.

SEASON FOUR: EPISODE 92
IDENTITY CRISIS
Teleplay by Brannon Braga
Story by Timothy DeHaas
Directed by Winrich Kolbe

La Forge is contacted by Susanna
Leitjen, a colleague who accompanied
him on an away team to Tarchannen
III five years earlier. According to
Leitjen, the rest of the team disappeared, apparently after returning to
Tarchannen III. After Leitjen falls
ill, Dr. Crusher discovers that
Susanna's DNA is being rewritten by
a parasite, transforming her into a
different species. When Geordi
studies the logs of the mission, he
finds evidence of an unknown entity
shadowing the away team. Then he,
too, falls ill and beams down to
Tarchannen III. Crusher restores
Susanna by removing the parasite;
then she and Susanna follow
La Forge down to the planet. There,
they find a nearly transformed
La Forge and manage to convince
him to return to the ship. Crusher
removes his parasite, and cures him.

sci-fi, tawdry kind of thing. But then, the first tape I watched of *The Next Generation* was 'The Defector' [second season, episode 58, by Ronald D. Moore], and I was stunned. It was this beautifully crafted, finely honed, intelligent, per-ceptive piece of human drama. Very sophisticated. And I was just bowled over.

"Then I started reading the scripts and I realized how much in error I had been. My ignorance had led me completely down the wrong path, and I began to realize what a remarkable series this was. Then, as I got back into *The Original Series*, I saw what an incredible universe Gene Roddenberry had created. I saw why it was so timeless and so pervasive."

Of all that has been written about *Star Trek* in all its guises, perhaps no aspect of it has been addressed more often than the one Jeri Taylor had inde-pendently stumbled upon—its capacity to arouse passionate interest.

Most people explain *Star Trek*'s unprecedented appeal to its fans as a result of its optimistic view of the future. But Taylor, who absorbed almost twenty-five years' worth of *Star Trek* in a matter of weeks, has a slightly different theory.

"One of the reasons for *Star Trek*'s success is the commonly accepted pos-itive view of the future, that most people feel good to think that things can get better than they are now. But I also have a feeling that there's something a lit-tle more deep-seated going on, which has to do with heroes in our lives.

"We don't have them anymore," she says. "We have lost the traditional are-nas of heroes. We don't have gods and legends and myth anymore. We have lost sports figures as heroes—they have proven all too human and vulnerable. We have lost politicians. We have lost movie stars. We've even lost royalty, who have feet of clay also.

"So, there don't seem to be those icons, now, that are the role models, larg-er-than-life people who are better than we are, who are heroic, who stand for something. I think that what Gene gave us in the *Star Trek* characters is these larger-than-life people who are committed to an ethical and moral way of life, who are not afraid to go into the wilderness and to confront the fears and ter-rors of the demons and dragons that are out there, who have a moral principle

This Robert Blackman design for
a Gates McFadden costume in
"The Nth Degree" was sketched
on the back of an old script page.
COURTESY OF THE ARTIST.

and a moral center and who will not stray from that, no matter what. *Star Trek* presents godlike figures for us to admire and emulate. And I think that is a need that people have deep inside them that is not being satisfied otherwise today."

This outlook on the exemplary nature of the *Next Generation* characters raises a question that was hotly debated over the course of the series' entire run, and which was often cited as one of the reasons why so many writers found the series difficult to write for—that is, the lack of conflict between the characters.

Ask any writer, for television, novels, or film, and the answer will be that the heart of any story is conflict—the tension that arises when characters confront obstacles. But Gene Roddenberry had decreed that one of the most vital wellsprings of drama—interpersonal con-

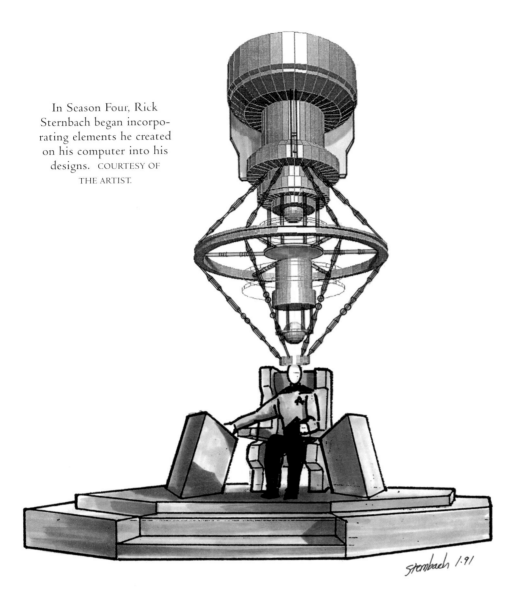

In Season Four, Rick Sternbach began incorporating elements he created on his computer into his designs. COURTESY OF THE ARTIST.

Dr. Crusher and Lieutenant Reg Barclay, played by Dwight Schultz. ROBBIE ROBINSON.

SEASON FOUR: EPISODE 93
THE NTH DEGREE
Written by Joe Menosky
Directed by Robert Legato

Engineer Reg Barclay becomes a genius when he and La Forge are struck by an energy surge from an alien probe while they are repairing a dysfunctional telescope. With his new mental powers, Barclay is able to explain how to destroy the dangerous probe, and repair the telescope in a fraction of the time. Before long, the superadvanced Barclay has taken control of the ship's computer and hurls the ship 30,000 light-years distant. Before Picard can confront Barclay, the image of an alien appears to tell him that he and his crew have been part of a routine Cytherian study of alien civilizations. Barclay is returned to normal. Picard and the Cytherians agree to an information exchange.

SEASON FOUR: EPISODE 94
QPID
Teleplay by Ira Steven Behr
Story by Randee Russell and Ira Steven Behr
Directed by Cliff Bole

To repay a favor to Picard, Q turns Picard into Robin Hood and Picard's former flame, Vash, into Maid Marian. Casting himself as the Sheriff of Nottingham, Q challenges Picard to rescue Vash—at the possible expense of the lives of his crew. Vash is uncooperative and says she'll marry her captor, Sir Guy, but then secretly signals the crew for help. The arrival of the crew, as Robin's Merry Men, helps avert disaster and Picard dispatches Sir Guy with skilled swordplay. The game over, Vash tells Picard she's decided on her next adventure—a galactic expedition with Q. Picard and she kiss farewell and vow to meet again.

flict—no longer existed among Starfleet personnel in the twenty-fourth century.

To be fair, Roddenberry's arrival at this conclusion had been slow to develop. The first-season Writers/Directors Guide states:

> The crew of the *Enterprise* are intelligent, witty, thoughtful, compassionate, *caring* human beings—but they have human faults and weaknesses, too—although not as many or as severe as in our time. They have been selected for this mission because of their ability to *transcend* their human failings. We should see in them the kind of people we aspire to be.

But by the series' third season, that passage had been amended to be much more specific:

> Our continuing characters are the kind of people that the *Star Trek* audience would like to be themselves. They are not perfect, but their flaws do not include falsehood, petty jealousies, and the banal hypocrisies common in the twentieth century.

THE DRUMHEAD
Written by Jeri Taylor
Directed by Jonathan Frakes

An unexplained explosion onboard the *Enterprise* brings retired Admiral Norah Satie to the ship to investigate. Though the explosion is ultimately proven to be an accident, Satie continues to harass a crewman who Picard feels is innocent. Challenging Satie's conclusions, the angry admiral accuses Picard of treason. Picard's rebuttal of her charges, using her own father's words against her, provokes Satie to ruin her own career and ends the pointless search for phantom co-conspirators among Federation officers.

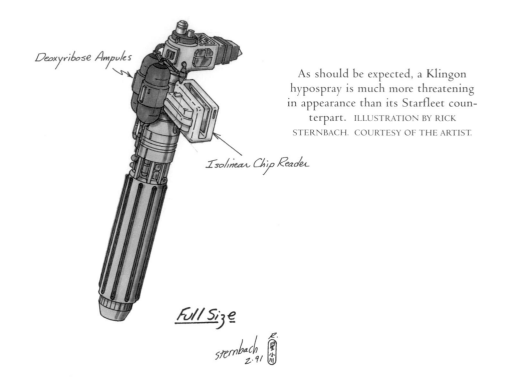

Deoxyribose Ampules

Isolinear Chip Reader

As should be expected, a Klingon hypospray is much more threatening in appearance than its Starfleet counterpart. ILLUSTRATION BY RICK STERNBACH. COURTESY OF THE ARTIST.

Full Size

sternbach 2.91

In the first and second seasons, then, the challenge writers felt they faced was in coming up with stories in which all the conflict arose from external events, even though that still left a dramatic void within which seven regular characters were never supposed to argue with each other. Considering that *Star Trek*'s legacy includes the fondly remembered verbal sparring of Spock and McCoy, that lack of interpersonal conflict seemed, at first, to be out of place. And to writers, especially, it seemed maddening.

Then Michael Piller joined the series.

He remembers a departing writer who said at the time that *The Next Generation* was a doomed franchise because Gene refused to allow his characters to have any conflict between them. "But that really wasn't true," Piller says. "My take on that always was: Look, it's Gene's universe. Gene can make any rules he wants to. Our job is to find ways of creating conflict, as long as we remained true to the characters.

"You may not have an easy time getting conflict between Riker and Geordi," Piller concedes, "but the whole issue of the evolution of humans was very important to Gene, and he didn't want any petty jealousies going on, on board his ship. So we had to find ways of creating conflict through other means."

In particular, Piller recalls the third-season episode "The Enemy," for which he shared writing credit with David Kemper.

In the episode, a dying Romulan requires a transfusion that only Worf can provide. And Worf refuses to give the transfusion, because of the long history of hatred between the Klingons and the Romulans.

"That came out of straight character motivation," Piller says. "It was honest and truthful and Gene didn't blink an eye, even though I put Worf into direct conflict with Beverly Crusher, the doctor who absolutely refused to accept no as an answer."

A new medical kit was introduced in the fourth season. The empty top slot holds a medical tricorder. ROBBIE ROBINSON.

Tricorders acquired new details in the fourth season. Above is a medical tricorder showing the detachable scanner. To the lower left is a "hero" version of a standard tricorder in which all lights work. To the upper left is a less expensive version, used for extras or during action sequences, in which details are simply painted onto a plastic shell. ROBBIE ROBINSON.

SEASON FOUR: EPISODE 96
HALF A LIFE
Teleplay by Peter Allan Fields
Story by Ted Roberts and Peter Allan Fields
Directed by Les Landau

Troi's mother, Lwaxana, returns to the *Enterprise* and succeeds in making Dr. Timicin, a shy scientist, fall in love with her. Timicin is aboard to test theories that could save his planet's dying sun. The test fails, though he could be on the right path—but Timicin shocks Lwaxana when he tells her he must return home to commit ritual suicide. Once 60, adults of his world must die so they will not become burdens to their children. Lwaxana urges him to rebel, continue his work, and seek asylum aboard the *Enterprise* instead. Timicin's brief rebellion lasts until his daughter arrives and reminds him of what he has taught her about honoring their heritage, after which he agrees to go home to die. Lwaxana decides to go with Timicin, to be among his loved ones when he says goodbye.

SEASON FOUR: EPISODE 97
THE HOST
Written by Michel Horvat
Directed by Marvin V. Rush

Odan, a Trillian mediator, en route to oversee negotiations between Peliar's Alpha and Beta moons, becomes romantically involved with Dr. Crusher. When Odan suffers lethal injuries in an attack on his planet-bound shuttlecraft, Crusher learns Odan is a joined Trill, a combination of humanoid host and symbiotic intelligent life-form. With his host dying, the Odan symbiont accepts Riker's offer to be temporary host until a replacement arrives from Trill. After initially spurning Odan-within-Riker, Crusher and Odan experience a last night together before his permanent host arrives—a female, this time. Crusher declares that she cannot adjust to the changing versions of the man she fell in love with, and the two part.

The solution to the dilemma was equally new for *The Next Generation,* and indicative of the fresh life that the new stream of writers were bringing to the series.

"Ultimately, it was a very interesting argument," Piller says, "and it was extensively discussed. What would change Worf's mind? And I'm sitting there listening to the staff's conversation and I finally say, "Umm, what if he *doesn't* change his mind? Why doesn't he let the guy die?' And they all looked at me like I was crazy.

"They said, 'Wait a minute, this is *Star Trek.* We don't do those kind of things on *Star Trek.*'

"I said, 'But why not? If it's honest, it's truthful.'"

Worf's decision was put in a revised script, and the first person to respond was the actor who played Worf, Michael Dorn.

La Forge is subjected to Romulan mind-control. MICHAEL PARIS.

SEASON FOUR: EPISODE 98
THE MIND'S EYE
Teleplay by René Echevarria
Story by Ken Schafer and René Echevarria
Directed by David Livingston

Geordi is placed under mind control and conditioned to become an assassin in a Romulan plan to break up the Federation-Klingon alliance. Meanwhile, a Klingon ambassador arrives on board the *Enterprise* to investigate charges that Starfleet is aiding rebels in a Klingon colony. His suspicions seem confirmed when an illegal arms shipment is detected in transit from the ship. Data discovers that Geordi is responsible for the activity, and reveals the truth to Picard just in time for him to avert Geordi's assassination of a Klingon governor.

SEASON FOUR: EPISODE 99
IN THEORY
Written by Joe Menosky and Ronald D. Moore
Directed by Patrick Stewart

At shipmate Jenna D'Sora's urging, Data investigates the course of true love by following a self-devised personal behavioral program to better understand the phenomenon. But Jenna finds that the romantic relationship between herself and the android can never be anything but artificial and realizes that she needs more than Data can deliver. Data responds logically by erasing his special program, the android equivalent of "breaking up."

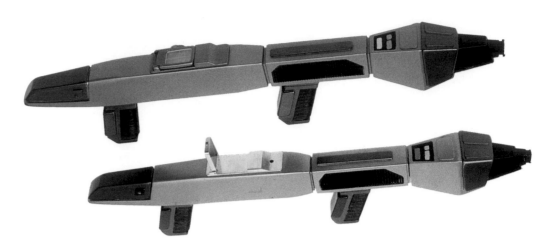

Phaser rifles built for "The Mind's Eye." ROBBIE ROBINSON.

Piller recalls that Dorn called him to ask what he thought he was doing. "You're assassinating my character!" But Piller said to Dorn, "Michael, trust me. This is what Worf would do in that situation. We can't write something to make everybody feel comfy and cozy at the end of this show. If that's what Worf would do, we have to listen to what the character tells us to do."

Dorn even questioned Rick Berman about Worf's decision. "I said, Rick, are you sure you want to do this?" Dorn remembers Berman replied by saying, "We just wanted to show that Worf is not human." And that gave Dorn a new way to look at the character and what the decision would mean.

"I had my trepidations about it," Dorn says, "but Rick was right about that. I think it was one of the bright moments in the character, where people looked at Worf and said, 'Wait a minute. He is *not* a human. He is not constrained by the same type of moral dilemmas that humans are.' I mean, Worf has his own moral dilemmas but they are a completely different set."

Piller agrees with Dorn's assessment. "Ultimately," Piller says, "I look

Patrick Stewart directed his first episode of *The Next Generation* with "In Theory." Here he works with Brent Spiner and Michele Scarabelle in Ten Forward. ROBBIE ROBINSON.

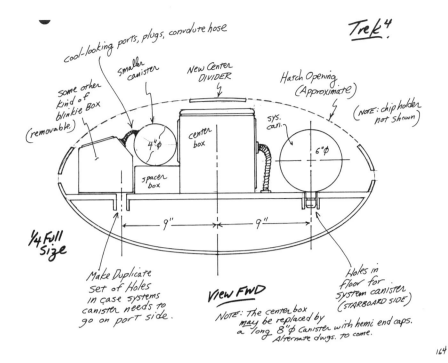

Trek⁴

cool-looking ports, plugs, convolute hose

Some other kind of blinkie Box (removable).

smaller canister

New Center DIVIDER

center box

4"ϕ

spacer box

sys. can.

6"ϕ

Hatch Opening (Approximate)

(NOTE: chip holder not shown)

¼ Full Size

9"

9"

Make Duplicate Set of Holes in case systems canister needs to go on port side.

View FWD

NOTE: The center box may be replaced by a long 8"ϕ canister with hemi end caps. Alternate dwgs. to come.

Holes in floor for system canister (STARBOARD SIDE)

164

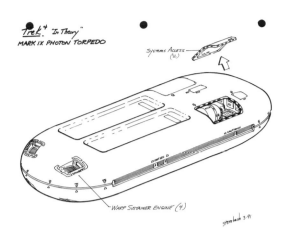

Trek⁴ "In Theory"
MARK IX PHOTON TORPEDO

Systems Access (2)

Warp Sustainer Engine (4)

sternbach 3-91

For "In Theory," Spock's photon-torpedo coffin was reused once again.
ILLUSTRATIONS BY RICK STERNBACH.
COURTESY OF THE ARTIST.

PHOTON TORPEDO MODIFICATIONS 8063

11-4077												
24Z2670	04	88754	38409823408Z348	88754	95485	04	4353	983	23	48098346908569088898908	95485	98754	95485
	05	234	4005723823808443	234	34	05	5	8	458	05976389489849408	34	234	34
	06	0785	1263186308742323	0785	3458	06	67	9		8768858	3458	0785	3458
	07	03499	0934721848301	03499	0977	07	5875	345	78	83480838408849034834	0977	03499	0977
	08	0058	0089090987712332	0058		08	09		458	4123409824288312838423		0058	
488-5851	09	34558	4834208835780908	34558	80875	09	0098	098	088	875388830498	80875	34558	80875
40273													
7876-18834													

SUSTAINER ENGINE MODULES — — DEUTERIUM SUPPLY — ANTIMATTER SUPPLY

REACTION CHAMBERS

GUIDENCE

MARK XXI TORPEDO DEVICE

back at that episode as the show that began the genuine emergence of Worf as a major player on the cast. Until then, he'd spent too much time in the background."

As the fourth season began, Jeri Taylor found herself at home with Piller's approach to conflict. "If we were to posit a supremely positive view of the entire galaxy, we would not have a series," she says. "But in *Star Trek* there is room for disagreement or differences of opinion that are credible and well thought out on each side. That is perfectly legitimate and we endowed our people with exactly those kinds of things. But we did get rid of the petty bickering, the small niggling feelings that get in the way of most of us every day, and the concern for things like: Where is my next meal coming from? Am I going to have a job next year?

"Those concerns had been eliminated, so humans could focus on their own inner growth, improving their minds, and on studying and research and all those kinds of things. When you take away the need to make a living, a lot of other things are possible."

REDEMPTION, PART I

Written by Ronald D. Moore
Directed by Cliff Bole

Picard and Worf are again involved in the politics of honor and succession on the Klingon homeworld when Picard arrives to oversee Gowron's installation as Emperor. Gowron reveals that the family of Duras, who accused Worf's father of treason at Khitomer, is challenging him for leadership of the Empire. When Picard refuses to help him fight Duras's sisters and bastard son, Gowron refuses to redeem Worf's family honor, although he changes his mind when Worf and Kurn rescue him from an ambush set by the Duras clan. Yielding to the demands of his heritage, Worf resigns from Starfleet to fight for Gowron. In the meantime, the Duras family meets with its Romulan supporters, one of whom looks like the late Tasha Yar.

What it comes down to is that Gene Roddenberry's dictate not to involve the regular characters in petty conflicts was not an outrageous affront to dramatic structure, provided his intention was interpreted in a way that generated appropriate *Star Trek* stories. And neither was Roddenberry's vision of how his characters should behave something that didn't belong in *Star Trek*. Indeed, what he had suggested is the very heart of science fiction.

Gene Roddenberry felt it was much easier for the audience to contemplate some of the issues they faced in their own life if those issues were set in the future, and science-fiction fan LeVar Burton agrees. "It gives us a safe distance from which to observe our own behavior in the now. It's what storytelling at its essence is all about."

The first storytelling task in the fourth season was, of course, the conclusion of "The Best of Both Worlds." Over hiatus—the break between one season and the next—Michael Piller had decided to return to the series, but hadn't thought about how he would resolve the story until he physically returned to the lot. He only came up with the strategy used to defeat the Borg—by sending a command to the Collective telling the Borg to "sleep"—two days before production began.

Though rumors had flourished over the summer, suggesting that Picard might not be rescued from the Borg because Patrick Stewart wanted to leave the show, or that the popular Lieutenant Commander Shelby, played by Elizabeth Dennehy, would become a new regular, the fourth season was the first to begin with no cast changes. However, there were several comings and goings behind the scenes.

Ira Steven Behr left the series to work on a feature project. But he was missed and eagerly invited back to the *Star Trek* family when *Deep Space Nine* began production. At the time of *The Next Generation*'s tenth anniversary, Behr now shared executive-producer credit for the series with Rick Berman.

Richard Manning and Hans Beimler, a writing/producing team who had written for the series since the first season under a variety of on-screen credits, left in the fourth season to develop a science-fiction series of their own—*Beyond Reality,* a series whose open-minded, male investigator of the unknown, paired with a skeptical female partner, prefigured *The X-Files* by two years. Like Behr, Manning and Beimler would be invited back as producers on *Deep Space Nine*'s fourth season.

In addition to Jeri Taylor, who had joined *The Next Generation* as supervising producer, new writers for the fourth season included producers Joe Menosky and, briefly, Lee Sheldon, and the talented team of David Bennett Carren and J. Larry Carroll, who came on staff as story editors.

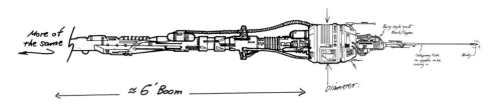

Season Four began with the long-awaited conclusion of "The Best of Both Worlds."
Ending months of unfounded speculation, Patrick Stewart returned to the series.
ILLUSTRATIONS BY RICK STERNBACH. COURTESY OF THE ARTIST. PHOTOGRAPHY BY JULIE DENNIS.

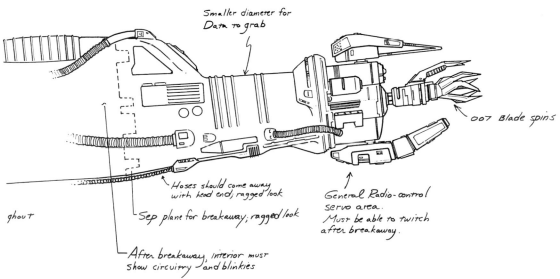

Smaller diameter for
Data to grab

007 Blade spins

General Radio-control
servo area.
Must be able to twitch
after breakaway.

Hoses should come away
with head end; ragged look

Sep plane for breakaway; ragged look

After breakaway, interior must
show circuitry and blinkies

ghout

In "Brothers," Brent Spiner played three roles, including the aged Dr. Soong. MAKEUP BY MICHAEL WESTMORE. FRED SABINE

Ongoing *Star Trek* writer, Hilary J. Bader, began her association with *Star Trek* as an intern that season, as did Brannon Braga, who would get his first full-time position with the series in Season Five.

Other than receiving an infusion of fresh writing blood, the stability that had been so hard-won in the early seasons remained. Credits changed—Rick Berman's name accompanied Gene Roddenberry's as executive producer in the end titles, and David Livingston went from line producer to producer. But virtually the entire proven *Star Trek* team who toiled behind the scenes remained intact at the beginning of Season Four.

Notable episodes that season included "Brothers," the first to be written by Rick Berman. The episode was a tour de force for Brent Spiner, who carried whole scenes by playing three roles—Data, Data's android brother, Lore, and their creator, the elderly human, Dr. Noonien Soong. The episode also introduced the "emotion chip," which would play an important role in both the two-part episode "Descent," and the first *Next Generation* movie, *Star Trek Generations.*

As examples of ways in which Michael Piller liked to stretch the boundaries of television writing, three fourth-season episodes stand out as important deviations from *Star Trek* tradition. "Family," which dealt with Picard's recuperation from assimilation by the Borg, was set on Earth, and was the first and only episode from both *The Original Series* and *The Next Generation* that had no scenes on the bridge of the *Enterprise.*

Another exception to traditional *Star Trek* storytelling was "First Contact," which was pitched by freelance writer, Marc Scott Zicree, as the opposite of all the stories in which the crew of the *Enterprise* struggled to avoid breaking the Prime Directive. At what point in a planet's development, Zicree asked, was it finally *allowable* for the Federation to openly contact a world for the first time? Piller decided that the story should be told from the aliens' point of view, something that had never been done before on *Star Trek,* but which worked perfectly in this story.

A third change-of-pace episode was the delightful "Data's Day," which followed the android through a typical day's events on the *Enterprise,* including the wedding of Miles O'Brien and Keiko Ishikawa, and the not-so-typical discovery of a Romulan spy. This episode also introduced Data's cat, Spot.

A life-form slightly more important than Spot was introduced in "The Host," which was the first *Star Trek* episode to feature the symbiont life-form known as a Trill. Jeri Taylor recalls it as one of those episodes that turned out much better than anyone had expected. Though her writing contribution to the episode is uncredited, Taylor recalls, "I poured a lot of good stuff into it, and everything came together. It became a wonderful, memorable episode." Then she adds with a laugh, "Memorable enough that the Trill were then coopted for *Deep Space Nine.*"

"The Host" was the first *The Next Generation* episode to touch, even lightly, on the topic of homosexuality—Beverly Crusher falls in love with a Trill when its symbiont is in a male body, but later

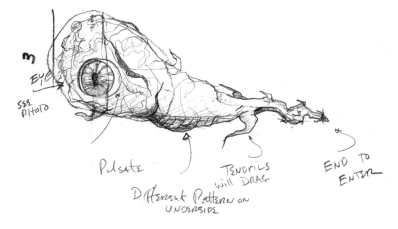

One of Michael Westmore's first concept sketches for a Trill symbiont, first seen in "The Host." COURTESY OF THE ARTIST.

decides not to continue the relationship when the symbiont moves to its new host: a female body.

Another major element introduced into the *Star Trek* universe this season was the Cardassians, first seen in "The Wounded." With eerie and elaborate makeup designed by Michael Westmore, matched to ominous, militaristic uniforms designed by Robert Blackman, the Cardassians became one of the most visually striking alien races seen thus far. They would also go on to become a critical part of *Star Trek: Deep Space Nine.*

Marco Rodriguez as Glinn Telle, and Marc Alaimo as Gul Macet, in "The Wounded," the episode which introduced Cardassians to the *Star Trek* universe. Alaimo went on to portray Gul Dukat in a continuing role on *Deep Space Nine.* MICHAEL PARIS.

Like "The Child" in the second season, this season's "Devil's Due" was also rewritten from an unproduced script from the lost series of the seventies, *Star Trek: Phase II.* In this case, Picard replaced Kirk, and Data took over the role originally written for the *Enterprise*'s computer.

But perhaps the most notable episode of the season, at least symbolically, was "Legacy." In it, Picard's opening log states that the *Enterprise* is bypassing a scheduled archaeological survey of planet Camus II. An archaeological dig on Camus II is where the seventy-ninth and final episode of *The Original Series* began, and with "Legacy," *The Next Generation*'s eightieth episode, the child had surpassed its parent.

As the fourth season came to an end with *The Next Generation* continuing to set records as its ratings climbed, Ron Moore took up the challenge of writing a season-ending cliffhanger that centered on the threat of a Klingon civil war. Not only did "Redemption, Part I" introduce the deadly Duras Sisters, it also ended with a tantalizing glimpse of a blond Romulan who looked surprisingly like Tasha Yar.

After four years, *The Next Generation* had at last gathered a writing team that was every bit as strong as its cast, its production staff, its technical crew, and its ratings, while never straying from what Gene Roddenberry had first put into place, and what Piller and Taylor so clearly understood.

"At the core of *Star Trek* is people," Taylor says. "Stories about the human condition. Stories about relationships. Stories about the struggles that we all have. The science-fiction aspects are those sort of wonderful, provocative, intriguing kinds of veneer, but I believe if you look at the core of most of our stories, it's all about us, and that's important to me."

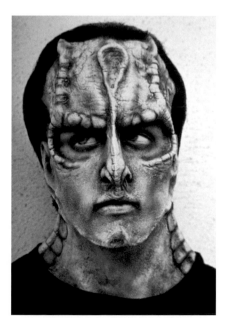

An early Cardassian makeup test.

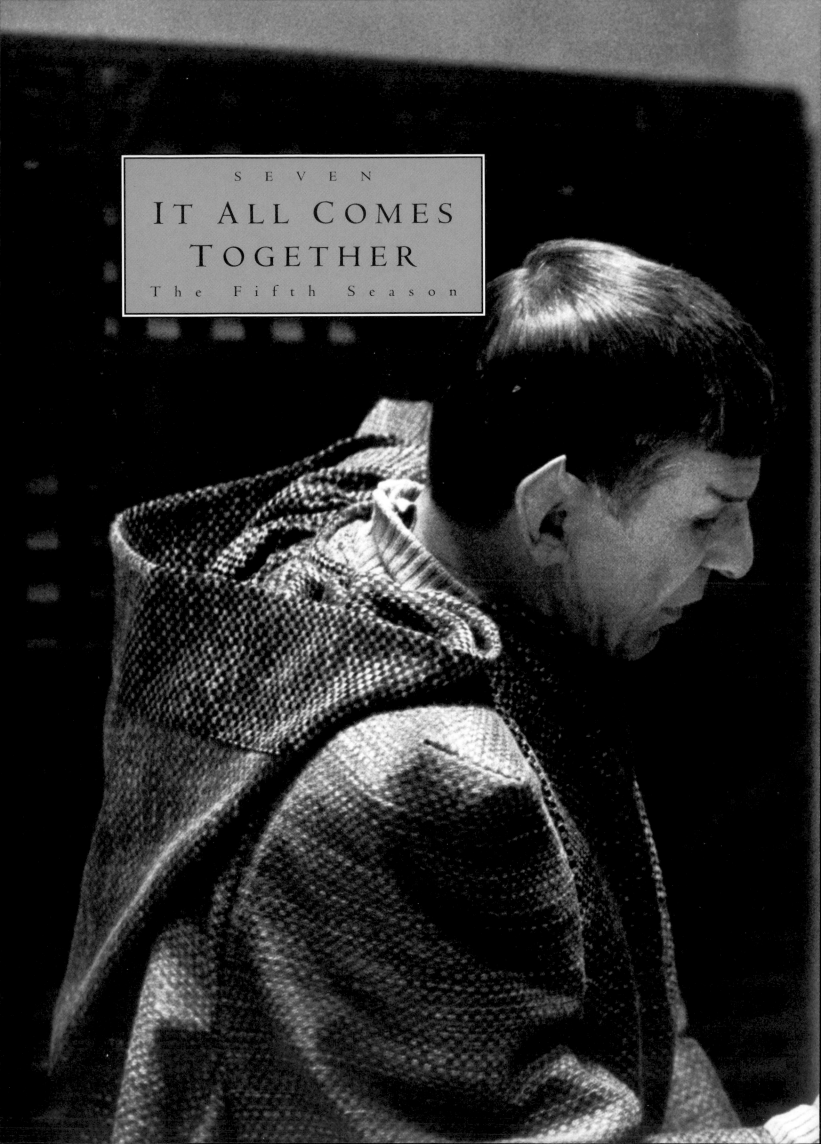

SEVEN

It All Comes Together

The Fifth Season

I T was the best of times, it was the worst of times. In October 1991, *Star Trek* was poised to celebrate its twenty-fifth anniversary. A sixth *Star Trek* film was ready for release. *The Next Generation* was on the brink of achieving its highest-ever ratings.

And on October 26th, at the age of seventy, Gene Roddenberry died.

It was a moment that brought sadness to those who loved him and his visionary work. For Gene Roddenberry had, through talent, hard work, and not a little luck, been blessed with a lifetime achievement that few creative people attain.

Like Walt Disney, Bob Kane, George Lucas, and a mere handful of others, Roddenberry had been fortunate enough to see one of his

In the year of *Star Trek*'s twenty-fifth anniversary, the world was closer to attaining global peace than it had been for decades. The culminating event was the formal break-up of the Soviet Union in December 1991, with the majority of its members then forming the Commonwealth of Independent States.

Even as the international scene calmed, the United States faced more turmoil at home. Most troubling were the riots that spread through Los Angeles at the end of April 1992, following the acquittal of four white police officers who had been video-taped beating black motorist, Rodney King. In the aftermath of those riots, once again *Star Trek* writers would draw inspiration from the daily news as they began the process of creating an as-yet-untitled new chapter in the saga, which would become *Star Trek: Deep Space Nine*. The image of Los Angeles neighborhoods in ruin served to fuel Rick Berman and Michael Piller's vision of the planet Bajor and the *Terek Nor* space station devastated by the Cardassians.

In addition to the fall release of *Star Trek VI: The Undiscovered Country*, science fiction continued to prove its popularity at the box office with James Cameron's summer blockbuster *Terminator 2: Judgment Day*, with Arnold Schwarzenegger and Linda Hamilton. Non-science-fiction films included Michael Hoffman's *Soapdish*, with Sally Field, Kevin Kline, and *The Next Generation*'s own Whoopi Goldberg.

But despite the continual appeal of the genre in movies, and the non-stop ratings gains of *The Next Generation*, science fiction remained sparse on network television. The half-hour, comedy-sf series *Eerie, Indiana* was the only genre series on a major network in the 1991-92 season, and destined to last only one season. On the smaller USA Network, *Beyond Reality*, a forerunner of *The X-Files* created by *Next Generation* alumni Richard Manning and Hans Beimler, would enjoy only two years of production.

Whatever it was that *Star Trek* did so well, no one else seemed to have the slightest idea of how to match its success.

Yet.

creations spring from his imagination to become part of the lives of tens of millions of people, effortlessly transcending national boundaries, generations, and decades.

Death is inescapable for us all, but for a parent, how reassuring to know that a child will continue on past one's own lifetime, thriving, protected, and secure.

So it was for Gene Roddenberry and his child—*Star Trek*.

Two days before his death, Roddenberry attended a screening of *Star Trek VI: The Undiscovered Country* at the Paramount lot. At the time, it was expected to be the final outing for the cast of *The Original Series,* the last time Kirk, Spock, and McCoy, Scotty, Sulu, Chekov, and Uhura would answer adventure's call together. And that expectation would become reality.

Twenty-five years, almost to the day, after *Star Trek* had premiered, Roddenberry watched what would be his characters' final joint appearance. In the history of many other creative endeavors, it might have been a bittersweet, nostalgic moment—that as the creator faced death, so did his creation.

But the last words in that movie clearly expressed what everyone knew for fact—*Star Trek* was something special. And it still had a future.

As the first crew's *Enterprise* slowly faded into the beckoning light of a distant star, in the protective darkness of the theater, Captain James T. Kirk made his last log entry.

"This is the final cruise of the *Starship Enterprise* under my command. This ship and her history will shortly become the care of another crew. To them and their posterity we will commit our future. They will continue the voyages we have begun, and journey to all the undiscovered countries, boldly going where no man ... where no *one* has gone before."

With that sixth film, only *one* chapter of the *Star Trek* saga had ended. Gene Roddenberry knew that the next chapter was solidly under way, and had even been told about the possibility of new chapters for the future.

Secure in that knowledge, knowing the scope of his achievement in a way few others have been privileged to experience, two days later he was gone.

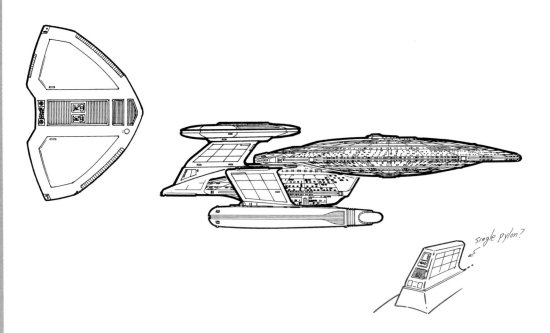

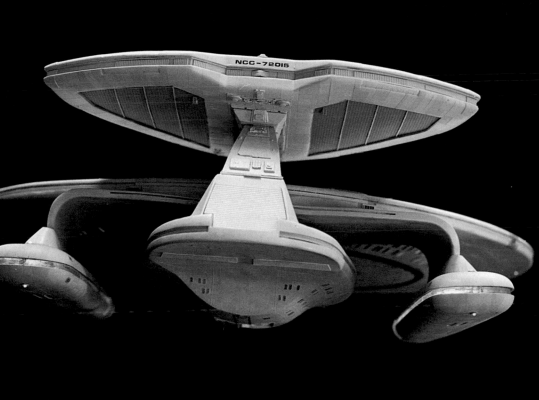

SEASON FIVE: EPISODE 101
REDEMPTION,
PART II
Written by Ronald D. Moore
Directed by David Carson

To expose Romulan attempts to dis-
rupt the Federation-Klingon alliance
(first revealed in "Redemption, Part
I") Picard deploys a Starfleet-
approved blockade of starships along
the Neutral Zone—an active tachyon
web will detect even cloaked
Romulan ships. After being kidnapped and tortured by the
Romulans, Worf realizes his future
lies in Starfleet, and decides to rejoin
the *Enterprise*. Gowron takes his place
as leader of the Klingon Empire and
his rivals the Duras family fail. The
motivation, actions, and existence of
the chief Romulan instigator, Tasha
Yar's half-human, half-Romulan
daughter, Sela, puzzle all who served
on the *Enterprise* with her mother.

Rick Sternbach's design for the *Nebula*-class *Sutherland* from "Redemption, Part II" resulted
in a highly detailed model from Greg Jein. ILLUSTRATION COURTESY OF THE ARTIST.
PHOTOGRAPHY COURTESY OF GREG JEIN.

SEASON FIVE: EPISODE 102
DARMOK
Teleplay by Joe Menosky
Story by Philip Lazebnik and Joe Menosky
Directed by Winrich Kolbe

Picard learns firsthand the importance of communication when he and the leader of the Children of Tama, whose language of allusion and metaphor has been an insurmountable barrier for the Federation, are isolated on a planet by the Tamarians so that the two may establish contact. When they are attacked by a savage electromagnetic predator, the Tamarian leader is fatally injured. But when the Children of Tama threaten to destroy the *Enterprise,* Picard saves his ship by expressing the correct eulogy to their fallen captain in the appropriate Tamarian way, thus proving their leader's sacrifice was meaningful.

Michelle Forbes as Ensign Ro. Because *Next Generation* uniforms were designed without obvious closures, this scene in which Ro takes off her uniform jacket to give it to a Bajoran refugee child required extensive consultation between costume designer Robert Blackman and director Les Landau, to allow modifications to be made to the jacket off-camera.

To be sure, as *The Next Generation*'s success had become apparent, Roddenberry had realized his creation would survive him. And graciously, he had spoken of the day that *Star Trek* would continue under the creative control of others.

At a 1990 *Star Trek* convention at the Los Angeles Airport Hilton Hotel, Roddenberry told an enthusiastic audience that he expected—indeed, he hoped—that in the years to come, new generations of fans would look at the new forms of *Star Trek* being produced and say, " 'This is real *Star Trek.* Those other people back there at the beginning, they didn't do it half as well.' "

One *Next Generation* makeup artist could handle four Bajoran noses—*if* they were to be put on adults. If they were to be put on children, though, the artists were expected to handle only two noses in the same time period.

When Roddenberry spoke those words during *The Next Generation*'s fourth season, *Star Trek,* of course, had already been under the creative control of his chosen successor, Rick Berman, for almost the full four years. Roddenberry's remarks clearly indicated his support and appreciation for what Berman had done to manage *Star Trek*'s future in that time, as the series' executive producer.

Which raises an interesting question, especially for those who read the seemingly endless parade of credits that have become *de rigueur* for television in the nineties.

What exactly *is* a producer?

In Hollywood, perhaps no other term is as often misused and misunderstood,

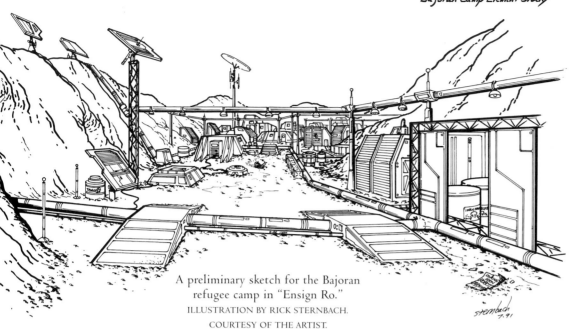

Trek⁵
Bajoran Camp Element Study

A preliminary sketch for the Bajoran
refugee camp in "Ensign Ro."
ILLUSTRATION BY RICK STERNBACH.
COURTESY OF THE ARTIST.

Michelle Forbes in the title
role. ROBBIE ROBINSON.

SEASON FIVE: EPISODE 103
ENSIGN RO
Teleplay by Michael Piller
Story by Rick Berman & Michael Piller
Directed by Les Landau

Starfleet Command sets up an operation designed to preserve the peace
treaty with the Cardassians by bringing in line militant Bajoran rebels
suspected of raids on a Federation
colony. The Bajorans were displaced
from their homeworld by the
Cardassians decades earlier. Ensign
Ro, a Bajoran Starfleet officer court-
martialed for causing eight deaths on
an away-team mission, is assigned by
Admiral Kennelly to lure the leader
of the Bajoran rebels into an ambush
by Cardassians. After initially distrusting Ro, Picard learns Kennelly's
plan and amends it to save the
Bajoran leader's life. Picard then
reveals that the attack on the
Federation colony was actually staged
by the Cardassians. Recognizing
Ro's integrity in a difficult situation,
Picard offers her a post on the
Enterprise, which she accepts.

Patrick Stewart and Michelle Forbes on location for "Ensign Ro." ROBBIE ROBINSON.

especially in all its myriad forms—executive producer, co-executive producer,
co-producer, supervising producer, co-supervising producer, associate produc-
er, visual effects producer, line producer, and even just plain producer.

Part of the confusion lies in the fact that unlike the industry guilds for
writers, actors, and directors, the Producers' Guild has not established a clearly defined hierarchy of job descriptions. Therefore, since job titles do not set
job responsibilities and minimum pay scales as they do for other guilds, a producer credit can sometimes be a loosely defined honorific that is awarded in
lieu of extra money, as a favor, or for other reasons having little to do with the
recipient's actual contribution to a production.

Change is under way, however, at least in the television industry. Under new
guidelines adopted in 1997 by the Academy of Television Arts and Sciences gov-
erning eligibility for Emmy Awards, only those people who are directly respon-

sible for arranging or making possible the production of a television project, or who have creative control over some aspect of a production, will be considered producers, no matter what their titles might read.

Under those stricter definitions, Gene Roddenberry easily earned his executive-producer credit on *The Next Generation,* first as the person who was directly responsible for initiating its production, and then as an adviser who provided ongoing creative direction and inspiration to the production team, even as his health failed and his day-to-day involvement with the series waned. Under the same definitions, Rick Berman earned his credit of executive producer for serving as the ultimate authority for *The Next Generation,* in all aspects of its production, technical and creative.

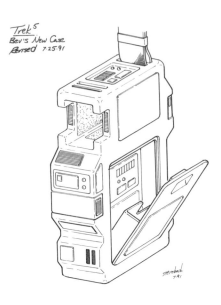

Refinement was ongoing. This sketch shows fifth-season additions to the medkit introduced in Season Four.
ILLUSTRATION BY RICK STERNBACH.
COURTESY OF THE ARTIST.

During the series' run, Rick Berman discussed his role as executive producer and suggested that another reason for the confusion surrounding the meaning of "producer" is that "the role of a producer is quite different in different media.

"In the motion-picture world, a producer is much more of a packager and an overseer," Berman said. "But in television, a producer has responsibilities that are more like those of a movie's director." In other words, a television producer, especially at Berman's executive level, is the one who is ultimately responsible for every aspect of what viewers see and hear on the screen.

Berman put it succinctly when he described his position by saying, "I'm involved in *everything.*" With *The Next Generation,* as with the other series, the amount of Berman's involvement varied from one area to another, but his authority started with the single element that begins every episode. In reference to *The Next Generation,* he said, "I am very involved in the scripts. I get involved conceptually in the stories, and then, when the stories go to the various drafts, I sit down with Michael [Piller] and the writer and I give notes, usually copious. I also get involved with the final dialogue polishing of the script, though I'm not anywhere near as involved with the structural work on the scripts as Michael is.

"Then, I'm in charge of all the production meetings, and all the elements of design, whether it be set design, or costume design, or makeup design, or hair design—all of those things come through me. During the course of filming, I view the dailies, and discuss them with the directors and with supervising producer David Livingston. Then I get very involved in the postproduction, including the opticals [visual effects] as they come in in various stages. I sit for two or three days with each episode, working with the editor and the supervising editor on the final cut.

"*Then,* I get involved with the spotting [placement and design] of the

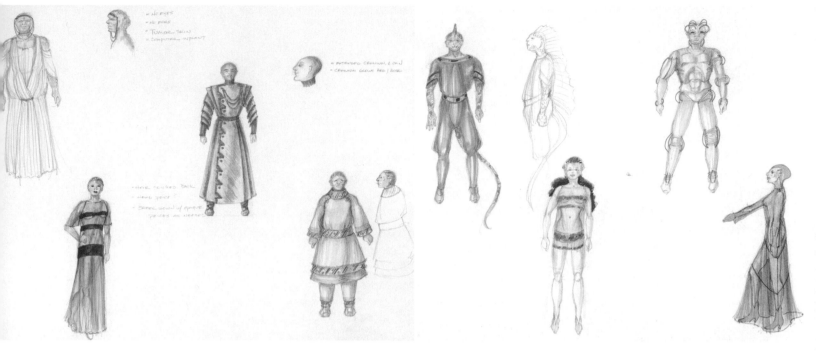

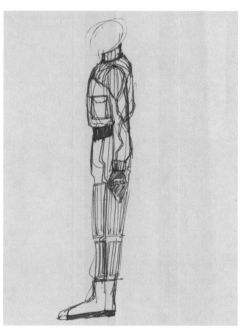

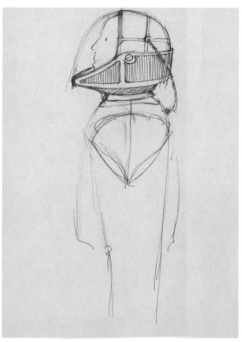

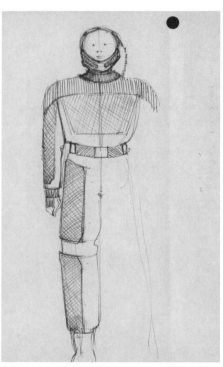

All the designers working on *The Next Generation* were engaged in a constant creative process, and some of the thousands of designs produced invariably fell by the wayside. These rough sketches by Robert Blackman reflect the artist's imagination at work. Interestingly, an "Away Suit" was something that would never be seen on *The Next Generation* during its television run. Some viewers saw this as an unusual omission for a series set in space, but given the difficulties of realistically portraying an outer space environment on a television budget and schedule, it was probably a wise decision. Away Suits made their *Next Generation* debut in the feature, *First Contact*. ILLUSTRATIONS COURTESY OF THE ARTIST.

Deanna Troi and her first
love—chocolate.
ROBBIE ROBINSON.

SEASON FIVE: EPISODE 106
THE GAME
Teleplay by Brannon Braga
Story by Susan Sackett, Fred Bronson,
and Brannon Braga
Directed by Corey Allen

The crew of the *Enterprise* is exposed
to an addictive game that is introduced to them by Riker after a trip
to Risa. Riker receives the game
from Etana Jol, who plans to use the
game to bring the Federation under
control, starship by starship. The
only unaffected crew members are
Data, who is soon put out of commission under mysterious circumstances; Robin Lefler, a young engineering ensign; and Wesley Crusher,
on leave from Starfleet Academy.
When the crew captures and converts
Robin, she betrays Wesley. Just as
Wesley is about to be infected, Data
appears, and restores the crew to normal with a neuro-optic burst device.

HEATHER
BLOND

SHAUNA
BRUNETT

For the barroom scene in "Unification," costume designer Robert Blackman was able to
temporarily leave behind the elegant simplicity of Starfleet uniforms to have some fun with
costumes reminiscent of *The Original Series.* ILLUSTRATIONS COURTESY OF THE ARTIST.

sound effects and the music, and finally I review each one of the dubs [versions
of each episode at various stages of completion]. As well, I'm the final voice
when problems occur with the actors or with
the crew or with anything that has to do with
the studio. I tend to be the person who has to
work those things out."

Berman's responsibilities also extended
into areas that had little immediate connection
with what appeared on the screen every week.
As executive producer of *The Next Generation,* he
was also responsible for its future, and as the
fifth season began, the same financial factors
that had played such an important part in the
series' creation now pointed to an inevitable
conclusion, one that remains controversial to
the series' most devoted fans even today—

The series could not continue forever.

Five years earlier, independent stations
had experienced great success by airing only
the seventy-nine existing episodes of *The*

SAREK
AMARIE

A Vulcan ship built by Greg Jein for "Unification." Note the IDIC symbol from *The Original Series* on the side of the ship. COURTESY OF GREG JEIN.

SEASON FIVE: EPISODE 107

UNIFICATION, PART I

Teleplay by Jeri Taylor
Story by Rick Berman and Michael Piller
Directed by Les Landau

Following up on Starfleet's fears that Ambassador Spock has defected to the Romulan Empire, Picard learns from Sarek, the Vulcan's dying father, that Spock may actually be trying to heal the ancient Vulcan-Romulan rift. Picard and Data, disguised as Romulans, take a cloaked Klingon ship to Romulus to meet Pardek, known to be a peace advocate and Spock's contact. The pair are captured by underground supporters of Pardek, who take them to meet Spock. In the meantime, Riker and the *Enterprise* crew trace some stolen Vulcan equipment to a ship junkyard, from which several Vulcan ships have also disappeared. Discovering an unknown ship in one of the Vulcan berths, the *Enterprise* fires a warning shot at the ship, which immediately self-destructs.

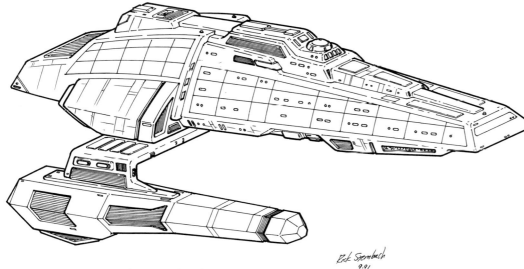

Vulcan starship designs by Rick Sternbach.
COURTESY OF THE ARTIST.

TREK⁵: "UNIFICATION II"
VULCAN STARSHIP

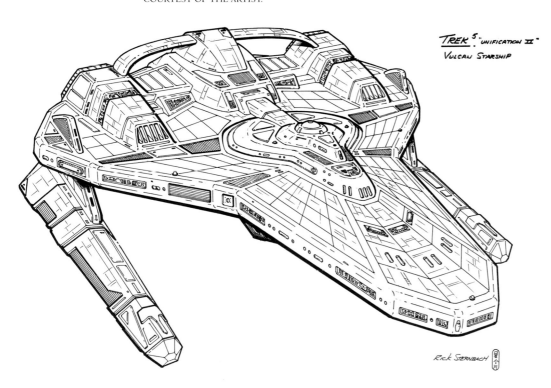

Denise Crosby as Sela, the half-human, half-Romulan daughter of the alternate-time-line Tasha Yar introduced in "Yesterday's *Enterprise*." ROBBIE ROBINSON.

SEASON FIVE: EPISODE 108
UNIFICATION,
PART II
Teleplay by Michael Piller
Story by Rick Berman and Michael Piller
Directed by Cliff Bole

Picard learns that Sarek was right: Spock was trying, unofficially, to unite the Romulans and Vulcans. Riker and Picard discover that the Vulcan ships stolen from the junkyard investigated by the *Enterprise* are to be used as decoys in a Romulan attack on Vulcan. The plan has been set in motion by Sela, Tasha Yar's half-Romulan daughter and the new Romulan Proconsul. Sela seizes Spock, Picard, and Data, but cannot force Spock to endorse the fake mission. Spock and Data find a way to secretly signal Riker, who intercepts the Vulcan ships, which are destroyed by their cloaked Romulan escorts, eliminating evidence of the mission. Spock decides to continue his work on Romulus. Picard invites the Vulcan to mind-meld with him to experience some thoughts and memories of Sarek.

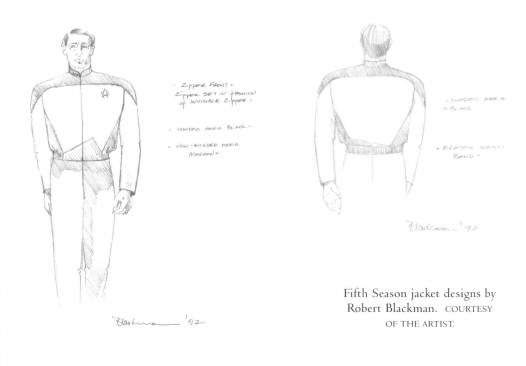

Fifth Season jacket designs by Robert Blackman. COURTESY OF THE ARTIST.

Original Series. Even network stations profited from showing *Star Trek* episodes outside of network programming hours. But after twenty years, the audience for those episodes was diminishing. That was why stations constantly had asked Paramount for more episodes, new episodes.

So Paramount delivered. By the end of the 1991-1992 television season, those seventy-nine original episodes would be joined by 126 additional hours of *The Next Generation.*

And it was here that a problem appeared on the horizon. Syndicators could get by with sixty-five episodes. Paramount had almost doubled that number, making everyone happy. But with no sign of *The Next Generation*'s popularity waning, each year to come could result in an additional twenty-six episodes being added to the pot.

The availability of new episodes increased the cost of the series to stations who wanted to strip *The Next Generation* for viewing five days a week. And as the fifth season began, for the first time Paramount was beginning to hear grumblings from some stations that they had enough episodes and weren't particularly interested in continuing to pay for additional ones that were not required to maintain the ratings they wanted.

The turnaround in thinking that Paramount executives faced was astonishing.

Five years earlier, they had sweated over creating a business plan that would cover a potential loss of almost $16 million—about half the first season's production budget[2]— if *The Next Generation* failed after thirteen episodes.

Now, with the series bringing the studio gross revenues approximately $30 million more than the cost of producing the series *each year,* the executives confronted the possibility that they were in danger of saturating the market. Not in the sense of fan enthusiasm—which then and now shows no sign of

= ALSO ZIPPER FRONT
= SHADED AREA BLACK
= NON-SHADED AREA
MAROON

Blackman '92

JACKET BASED ON CAPT. PICARDS

waning—but in strictly dollars-and-cents terms. Brandon Tartikoff, chairman of Paramount Pictures at the time the future of *The Next Generation* was being decided, said the ultimate conclusion was apparent. "After about seven years, the show, even as successful as it was, was probably going to have to be taken off the market, just because stations already had too many episodes."

Kerry McCluggage, current chairman of Paramount TV Group, confirms that conclusion. "We didn't want stations to choke on all those episodes. The original episodes have been outstanding, but once they start repeating five days a week, we're usually looking at declining ratings over time."

What's more, it was no secret that Paramount—a publicly traded corporation—was earning substantially more than the cost of the series each year. "When you looked at the books," said Brandon Tartikoff, at the time chairman of Paramount Pictures, "you saw that *Star Trek: The Next Generation* was a twenty-five-million-dollar goody, every year. That's the profit it would generate for Paramount." And with the cast members' original contracts coming to an end, it was only reasonable that new salary negotiations for the inevitable sixth season would take the series' spectacular earnings into account. The cast of *The Next Generation* had helped create one of the most financially successful syndicated series in television history, and it was only fair that they share that success with appropriate increases in their per-episode fees.

The bottom line for Paramount was that though *The Next Generation* had been a profitable series over the first four seasons, and would continue to be through the fifth season, once renegotiated cast and crew pay increases were factored into the equation, along with the hint of syndicator resistance to additional episodes, the series was projected to become both more expensive to produce, *and* harder to sell.

Only in Hollywood could success be so counterproductive.

Matt Frewer, whose own science-fiction series, *Max Headroom,* debuted the same year as *The Next Generation,* portrayed time-traveler Berlingoff Rasmussen in "A Matter of Time," a character originally written for *Star Trek* fan Robin Williams. ROBBIE ROBINSON.

HERO WORSHIP

Teleplay by Joe Menosky
Story by Hilary J. Bader
Directed by Patrick Stewart

The lone survivor of a wrecked Federation research ship is a young boy named Timothy who identifies with his new friend Data, even to the point of pretending to be an android. When Picard pushes for details about the cause of the disaster, the child holds to a tale of alien invaders, so Troi encourages Data to win the boy's trust and get him to tell the truth. As the *Enterprise* enters the same region of gravitational shock waves Timothy's ship encountered, the boy reveals that he caused the disaster by accident. However, as the *Enterprise* combats the effect of the gravity waves with their shields, the boy recollects that his ship did the same, just before being destroyed. Data realizes shield power magnifies the waves, and orders the lowering of shields just in time, saving the ship and clearing Timothy's conscience.

VIOLATIONS

Teleplay by Pamela Gray and Jeri Taylor
Story by Shari Goodhartz and T. Michael Gray and Pamela Gray
Directed by Robert Wiemer

The *Enterprise* takes on board three telepathic Ullians, members of a race of historians who research memories not easily accessed by conventional means. The lead historian seeks permission to probe the crew's memories, but there is little support for the request. Then, suddenly, Riker and Crusher relive traumatic death-related events, while Troi experiences a flashback of a past romantic interlude in which Jev, the lead historian's son, takes on Riker's role. Her struggles against him place her in a coma. Picard suspects the telepaths, and to test them, when Troi is revived she undergoes a mind probe by Jev. This time it is not Jev but his father who takes Riker's place. Picard has the older historian arrested, but when Jev later visits Troi, she realizes that he is the true aggressor. Worf and Data save her, explaining that their research turned up his involvement in earlier memory-rape coma cases.

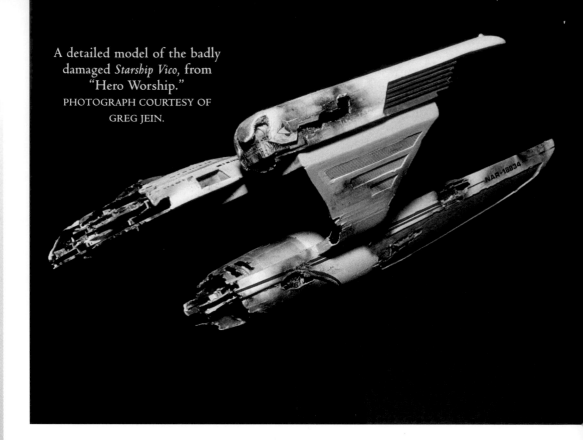

A detailed model of the badly damaged *Starship Vico*, from "Hero Worship."
PHOTOGRAPH COURTESY OF GREG JEIN.

If there was any light at the end of the tunnel, it was the continuing success of the *Star Trek* movies featuring the *Original Series* cast—a series that had now, ostensibly, come to an end.

In light of those three elements—increased costs, television sales resistance, and a movie franchise in need of a new twist—the solution was obvious.

Even as the fourth season ended, strategies were already being explored to have *The Next Generation* follow in the footsteps of *The Original Series* by leaving television and making the transition to the movie screen.

Of course, that would leave a hole in the television side of the *Star Trek* franchise, and, using Taritikoff's figures, with potential gross revenues of $25 million a year over production costs, it was not a hole Paramount was willing to leave unplugged.

Thus, in the summer of 1991, Brandon Tartikoff and other Paramount executives had their first conversations with Rick Berman about developing a third *Star Trek* series to take over from *The Next Generation*. Berman had a chance to sound out Roddenberry on how he felt about the idea of a third *Star Trek* series and Roddenberry, Berman reports, thought it would be great and that they should talk about it soon.

Roddenberry's failing health prevented those additional conversations from taking place. But, Brandon Tartikoff recalls, after Roddenberry's death, his widow, Majel Barrett-Roddenberry, "was very open to the idea of having this deal happen and happen quickly."

The result was that after four years of heroic effort which had resulted in *The Next Generation* assembling solid and seasoned teams in all areas of its production, what should have been its smoothest year yet took on the added complication of having its top people begin the preparations for its inevitable end.

What's surprising is that the situation in no way led to a lowering of standards, nor neglect of the franchise. For even as Rick Berman and Michael Piller met in Berman's office over box lunches from the Paramount commissary and began sketching out the series that would become *Star Trek: Deep Space Nine, Star Trek: The Next Generation* enjoyed its best season to date, not only in terms of ratings and demographics, but in creative terms as well.

Gene Roddenberry's hope for the future had indeed been realized. His successor was guiding *Star Trek* to new levels of excellence, imagination, and appeal, with no sign of any limits to the heights it might reach.

Just as for Season Four, there were no cast changes for the fifth season, and only a relatively few comings and goings in the production staff. Herbert Wright, whose writing credits in the first season included "The Last Outpost," "The Battle," and "Heart of Glory," returned for six episodes in the middle of the season. His replacement for the end of the season, Peter Allan Fields, would continue to be an important *Star Trek* writer, especially for his contributions to *Deep Space Nine* as co-producer.

But the most influential addition to the *Star Trek* family that season was Brannon Braga. Braga had earned his first television writing credit as a summer intern in Season Four, working with Ron Moore on "Reunion," the episode that introduced Worf's son, Alexander. As someone once said, it was the beginning of a beautiful relationship. As a writing team, Moore and Braga went on to write "All Good Things...," the series' acclaimed, two-hour final episode in Season Seven, as well as the first two *Next Generation* movies, *Generations* and *First Contact,* for which they shared story credit with Rick Berman.

Ongoing *Star Trek* writers like Moore and Braga are rare. As Jeri Taylor explains, "*Star Trek* is a unique kind of animal in terms of the people who can write it. I know and have hired some very, very good writers, some very senior, experienced writers who have been showrunners on other series, who cannot write *Star Trek,* who absolutely crash and burn with the show.

"So, when we find someone who, for whatever synapse in the brain works, can write this show, then we gobble them up, put them on staff, nurture them, teach them, love them, and bring them up through the ranks because they are a prized commodity."

Each writer who has thus remained with *Star Trek* as a regular contributor brings a particular slant to his or her work: Michael Piller and his emphasis on characters' personal issues; Jeri Taylor and character development; the wry humor of Ira Steven Behr; the tight plotting of Peter Allan Fields; the political intrigue and understanding of *Star Trek* history of

STARBASE 32

15850 GENE RODDENBERRY	35951 DAVE ROSSI	55154 JOE CHESS
15037 RICK BERMAN	35951 CHERYL GLUCKSTERN	55154 MARICELLA RAMIREZ
15037 TERRI MARTINEZ	35787 ERNIE OVER	85114 MICHAEL STRADLING
15810 MICHAEL PILLER	35951 BRAD YACOBIAN	85146 BILL PEETS
15810 KIM FITZGERALD	35951 DOUG DEAN	85146 PHIL JACOBSON
14744 JERI TAYLOR	35951 ADELE SIMMONS	85146 RALPH JOHNSON
14744 LOLITA FATJO	35951 ARLENE FUKAI	85146 SCOTT MCKNIGHT
24870 DAVID LIVINGSTON	35951 COSMO GENOVESE	85146 MURPHY WILTZ
24870 HEIDI JULIAN	35258 RICHARD JAMES	85146 JIM THORPE
24463 RON MOORE	45268 ANDY NESKOROMNY	85114 BOB SORDAL
24523 JOE MENOSKY	45248 RICK STERNBACH	85114 WAVERLY SMOTHERS
24597 HERB WRIGHT	45244 CARI THOMAS	85114 TOM CONLEY
25882 PETER LAURITSON	45254 GARY SPECKMAN	85114 EDMOND WRIGHT
35682 WENDY NEUSS	45245 LOUISE NIELSEN	85114 TOM MOORE
35709 BRANNON BRAGA	45252 JIM MAGDALENO	85993 RICK ROWE
34429 ERIC STILLWELL	45241 AL SMUTKO	75274 JIM MEES
35871 RICHARD ARNOLD	44398 TOM PURSER	75274 FERNANDO SEPULVEDA
35682 ROB LEGATO	45197 ED CHARNOCK JR.	75274 DICK D'ANGELO
35682 DAN CURRY	45197 GEORGE STUART JR.	75274 JOHN NESTEROWICZ
35982 WENDY ROSENFELD	43984 DICK BROWNFIELD	75260 JOE LONGO
35559 SUZI SHIMIZU	53984 RICHARD CHRONISTER	75260 ALAN SIMS
35680 DOLORES ARCE	53984 BILL THOMS	75260 CHARLIE RUSSO
35951 MERRI HOWARD	53984 RICHARD BALDER	83412 BOB BLACKMAN
35951 DIANE OVERDIEK	55154 MARVIN RUSH	83412 CAROL KUNZ

STARFLEET OPERATIONAL SUPPORT SERVICES • MAXIA SECTOR

The sheer number of people required to produce an episode of *The Next Generation* meant that the art department was never at a loss for names to fill in duty rosters. Starbase 32 appeared in "Violations."

SEASON FIVE: EPISODE 113
THE MASTERPIECE SOCIETY
Teleplay by Adam Belanoff and Michael Piller
Story by James Kahn and Adam Belanoff
Directed by Winrich Kolbe

When a stellar core fragment threatens the colony of Moab IV, the *Enterprise* crew is surprised by the colonists' refusal to evacuate. The colony has been genetically planned and engineered to be "perfect," and they have no desire to leave. La Forge works with Hannah Bates, the chief scientist of the colony, to develop a tractor beam to deflect the fragment. Troi becomes intimate with the colony leader, Aaron Conor, and learns more about their "perfect" society. Troi and La Forge both realize that, as part-Betazoid and sight-deprived beings, respectively, they would never have been permitted to remain within the community. The tractor beam saves the colony but exposure to the outside influences has made Bates and 23 other colonists decide to leave with the *Enterprise.*

SEASON FIVE: EPISODE 114
CONUNDRUM
Teleplay by Barry M. Schkolnick
Story by Paul Schiffer
Directed by Les Landau

A scan of the *Enterprise* by a mysterious alien ship wipes the memories of the crew, leaving their instincts to direct them to new roles: Worf feels comfortable at command; Picard, at navigation; Data, bartending in Ten-Forward. Eventually, the computer retrieves a crew manifest that lists a Commander Kieran MacDuff as first officer, and also details a secret mission: to destroy the Lysians, an enemy of long standing. Picard, however, distrusts the unequal match-up of technology against their weaker foe and he aborts the attack. When MacDuff tries to seize command, Worf stuns him, and reveals MacDuff to be an alien. After Crusher restores the crew's memories, they learn that MacDuff is a member of the Sartaaran race, which captured the *Enterprise* for a technological edge over the Lysians.

Ensign Ro in one of the *Enterprise*'s Jefferies Tubes. ROBBIE ROBINSON.

SEASON FIVE: EPISODE 115
POWER PLAY
Teleplay by Rene Balcer and Herbert J. Wright & Brannon Braga
Story by Paul Ruben and Maurice Hurley
Directed by David Livingston

Responding to a distress call via shuttlecraft, Riker, Troi, and Data crash-land on what appears to be an uninhabited moon, injuring Riker. As the *Enterprise* rescues the away team, all but Riker are taken over by alien entities, who, once on board, hold hostages in Ten-Forward. Picard discovers that the entities are prisoners from an alien penal colony, trying to escape the moon via the *Enterprise*. However, Picard refuses to give in to their demands and threatens to blow them all out the cargo-bay doors, killing himself along with them. Fearing death more than imprisonment, the entities return to the penal colony, freeing their human hosts.

SEASON FIVE: EPISODE 116
ETHICS
Teleplay by Ronald D. Moore
Story by Sara Charno & Stuart Charno
Directed by Chip Chalmers

When an accident leaves Worf paralyzed, he considers ritual suicide to be the only honorable course, since conventional medical treatment will not reverse his condition. Worf asks a reluctant Riker to assist him, but Riker knows that a Klingon's son is the customary choice in such situations. Since Worf does not wish this role for his seven-year-old son, Alexander, he agrees to the dangerous, experimental surgery offered him by Dr. Toby Russell, a specialist whose work Crusher considers unacceptably risky and unethical. Worf dies during surgery, but his Klingon anatomy has a number of redundant backup systems and one of them brings him back to life.

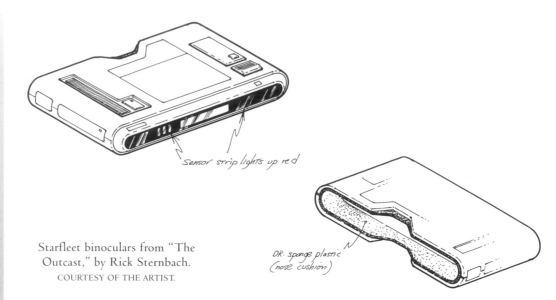

Sensor strip lights up red

Dk. sponge plastic (nose cushion)

Starfleet binoculars from "The Outcast," by Rick Sternbach. COURTESY OF THE ARTIST.

Ron Moore. Certainly, all these writers shine in many areas of storytelling expertise and overlap in the qualities they bring to their scripts, but attentive viewers of *The Next Generation* and the current *Star Trek* series have little trouble picking out the style of story most usually associated with a familiar writer.

Brannon Braga is no exception to this observation. To the simultaneous delight and consternation of different groups of viewers, Braga's stories are most often characterized by a fascination with the disruption of the flesh and mind, echoing themes similar to those in the early work of film director David Cronenberg. Braga has fun maintaining his image as "*Star Trek*'s bad boy," as he was depicted in an interview published in *Details* magazine at the time of *First Contact*'s release. And the fun is shared by those who work with him. One producer, in discussing an approach to creating believable villains for a *Star Trek* episode, says, "The key to writing villains is to make them feel that they are the heroes of the piece. I don't care what show you're on, there are very few people who look at themselves as villains, who say, 'I am evil.'" Then the producer adds with a laugh, "Now, Brannon Braga is not included in this group."

Perceptions of notoriety aside, Braga's ongoing success as a writer and producer for a franchise known for its family appeal clearly comes from working within the nurturing environment of the *Star Trek* family, and it is that element more than any other that is most strongly reflected and appreciated in his work.

Of the many notable episodes that were part of the fifth season, one in particular took on a life of its own, in an unusual arena.

"The First Duty," written by Ron Moore and the series' science adviser, Naren Shankar, marked the first time in *Star Trek*'s history that viewers saw the famous Starfleet Academy, an institution first mentioned in *The Original Series*. In the episode, Wesley, a cadet, faces the dilemma of either withholding the truth about a tragic accident in order to protect his fellow cadets, or revealing the truth, which could result not only in the end of his Starfleet career, but those of his friends as well.

It was exactly the kind of issue Michael Piller sought to showcase on the series, and he recalls with enthusiasm the storybreaking session he went through with Ron Moore.

"We got into one of the most rewarding arguments in the history of the production of this show," Piller says. "Ron argued, 'Wesley can't turn his friends in. It is absolutely the worst possible thing. People are going to be watching this and they are never going to forgive Wesley for turning his friends in after he agreed to a code of silence. Your honor to your friends is the most important thing you could ever have in your life.'

"And I said, 'Ron, it's not true. The truth, your dedication to the truth, and honesty is the most important thing in your life.' We went on for an hour and a half, and afterward I said, 'Ron, everything that's just been said in this hour and a half should be in this script so that your argument is as understandable to the audience from the antagonist's point of view as it can be. You should not shortchange the antagonist in that piece one bit. But *I'm* speaking for Picard, now, and since I'm the executive producer, I'm going to say this is how the show's going to end—Picard's going to give the speech that I gave.' That's how it was done," Piller concludes, "and as it turned out, it was really one of the great episodes."

Indeed, surpassing Piller's goal that the issues presented in *The Next Generation* stories could be discussed at the breakfast table, "The First Duty" has aired at the Air Force Academy as part of real cadets' introduction to the honor code.

Another pivotal script was "I, Borg," by René Echevarria, in which *The Next Generation*'s favorite villains made their first appearance since "The Best of Both Worlds." But this time, viewers' perception of the Borg underwent the same subtle change that Worf's presence on the *Enterprise* had brought to the Klingons. The episode took a closer look at the Borg in the guise of one individual who was cut off from the Collective. With no immediate threat of attack, the crew of the *Enterprise* was finally able to observe and communicate with a Borg, and in a surprising twist that fit in perfectly with the ethos of Gene Roddenberry's *Star Trek,* the Borg were revealed to be no different from any other beings. And where there are no differences, how can there be enemies?

"I, Borg" was Michael Piller's favorite episode of the season. To Jeri Taylor, the legacy of the episode was that the Borg could never again appear as they had in

Jonathan Del Arco as Hugh, the first Borg individual to be encountered by the Federation—but not the last.

Riker awakens a forbidden taboo of the J'naii, sexual love, in Soran, played by Melinda Culea.
ROBBIE ROBINSON.

SEASON FIVE: EPISODE 117
THE OUTCAST
Written by Jeri Taylor
Directed by Robert Scheerer

Soren, a shuttle pilot of an androgynous species, becomes good friends with Riker when the two work together to save survivors on board a missing shuttlecraft. Soren explains that her people, the J'naii, penalize those who have a sexual preference, by treating them with a brainwashing cure. Nevertheless, Soren admits that she has always had female tendencies, and is attracted to Riker, who feels the same. When Soren's people capture and try her, Riker attempts to defend Soren, to no avail. Riker's and Worf's attempt to rescue her is too late; Soren's "cure" causes her to deny what developed between herself and Riker.

CAUSE AND EFFECT
Written by Brannon Braga
Directed by Jonathan Frakes

The *Enterprise* is caught in a time loop in the Typhon Expanse, causing the crew to experience the same sequence of events over and over again, beginning with a poker game and ending with a destructive collision with another spaceship caught in the same loop. Catching on to what is happening, Data plants a clue for himself that he hopes will eventually allow them to break free of the loop. The clue—which suggests to him that Picard must follow Riker's plan, not Data's—succeeds, and the ship alters its course at the last minute to avoid collision. Later they realize that the *Enterprise* has been trapped for 17 days, but the other ship, the *Bozeman*, has endured 90 years in the time loop.

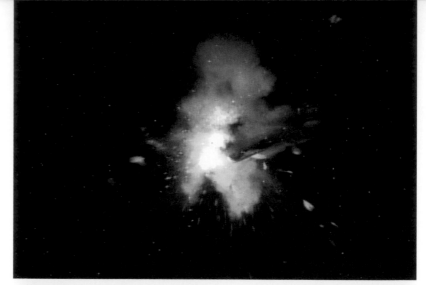

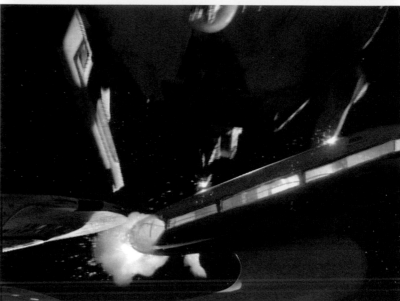

For "Cause and Effect," Brannon Braga wrote what is arguably the best teaser in the history of *Star Trek*—a starship collision that results in the complete destruction of the *Enterprise*. Who wouldn't stay tuned?

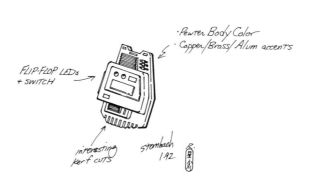

Two crucial props from "Cause and Effect." ILLUSTRATIONS BY RICK STERNBACH. COURTESY OF THE ARTIST.

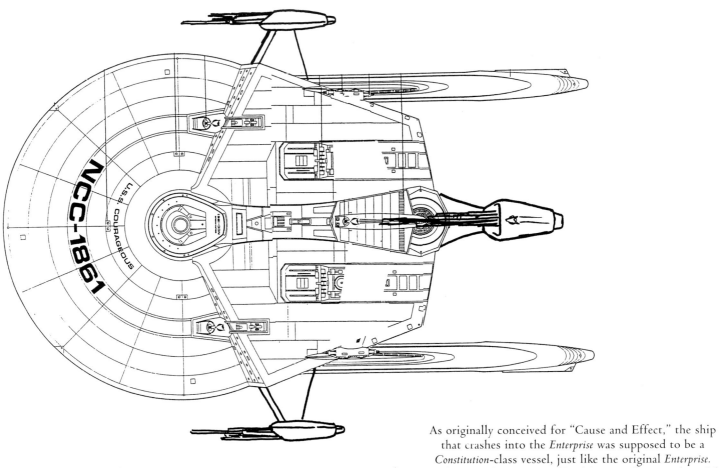

As originally conceived for "Cause and Effect," the ship that crashes into the *Enterprise* was supposed to be a *Constitution*-class vessel, just like the original *Enterprise*. Unfortunately, the cost of building an all-original model for the episode was prohibitive, so the art department was once again asked to modify an already existing model—the ever-reliable *Reliant*. ILLUSTRATIONS BY MICHAEL OKUDA. COURTESY OF THE ARTIST.

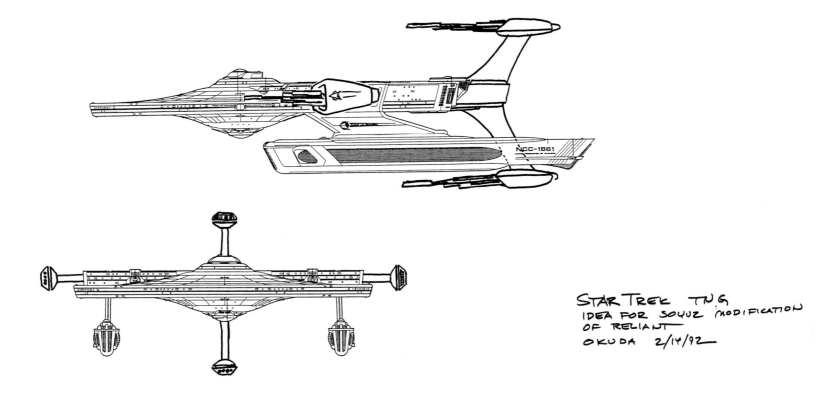

STAR TREK TNG
IDEA FOR SOYUZ MODIFICATION
OF RELIANT
OKUDA 2/14/92

THE FIRST DUTY

Written by Ronald D. Moore &
Naren Shankar
Directed by Paul Lynch

Wesley is involved in the cover-up of
an accident that has taken the life of
a member of his flight squadron.
Although the blame rests primarily
on Nick Locarno, the squadron
leader, who had encouraged the team
to attempt a banned flight maneuver,
Locarno shifts the blame to the student who died. Though Wesley
protests the lie to the rest of his
team in private, he supports
Locarno's version before the investigating panel, despite the fact that it
contradicts satellite evidence.
Visiting the Academy to give the
commencement address, Picard tells
Wesley he has guessed the truth, and
demands it be revealed. Agreeing
with Picard about what his duty
must be, Wesley makes the difficult
choice to expose his friend, who is
expelled, and prepares to face the
consequences of his action, along
with the rest of the team.

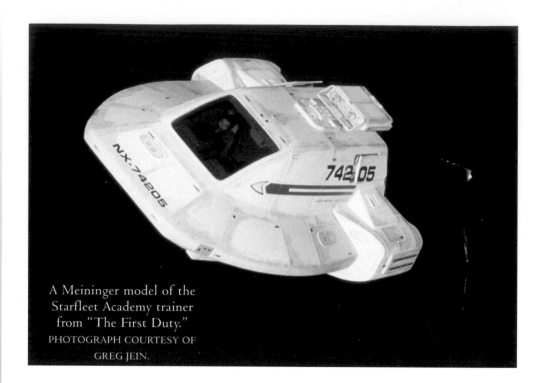

A Meininger model of the
Starfleet Academy trainer
from "The First Duty."
PHOTOGRAPH COURTESY OF
GREG JEIN.

"Q Who?" or "The Best of Both Worlds"—as relentless, inhuman monsters
who deserved to be eradicated.

Indeed, the script's new look at the Borg as individuals played into the
two-part cliffhanger episode that ended the sixth season and began the seventh,
as well as the film *First Contact,* a third-season episode of *Voyager,* and, ultimately, a profound addition to the cast in *Voyager's* fourth season.

Twenty-five years earlier, when *The Original Series* had first aired, the rule in
weekly television drama was that characters and basic situations never changed
from week to week. But for the sophisticated audiences of the nineties, as "I,
Borg" illustrates, that creative roadblock had long been abandoned by the producers and writers of *The Next Generation.*

As the fifth season progressed and *Deep
Space Nine* grew from an idea to a bible, it was
clear that what viewers responded to was the
context of *Star Trek,* not a rigidly defined set of
characters and situations. That suggested
that the *Star Trek* universe could also be
opened up to become as dynamic as any real-
life situation. In the next two seasons, the
creative team behind *Star Trek* would use that
freedom to great extent, and not just in *The
Next Generation.*

For example, the third episode of the
fifth season, "Ensign Ro," was written by
Michael Piller, from a story by Berman and
Piller, specifically to introduce a new, recurring member of the *Enterprise* crew who would
have an edge to her personality and to her
interactions with the other regulars. The
backstory created for the Ro character, bring-

Acclaimed actor Ray Walston
appeared as Picard's mentor,
Boothby, the Starfleet Academy
gardener, in "The First Duty."
ROBBIE ROBINSON.

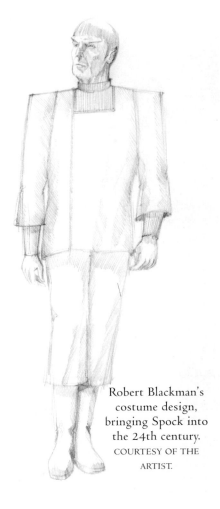

Robert Blackman's costume design, bringing Spock into the 24th century.
COURTESY OF THE ARTIST.

ing back the ominous Cardassians as conquerors who had occupied her homeworld of Bajor, quickly became incorporated into the setting of *Deep Space Nine,* which would be a series in which almost everyone had an "edge."

The most important installment of the fifth season, perhaps of the entire series, was, of course, the two-part episode "Unification."

In Season Three, long hours of debate had centered on a single word in "Sarek"—the mention of Sarek's son, Spock.

Now, two years later, there was no debate, only eager anticipation at the prospect that Spock would actually appear on *The Next Generation.*

Fittingly, the logic was perfect— Vulcans did have long lives, and Spock's age had been established to be young enough in *The Original Series* that he would be in Vulcan middle age at the time of *The*

Riker, Crusher, and Picard attend the wedding of Lwaxana Troi.
ROBBIE ROBINSON.

After destroying an asteroid on which some metallic parasites were feeding, the *Enterprise* finds itself infested with the creatures, which instigates life-threatening breakdowns on the ship until Data finds a way to send them home. In the meantime, Lwaxana Troi comes on board to marry a man she has never met, who turns out to be stuffy and old, and Deanna tries to help Worf rein in his rebellious young son, Alexander. Ironically, spending some time with Alexander ends up being therapeutic for both Lwaxana and the young Klingon, and Lwaxana ultimately decides she must be herself with her new fiancee, which promptly sends him packing after she shows up nude—in traditional Betazoid style—for their wedding.

On board the *Enterprise,* two Ferengi try to steal a "priceless" peace offering that will mark the end of the Kriosian-Valtese war The offering is Kamala, a beautiful, empathic mesomorph raised since birth to become what any man desires and to bond with the leader of the Valt. Revelation of Kamala's situation causes controversy among the crew of the *Enterprise.* Crusher argues that such surrender of the individual's rights is, in fact, prostitution. Picard, though deeply affected by Kamala, and she, in turn by him, reasons that all peoples have a right to their own beliefs and practices. Kamala bows to her duty, but tells Picard that she will always consider herself bonded to him.

Famke Janssen as Kamala in "The Perfect Mate." Costume designer Robert Blackman recalls that the script described her wedding gown only as "the most beautiful dress in the galaxy," a description that was challenging because it gave absolutely no indication of what the gown should actually look like.

IMAGINARY FRIEND
*Teleplay by Edithe Swenson and
Brannon Braga
Story by Ronald Wilderson & Jean
Matthias and Richard Fliegel
Directed by Gabrielle Beaumont*

Clara, a ship's officer's young daughter, is delighted when "Isabella," her imaginary friend, takes physical form as a child. But Isabella soon moves from pranks to lethal interference with the *Enterprise*. Isabella leads Clara into off-limit areas of the ship, interferes with Clara's friendship with Worf's son, Alexander, and then threatens the lives of all on board. Picard discovers that there is a link between Isabella and the mysterious energy drain the ship is experiencing in the FGC-47 nebula. The inhabitants of the nebula, of which Isabella is one, consider the *Enterprise* a source of energy from which they can feed. Although Picard offers alternate energy sources, Isabella is finally swayed by Clara's pleas for her friends and leaves the ship.

Guinan confronts the captive Borg, Hugh, played by Jonathan Del Arco. ROBBIE ROBINSON.

I, BORG
*Written by René Echevarria
Directed by Robert Lederman*

Dr. Crusher argues to save the life of an injured Borg the *Enterprise* retrieves from a crash site. Despite objections from the rest of the crew, particularly Picard and Guinan, Crusher's humanitarian spirit wins, and the Borg, which calls itself "Three of Five," begins to exhibit signs of individualism. Taking on the new name "Hugh," the Borg becomes friends with La Forge and eventually convinces Picard of his sincerity. Although he had originally intended to implant a computer virus in Hugh to infect his collective, Picard decides to gamble that Hugh's new individuality will be a potent force for change, and he directs La Forge to return Hugh to the crash site, where he will be retrieved by his kind.

Eve Brenner as Inad, with Jonathan Frakes in "Violations." ROBBIE ROBINSON

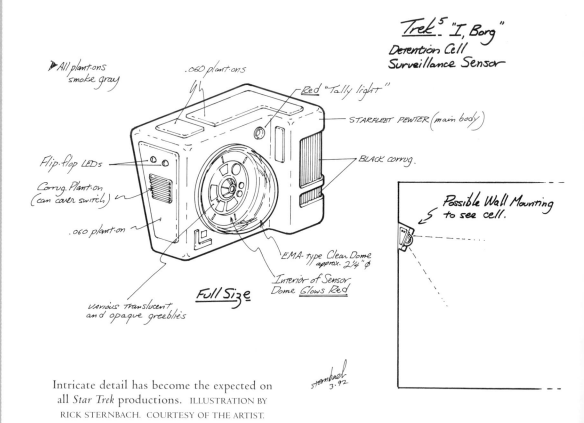

Intricate detail has become the expected on all *Star Trek* productions. ILLUSTRATION BY RICK STERNBACH. COURTESY OF THE ARTIST.

The Kataanian probe from "The Inner Light," on its mount at Image G.
COURTESY OF GREG JEIN.

SEASON FIVE: EPISODE 124
THE NEXT PHASE
Written by Ronald D. Moore
Directed by David Carson

La Forge and Ro appear to die in a transporter accident while the *Enterprise* is in the midst of aiding a Romulan science vessel. They have been caught up in the effects of a Romulan science experiment that actually cloaked them. Invisible to their grieving crewmates, they must find a way to reveal their plight to Data before the Romulans can complete a plan that will intentionally destroy the *Enterprise*. Complicating matters is a cloaked Romulan who is also aboard the *Enterprise*. Ro and La Forge succeed in getting Data to create the circumstances that will allow them to uncloak and reappear.

Picard experiencing the life of Kamin, an inhabitant of the dying world, Kataan.
ROBBIE ROBINSON.

SEASON FIVE: EPISODE 125
THE INNER LIGHT
Teleplay by Morgan Gendel and Peter Allan Fields
Story by Morgan Gendel
Directed by Peter Lauritson

The effects of an energy beam launched by a probe cause Picard to experience a life of thirty years in the span of twenty-five minutes. While his crew attempts to revive him, Picard lives the life of an iron weaver named Kamin on the long-dead planet of Kataan, whose sun eventually goes nova. When Kamin's life ends, Picard awakes with the memory of a wife, friends, two children, and a futile, lifelong struggle to combat an inescapable drought. He realizes that his experience was the means by which the doomed people of Kataan were able to share their existence and their history with others.

TIME'S ARROW, PART I

Teleplay by Joe Menosky and Michael Piller
Story by Joe Menosky
Directed by Les Landau

An excavation in the caverns beneath San Francisco turns up Data's head, apparently buried there for centuries along with a number of alien relics. Triolic wave traces on the relics lead the *Enterprise* to Devidia II, where they pick up signs of invisible life-forms and a possible time rift. Data reasons that the life-forms may not be invisible but time-shifted and he uses a mobile forcefield to align himself with them. Before he can complete a report, he is propelled backward in time to nineteenth-century San Francisco. Making use of his poker skills to gain funds, Data begins work on a device to contact the *Enterprise*. He encounters Guinan, who does not yet know him, and tells her of their acquaintance in the future; their conversation is overheard by Samuel Clemens. Data's crewmates set up a second mobile forcefield, and an away team led by Picard enters the vortex.

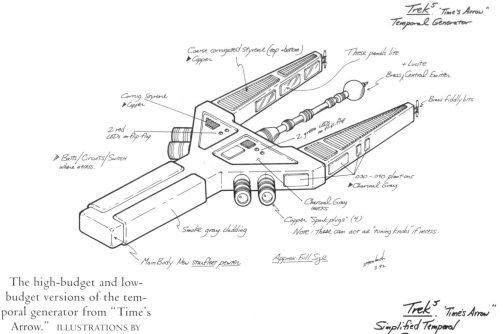

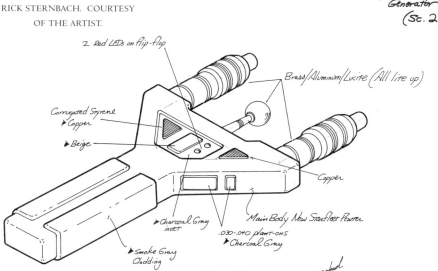

The high-budget and low-budget versions of the temporal generator from "Time's Arrow." ILLUSTRATIONS BY RICK STERNBACH. COURTESY OF THE ARTIST.

Next Generation. The timing was perfect as well, with both the twenty-fifth anniversary and the release of the sixth film occurring in the first half of the season.

Leonard Nimoy, who before the writers' strike had discussed the possibility of Spock's appearing in a second-season episode to be written by Tracy Tormé, was an executive producer of *The Undiscovered Country*. And just as the first episode of *The Next Generation* undoubtedly received a ratings boost because of the ads for the series placed on the home-video release of *Star Trek IV*, certainly *Star Trek VI* would profit from a cross-promotion link with the now hugely successful series.

In "Unification," Rick Berman and Michael Piller developed a story that drew not only from *Star Trek*'s history—the schism between the Vulcans and the

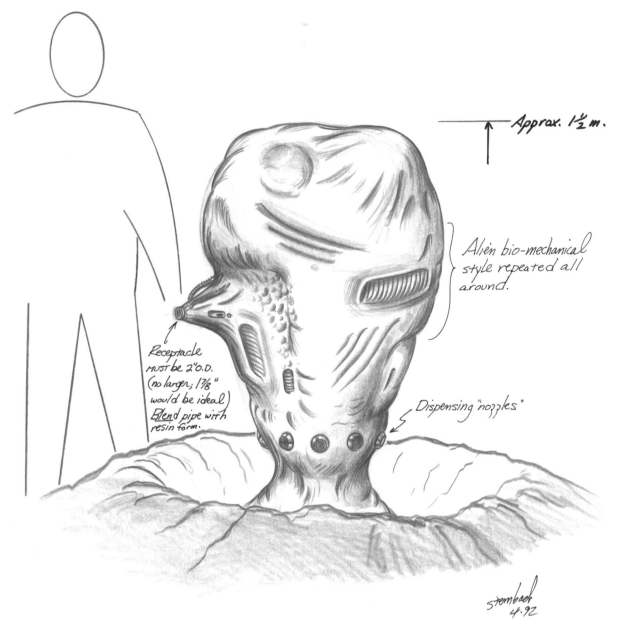

Approx. 1½ m.

Alien bio-mechanical style repeated all around.

Receptacle must be 2" O.D. (no larger; 1⅞" would be ideal) Blend pipe with resin form.

Dispensing "nozzles"

sternbach 4.92

Sometimes alien technology is *supposed* to look alien. ILLUSTRATION BY RICK STERNBACH. COURTESY OF THE ARTIST.

Romulans—but recent, real-world events as well: the reunification of Germany. With *Star Trek VI* also reflecting the collapse of the Soviet Union with its tale of a faltering Klingon Empire, an elegant interweaving of history, real and imaginary, took place within *Star Trek,* on both television and movie screens, solidly linking the two generations so that at last, there was no distinction between the two—only an ongoing continuum that fans of both series could enjoy. In true *Star Trek* fashion, there were no longer differences between them.

Though this was the season in which the dreamer had died, his dream lived on, a legacy to the world.

EIGHT

APPROACHING DEEP SPACE

The Sixth Season

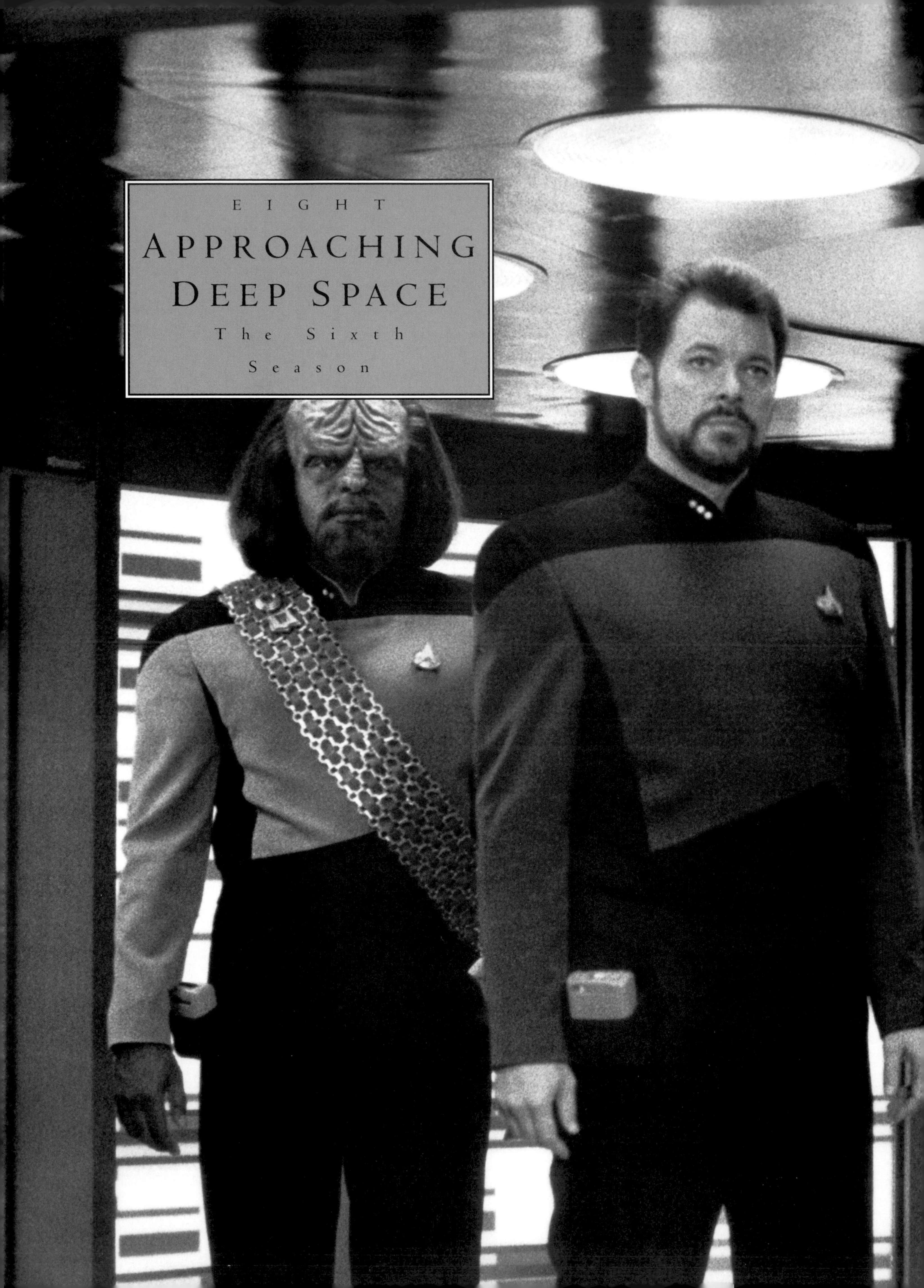

GENE Roddenberry was gone, but he was not forgotten. On the Paramount lot, in every storybreaking session that followed, in every creative meeting, the question constantly asked was: Is this true to Gene Roddenberry's *Star Trek*?

The deference was not lip service. It was policy.

And as *The Next Generation* entered its distinguished sixth season, the question was asked just as often, and answered just as thoughtfully, as when Roddenberry had been working in his office down the hall, and had been available to answer it himself.

Fortunately, the question had been addressed often enough during his lifetime that many other people involved with *Star Trek* already knew the answer. Chief among them were *The Next Generation*'s executive producers, Rick Berman and Michael Piller.

In the fall of '92, Clinton beat Bush in the American presidential election, Larry Bird retired from basketball, and in a historic development that might be a harbinger of *Star Trek*'s prediction of the demise of major league baseball by the year 2042, the Toronto Blue Jays became the first non-U.S. team to win the World Series.

In movie theaters, science fiction was not as strong a presence as it had been in earlier years, or as it would be later. *Batman Returns* was a summer blockbuster. *Alien 3* was a stylish though disappointing follow-up to the first two installments. And Paramount launched a new series of successful films based on another television property—*The Addams Family.*

On television itself, an era came to an end as Johnny Carson retired after twenty-nine years of hosting *The Tonight Show.* And yet again, network television continued to be conspicuously devoid of science-fiction programming. Only on Fox did anything close to genre shows surface—the short-lived, post-apocalypse sitcom *Woops!,* and the pseudo-documentary series *Sightings.*

But in the syndication market, the success of *The Next Generation* had finally been noticed, and three science-fiction series were poised to appear in January 1993. The first was *Time Trax,* created by Harve Bennett, producer of four *Star Trek* films. Unfortunately, the show would run only two seasons.

The second series was one of the few in twenty-six years which could actually be considered on a par with *Star Trek* in the arena of intelligent, well-produced, serious science-fiction drama. In January 1993, the two-hour pilot for J. Michael Straczynski's *Babylon 5* aired, and the response from viewers and critics was strong enough for the series to begin full production by the next season.

But it was the third series which set syndicated-ratings records, and which is still going strong today, helped no doubt in the beginning by a visit from Jean-Luc Picard and the *Starship Enterprise.*

Arriving halfway through *The Next Generation*'s sixth season, the unprecedented and much-anticipated *third Star Trek* series, *Deep Space Nine,* became an instant hit.

But that did not necessarily mean that the sixth season would automatically run smoothly.

What had been fanciful discussion in the summer of 1991 had become reality by the summer of 1992: a television series with a twenty-episode order. *Star Trek: Deep Space Nine,* created by Rick Berman and Michael Piller, was scheduled to begin principal photography in mid-August, which basically meant that all the work which Berman and Piller would normally do for *The Next Generation* had more than doubled. Not only would two complex series be produced simultaneously, but the newer one would require a myriad of start-up decisions regarding sets, costumes, makeup designs, and casting.

That level of intense involvement on the part of the two people most responsible for a series might have led to difficulties, like those that had plagued *The Next Generation*'s first season, when Roddenberry had been not been able to meet the demands on his time and energy.

But the truth was that *Deep Space Nine* was not like any other first-season series. Berman and Piller carefully split their in-house writing, creative, and production teams, giving some people, like Supervising Producer David Livingston, double duty on both series, and assigning others from *The Next Generation*, like Visual Effects Supervisor Robert Legato, exclusively to the new series. The production team Berman and Piller created for *Deep Space Nine*, in effect, brought to that series' first season the experience and assurance of a team going into the sixth season of their veteran series.

A special appearance by Captain Picard and the *Starship Enterprise* helped launch *Star Trek: Deep Space Nine* on its own stellar course during *The Next Generation*'s sixth season. From the pilot episode, "Emissary," Avery Brooks as Commander Benjamin Sisko has his second meeting with Picard. Their first meeting was during the battle of Wolf 359 in "The Best of Both Worlds."

An unrealized design for new ready-room art in the sixth season—Order-from-Chaos: The *Enterprise* is born from Mars. ILLUSTRATION BY RICK STERNBACH. COURTESY OF THE ARTIST.

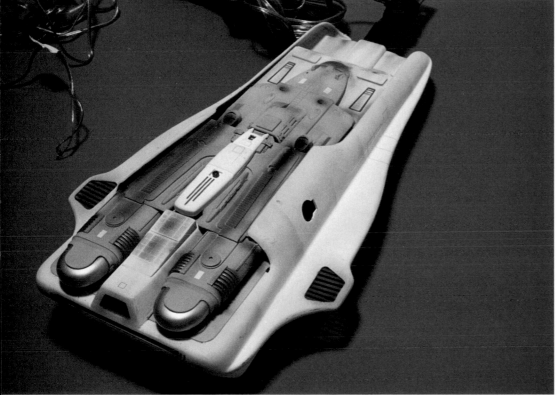

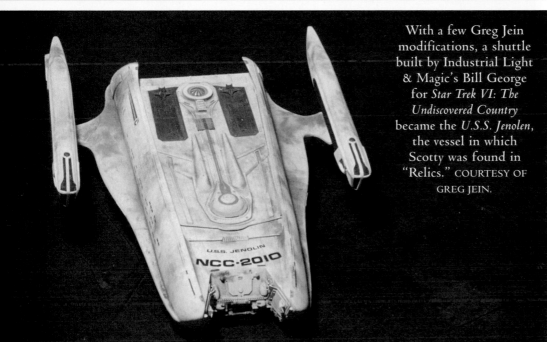

With a few Greg Jein modifications, a shuttle built by Industrial Light & Magic's Bill George for *Star Trek VI: The Undiscovered Country* became the *U.S.S. Jenolen,* the vessel in which Scotty was found in "Relics." COURTESY OF GREG JEIN.

Riker, Troi, and Picard in 1890s San Francisco. ROBBIE ROBINSON.

SEASON SIX: EPISODE 127
TIME'S ARROW, PART II
Teleplay by Jeri Taylor
Story by Joe Menosky
Directed by Les Landau

Concluding the *Enterprise* crew's time-travel adventure in 1890s San Francisco, Picard's away team heads to Earth's past to rescue Data and discovers that the aliens from Devidia II are feeding on energy from cholera victims. Picard seizes the cane that activates the aliens' time-vortex and, followed by Samuel Clemens, goes to the underground cave where Data's head will be found in the future. The aliens recover the cane and open the vortex with an explosion that separates Data's head from his body. Clemens and the away team escape back to Picard's time; Picard does not. He places a message for help in Data's head that he hopes will be found in the twenty-fourth century. Eventually Clemens changes places with Picard to restore history, and the *Enterprise* destroys the alien's time portal.

SEASON SIX: EPISODE 128
REALM OF FEAR
Written by Brannon Braga
Directed by Cliff Bole

Engineer Reg Barclay must overcome his fear of transporting in order to save the lives of four crew members of the *Yosemite.* Dr. Crusher discovers that, in transporting over to the deserted ship, Barclay's body has been infused by an energy life-form that can only be removed by molecular separation—a procedure which can occur only in mid-beam. When Barclay resubmits to beaming, he is separated from what turns out to be the life force of a *Yosemite* crew member who had been thought deceased. The discovery leads the *Enterprise* crew to locate and save the remaining *Yosemite* crew members in the same way.

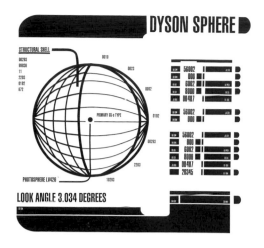

DYSON SPHERE

STRUCTURAL SHELL

PRIMARY G5-a TYPE

PHOTOSPHERE LV426

LOOK ANGLE 3.034 DEGREES

In "Relics," not only did writer Ron Moore create a moving story about Scotty's rescue in the 24th century, he also incorporated a science-fiction concept that the writing staff had been trying to fit into an episode for years—a Dyson sphere. Named for scientist Freeman Dyson, who first described it, the Dyson sphere is, in effect, an immense artificial shell built around a star by a sufficiently advanced culture that wants to collect all the energy its sun produces.

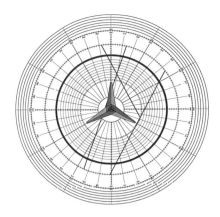

For "Relics," the *Next Generation* art department re-created several graphic elements from *The Original Series,* including this central helm display.

James Doohan and "Relics" writer Ronald D. Moore. ROBBIE ROBINSON.

Visual Effects Supervisor Dan Curry makes last-minute adjustments to the model of the Dyson Sphere's surface from "Relics."

SEASON SIX: EPISODE 129
MAN OF THE PEOPLE
Written by Frank Abatemarco
Directed by Winrich Kolbe

When the ship's counselor becomes the repository of a Lumerian ambassador's negative thoughts, Troi begins to age dramatically and loses emotional control and judgment. Picard discovers that the ambassador has done this before; feeling that it makes him a purer diplomat, although his victims always die. Near the end of the ambassador's latest interplanetary-war negotiations, Picard breaks the deadly link by faking Troi's death. The ambassador himself ages and dies when he tries to replace Troi with one of his aides, whom Picard transports safely out of range.

Picard and Chief Engineer Montgomery Scott of the original *Starship Enterprise.* ROBBIE ROBINSON.

SEASON SIX: EPISODE 130
RELICS
Written by Ronald D. Moore
Directed by Alexander Singer

The crew of the *Enterprise* finds Montgomery Scott, the chief engineer from the first *Enterprise,* preserved alive for 75 years in a transporter loop on a downed shuttle. The shuttle had been trapped on a Dyson sphere, an artificially constructed habitat built with a star at its center. When Scotty begins to feel that he has no useful role in the twenty-fourth century, Picard asks La Forge to use the veteran to investigate the old shuttlecraft. But Scotty's skills become vital when the *Enterprise* is drawn into the Dyson sphere after it triggers the sphere's tractor beam, just as happened to Scotty's vessel 75 years earlier. Scotty helps to free the *Enterprise* by wedging the sphere's doors open with his shuttle. As a reward, Scott leaves the *Enterprise* with a new shuttle—a gift from the crew.

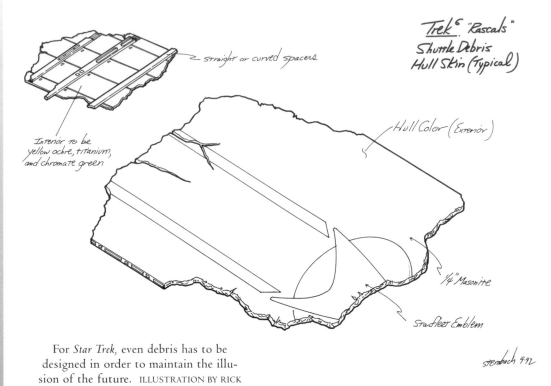

SEASON SIX: EPISODE 131
SCHISMS
Teleplay by Brannon Braga
Story by Jean Louise Matthias &
Ron Wilkerson
Directed by Robert Wiemer

After La Forge performs an experiment with the ship's deflectors, *Enterprise* crew members begin to experience mysterious bouts of anxiety and lapses in their sense of the passage of time. Troi's re-creation of events from crew members' memories leads to the realization that they have been abducted and experimented upon by aliens from another universe. Volunteering to serve as decoy, Riker allows himself to be taken to an alien lab, where he sees aliens battling to close a rupture between their universe and ours, which La Forge's experiment triggered. Riker escapes after retrieving the remaining "lost" crew of the *Enterprise.*

SEASON SIX: EPISODE 132
TRUE Q
Written by René Echevarria
Directed by Robert Scheerer

Q returns to the *Enterprise* to retrieve Amanda, an orphaned student, who is the offspring of two members of the Q continuum. Although she believes her parents died in an accident, Q reveals they were executed by the continuum—and the same fate could await her, unless she comes with him. Q gives her a choice: Join the continuum as a superbeing, or give up her powers to remain with humanity. Amanda tries to abstain from using her powers but is unable to passively stand by in the face of sure disaster. Sadder but wiser, she decides to join the Q.

Trek⁶ "Rascals"
Shuttle Debris
Hull Skin (Typical)

straight or curved spacers

Interior to be
yellow ochre, titanium,
and chromate green

Hull Color (Exterior)

¼" Masonite

Starfleet Emblem

sternbach 9·92

For *Star Trek,* even debris has to be designed in order to maintain the illusion of the future. ILLUSTRATION BY RICK STERNBACH. COURTESY OF THE ARTIST.

But that still didn't mean that there would not have to be changes. Though the days on the station *Deep Space Nine* might be twenty-six hours long, Berman and Piller were limited to twenty-four, and it was not possible to split their time equally between the two series. Their main concentration had to be focused on the newcomer, which meant that other members of the *Next Generation* team had to assume more responsibility for the ongoing series.

On the writing side, Jeri Taylor was elevated from supervising producer to co-executive producer for *The Next Generation,* taking on Berman's casting decisions, and Piller's management of the storybreaking sessions. Her touch was quickly apparent in that actors cast as "atmosphere"—that is, extras who are seen in the background—were now, by Taylor's specific request, to include people who appeared to be older than thirty. Also, sixth-season episodes were less likely to feature what some writers referred to as the "soap opera" stories of previous years. And by the end of the season, not one story had relied on the breakdown of some part of the *Enterprise*'s equipment to provide a story point— as exciting as those story points can be.

Yet for all the changes reflecting the realignment of staff to encompass the production of two series, the core of *The Next Generation* remained intact and the series' ratings kept it the top-rated syndicated drama throughout the season, a category marked by much more competition than in 1987.

Where once Paramount executives had feared that only one person would ever know what gave *Star Trek* its appeal, it was clear now that Rick Berman had assembled an entire team of people who understood the secret.

Which meant it wasn't a secret anymore.

In fact, it never had been.

Another "back-of-the-script-page" sketch by costume designer Robert Blackman gave Worf this Sergio Leone look for "A Fistful of Datas." COURTESY OF THE ARTIST.

Because there wasn't *one* reason for *Star Trek*'s appeal; there were many.

As more and more specialized viewing choices had become available, television audiences had grown more fragmented, watching specialty interest cable channels, dozens of movie channels, scores of sports channels. For a series like *The Next Generation* to achieve the ratings it did—and still does in syndication—it had to attract a variety of *different* audiences, all at the same time.

The simplest illustration of that broad appeal can be found by looking at two people who worked on *The Next Generation* and the series that have followed it—Visual-Effects Supervisor Dan Curry and Science Consultant André Bormanis. Each comes from a different background, one leaning more to the arts, one more to the sciences. Yet each was able to make unique contributions to the series based on his own different interests and experience. And those different contributions helped maintain *The Next Generation*'s appeal to two different segments of its audience.

In 1986, Dan Curry was Director of Creative Services at Cinema Research Corporation, a company that produced visual-effects and title sequences for movies. One of his friends in the industry was Peter Lauritson, the junior

Patrick Stewart took another turn as director, enthusiastically embracing the conventions of American Western films for "A Fistful of Datas." ROBBIE ROBINSON.

Keiko, Ro, and Picard as children, played by Caroline Junko King, Megan Parlen, and David Tristen Birkin. ROBBIE ROBINSON.

SEASON SIX: EPISODE 133
RASCALS
Teleplay by Allison Hock
Story by Ward Bostock & Diana Dru Botsford and Michael Piller
Directed by Adam Nimoy

Beaming through an energy field unexpectedly gives Picard, Ro, Keiko, and Guinan the bodies of twelve-year-olds, though their minds are unaffected. Complicating matters is a takeover of the *Enterprise* by a group of renegade Ferengi. The child guise of Picard and the others ultimately allows the crew to reclaim the ship, after which O'Brien and Crusher work together to use the transporter to restore the "children" to their adult forms.

SEASON SIX: EPISODE 134
A FISTFUL OF DATAS
Teleplay by Robert Hewitt Wolfe and Brannon Braga
Story by Robert Hewitt Wolfe
Directed by Patrick Stewart

After Geordi begins an experiment to use Data as backup for the ship's computer, strange glitches begin to occur throughout the ship—particularly in a Western holodeck scenario that Alexander has convinced Worf to participate in. Within the suddenly lethal simulation, Worf and Troi must work together to save the kidnapped Alexander. Outside the game, La Forge discovers the connection between a now drawling Data and the holodeck database to save his friends from the simulation's Data-based villains.

Picard is captured by
Cardassians. ROBBIE ROBINSON.

executive whom Bob Justman had talked into leaving a secure position in Paramount's television post-production department to take a flyer on *The Next Generation.*

In the early planning stages of the series, one the strategies that was developed was supposed to provide the high-quality visual effects the audience had come to expect from filmed science fiction, while saving money at the same time.

Industrial Light & Magic, then as now the foremost visual-effects house in the industry, had been hired to build the new *Enterprise,* and also to shoot a series of "stock" shots of the starship and various planets, which could then be reused, week after week. Theoretically, after paying once for a shot of the *Enterprise* orbiting a planet, Paramount could use the shot an unlimited number of times in new episodes, perhaps only changing the color of the planet in the background as had been done so often on *The Original Series.*

As Sarek had explained his decision to marry an emotional human woman, it seemed like a good idea at the time.

But while the image of the *Enterprise* orbiting a different-colored world each week might have worked in the sixties, it soon became apparent that it wasn't going to work in the eighties. Given the scope of the scripts being written, hundreds of other visual effects shots of the *Enterprise* and other craft would be required each season, many so specific to a particular episode that they could not be reused.

But that realization did not occur until the series actually began production.

What was known during the preproduction period was that careful planning would be required to make the most of those initial ILM shots. Dan Curry specialized in creating storyboards for visual-effects shots—comic-book-like series of drawings which showed exactly how a visual-effects sequence should be put together. Knowing of his friend's expertise, Lauritson asked Curry if he would create the storyboards for *The Next Generation*'s stock shots.

Though the assignment was originally intended to be something that Curry could take on in the evenings and on weekends, by the time the first few episodes had been completed, Visual-Effects Supervisor Rob Legato was, in Curry's words, "totally overwhelmed" by the visual-effects requirements of the show. Having already had the benefit of seeing the creativity and technical proficiency of Curry's work, *The Next Generation* producers then asked Curry if he would consider leaving CRC to come work on the series full-time as another visual-effects supervisor, alternating episodes with Legato.

Excited about an opportunity to contribute to *Star Trek,* Curry jumped at the chance. As he explains, "Because it was *Star Trek* and science fiction and space, I looked at it as an opportunity to go on a journey and explore areas of my own imagination that *Star Trek* would enable me to apply to my professional life. I think the reason I'm in this industry is that I've always been interested in science fiction. As a kid, I made crude optical printers. I'd seen *The Beast from 20,000 Fathoms* and *Forbidden Planet,* and they made me aware that not everything on the screen was really there at the same time. There were generation differences, image-quality differences, and I began to realize that you can create this."

Like so many others drawn to *Star Trek,* Curry's passion is not just focused on the artistic and technological processes of his work, but on the effect that work can have on those who view it.

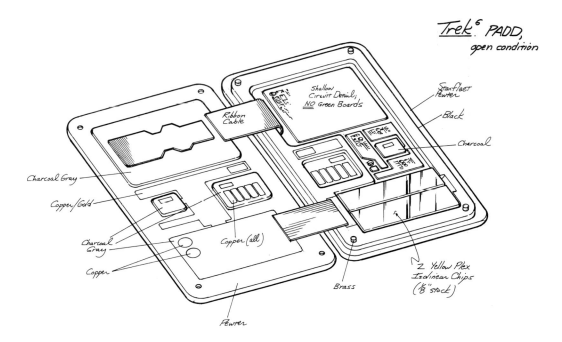

Trek⁶ PADD,
open condition

Charcoal Gray

Copper/Gold

Charcoal
Gray

Copper

Pewter

Ribbon
Cable

Shallow
Circuit Details;
NO Green Boards

Copper (all)

Brass

Starfleet
Pewter

Black

Charcoal

2 Yellow Plex
Isolinear Chips
(⅛" stock)

Under Production Designer Richard James, the level of realistic
detail achieved in *The Next Generation*'s prop design was unsurpassed.
ILLUSTRATION BY RICK STERNBACH. COURTESY OF THE ARTIST.

"I think what the medium of film, and television, does best," he says, "is
to enable an audience to experience not only a time and place, but a level of
intensity of situations that are outside daily life. And I think that's what *Star
Trek* does. I think one of the reasons *Star Trek* is so important, not just as an
entertainment, but as a philosophy, is because it offers the promise of a future
where as a species we have our act together. We've conquered poverty. We've
conquered racism. We've conquered disease, for the most part. And people are
then put in a position where they define their success by the quality of their
achievements as a person, rather than by the numbers in a bank book and the
square footage of their residence and what brand of vehicle they tool around
in. So I think that promise of *Star Trek* is good."

Curry finds that the promise of *Star Trek* is not only evident in the finished
episodes, but behind the scenes as well, as an attitude shared by all those who
contribute to its production. "For me, working with the casts that we've had,
the other people on our crew, the astonishing degree of freedom that we have
not only to work within our own department, but to overlap with other departments—there's a feeling of collaboration and welcome that is not usual on
other productions."

That openness and sense of collaboration is extremely important to Curry,
for his function in a series with such extensive visual-effects requirements is not
cut-and-dried. For one episode, he might be called upon to devise a photographic means of creating a forcefield effect, for the next he might be required
to sculpt a model of a new alien, and yet another might call for a new school of
alien martial arts, complete with alien weapons and ritualized movements.

First as visual-effects producer for *The Next Generation,* and then for *Deep
Space Nine* and *Voyager,* Curry has met all these challenges and more, drawing on
a background every bit as eclectic as his job requirements.

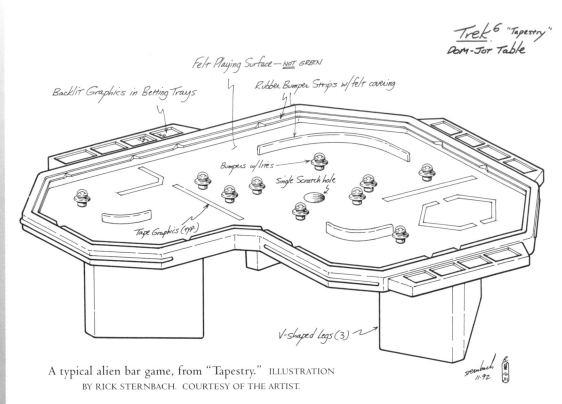

A typical alien bar game, from "Tapestry." ILLUSTRATION BY RICK STERNBACH. COURTESY OF THE ARTIST.

"I was always a painter," Curry recalls, "even as a little kid. And interestingly enough, my early artwork—which my mother has saved for me," he adds with a smile, "was very cinematic. Some of it was almost like storyboards, or I'd draw illustrations from a movie I'd just seen, like *The Time Machine* or *Spartacus.* So I think my visual imagination is expressed in any medium, and film is the medium that I believe is the most powerful mode of artistic expression developed by our species. It enables me to draw upon everything that has preceded this moment in life."

And when Curry says "everything," he means *everything.* "When I got out of college," he explains, "I went into the Peace Corps and built small dams and bridges in Thailand. You would not think that that relates to *Star Trek* at all, yet it's been a heavy influence."

The influence Curry refers to is most evident in his interest in serious martial arts. "I had some friends in Thailand who were genuine thugs and I was impressed with their ability to inflict bodily harm in a formal but creative way," Curry says dryly. "So, I studied *tae kwon do,* which is Korean martial arts, and have a black belt in that. And I studied, sometimes formally, sometimes informally, with Thai and Chinese instructors, learning things like quick kill, how to use anything at hand to send somebody off to the nonbiological phase of existence. How to slit throats with paper, stuff that you need in dark alleys."

In Thailand, Curry had many other experiences that shaped his contributions to *The Next Generation.* "When I got out of the Peace Corps I did documentary films. I directed some Thai-language TV shows and got involved in their film industry. I also did a lot of live theater. In Thailand, I designed sets for their Bangkok Opera Society. I designed the Ball for the King one year. I also spent a lot of time in Laos, and a lot of time in the Himalayas."

Followers of *The Next Generation* can easily recognize the seeds that were

Until Dan Curry designed the *bat'leth*, Klingon weapons, such as these knives based on designs from *Star Trek III: The Search for Spock,* tended to be modifications of more familiar forms. ROBBIE ROBINSON.

The art department saw to it that not every aspect of Klingon culture was based on war and destruction.

Q takes Picard back to observe the bar brawl in which Picard almost died as a young officer. ROBBIE ROBINSON.

SEASON SIX: EPISODE 141
TAPESTRY
Written by Ronald D. Moore
Directed by Les Landau

When his artificial heart is damaged, Picard is snatched from the brink of death by Q, who returns him to the period in his past when he received the heart after a near-fatal bar brawl. This time, Picard chooses to avoid the fight. The undesirable consequence of that choice is a new life as a junior science officer whose chances of obtaining command position are overruled by his conservative attitude toward risk-taking. Q agrees to give Picard another chance to restore the life he knew and he revisits the bar scene and is mortally wounded once again. When Picard wakens in his familiar life, recovering from his latest injuries, he has a new sense of what led to his becoming the man that he is.

planted in Curry which grew into the rich cultural heritage of one of *Star Trek*'s most popular aliens—the Klingons.

Curry's first major involvement in adding to Klingon culture began with the fourth-season episode "Reunion," which centered on the succession ceremony for the new Klingon leader. In the episode, Worf was required to use a *bat'leth*—an ancient Klingon sword. Curry recalls, "I looked at some of the designs that were proposed and they were wonderful, but there was a degree of familiarity about them. And I thought to myself, 'Well, you know, it's not really my job to get in people's faces about this, but because I care passionately about martial arts, and I have a strong feeling for the ergonomics of bladed weapons, let's have something that we've never seen before.'"

The distinctive, crescent-shaped weapon that resulted was not an overnight creation. "I had been imagining a weapon for a long time," Curry says, "that was kind of a staff weapon but had some of the interesting ergonomics of Himalayan blades that curve away. There's also some influence of Northern Chinese hook weapons. So I sketched it out, went home and made a foamcore mock-up of what I had in mind, and showed it to Rick."

Curry, who had studied *tai chi* for many years, also made up an instant *kata*—a series of standardized moves for using the weapon—which he also demonstrated. "I really like the fluidity of *tai-chi* sword, where instead of being a chop-chop-hack-hack action like some of the external martial arts, the con-

Data experiences "dreaming" when Dr. Bashir tests a Gamma Quadrant device that stuns Data and shuts him down, activating images of his "father-creator," Dr. Soong. At the same time, Worf learns that his father may have been captured rather than killed at Khitomer and may still be alive in a Romulan prisoner-of-war camp. Disturbed that his father would submit to being captured rather than die with honor, Worf seeks out the prison camp, where he is captured by the Klingon descendants of the Khitomer prisoners. An astonished Worf learns that the descendants no longer consider themselves prisoners, and that the prison camp is now a Klingon-Romulan colony.

Held captive in the Romulan prison that is now a Klingon-Romulan colony, Worf learns that his father is not among the "colonists." Unable to forget the Romulan slaughter of his family at Khitomer, he is upset to discover that one of the "colonists," Bael, to whom he is attracted, is half-Klingon, half-Romulan. Unrest grows among the Klingon youth when Worf introduces them to their Klingon-warrior heritage. When the Romulan leader decides that Worf is a threat to peaceful coexistence and must die, the Klingon elders help Worf to take the rebellious Klingon youths with him, posing as "crash survivors." In return, Worf agrees to keep the colony's existence secret, sparing their families shame.

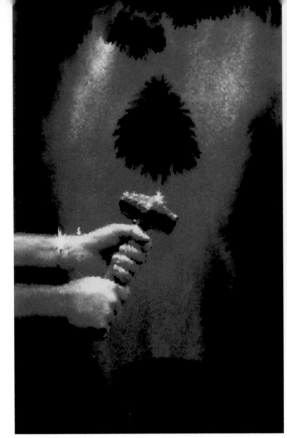
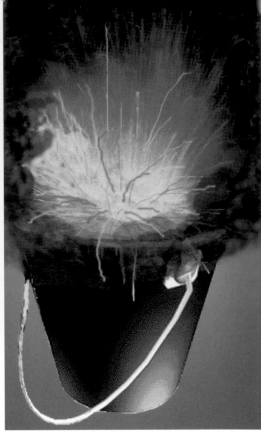

As befits their fictional source, Data's paintings, reflecting his troubled dreams in "Birthright, Part I," originated as computer collages.

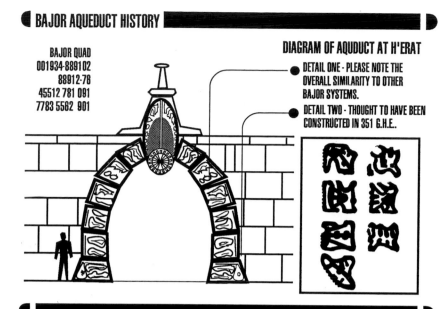

BAJOR AQUEDUCT HISTORY

BAJOR QUAD
001934-88910 2
88912-78
45512 781 091
7783 5562 901

DIAGRAM OF AQUDUCT AT H'ERAT

● DETAIL ONE - PLEASE NOTE THE OVERALL SIMILARITY TO OTHER BAJOR SYSTEMS.

● DETAIL TWO - THOUGHT TO HAVE BEEN CONSTRUCTED IN 351 G.H.E.

PLEASE SHOOT 1 FILM NEG AT 100 %
BAJOR HISTORY FOR PICARD'S DESK VIEWER
BIRTHRITE 12/8/92

Captain Picard's interest in archaeology and his return visit to Bajoran space in "Birthright, Part I," prompted this display.

One of the reasons actors enjoy getting guest roles on *Star Trek* series is that the typical industry restrictions on the number of years they must wait before being eligible for a second role (so audiences won't recognize them) are often not applicable because of extensive make-up. For example, *First Contact*'s Zefram Cochrane was played by James Cromwell, who first appeared with his own features in the Third-Season episode, "The High Ground." Then, Cromwell was unrecognizable as the alien, Jaglom Shrek, in "Birthright," and later reappeared without extensive make-up in the second *Next Generation* feature.

Picard is the sole defender of the *Enterprise*. ROBBIE ROBINSON.

SEASON SIX: EPISODE 144

STARSHIP MINE
Written by Morgan Gendel
Directed by Cliff Bole

As the *Enterprise* undergoes a routine baryon sweep, she's taken over by thieves after the ship's trilithium resin, and Picard is trapped as the only crew member on board. Staying ahead of the lethal baryon sweep, Picard bests the thieves, one by one. When his last adversary, Kelsey, will not negotiate, Picard fights her for the resin but loses. Kelsey, who intends to sell the resin for personal profit, escapes in a shuttlecraft. However, Picard has removed the volatile resin's stabilizer and her shuttle explodes.

SEASON SIX: EPISODE 145

LESSONS
Written by Ronald Wilkerson &
Jean Louise Matthias
Directed by Robert Wiemer

Picard chooses duty over personal feelings when he falls in love with a subordinate, Dr. Nella Daren, a chief of stellar sciences who also shares his love of music. An evacuation operation to save the inhabitants of a planet threatened by firestorms requires Dr. Daren's presence on the away team. Picard anguishes over sending her on such a dangerous mission and then suffers when she is presumed dead. Upon her return, they both acknowledge that their professional relationship must take precedence over their personal wishes, and they end their romance.

The model of the shuttlecraft *Magellan*, from "Starship Mine." COURTESY OF GREG JEIN.

As a mark of the constant improvement in technology between the time of *The Original Series* and *The Next Generation*, here we see how the old magnetic bottles for antimatter have been replaced by Thermos bottles. ILLUSTRATION BY RICK STERNBACH. COURTESY OF THE ARTIST.

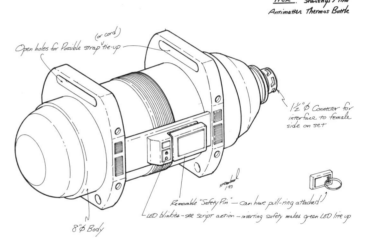

The portable piano keyboard from "Lessons" required two versions to be made, to create the illusion of a thin membrane that could unroll into solidity. ILLUSTRATION BY RICK STERNBACH. COURTESY OF THE ARTIST.

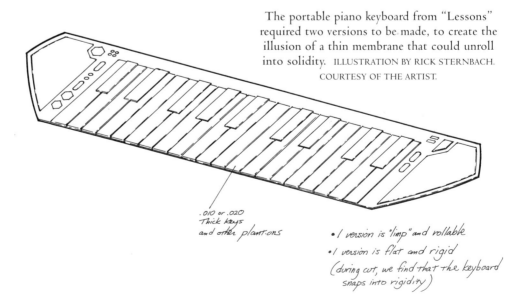

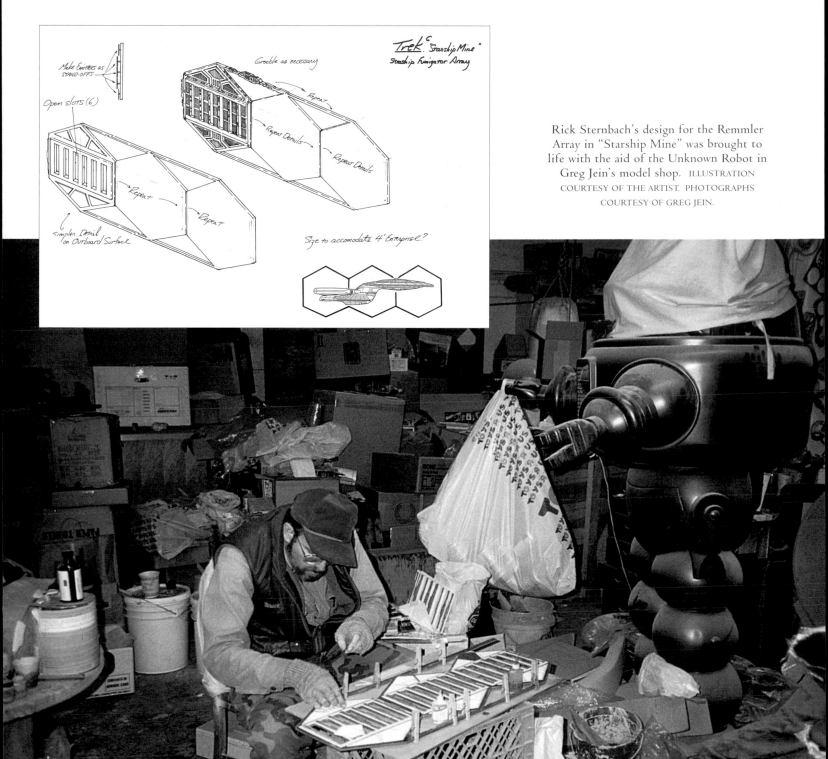

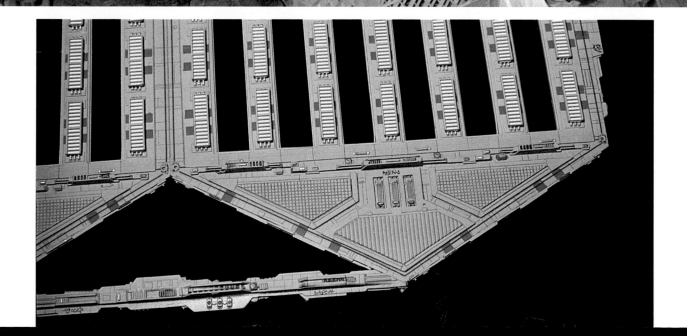

Rick Sternbach's design for the Remmler Array in "Starship Mine" was brought to life with the aid of the Unknown Robot in Greg Jein's model shop. ILLUSTRATION COURTESY OF THE ARTIST. PHOTOGRAPHS COURTESY OF GREG JEIN.

Picard and Crusher listen to the
message of a long-dead race.
ROBBIE ROBINSON.

THE CHASE
Teleplay by Joe Menosky
Story by Joe Menosky & Ronald D. Moore
Directed by Jonathan Frakes

Picard is caught up in solving a
genetic puzzle uncovered by his
former professor of archaeology,
Richard Galen. After Picard declines
Galen's invitation to help prove a
startling theory of how life developed throughout the galaxy, Galen's
ship is attacked by raiders and he
dies. Picard enlists the aid of unlikely allies—Klingon, Romulan, and
Cardassian—to take up Galen's
quest. Together they discover that
collected DNA samples, theirs and
Galen's, when studied as a group,
create a message that reveals that
an ancient race seeded their home
planets and that they share an
ancestral link.

FRAME OF MIND
Written by Brannon Braga
Directed by James L. Conway

Captured and neurologically tortured
while on an undercover mission to
rescue Federation hostages on
Tilonius IV, Riker preserves his sanity by drawing on memories of the
Enterprise and Dr. Crusher's play
"Frame of Mind." In the play, Riker
is a mental patient in an insane asylum. Tilonian brainwashing causes
him to confuse reality and illusion.
Even when Worf and Data appear to
rescue him, Riker continues to shift
back and forth between the ship and
the play, distrusting all realities he is
presented. At last, he awakens within
the Tilonian torture lab, then escapes
in an emergency beam-out.

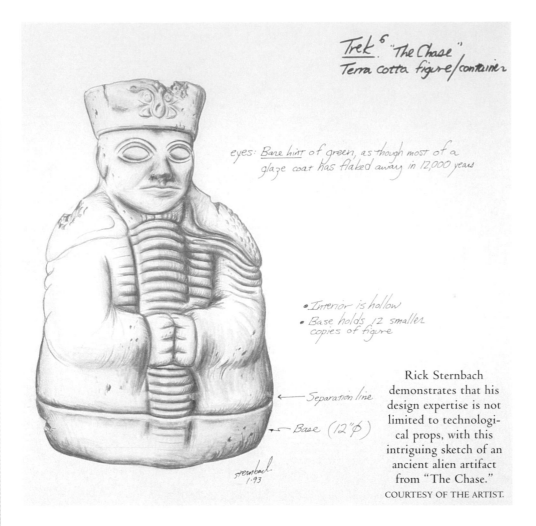

Trek 6 "The Chase"
Terra cotta figure/container

eyes: Bare hint of green, as though most of a
glaze coat has flaked away in 12,000 years

• Interior is hollow
• Base holds 12 smaller
copies of figure

← Separation line

← Base (12"ø)

sternbach
1-93

Rick Sternbach
demonstrates that his
design expertise is not
limited to technologi-
cal props, with this
intriguing sketch of an
ancient alien artifact
from "The Chase."
COURTESY OF THE ARTIST.

clusion of each movement is the beginning of another motion. I wanted to be
able to achieve that fluidity but with a heavy blade that was in keeping with
Michael Dorn's character."

Rick Berman liked Curry's invention. Prop versions of the *bat'leth* were
quickly made up. And Dan Curry began instructing Michael Dorn in the
weapon's use.

A ripple effect then spread out through the series' creative team. "The
writers started to pick up on the martial potential," Curry says, "and the
Klingons started to have a more Bushido quality about them. Then they came
up with *Mok'bara*, the Klingon hand martial arts, so they came to me and said,
'Well, Dan, what about that?' So I kind of adapted *tai chi*, but made it a little
bit more vicious, and a little bit more theatrical."

Once again, Michael Dorn became Curry's student, to the extent that in
several *Next Generation* episodes, as Worf goes through *Mok'bara* and *bat'leth* exer-
cises onscreen, Curry was just off camera, performing the movements to guide
the actor.

But Curry's influence on things Klingon was not limited to the more
physical aspects of their culture. "Klingon architecture became influenced by
Thai architecture and Himalayan architecture," Curry says. "I did that matte
painting of the Klingon lamasery where Worf encounters Kahless [in the sixth
season's 'Rightful Heir']. I kind of made it up, with just a little bit of Thai,
and a little bit of Nepali architecture, with some Tibetan thrown in."

Neither was Curry's influence limited to *Star Trek.* Though created for a science-fiction series where it would be wielded by aliens, the *bat'leth* is the first new bladed weapon in decades to be accepted in certain Korean associations' martial-arts competitions. With considerable bemusement, Curry also reveals, "Government agencies have contacted me to explore the *bat'leth*'s design, you know: 'Why did you think about that? Would you send us a tracing?' Stuff like that."

Curry's *tai chi* expertise also served *The Next Generation* in areas not as apparent as the development of Klingon martial arts. In the first-season episode "Arsenal of Freedom," the script called for a small drone robot to fly around the cast. "We had a sculptor make the drone," Curry remembers, "and it was big and heavy and unwieldy, and we were out of time and out of money. So, I threw a couple of ideas together and I took a plastic Easter egg, a *Sesame Street*–brand shampoo bottle, and a L'Eggs pantyhose container, and glued this thing together. This was another case where *tai chi*, which I'd studied for more than twenty years, came into account, because I decided that instead of shooting the robot floating through motion-control photography, I was going to do it all as a puppet. At the time, everybody thought I was insane.

"But I put this goofy robot upside-down on a stick, made a large shield for myself out of green screen, and put a green background behind me. Then I did all the

Dan Curry's son, Devin, demonstrates what will become a deadly and sophisticated drone robot, made of a plastic Easter egg, a *Sesame Street* shampoo bottle, and a L'Eggs pantyhose container. In addition to testing killer robots, Devin was also the test audience for the gruesome first-season episode, "Conspiracy." After viewing the episode, Devin suggested that a Remmick action figure with an exploding head would make a fine addition to the range of wholesome *Next Generation* toys. COURTESY OF DAN CURRY.

The finished version of Dan Curry's killer robot, animated by *tai-chi* movements in the first-season episode "The Arsenal of Freedom."

SEASON SIX: EPISODE 148
SUSPICIONS
Written by Joe Menosky and Naren Shankar
Directed by Cliff Bole

To vindicate a Ferengi scientist whose suicide she doubts, Dr. Crusher faces court-martial for performing an unauthorized autopsy on the Takaran scientist, Jo'Bril, who was killed testing the Ferengi's metaphasic-shield technology. When the evidence she finds is inconclusive, Crusher must risk testing the shield herself to prove sabotage was the cause of the first death. Her test flushes out the real killer, Jo'Bril, whose race can feign death, and who wants the shield for use as a weapon. During the subsequent struggle, Jo'Bril is killed, but Crusher succeeds in restoring the dead Ferengi scientist's reputation.

Worf in the Klingon monastery on Boreth. ROBBIE ROBINSON.

SEASON SIX: EPISODE 149
RIGHTFUL HEIR
Teleplay by Ronald D. Moore
Story by James Brooks
Directed by Winrich Kolbe

To strengthen his Klingon spiritual beliefs, Worf takes leave from his duties to travel to a Klingon temple, where clerics await the return of the legendary and long-dead Klingon leader—Kahless. To Worf's amazement, Kahless appears and vows to rally the Klingon people around him. Gowron, the High Council Leader, asks the *Enterprise* to bring Kahless to him to be verified. A DNA analysis proves Kahless's identity, but when Gowron defeats the mythic warrior in battle, the head cleric admits that this Kahless is a clone of the original programmed with sacred texts. All present realize, however, that the Klingon people, like Worf, are seeking new purpose in their lives. The decision is made for Kahless to rule as Emperor and moral leader, while Gowron and the council retain political power.

robot movement for the show in one morning, doing *tai-chi* motion."

Curry used the same basic technique to create the energy beings in the fifth season's "Power Play." Though instead of manipulating a "goofy" prop, Curry donned Day-Glo green mittens to serve as the initial image for the energy beings. When the images of Curry's moving hands were added to the live-action footage shot for the episode, they were first blurred far out of focus to create a glowing element, and then printed in a slightly more in-focus version with a color change, as if a hot central core existed in each being.

Two other memorable visual effects which reflect Curry's hands-on approach to his work are the *Enterprise* forcefields he created by shooting out-of-focus silver mylar pom-poms, and the mining planet whose mottled brown and yellow surface came from a photograph of something uniquely earthy his fellow visual effects producer, Ronald B. Moore (not the writer Ronald D. Moore), had stepped in on a sidewalk.

Curry credits his Renaissance-man approach to visual effects to "having worked in live theater a lot, where you have to make it happen *now*." Effects created with hand puppets or pom-poms arise from those situations where Curry asks, "How can we do something that looks cool without instantly jumping to the computer or reinventing the wheel? The fact that I can paint, sculpt, and make movies has only made *Star Trek* an even more wonderful opportunity for me, because I get to draw on all those things."

Kevin Conway as a clone of the Klingon spiritual leader, Kahless, in "Rightful Heir." A substantially different version of Kahless appeared in *The Original Series* episode "The Savage Curtain." ROBBIE ROBINSON.

To create an establishing shot for "Rightful Heir," Dan Curry began with a real photograph of the Himalayas, then digitally painted in a Klingon monastery. COURTESY OF THE ARTIST.

Nichelle Nichols and Dr. Mae Jemison visit on the set of "Second Chances." As Uhura in *The Original Series,* Nichols not only inspired a generation of actors like Whoopi Goldberg and LeVar Burton, but also scientists and space travelers like Jemison. In such positive ways, *Star Trek* is helping to create a real version of its own future today. ROBBIE ROBINSON.

The present and future of space exploration intertwined when space shuttle astronaut, Dr. Mae Jemison, the first African-American woman in space, played Ensign Palmer in "Second Chances."

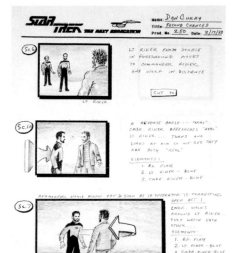

Dan Curry's storyboard and a final frame for the meeting of the two William Rikers in "Second Chances." COURTESY OF THE ARTIST.

SEASON SIX: EPISODE 150
SECOND CHANCES
Teleplay by René Echevarria
Story by Michael A. Medlock
Directed by LeVar Burton

When Riker returns to an isolated starbase that can be visited, via transporter, only every eight years, he encounters his "twin," Lieutenant William Thomas Riker. Lieutenant Riker was created in a transporter accident eight years earlier when Riker arrived on the *Potemkin* seeking a particular database. Riker's mission is again to obtain the same database. Disconcerting to all concerned, Troi and Lieutenant Riker resume the affair the original Riker began and ended years earlier. After Commander Riker saves his double's life while trying to complete his mission, Lieutenant Riker leaves the *Enterprise* for a new posting on the *Gandhi.*

SEASON SIX: EPISODE 151
TIMESCAPE
Written by Brannon Braga
Directed by Adam Nimoy

The *Enterprise* is frozen in time as it is being boarded by Romulans, its partially raised shields about to be hit by a Warbird's disruptor bolt, and its warp core about to breach. Fortunately, Picard, Data, La Forge, and Troi are not on board, but in a runabout on their way back from a conference. Aware of time-distortion pockets in the area, they adapt emergency transporter armbands to create personal forcefields of "real time," allowing them to beam to both ships. In the Warbird's engine core, they discover an alien vortex that Data's tricorder activates, alternately advancing and reversing time. They see the *Enterprise* destroyed and reformed. The mystery is explained when an alien informs them that his offspring are responsible for the area's time distortions. After normal time is restored, Picard acts to avert the warp-core breach and send the aliens back to their own time.

Picard and his crew, about to discover the aftermath of their previous release of the Borg Hugh.
ROBBIE ROBINSON.

SEASON SIX: EPISODE 153
DESCENT, PART I
Teleplay by Ronald D. Moore
Story by Jeri Taylor
Directed by Alexander Singer

Data experiences his first emotion when he feels pleasure at killing a Borg he encounters in a devastated outpost that had summoned the *Enterprise* for help. These Borg are different from the ones encountered in the past. They appear to have been infected by individuality, which may stem from the influence of Hugh, the Borg previously captured and released by Picard. Later, after a Borg is captured while boarding the *Enterprise*, Data stuns the ship's crew by leaving with the Borg in a stolen shuttlecraft. Pursuing Data, Picard leads most of his crew on an intensive search of a sensor-shielded planet where they find both Data and Lore, the android's malevolent "brother." Backed by an army of Borg, Data and Lore boast that they will conquer the Federation and destroy it.

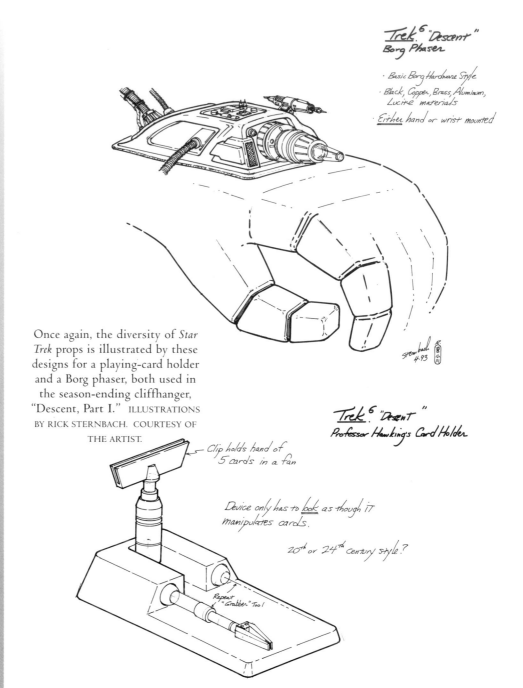

Trek[6] *"Descent"*
Borg Phaser

· Basic Borg Hardware Style
· Black, Copper, Brass, Aluminum, Lucite materials
· Either hand or wrist mounted

sternbach 4.93

Trek[6] *"Descent"*
Professor Hawking's Card Holder

— Clip holds hand of 5 cards in a fan

Device only has to *look* as though it manipulates cards.

20th or 24th century style?

Repeat "Grabber" Tool!

Once again, the diversity of *Star Trek* props is illustrated by these designs for a playing-card holder and a Borg phaser, both used in the season-ending cliffhanger, "Descent, Part I." ILLUSTRATIONS BY RICK STERNBACH. COURTESY OF THE ARTIST.

Curry recalls that it was in the first season that Gene Roddenberry set the tone for the level of interaction and self-direction that defines the operation of *Star Trek*'s visual-effects teams.

"Gene was very cordial and friendly," Curry says, "a very pleasant person and I, of course, had immense respect for him. He would approve everything, and watch everything closely, but he would rarely dictate things that he specifically wanted to see. I think he realized that you could get a lot out of people if you gave them the opportunity to do what they do best."

Curry says that attitude continued throughout the run of *The Next Generation* and exists today on *Deep Space Nine* and *Voyager*.

"Every visual-effects supervisor has a different way of going about the same thing, yet there's considerable harmony in the way the show looks and feels. I try to do what I do best. I'm hands-on where appropriate, but I also try to make sure that I help create an environment where each individual can excel on his or her own terms. That way, we benefit from everybody's creativity and imagination."

That approach to behind-the-scenes *Star Trek* is a fitting match to what appears on the screen— there's room for everyone who supports the mission.

Curry says it best. "Everybody on a *Star Trek* show that's been on the show for a while and continues to be a part of what *Star Trek* is, they bring a lot more to the party than just a body to do work. That goes for everybody, whether it's the writers, the art department, costume, camera crew, everybody. And despite any cynical façade or curmudgeonly exchanges at a production meeting, everybody's still aware of not only the wonder of our medium, but the wonder of what *Star Trek* is.

"I don't think there's a single person here who is not self-supervised and makes a greater demand of themselves than what is required to satisfy a paycheck. And I think the audience sees that and is aware of that: the homework done, the thought given. I don't think there's a person who does not exploit who they are way beyond whatever their job category is, to make the show better."

Dan Curry worked on *The Next Generation* as an artist, and as an artist he appreciated the series' passionate view of humanity's future, and the challenges of making that future visually come to life.

But Curry's contributions to the series were just one aspect of *Star Trek*'s appeal. For in addition to all the artists and dreamers who were in *The Next Generation*'s audience, there was a more pragmatic component as well— equally creative, equally passionate, but in different areas and for different reasons. These were the people who were drawn more to the science of *Star Trek* than the art of it. André Bormanis, who joined the series as science consultant in the sixth season, is a perfect example of another of *Star Trek*'s many audiences.

Like many of the people who came together to put *The Next Generation* on the air, from Gene Roddenberry the pilot to Herman Zimmerman the actor, André Bormanis came to the television industry in a roundabout route. He earned his B.Sc. in Physics from the University of Arizona, did graduate work there and at Arizona State in physics and astrophysics, became a research assistant in infrared astronomy, also at the University of Arizona, then went into the microcomputer industry as a technical writer, software developer, and teacher.

In "Descent, Part I," the Borg returned to *The Next Generation*, but just as Jeri Taylor had said after "I, Borg," they would never be the same again.

But immediate job concerns aside, Bormanis had always enjoyed non-technical writing as well, and in the midst of his science and technology career, he also took several creative-writing courses. Then, in time-honored Hollywood tradition, he wrote some spec scripts and went looking for an agent.

About the time he found an agent willing to represent an unknown scientist who had yet to make his first script sale, Bormanis was also offered a NASA fellowship to spend two years at the Space Policy Institute, in Washington, D.C. he recalls that the opportunity "struck me as being very intriguing because it combined many of my interests—science and space interest with writing and setting policy. Why do we do things in space? Why do we spend public money on it? Those kinds of high-level-debate issues are always engaging to me."

Without knowing it, Bormanis's interests and background already made him part of the *Star Trek* family.

NASA and *Star Trek* had been linked ever since the days of *The Original Series,* when Gene Roddenberry had sought the technical advice of space scientists and engineers to help make his series more accurate. In 1976, a tremendous letter-writing campaign by *Star Trek* fans—who wrote up to half a million letters according to some counts—had resulted in President Gerald Ford officially designating NASA's first flight-test space shuttle as the *Enterprise.* And on January 30, 1993, in the midst of *The Next Generation's* sixth season, Majel Barrett-Roddenberry accepted on her husband's behalf the Distinguished Public Service Medal from NASA's chief administrator, Dan Goldin. The medal's citation read: "For distinguished service to the Nation and the human race in presenting the exploration of space as an exciting frontier and a hope for the future."

Though he was gainfully employed at the time, Bormanis also responded to *The Next Generation's* call. While at the Space Policy Institute, one of the first requests he made of his new agent was to have her set up a pitch meeting at the show. "Months went by," Bormanis recalls with a laugh, "before I heard anything from my agent, and every time I would call, she would tell me they weren't looking for any new people to pitch at the moment."

But during one phone call, when Bormanis had almost reached the point of giving up on the idea of pitching to the series, his agent told him that the producers were looking for a new science consultant, because the previous consultant, Naren Shankar, had joined the writing staff as a story editor.

After meeting with Jeri Taylor, Michael Piller, and Ira Behr, Bormanis was given the chance to "audition." Piller gave him a copy of a *Deep Space Nine* script, "If Wishes Were Horses," and asked him to write notes on the science in it.

A day and a half later, Bormanis faxed Piller nine page of notes, and a few weeks later, he was hired. Fortuitously, he was needed at *The Next Generation* just at the time his NASA fellowship came to an end.

With his new job, André Bormanis had come full circle. He was hired in his role as a scientist, to work on the latest incarnation of the series which had inspired him to go into science in the first place.

"One of my earliest memories," Bormanis says, "is seeing *Star Trek* for the first time when I was seven years old, and thinking, 'Wow. That's just incredible. What is this thing, this huge ship?' I thought the ship was so big that there were parts of it they hadn't even explored yet. I had all these weird ideas about what went on in *Star Trek,* but it just pulled me in in a way that nothing else had.

"Clearly, it helped motivate my interest in astronomy and space science. So I think it's inspirational, very inspirational for kids to see people who are scientists and engineers as the principal characters of a television show that's fun and exciting and engaging. It shows that science and engineering are an important part of our lives. That it's important, at least on some level, to understand scientific reasoning, to understand technical issues. Not everybody has to be a scientist, but clearly people have to have some sort of basis for making informed decisions about science when it has an impact on the social sphere."

Speaking with the same conviction as LeVar Burton when recounting his excitement as a child at seeing a future in which people of color were present, Bormanis describes his own excitement for another aspect of *Star Trek's* vision of inclusion. "These people in *Star Trek,* these scientists and engineers, they really enjoy what they do. They find it rewarding, and they ultimately are rewarded with the greatest adventure of their lives by virtue of the fact that they have chosen this profession.

"I think that's the implicit message of *Star Trek,* and I think that has a lot of resonance for people in the sciences. I know many people with Ph.D.s in engineering and physics who are big fans of *The Next Generation,* and sometimes they'll complain about a certain technical detail, but they love the show. They love the fact that *Star Trek* is the only show on television that has scientists and engineers as its principals, and those principals spend much of their time doing science and engineering."

From those fascinated by the rituals and settings of different cultures, to those who wish a chance to glimpse the scientific possibilities of the future, *Star Trek,* unlike almost any other television series, throws a wide net, effortlessly encompassing its diverse audience with all the ease with which Gene Roddenberry assembled the first diverse crew of the *Enterprise.*

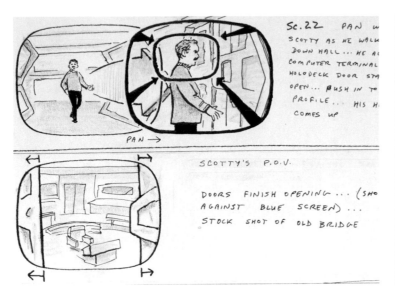

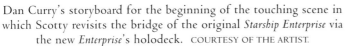

Dan Curry's storyboard for the beginning of the touching scene in which Scotty revisits the bridge of the original *Starship Enterprise* via the new *Enterprise*'s holodeck. COURTESY OF THE ARTIST.

Once again the generations meet in "Relics."

The scientific principles underlying the physics of *Star Trek* have inspired several books, including one by André Bormanis to be published in 1998. Other books have analyzed the future of the legal system under the Federation, or presented management skills drawn from the actions of Jean-Luc Picard.

The strength of *Star Trek*'s appeal is that it is a mirror, reflecting whatever we bring to it, whatever we wish to see.

Given that scope, is it any wonder so many are drawn to it?

Like the fifth season's "Unification," two of the most notable episodes of the sixth season harkened back to *The Original Series.* One in terms of character, the other in subject matter.

The first was "Relics," in which the original *Enterprise*'s chief engineer, Montgomery Scott, came aboard the *Next Generation*'s *Enterprise* after being released from a transporter-beam loop in which he had been trapped for seventy-five years.

Written by Ron Moore, the episode is not only a taut *Next Generation* story in which the *Enterprise* is placed in danger of destruction, it is also an affectionate tribute to *The Original Series,* especially in one particularly challenging and touching scene.

Feeling out of place in the future, Scotty goes to the holodeck and calls up a re-creation of the original *Enterprise*'s bridge in which he toasts his absent colleagues. The heroic effort that went into realizing that set is a telling example of the passion for *Star Trek* shared by everyone on the *Next Generation* team.

First of all, only a year before, a proposal to construct an *Original Series*–style bridge for "Cause and Effect" had been turned down because of the expense, and once again it appeared such a set would prove too costly.

One solution would have been to use the most recent bridge set from *The Undiscovered Country,* though that would hardly hold the same sentimental meaning for Scotty and the audience. Piller, Taylor, and Moore even thought about renting a fan-built replica bridge, made to be used as a backdrop at *Star Trek* conventions.

But Production Designer Richard James saw a unique solution in the design of the original bridge. He suggested building only the single pie-wedge section of the bridge which contained Scotty's engineering station, then matching it to a photographic image of the rest of the bridge taken from an *Original Series* episode.

Dan Curry knew just which episode, too. "This Side of Paradise" featured a scene that opened with

Careful planning meant that only this small section of the original bridge had to be reconstructed for "Relics." The rest was added during postproduction by utilizing an image of the deserted bridge taken from *The Original Series* episode "This Side of Paradise." ROBBIE ROBINSON.

a brief pan of the empty bridge. Those few frames were then digitally processed and matched to the small bridge section that was subsequently physically constructed—Scotty's station and the turbolift doors.

As for building that section of the bridge, no plans existed to guide Richard James's staff. All the measurements had to be inferred from painstaking examination of the original episodes, conducted in long, after-hours and weekend sessions that would never result in overtime pay. Control consoles and displays were similarly and exactly reproduced, helped by the addition of some actual, jewel-like control buttons that had been kept as souvenirs from the original sets. In the end, though, the production team did rent one part of a fan-built replica—a center console and captain's chair constructed by Steven Horch.

Scotty's scene in the holodeck was a magical moment, with Picard's presence on the original bridge movingly bringing the two generations of the *Star Trek* series even closer together, making all the effort well worthwhile. Along with the two-part "Best of Both Worlds," "Yesterday's *Enterprise*," and "The Inner Light," "Relics" was voted among the five best *Next Generation* episodes of all time, in a national poll taken at the end of the series' seventh season.

The episode that harkened back to *The Original Series* in terms of content was another in which Ron Moore played a part—"The Chase." With a script by Joe Menosky, from a story by Menosky and Moore, it addressed a topic that had been the subject of much discussion and debate among *Star Trek*'s devoted followers—the similarity of most alien species.

Of course, the real reason why *Star Trek* aliens look so much like humans is because of budgetary practicalities. It can cost up to $200 to apply a simple nose prosthetic to a *Star Trek* extra. Full Cardassian makeup can add $2000 to the budget per day, and they're still humanoid bipeds with a standard number of eyes. Unless there was a compelling story reason, truly alien aliens were seldom seen in the *Star Trek* universe.

During the time of *The Original Series*, though, Gene Roddenberry made a virtue of this necessity by suggesting in a few episodes that some of the planets in the galaxy had been deliberately seeded with life by an ancient and mysterious race called the Preservers. Certainly the fact that humans and Vulcans could procreate strongly implied that the two races were closely related.

In "The Chase," that premise is finally shown to be more than a possibility as it's discovered that the DNA of humans, Klingons, Cardassians, and Romulans contain deliberately engineered segments that when combined and decoded reveal a message from the long-dead race which had indeed seeded all those worlds with life.

An important mystery of the *Star Trek* universe had been cleared up, and once again the connections between the two series had grown stronger.

Other notable episodes included the two-part "Chain of Command," which served to set up the backstory of the soon-to-premiere *Deep Space Nine* by revealing that the Cardassians had withdrawn from the occupation of Bajor. The second part, especially, is called out as one of Patrick Stewart's most powerful performances as Picard endures intense torture at the hands of his Cardassian captor.

Stewart also took Picard in a new direction in the episode "Starship Mine," which was essentially a retelling of the *Die Hard* movie, set on the *Enterprise*. Trapped on his deserted vessel with six thieves intent on extracting a deadly substance from the warp engine, Picard takes on the John McClane role with relish, sneaking through the darkened ship's corridors, phaser rifle in hand, to confront the thieves one by one. It would not be until the second *Next Generation* film, *First Contact*, that Picard would assume such an action-oriented role again.

Deep Space Nine's presence was also felt in *The Next Generation*'s half of the *Star Trek* universe. In addition to "Chain of Command," another two-part episode, "Birthright," brought the *Enterprise* to the former Cardassian station. *The Next Generation*'s contributions to its sister series were featured in the pilot episode, "Emissary," in which the Battle of Wolf 359 from "The Best of Both Worlds" was re-created, and Patrick Stewart appeared as both Locutus and as Picard. And of course, Chief O'Brien and his wife, Keiko, transferred from the *Enterprise* in that first episode to take up residence on the *DS9* station.

But the true high point of the season came in a single scene in the final episode, "Descent, Part I," another season-ending cliffhanger in which a new type of Borg made its debut.

The scene in question was the opening teaser, in which Data plays poker with an assemblage of great scientists—Sir Isaac Newton, Albert Einstein, and Stephen Hawking. But in this case, Hawking wasn't a holographic reconstruction or an actor—he was the real thing.

Considered to be the leading physicist of our time, Hawking is also a *Star Trek* fan, and had suggested the possibility of appearing in a cameo while on a tour of the sets.

When he was shown the engine room with its two-story warp-engine core that could propel the starship faster than the speed of light, Hawking is reported to have said, "I'm working on that right now."

With those words of appreciation and promise from one of the world's greatest intellects, *Star Trek* was no longer merely an entertainment franchise with a solid core of "Trekkers" to support it. It had passed into the realm of world culture.

But though Gene Roddenberry's vision of the future had no more limits than the scientific imagination of Stephen Hawking, the business of syndicated television was another matter.

After six years, the continuing mission of the *Starship Enterprise* was drawing to an untimely, but inescapable, end.

Some advice for *Star Trek* fans who'd like a part on a *Star Trek* production—it helps if you're one of the leading physicists of the day. Professor Stephen Hawking as himself, during a holodeck poker game sequence in "Descent, Part I." DANNY FELD.

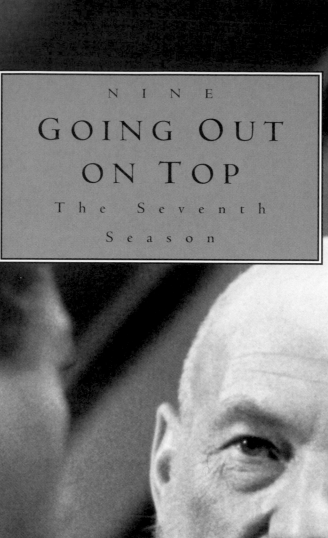

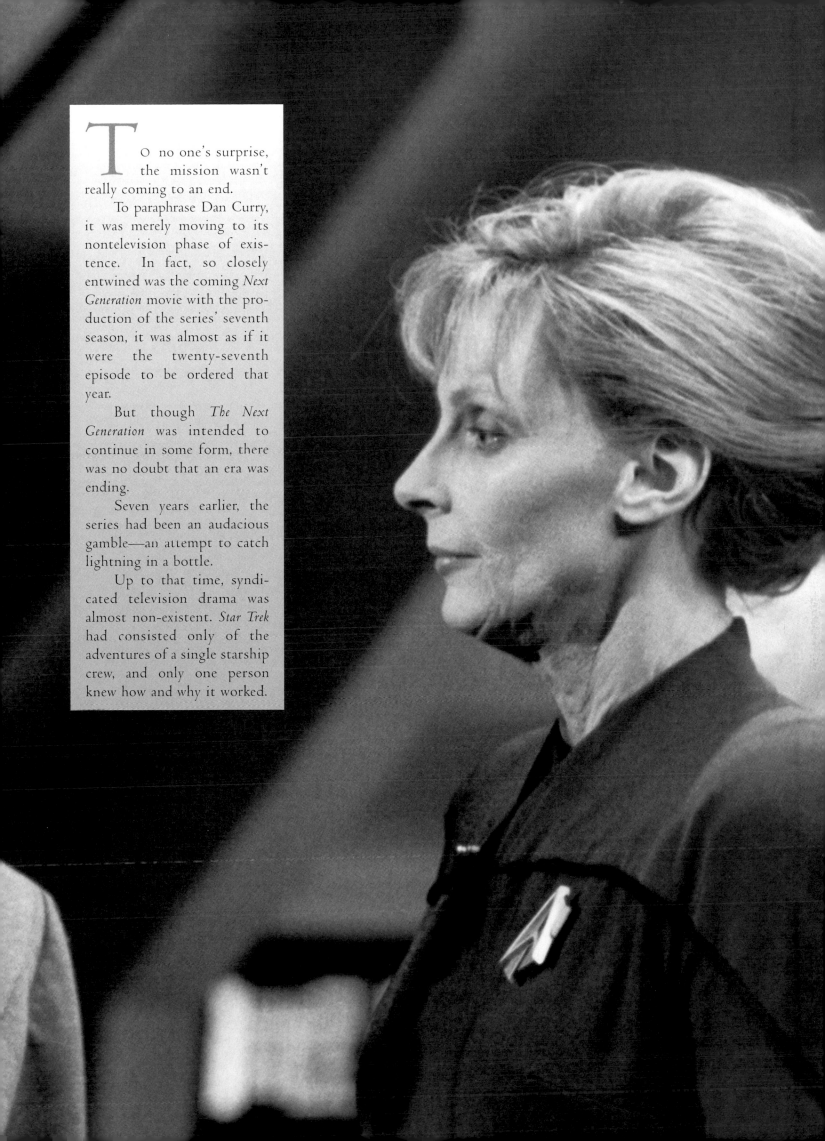

To no one's surprise, the mission wasn't really coming to an end.

To paraphrase Dan Curry, it was merely moving to its nontelevision phase of existence. In fact, so closely entwined was the coming *Next Generation* movie with the production of the series' seventh season, it was almost as if it were the twenty-seventh episode to be ordered that year.

But though *The Next Generation* was intended to continue in some form, there was no doubt that an era was ending.

Seven years earlier, the series had been an audacious gamble—an attempt to catch lightning in a bottle.

Up to that time, syndicated television drama was almost non-existent. *Star Trek* had consisted only of the adventures of a single starship crew, and only one person knew how and why it worked.

The nineties concept of cocooning—making one's home a refuge of comforting food, shelter, and entertainment options, and rarely venturing from it—seemed to be becoming a better idea every day in the United States.

In February 1993, five people were killed and hundreds injured when a terrorist bomb was detonated at New York's World Trade Center. American missiles once again flew against Baghdad in retaliation for Iraq's attempt to assassinate former President George Bush on a visit to Kuwait. Twelve U.S. soldiers died in a tragic operation in Somalia.

It was as if the whole country were trapped in *Deep Space Nine,* cringing at the nightmare evidence of the Cardassian-Bajoran conflict still exacting such a heavy toll on a devastated planet. The mood of the country was the mood of the show.

But there were real-world wonders to be seen as well. Astronauts on the space shuttle *Endeavor* performed one of the most complex spacewalks ever and successfully repaired the Hubble Space Telescope, ushering in a new era of magnificent astronomical photography. And the world of science-fiction again made its presence known at the box office with the record-setting opening of Steven Spielberg's *Jurassic Park,* based on Michael Crichton's novel.

At long last, network television began to see the light about science fiction's deep and broad appeal, and the season began with four genre series making their debuts: the comic-book inspired *Lois & Clark, seaQuest DSV,* the borderline *Adventures of Brisco County, Jr.,* and *The X-Files,* one of the few series destined to develop a diverse fan base as intensely devoted as *Star Trek's.*

The Next Generation's influence on the syndication market also could be seen in the celebrated first season of J. Michael Straczynski's *Babylon 5.* With its strong emphasis on science-fiction storylines, its ground-breaking use of sophisticated computer-generated effects, and the intriguing twist of a background story arc initially projected to run five seasons, the new series offered viewers intelligent science-fiction drama—an arena few broadcasters had been willing to consider until *The Next Generation* paved the way.

But now, seven years later, *Star Trek* was a machine. In fact, according to Supervising Producer David Livingston, that's what the production staffers called it——*The Machine.* An unstoppable phenomenon, almost Borg-like in its ability to assimilate production facilities at the Paramount lot. By the end of the seventh season, as the final episodes of *The Next Generation* were being made side by side with second-season episodes of *Deep Space Nine,* while preproduction work was under way on the feature film *Generations,* and planning began for a still-under-wraps *fourth Star Trek* series, more than five hundred people on the lot were working directly for the franchise, with hundreds more working off the lot for outside suppliers.

But though the executives who had clenched their jaws and crossed their fingers when they had given the go-ahead for the first thirteen episodes of the series would never have believed it, in the midst of this plenty *The Next Generation* had become *too* successful. As Rick Berman has said, in Hollywood "numbers" is the name of the game, and as the executives had foreseen back at the beginning of season five, those numbers had finally turned against the show.

The renegotiated fees for the actors and key creative personnel had led to an increase in the series' cost—from about $1.2 million in the first season[2] to about $2 million in the seventh.[3] That did not mean that Paramount was losing money. But it did mean the studio would be spending more to earn less, with its return on investment continuing to diminish into the future as—and *if*—*The Next Generation* continued.

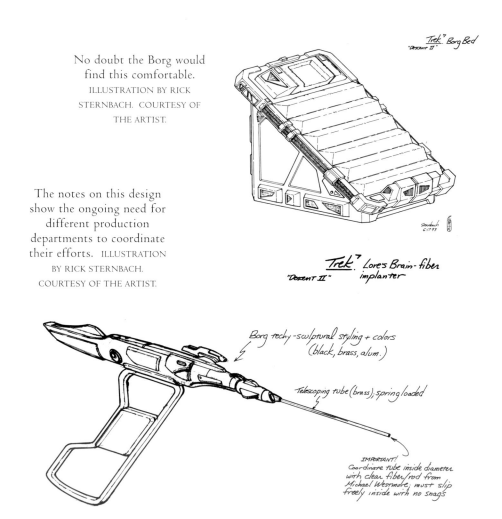

No doubt the Borg would find this comfortable. ILLUSTRATION BY RICK STERNBACH. COURTESY OF THE ARTIST.

The notes on this design show the ongoing need for different production departments to coordinate their efforts. ILLUSTRATION BY RICK STERNBACH. COURTESY OF THE ARTIST.

Behind the scenes on "Descent, Part 2." ROBBIE ROBINSON.

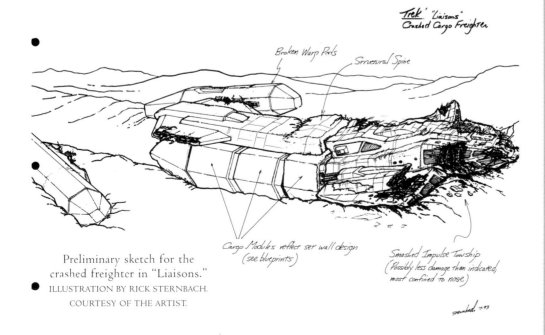

Trek "Liaisons"
Crashed Cargo Freighter

Broken Warp Pods

Structural Spine

Cargo Modules reflect set wall design
(see blueprints)

Smashed Impulse Township
(Possibly less damage than indicated,
most confined to nose)

sternbach 7-93

Preliminary sketch for the
crashed freighter in "Liaisons."
ILLUSTRATION BY RICK STERNBACH.
COURTESY OF THE ARTIST.

DESCENT, PART II
Written by René Echevarria
Directed by Alexander Singer

Picard, Troi, and La Forge are prisoners of Data, his "brother" Lore,
and a branch of the Borg originally
contaminated with individuality by
Hugh. Lore has capitalized on the
confusion the group felt at being cut
off from their brethren by offering
them a different kind of unity.
Hugh was appalled by the atrocities
Lore carried out in the name of
research, and went into hiding along
with some other Borg. Riker and
Worf are captured by this group and
convince Hugh and his followers to
help them overthrow Lore.
Meanwhile, Crusher must take the
Enterprise into a star's corona to
destroy a pursuing Borg vessel.
Hugh stops Lore from killing Data,
whose ethical program has been reac-
tivated by his crewmates. Then Data
fires upon Lore and deactivates him.
On La Forge's urging, Data recovers
Dr. Soong's emotion chip and sets it
aside for future consideration.

LIAISONS
*Teleplay by Jeanne Carrigan Fauci and
Lisa Rich
Story by Roger Eschbacher and
Jaq Greenspan
Directed by Cliff Bole*

On board the *Enterprise*, Worf and
Troi play host to two Iyaaran ambas-
sadors whose desire to experience
sensation leads them into poker and
gourmandise, respectively.
Meanwhile, on his way to meet the
Iyaaran leader, Picard's shuttle crash-
lands on an inhospitable planet and
Picard's Iyaaran pilot is rendered
unconscious. Picard finds himself
being cared for by a mysterious
human woman who says she is a
crash survivor herself from seven
years back. Although she claims to
love him, Picard turns against her
after he realizes she is trying to keep
him captive on the planet. Picard
soon discovers that the "woman" is
really the Iyaaran pilot, who was only
using him, as Worf and Troi were
being used on the *Enterprise*, to
experience emotional sensation.

INTERFACE
Written by Joe Menosky
Directed by Robert Wiemer

Using a remote-"reality" interface that works with his VISOR inputs, La Forge works to retrieve a Federation vessel trapped within a gas giant's volatile atmosphere. On his first run, he finds the crew of the *Raman* dead. Incredibly, on his second run, he sees his mother, Captain Silva La Forge, who had been presumed lost along with her ship, the *U.S.S. Hera*. Refusing to accept that he may be suffering hallucinations, La Forge defies Picard's orders, to do as his "mother" asks: take the *Raman* into the lower levels of the planet's atmosphere, where Silva says the *Hera* is trapped. After he does so, Geordi instead finds that his "mother" is actually one of the planet's fire-based life-forms who'd been trapped aboard the *Raman* with others of its kind. The fire aliens must return to the lower levels if they are to survive. Though he realizes he is not dealing with his mother, La Forge helps them, and his rash actions are eventually understood and forgiven by Picard.

But the switch to movie production offered the chance of elevating the earnings potential of *The Next Generation* considerably. With an anticipated approximate cost of $30 million for a two-hour movie,[4] plus an additional expenditure of about $15 million to release the film (to pay for prints, promotion, and advertising), Paramount might actually spend less than what another season would cost. In an era of blockbusters, it was not inconceivable that if a *Next Generation* movie could reach at least the not impossible box office goal of $90 million in the domestic market, of which the studio would receive approximately half, the cost of the film would be covered. Paramount would then be well on its way to earning far more than $17 million from foreign box-office, home video, pay television, and network television receipts. And, of course, *The Next Generation* movie would be a perfect replacement for the now-discontinued *Original Series* movies.

In the meantime, the success of *Deep Space Nine* had established that the television audience could support two *Star Trek* series at the same time. Consequently, the studio reasoned that still another *Star Trek* series could take to the air to replace *The Next Generation*, come in at a lower production cost, and thus generate the higher earnings above cost that *The Next Generation* had once brought in.

But as sound as Paramount's rationale was for the studio's bottom line, for *The Next Generation*'s most devoted fans it was a controversial move. To those members of *Star Trek*'s audience who would much rather have had twenty-six new *Next Generation* episodes each year for five or six more seasons, the business strategy underlying Paramount's decision to stop production of the series seemed callous and cynical. They feared mere money was getting in the way of Gene Roddenberry's vision of the future.

But over the preceding fourteen years, it was that same careful business management which had brought forth *The Original Series* movies, and nurtured *The Next Generation*'s success. Even *The Original Series* itself had arisen from the belief that NBC could make money by selling advertising on the series and that Desilu Studios could make money on syndicating the series after its network run. So, contrary to the fans' fears, business concerns were not getting in the way of Gene Roddenberry's vision of the future—it was those same concerns which had brought that vision to the public in the first place. Paramount's new direction for *The Next Generation* was simply the next in a long line of decisions that had originally helped create the *Star Trek* phenomenon, making it available to all its tens of millions of fans for more than twenty-seven years.

Ironically, once it was announced that the seventh season of *The Next Generation* would be the last, ratings climbed again, prompting an increase in the cost of advertising on the series, making it the highest-earning season ever.

In the fifth season, *Variety*—a movie and television industry daily news publication—gave the quoted price for buying a thirty-second national commercial spot on the series as $100,000.[2] According to the same report, Leonard Nimoy's guest appearance as Spock on the two-part episode "Unification" doubled that price to $200,000.[2] But to buy the same commercial time on the final episode of the seventh season, the projected audience figures gave rise to a price of *$700,000!*[3] If Paramount executives had thought they could reach that level of earning all the time, the series would have been renewed until the real twenty-fourth century.

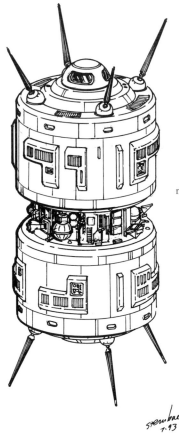

Initial design for the remote telepresence probe from "Interface."
ILLUSTRATION BY RICK STERNBACH. COURTESY OF THE ARTIST.

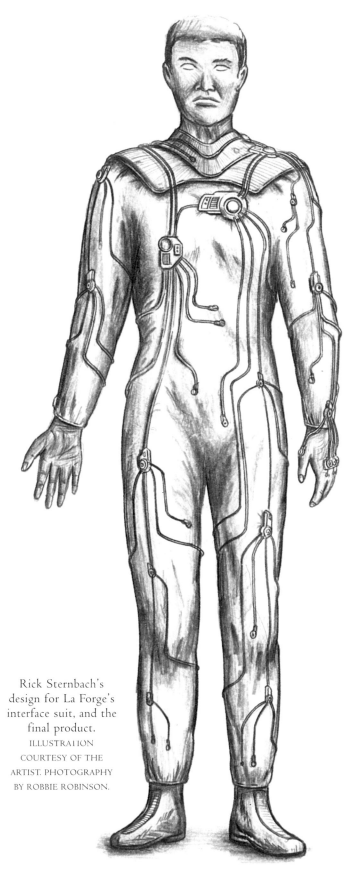

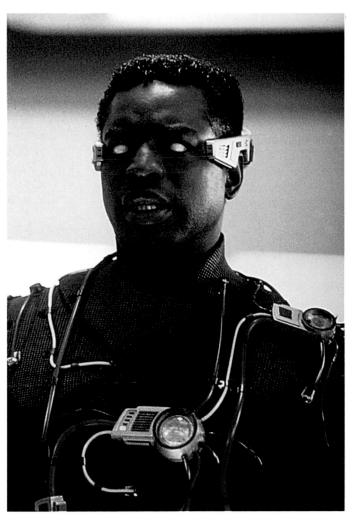

Rick Sternbach's design for La Forge's interface suit, and the final product.
ILLUSTRATION COURTESY OF THE ARTIST. PHOTOGRAPHY BY ROBBIE ROBINSON.

Picard undercover as a renegade archaeologist. ROBBIE ROBINSON.

SEASON SEVEN: EPISODE 156

GAMBIT, PART I

Teleplay by Naren Shankar
Story by Christopher Hatton and Naren Shankar
Directed by Peter Lauritson

While pursuing his archaeological interests, Picard is kidnapped by archaeological looters, who make it appear that he was disintegrated in a bar fight. Intent on justice, Riker pursues the criminals and is himself attacked and kidnapped by a band of mercenaries led by the smuggler, Arctus Baran. When Riker regains consciousness, he is on Baran's ship, wearing one of Baran's controlling pain-inducer devices. Amazingly, Picard is still alive, traveling with the band, though posing as a smuggler. Following a covert signal from Picard, Riker gains the trust of the band leader by "repairing" an engine deliberately damaged by Picard. Meanwhile, Data discovers the raiders' interest in Romulan ruins and follows the attackers to Calder II, where Riker unexpectedly orders the *Enterprise* to lower its shields and Baran forces Picard to fire on the *Enterprise*.

Baran's gang of archaeological raiders from the two-part episode "Gambit." PHOTOGRAPH BY ROBBIE ROBINSON.

After seven seasons, the long quest for the perfect Starfleet shuttlecraft had ended. Which meant it was time to take on the design of a Klingon shuttle. ILLUSTRATION BY RICK STERNBACH. COURTESY OF THE ARTIST.

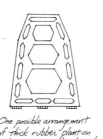

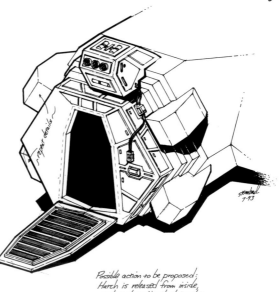

Trek⁷ "Gambit II"
Klingon Shuttle Aft Details

Corrugated
small plantons

Phaser Block Detail
Trapezoidal c.s.

One possible arrangement of thick rubber plant-on pads to protect hatch and shuttlebay floor.

Possible action to be proposed; Hatch is released from inside, makes dramatic thud to the floor, and then out steps the towering Klingon.

NBA star James Worthy gave a towering performance as the Klingon Koral, in "Gambit, Part II." ROBBIE ROBINSON.

GAMBIT, PART II
Teleplay by Ronald D. Moore
Story by Naren Shankar
Directed by Alexander Singer

Picard and Riker, while prisoners on Baran's ship, work together to stage a harmless yet convincing attack on the *Enterprise*. Data lets the pirates escape, having been tipped as to their next stop by Riker. On board Baran's ship, a Vulcan agent posing as a Romulan discovers that Picard is not a smuggler and reveals that the mercenaries, and she, are after an ancient psionic superweapon. The mercenaries raid the *Enterprise* for part of the weapon held by a Klingon contact detained on the vessel, after which the mercenaries' leader orders Riker to kill Picard. Instead, Picard "stuns" Riker. The Vulcan agent exposes Picard, but Picard reveals that she is actually a Vulcan isolationist out to destroy Vulcan's leaders and unwanted visitors. The dissident uses the negative-thought weapon to kill the mercenaries. Alerted by Picard, the crew of the *Enterprise* save their captain and the Vulcan government destroys the device.

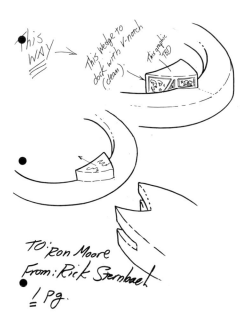

TO: Ron Moore
From: Rick Sternbach
1 pg.

In addition to preparing detailed drawings to serve as guides for the prop makers, Rick Sternbach sometimes would also make quick sketches for the writers to suggest ways in which the props might be used. ILLUSTRATIONS COURTESY OF THE ARTIST.

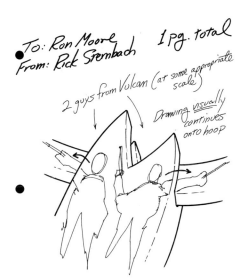

To: Ron Moore
From: Rick Sternbach   1 pg. total

2 guys from Vulcan (at some appropriate scale)

Drawing visually continues onto hoop

PHANTASMS
Written by Brannon Braga
Directed by Patrick Stewart

After La Forge installs a new warp core that fails, Data begins to experience nightmares that eventually provoke him to stab Troi. However, Crusher discovers that Troi's shoulder wound holds the possible solution to both the faulty warp core and Data's behavioral aberrations. Troi and many other members of the crew are infested with alien interphasic life-forms that act as leeches, drawing out cellular peptides from their hosts. Suspecting that Data's dreamworld holds the solution to eliminating the alien parasites, Picard and La Forge connect the holodeck to Data's dream program. Data, now awake, drives away the aliens with a high-frequency interphasic pulse, and frees himself from the disturbing dream images caused by their attacks on the crew and the warp core.

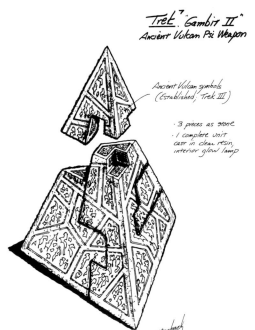

Trek "Gambit II"
Ancient Vulcan Psi Weapon

Ancient Vulcan symbols (Established, Trek III)

· 3 pieces as stone
· 1 complete unit cast in clear resin, interior glow lamp

sternbach 7-93

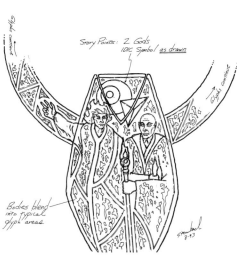

Story Points: 2 Gods
IDIC Symbol as drawn

Glyphs continue

Glyphs continue

Bodies blend into typical glyph areas.

sternbach 8-93

DARK PAGE
Written by Hilary J. Bader
Directed by Les Landau

Troi battles to save her mother's life when Lwaxana Troi falls into a coma induced by a psychic-trauma, the result of a triggered repressed memory. With the help of a member of a telepathic nonverbal species whom Lwaxana had been tutoring, Troi enters her mother's mind. There she encounters mental barriers in the form of Picard, a wolf, and her father, all of which try to dissuade her from learning something that occurred in her mother's past. When Troi discovers that her mother is still suffering guilt from the drowning death of a child who was Troi's older sister, she helps Lwaxana face and let go of the traumatic memory.

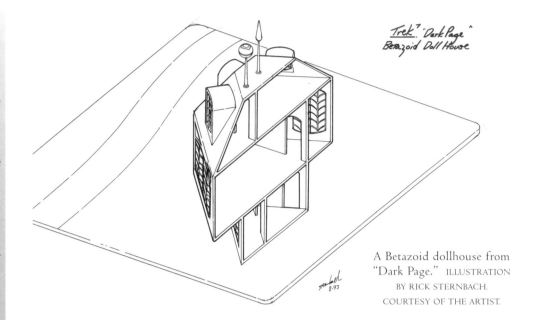

Trek: "Dark Page" Betazoid Doll House

A Betazoid dollhouse from "Dark Page." ILLUSTRATION BY RICK STERNBACH. COURTESY OF THE ARTIST.

But as the saying—and the title—goes, all good things must come to an end. And once again, though it had an expert and experienced creative staff and production team, *The Next Generation* was denied the chance to have just an ordinary season. In addition to everyone's usual responsibilities, for Producer Ron Moore and Co-Producer Brannon Braga there was a feature script to write; for the rest of the writing staff, there were loose ends to tie up; for the cast, movie negotiations to be suffered through; and for Rick Berman, Michael Piller, and Jeri Taylor, a new series to create.

In technical terms, the seventh was one of the best seasons yet. But on the stages and behind the scenes, as the season moved toward the final episode and the demands on everyone's time and energy increased, tension mounted.

Fortunately, the strong sense of family and very real friendship among *The Next Generation*'s company of players helped insulate them from what might have been a year of nerve-racking distraction.

Looking back on their journey from the first season to the seventh, Jonathan Frakes recalls that "as a breed, actors become family immediately. I think that's because actors are nomads by nature, and we bond fast and stay together." Part of that nomadic nature comes from the grueling search for work that is part of every actor's life in Hollywood. "You know," Frakes says, "pounding the pavement, going from guest spot to guest spot, and failed pilot to failed pilot."

For most of the actors, then, to have achieved the rare treasure of a steady job on *The Next Generation* was a thrilling accomplishment. To then have their natural inclination to form a close professional arrangement heightened by seven years of success made the unit even stronger.

Michael Dorn recalls the moment when that strong sense of community became established for the cast. "Probably the midway point in the first season. It was really tough for me because I was the last guy cast, so I was like the new kid on the block. The others had been cast for months before I was brought on. When I started my first interviews, they had just started working."

ROBBIE ROBINSON.

Over the seven-year run of the series, a strong sense of family and friendship grew among the cast.

KIM GOTTLIEB-WALKER

Picard and Crusher are tele-pathically linked on Kes-Prytt.
ROBBIE ROBINSON.

SEASON SEVEN: EPISODE 160
ATTACHED
Written by Nicholas Sagan
Directed by Jonathan Frakes

The Kes of the planet Kes-Prytt peti-tion the Federation for membership, despite the fact that another group on their planet, the Prytt, are against their application. While en route to meet the Kes, Picard and Crusher are captured by the Prytt. They escape, but discover that they have been implanted with devices that enforce a telepathic link between them. Any attempt to separate causes them to become ill. Their forced intimacy leads Crusher to learn that Picard suppressed his love for her when she joined his crew, because of his guilt over the death of her husband, Jack. Riker resolves the standoff between the Kes and the Prytt when he tells the Kes their membership bid will be denied and then tells the Prytt that Starfleet will forcibly insist on the return of Picard and Crusher. In the meantime, Crusher becomes the one to set the course of her relationship with Picard. For now, she chooses friendship.

Dorn remembers that as the newcomer, he at first felt left out of the cama-raderie that had already begun to develop among the cast, "but around mid-point, I started to enjoy it. Then by the end of the first season, it was a pretty neat thing. And it grew." Dorn laughs as he admits, "I mean, by the fifth sea-son, it had gotten out of hand."

Dorn confirms that the cast, unshakably secure from having worked so well together for so long, eventually developed a reputation for being a trifle "unruly" for certain first-time directors to work with. "We're a wild group of actors," he says. "I mean, a *really* wild group. Though it's hard to describe if you're not there." Dorn credits the mood on the set to the cast's predilection for "hijinks."

"Everybody on the show is a riot to be around," he says. "We're not prac-

Seven alternate-universe Worfs converge in a complex scene from "Parallels."

tical jokers, but we have a good time." One can but wonder whether or not directors shared that assessment when faced with a cast that would occasionally and seemingly spontaneously break into a song-and-dance show-tune number in the midst of a serious scene.

In a moment of philosophical introspection, Michael Dorn and Brent Spiner decided that there was a simple explanation for why the company developed its reputation for being hard on some first-time directors. "We're like animals," Dorn says. "We can smell fear."

It wasn't necessarily first-time directors who received the unruly treatment. Dorn continues, "I think we were pretty tough on directors who didn't pay attention to who we were. We all have a certain way of doing things. We know our characters very well from the start. And we were always very critical actors—perfectionists—because we had to be. We were very comfortable with our characters, and we knew them, and we weren't going to go out of character for anyone.

"For the most part, we had some wonderful directors and first-time directors who were very good, so we weren't hard on all first-timers. But if you came in thinking that you were going to enforce your will on these people, I think you were really asking for trouble. We were a tough group."

The "tough group" image only applied to those on the outside, though, because the chemistry viewers glimpsed on the screen among the *Next Generation* company was and is very real behind the scenes as well.

Reflecting on her years with her fellow cast members, Marina Sirtis says, "I think I'm one of the very few actors who has never had a bad experience with a company she works with." Sirtis agrees with Frakes that actors form families quickly, but for her, the fact that *The Next Generation* company has remained close for so long is rare.

"We began to realize it when people would say to us, 'You go out to parties, and you go out to functions, and to first-nights and premieres, and you don't talk to anyone else! You guys just stick together and talk to each other.'

"We were very cliquey," Sirtis admits. "We just had this nucleus and we didn't want to venture out from it. But I don't know why that happened." Sirtis says that in some way the relationship among the cast reminded her of a repertory company. "But usually with a repertory company, you're together a few months and then you swear to keep in touch and you never do. But with these people, we all live very close to each other so we see each other all the time."

Clearly, the closeness that exists among the company as a united group of actors adds extra impact to their portrayal of a united crew of a starship.

LeVar Burton believes that chemistry has its roots in the characters the actors portray. "I think all of these characters represent archetypes, aspects of the whole self. You can look at all of these characters and find an aspect of them that you relate to, as a whole being yourself.

"These people are just reflections of ourselves. Geordi is that part of us that is more loose, more relaxed, really loving life in a very freewheeling, uninhibited sort of way. Just as Picard is that aspect of us that is the father figure, authority figure, politician."

Without that archetypal foundation, Burton believes the characters would not have worked as well as they did. And that foundation is what enabled the chemistry among the actors to come to the fore.

"Within each of us hired to play these parts," he says, "there was a magic. There was an indefinable chemistry. There was something that cannot be orchestrated on a conscious level that just *happened.* You can't create it, you can't plan on it. You can hope for it, but I don't think in their wildest imaginings that the producers ever anticipated the chemistry working as well as it did. I don't think that kind of chemistry happens often, and so to expect it going in would be silly."

The company of *Next Generation* actors is larger than just the cast of seven regulars, including Denise Crosby, Whoopi Goldberg, and Wil Wheaton. Over the seasons, many actors in recurring roles felt themselves admitted to the exclusive club, by the openness of the regulars and the appreciation of the fans: Majel Barrett-Roddenberry as Lwaxana Troi; Brian Bonsall as Alexander (first played by Jon Steuer); Rosalind Chao as Keiko O'Brien; Daniel Davis as the holographic Professor Moriarty; Michelle Forbes as Ensign Ro; Andreas Katsulas as Romulan Commander Tomalak; Colm Meaney as Chief O'Brien; Eric Menyuk as the Traveler; Robert O'Reilly as Gowron; Suzie Plakson as K'Ehleyr and Dr. Selar; Dwight Shultz as Reg Barclay; Carel Struycken as Lwaxana's aide, Mr. Homn; Doug Wert as Jack Crusher; and Patti Yasutake as Alyssa Ogawa.

But of all the recurring characters in *The Next Generation,* the unquestionable favorite was John de Lancie in his role as Q, a part he played in ten episodes over seven years.

In terms of being part of the *Next Generation* family, de Lancie likens his position as being "like the wayward merchant marine uncle who visits the family once a year to the delight of the children and the horror of the parents."

Worf as first officer to Captain Riker in an alternate universe.
ROBBIE ROBINSON.

SEASON SEVEN: EPISODE 163
PARALLELS
Written by Brannon Braga
Directed by Robert Wiemer

When Worf begins to slip out of phase with the "real" universe, the Data and Wesley of the alternate existence discover a quantum fissure. Somehow the fissure, which is aggravated by La Forge's VISOR, has trapped Worf.

While he struggles to return to his own universe, Worf finds himself in many different existences, including some in which he is married to Troi, Cardassians kill La Forge, the Borg kill Picard, and Riker destroys himself and his *Enterprise* rather than return to Borg domination. When militant Bajorans further damage the fissure, dozens of Worfs and hundreds of *Enterprises* encounter one another as Worf flies his shuttlecraft home through the rift, sealing it.

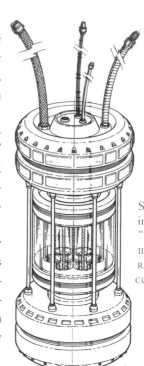

SEASON SEVEN: EPISODE 164

THE PEGASUS
Written by Ronald D. Moore
Directed by LeVar Burton

Riker faces an old cover-up when the *Enterprise* locates the *Pegasus*, the long-lost ship on which Riker served under Erik Pressman. After Picard takes his ship inside an asteroid to salvage the *Pegasus*, Pressman, now an admiral, tells Riker he plans to resume the unauthorized test that trapped their old ship and killed much of its crew. In defiance of a Federation treaty with the Romulans, the *Pegasus* was testing a cloaking device that permitted ships to pass through solid rock. When pursuing Romulans trap the *Enterprise* in the fissure, Riker tells Picard Pressman's secret and Picard uses the device to free the *Enterprise*. Picard alerts the Romulans to the treaty infraction and arrests Pressman.

SEASON SEVEN: EPISODE 165

HOMEWARD
Teleplay by Naren Shankar
Television story by Spike Steingasser
Based upon material by William N. Stape
Directed by Alexander Singer

Worf's human foster brother, Nicolai, a cultural observer, intervenes to save a people on a planet whose atmosphere is disappearing. Without Picard's approval, Nicolai beams the threatened people, including the mother of his unborn child, to the *Enterprise*'s holodeck re-creation of their cave shelters. Nicolai's plan to transport them, still unaware of their planet's destruction, to a new planet is disrupted when one of the natives leaves the holodeck and discovers the truth. Unable to cope with the knowledge, he commits suicide. Picard's crew locates a suitable new planet just before the atmospheric storms cause failure of the holodeck. Although Nicolai's violation of the Prime Directive disturbs Picard, Worf and his brother are ultimately able to reach an understanding.

By portraying a recurring character, de Lancie did not become as swept up in the *Star Trek* phenomenon as the regular cast, but *The Next Generation* did have its effect on him.

"I have very good memories and feelings about *Star Trek: The Next Generation*," de Lancie says, "and I have been taken aback by the enormous level of achievement, competence, talent, and skill of the people associated with it.

"I came in as someone who really didn't have much of a sense about *Star Trek*'s popularity, but if there had ever been a television series that I were ever to have wanted to be a regular on, this would have been it if for no other reason than it's so deeply loved."

In fact, John de Lancie recalls that his experience with *The Next Generation* was so positive when he learned the seventh season was to be the series' last, "It's the only time I actually felt motivated and sentimental enough to go to Rick and say, 'You know I've never asked you for a job, but I did the first episode, and I understand you're doing a two-hour last episode, and I'd love to be in that.'

De Lancie remembers that Rick Berman replied with amusement, " 'Say no more. You're already in it anyway, whether you like it or not.' "

An illegal Starfleet cloaking device from "The Pegasus." ILLUSTRATION BY RICK STERNBACH. COURTESY OF THE ARTIST.

After seven years, Michael Dorn at last got the chance to perform without his Klingon make-up in "Homeward," an episode in which Worf was altered to appear human. ROBBIE ROBINSON.

De Lancie attributes a great deal of Q's popularity with the *Star Trek* audience to the writing. "The people who have written the Q episodes have worked extra hard to make those episodes good. They recognize that for reasons that probably none of us truly knows, this character is a little larger than life, and they rise to the occasion in the same way I feel the responsibility to rise to the occasion.

"I don't take an opportunity of having a role like this lightly, and I know that the writers don't, either."

To many *Star Trek* fans, Q's appeal is inextricably bound to the fact that he was originally conceived by Gene Roddenberry. Indeed, the idea of an omnipotent alien who sits in judgment of humanity has been a recurring motif in *Star Trek*, especially in *The Original Series*. By including Q in *The Next*

Generation's final episode, writers Ron Moore and Brannon Braga not only brought closure to the television phase of the series, but paid respectful homage to *Star Trek*'s creator.

With the same fondness, de Lancie remembers two conversations in particular he had with Gene Roddenberry. The first was right after de Lancie's audition for the role. "Gene said, 'You make my words sound better than they are.' Which was a very generous thing for him to say."

Then de Lancie remembers being with Roddenberry on the set of the first *Next Generation* episode. "We were shooting and I heard a voice behind me say, 'You have no idea what you have gotten yourself into.' I turned around, and it was Gene. I asked, 'What do you mean?' And all he said was, 'Oh, you'll see.'"

In the years since, de Lancie has come to understand what Roddenberry meant as he has been swept up in appearances at *Star Trek* conventions. To de Lancie, those conventions are part and parcel of the actor's experience.

"A convention is not unlike the backstage door. You finish the show, you take off your makeup, and you walk out. But when you open the backstage door, there are three or four people there who want to talk about the play they've just seen.

"And when I was younger and had the time, sometimes I'd say, 'A couple of us are going over to Harry's Bar down the street. Why don't you join us? We'd love to hear what you have to say.' Conventions are the same thing."

For *The Next Generation*, after seven years the conversation between the audience and those who made the series continued, stronger than ever.

In some ways, *Star Trek: The Next Generation* was just beginning.

The episodes in that final year began as an unsettled mix of stand-alone stories and those which acknowledged that *The Next Generation* was on the brink of a profound change.

Setting up a story point to be explored in *Generations*, Data emerged from the conclusion of the "Descent" cliffhanger with an emotion chip, though he would not install it until the movie. In "Interface," La Forge, who was the last of the regular characters to have his backstory explored in detail, conversed with his father, played by Ben Vereen, and his mother—at least, an alien duplicate of his mother—played by Madge Sinclair.

The long-simmering attraction between Picard and Dr. Crusher was acknowledged in "Attached," written by Nicholas Sagan, son of famed and sorely missed astronomer Carl Sagan.

A notable change-of-pace

Ben Vereen as Commander Edward M. La Forge, Geordi's father, in "Interface."
ROBBIE ROBINSON.

Crusher learns unsuspected family secrets on Caldos IV.
ROBBIE ROBINSON.

SEASON SEVEN: EPISODE 166
SUB ROSA
Teleplay by Brannon Braga
Television story by Jeri Taylor
Based upon material by Jeanna F. Gallo
Directed by Jonathan Frakes

Following her maternal grandmother's funeral on Caldos IV, Crusher becomes the latest conquest of Ronin, the mysterious young lover of the women of her family for the past 800 years. Pursuaded to take her grandmother's place as healer on the planet, Crusher resigns from Starfleet. But when Picard investigates sabotage of the planet's weather net, Crusher learns the truth. Ronin is a noncorporeal, anaphasic life-form, drawing life and physical form from Crusher's family, a special candle, and the planet's weather net. Crusher then destroys the candle and her lover.

LOWER DECKS

Teleplay by René Echevarria
Story by Ronald Wilkerson &
Jean Louise Matthias
Directed by Gabrielle Beaumont

Picard, Riker, and Worf evaluate four crewmen facing competition for promotion and choose three of them for a top-secret mission. Worf successfully schools Ensign Sito Jaxa's progress in combat techniques, but Picard undermines her confidence by reminding the young ensign of her involvement in the Academy cover-up regarding Wesley Crusher's flight team. Riker is at odds with Lieutenant Sam Lavelle, whose nature closely resembles his own. Lieutenant Ogawa and Lieutenant Taurik, a Vulcan, complete their mission roles and are promoted. Jaxa pleases Picard by standing up to him and volunteering for a dangerous undercover assignment, but loses her life. Though saddened by Jaxa's death, Lavelle is promoted and receives comfort from his remaining friends.

episode by René Echevarria, "Lower Decks," focused on some of the thousand-plus other crew members who toiled in parts of the *Enterprise* other than the bridge. And in "Journey's End," Wesley Crusher, perhaps the most problematic of *The Next Generation*'s semi-regular characters, received a fitting send-off, reuniting him with the enigmatic alien known as the Traveler, who had appeared in the first season to say that Wesley faced a unique destiny.

Just as Season Six had incorporated background information about the Cardassians and the Bajorans to help set up the backstory of *Deep Space Nine,* the seventh season was given the task of helping in part to set up the next *Star Trek* series, *Voyager,* with "Preemptive Strike," a story involving the rebel settlers known as the Maquis.

This penultimate episode featured the return of Michelle Forbes as now-Lieutenant Ro, the Bajoran Starfleet officer with an edge, first introduced in Season Five.

Forbes's character had been so popular with *Star Trek* fans that Berman and Piller had planned to include her as a regular character in *Deep Space Nine,* well into the preproduction stages. But Forbes chose to pursue her career in feature films, and, like Denise Crosby and Wil Wheaton before her, turned down a chance to be part of an ongoing *Star Trek* series. On *Deep Space Nine,* Ro was replaced by the new character of Major Kira.

Finally, the time came for the last *Next Generation* episode, aptly titled "All Good Things … ." Fittingly, it was one of the finest installments of the series.

The two-part episode, in which the time-jumping Picard spanned more than thirty years from the past to the future, called for heroic efforts from every member of the production team, and every member came through brilliantly.

Most under the gun at the beginning were Ron Moore and Brannon Braga. Throughout the season they had juggled their writing duties on the series with

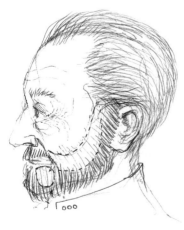

Michael Westmore's sketches planning the aging makeup to be used on LeVar Burton, Jonathan Frakes, and Gates McFadden in "All Good Things … ." COURTESY OF THE ARTIST.

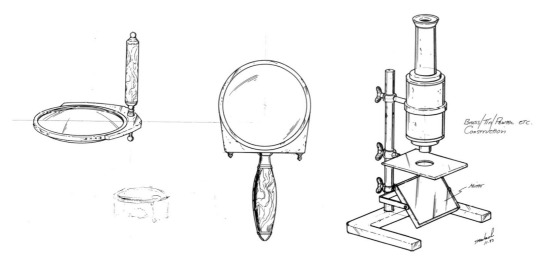

Designs for Data's rudimentary scientific apparatus in "Thine Own Self."
ILLUSTRATION BY RICK STERNBACH. COURTESY OF THE ARTIST.

Data and Gia, played by Kimberly Cullum, on Barkon IV.
ROBBIE ROBINSON.

SEASON SEVEN: EPISODE 168
THINE OWN SELF
Teleplay by Ronald D. Moore
Story by Christopher Hatton
Directed by Winrich Kolbe

Suffering from amnesia, Data makes new friends and enemies on a pre-industrial planet where he was sent to recover a wrecked radioactive probe. Without realizing it, Data infects the townsfolk with radiation sickness from the probe's debris and, true to his nature, begins work on finding the cause and the cure. At the same time, the town healer determines that Data is the source of the strange sickness and the townsfolk attack him. Before they "kill" him, Data discovers he is an android. When Riker and Crusher locate and reactivate him, they find out that Data had worked out the cure and saved the townsfolk. During the same time interval, Troi learns more about herself when she takes the bridge officer's test and passes it only after facing the necessity of a crew member's death.

their ongoing work on the feature script *Generations*. And then, with the complexity of the final episode requiring a major shift in production schedule, they were faced with less than a week to write a first draft—a process that normally would take place over a month.

The other demands on the rest of the production team were equally pressure-ridden. For the scenes set back at the time of the first episode, original sets and costumes had to be re-created, and old props and set decorations tracked down and hauled out of storage. For the scenes set twenty-five years in a possible future, new sets and costumes were required, in addition to new ships, and new "aged" makeup designs for the actors.

Underlying everything was the knowledge that this was the last outing. Television production is an ongoing process, and anything that is less than perfect one week can be corrected in the next week. But there would be no more "next week"s. Everyone worked on the episode with the desire to make it

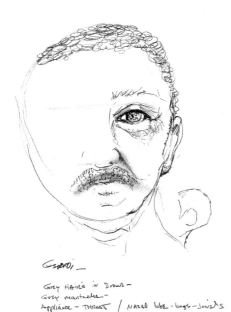

GSPARDI —
GRAY HAIRS IN BROWS —
GRAY MUSTACHE —
APPLIANCE — THROAT / NASAL LOBE—BAGS—JOWLS

Worf, twenty-five years older, in "All Good Things ... ." ROBBIE ROBINSON.

SEASON SEVEN: EPISODE 169
MASKS
Written by Joe Menosky
Directed by Robert Wiemer

When the *Enterprise* encounters the comet-based archive of an ancient society, Data suddenly assumes multiple, masked personalities from that culture. At the same time, the *Enterprise* undergoes a transformation of its own, assuming the settings of the ancient world, including its temple. By the time Picard gives the order to destroy the archive it is too late; they will have to deal with the program at its own level. After La Forge finds the archive's transformational program, Picard assumes one of the masked personas. He and the crew have discovered that the lead personalities are a pair of gods who, like the sun and moon, "chase" one another from the temple throne. Picard "chases" Data from the throne, restoring both Data and the ship to their customary states.

SEASON SEVEN: EPISODE 170
EYE OF THE BEHOLDER
Teleplay by René Echevarria
Story by Brannon Braga
Directed by Cliff Bole

Worf and Troi investigate the inexplicable suicide of Lieutenant Kwan, a young crew member on board the *Enterprise*. An empathic echo at the scene of Kwan's death suddenly gives Troi a glimpse of a frightened woman, her lover, and a threatening man in the same area of the *Enterprise*, but as it was eight years earlier, while the ship was under construction. She subsequently encounters the second man, Walter Pierce, on the *Enterprise* and he becomes the third, disruptive party in her recently initiated intimacy with Worf. Only after she "shoots" Worf in a jealous rage, and the real Worf stops her from committing suicide just as Kwan had, does she realize that she has experienced the tragic scenario only in her mind. Pierce, who was partially empathic, left the trace that affected Troi eight years later.

In the possible future of "All Good Things ... ," Dr. Crusher has command of her own vessel, the hospital ship *Pasteur*. ROBBIE ROBINSON.

Reflecting one possible future, the extensively refitted *Enterprise*, from "All Good Things ... ." COURTESY OF GREG JEIN.

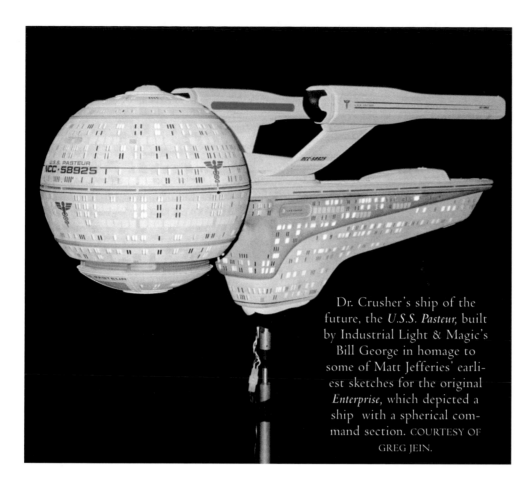

Dr. Crusher's ship of the future, the *U.S.S. Pasteur*, built by Industrial Light & Magic's Bill George in homage to some of Matt Jefferies' earliest sketches for the original *Enterprise*, which depicted a ship with a spherical command section. COURTESY OF GREG JEIN.

SEASON SEVEN: EPISODE 171
GENESIS
Written by Brannon Braga
Directed by Gates McFadden

The injection of a synthetic T-cell creates a new disease—Barclay's Protomorphosic Syndrome—which infects all but Data and Picard, who are off-ship, and causes the crew of the *Enterprise* to begin deevolving. Somehow the cell activates long-dormant introns in the crew, causing them to revert to much earlier forms of life. Barclay begins to turn into a spider; Worf, a primitive Klingon beast; Troi, an amphibian; Riker, an apelike proto-human. A pregnant Spot delivers normal kittens, but she herself becomes an iguana. Data successfully uses this information to work out the cure and restore the crew, while Picard, though beginning his own transformation, fends off the unruly crew-monsters.

perfect. And in the view of the vast majority of *The Next Generation*'s fans, they succeeded.

For those who enjoyed the big science-fiction ideas of *Star Trek,* once again the fate of humanity hung in the balance, not just in the future, but throughout all time. Once again, Jean-Luc Picard faced Q in the same post-apocalyptic court in which they had first encountered each other, seven years earlier, in the series' pilot.

For those who enjoyed *Star Trek*'s science-fiction action-adventure side, a new Klingon cruiser engaged a retrofitted, three-engined *Enterprise.* And Captain Beverly Crusher's medical vessel, the *Pasteur,* built as a labor of love by Industrial Light & Magic's Bill George, was based in part on never-used sketches for the original *Enterprise,* drawn thirty years earlier.

Finally, on March 31, 1994, six years and ten months since the first day of principal photography on "Encounter at Farpoint," the cast of *The Next Generation* gathered together in the same set for the final scene of the episode, the final scene in which they would all appear together on the television screen.

Then, for the first time, Captain Picard joined his crew in their regular poker game, first introduced in Season Two. And as the captain dealt his first hand, he spoke the episode's and the series' final words.

Words full of promise for all that was still to come.

"The sky's the limit."

"It was the most emotional moment of the series for me," Marina Sirtis recalls. "It was just so charged, so intense."

Yet unlike the last scene for so many other long-running series, when the

Picard confronts Gul Evek, played by
Richard Poe, over the fate of the
Dorvan V colony. DANNY FELD.

SEASON SEVEN: EPISODE 172
JOURNEY'S END
Written by Ronald D. Moore
Based on material by Shawn Piller &
Antonio Napoli
Directed by Corey Allen

Wesley Crusher finds his true destiny on a planet whose Indian colonists are being forced to evacuate to satisfy the terms of a new Federation-Cardassian peace treaty. While Picard tries unsuccessfully to dissuade the Federation Council from forcing the evacuation, Wesley encounters an Indian colonist who later turns out to be the Traveler, the transdimensional being, who is still interested in Wesley's destiny. After Wesley alerts the colonists to Starfleet's planned surprise mass beam-out, he resigns from Starfleet, citing a message from his late father, who appeared to him in a vision and told him to seek his own future. Picard picks up the pieces with the Federation, the Cardassians, and the colonists. The colonists decide to remain on the planet, under Cardassian rather than Federation supervision.

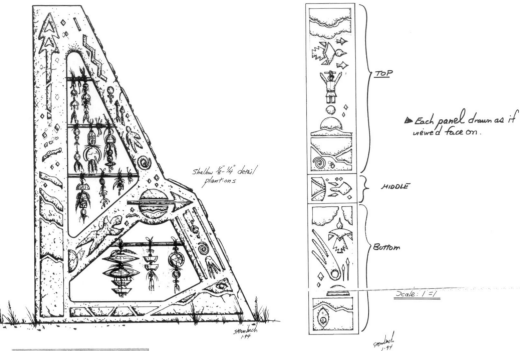

Shallow ⅛-¼" detail plantions

TOP

Each panel drawn as if viewed face on.

MIDDLE

Bottom

Scale: 1 = 1

Cruciform Arrangement of 4 Columns

Rick Sternbach used advanced computer modeling to develop structure designs for "Journey's End." Originally, the producers also had sought to base the illustrative designs on those from a specific Native American tribe, but concerns over the proper use of the images and how the Native characters would be portrayed in the episode led to the decision to create a fictional group of people as a blend of many different Native American cultures. ILLUSTRATIONS COURTESY OF THE ARTIST.

PRIMARDIAL EARTH — MATTE SHOT   DAN CURRY

Dan Curry's concept sketch of Picard and Q on primordial Earth, and the finished frame from "All Good Things ...." SKETCH COURTESY OF THE ARTIST.

SEASON SEVEN: EPISODE 173
FIRSTBORN
Teleplay by René Echevarria
Story by Mark Kalbfeld
Directed by Jonathan West

Worf has been worried that Alexander is not sufficiently interested in training to become a warrior, and has taken his son to a Klingon festival. However, he and his son are attacked by Duras supporters who are intent on killing Alexander. A helpful Klingon named K'mtar helps Worf and Alexander, then berates Alexander for his pacifist nature. When Worf discovers K'mtar is about to kill Alexander, the mysterious Klingon reveals that he is actually Alexander, returned from the future to kill himself in order to prevent tragedy. He reveals that Alexander's pacifistic ways cause him to grow into a diplomat, whose counsel eventually leads to Worf's assassination. But Worf convinces K'mtar that Alexander must follow his own path, with guidance but not interference.

SEASON SEVEN: EPISODE 174
BLOODLINES
Written by Nicholas Sagan
Directed by Les Landau

Picard and an old Ferengi adversary, DaiMon Bok, reengage in conflict when Bok seeks revenge for the death of his son, which he blames on Picard. Bok resequences the DNA of a young human, Jason Vigo, to trick Picard into thinking the boy is his previously unknown "son." Bok uses an unreliable new subspace transporter to kidnap Vigo, whom he then threatens to kill. Bok's deception is revealed when Vigo develops a genetic disease related to neither Picard nor his mother, a woman Picard once had an affair with. Picard turns Bok's crew against him for engaging in risk without profit, and saves Vigo, by making use of the unstable transporter.

SEASON SEVEN: EPISODE 175
EMERGENCE
Teleplay by Joe Menosky
Story by Brannon Braga
Directed by Cliff Bole

A new life force develops within the ship systems of the *Enterprise* when the ship encounters a magnascopic storm. The first symptoms of its growth are inexplicable failures of ship's systems and the appearance on the holodeck of a strange train simulation, complete with odd passengers and crew. Data and La Forge soon work out that the train and its crew symbolize the *Enterprise* and its functions and are a way the life force can communicate with the crew. When the life force weakens, requiring a source of vertions, the crew is able to convince the force to leave the ship for a nearby life-sustaining nebula.

Star Trek stunt coordinator Dennis Madalone, in makeup (but not costume) for his role as a Klingon in "Firstborn," choreographs a fight sequence with Brian Bonsall, as Alexander. ROBBIE ROBINSON.

Picard and Lieutenant Ro, about to set off on an undercover mission against the Maquis. ROBBIE ROBINSON.

SEASON SEVEN: EPISODE 176
PREEMPTIVE STRIKE
Teleplay by René Echevarria
Story by Naren Shankar
Directed by Patrick Stewart

Ro Laren, a recent graduate of Starfleet's Advanced Tactical Training, goes undercover as a rogue Bajoran to infiltrate the rebel Maquis colonists. With Picard's full awareness, Ro proves herself to the Maquis by raiding the *Enterprise* for Maquis medical supplies. After Ro confesses her sympathies for the Maquis and their cause against the Cardassians, Picard sends Riker to help her bring in the Maquis. Ro chooses to side with the Maquis when Cardassians kill her aged Maquis mentor. She holds Riker off until the Maquis can escape. She has Riker tell Picard she is sorry she betrayed his confidence in her.

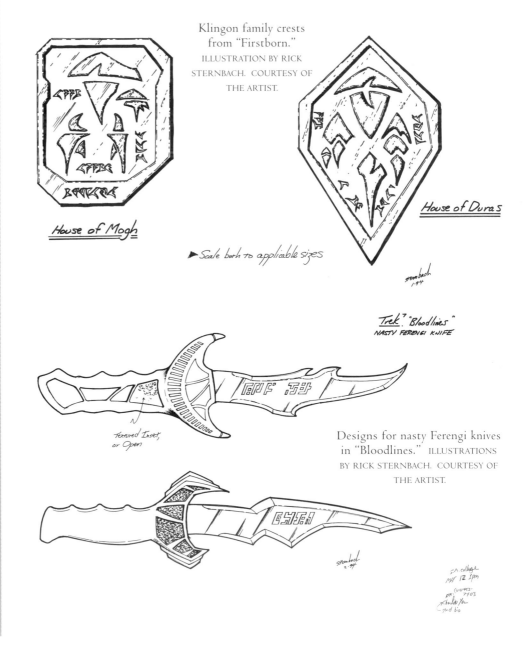

Klingon family crests from "Firstborn." ILLUSTRATION BY RICK STERNBACH. COURTESY OF THE ARTIST.

House of Mogh

House of Duras

▶ Scale both to applicable sizes

Trek "Bloodlines"
NASTY FERENGI KNIFE

Textured Inset, or Open

Designs for nasty Ferengi knives in "Bloodlines." ILLUSTRATIONS BY RICK STERNBACH. COURTESY OF THE ARTIST.

Close-up of a Maquis ship, important in "Preemptive Strike," the series *Deep Space Nine,* and the pilot episode of *Voyager.* COURTESY OF GREG JEIN.

cast and crew finally part to go their own ways, in less than three weeks this cast would be back together again, their mission far from over.

But even with a bright and limitless future beckoning ahead, Marina Sirtis is not alone as she expresses her feelings about the series' end. "I have to be honest. I mean, if it had gone on for twenty years, I would have been on it for twenty years. I was very happy doing the show. I miss not seeing those guys every day. And I was devastated when it was over. I mean, I just ... I didn't want it to ever end."

Her sentiments are shared by millions.

As the seventh season came to an end, Jonathan Frakes traded in his Starfleet uniform for street clothes to host a special presentation of the top five viewers'-choice episodes as determined by a national phone poll. In reverse order, viewers selected "Relics," "The Inner Light," "Yesterday's *Enterprise*," and the two-part episode "Best of Both Worlds."
ROBBIE ROBINSON.

Seven years after their first encounter, Picard is once again put on trial by Q. ROBBIE ROBINSON.

SEASON SEVEN: EPISODES 177
"ALL GOOD THINGS ..."
*Written by Brannon Braga &
Ronald D. Moore
Directed by Winrich Kolbe*

A strange anomaly in the Neutral Zone seems to be the cause of Picard's predicament: he is time-shifting among three different periods in his life—the present, seven years earlier when he first became captain of the *Enterprise*, and twenty-five years into the future, after he is retired. However, the appearance of Q, the superbeing who has tormented and provoked Picard for the past seven years, reveals that Picard is once again being tested by the Q as the representative of humanity. Eventually, Picard and his crews in their different times discover that the anomaly is a time rift focusing on the same temporal moment in Earth's primordial path, when it might prevent the evolution of life on Earth, wiping out humanity before the species had even evolved. But Picard's crews are able to close the rift by destroying the *Enterprise* in all three timelines. Human potential clearly demonstrated once more, Q then brings Picard back to his own time. Picard tells his crew of the strange future he experienced, but which may never occur, then for the very first time sits in on the crew's weekly game of poker.

STAR Trek is a universe of inventive story-telling, a creative vision of the future.

It is also a dollars-and-cents business whose various components must constantly earn more than their cost of production if that inventiveness and creativity are to continue to have expression.

For the most part, the blending of the art and commerce of *Star Trek* is a happy union. The audience responds to the art, which provides the commerce, which in turn insures the continued production of the art.

But at various times in *Star Trek*'s lifetime, there has come a branching point where the nature of its creative vision has been poised to change. At those times—for example, *Star Trek: Phase II, Star Trek: The Motion Picture,* and the development of *Star Trek: The*

Next Generation, among others—the needs of art and business can sometimes find themselves in collision. The making of the first *Next Generation* movie was one of those times.

Among *Star Trek* fans, conventional wisdom holds that the even-numbered films are better than the odd-numbered ones, with *Star Trek II: The Wrath of Khan* being superior to *Star Trek: The Motion Picture*, and with *Star Trek IV: The Voyage Home* continuing to hold its record of achieving the highest domestic gross of all *Star Trek* films to date.

Intriguingly, there might be a logical reason for this observation, having to do with the way movie stories are developed and budgets are determined. In a sense, business can be seen to be influencing art.

Star Trek: The Motion Picture was one of those branching points in which *Star Trek* was reinvented for a new medium—movies. At the time, there was nothing to point to to say what had worked in the past and what hadn't. The *Enterprise* was flying blind and for all the first movie's high points, the end result was a film that many fans thought was flawed.

However, the novelty of seeing Kirk and company on the movie screen led to an opening-weekend gross of $11.8 million—so spectacularly high that studio discussions for a second film began in the week after the first one was released. And this time, the producers had something to point to.

For instance, the first movie was overly long. The story of V'Ger's quest for its creator was not dramatic enough. There was too much talk and not enough action. The visual-effects budget had gotten out of hand. With clear examples of what hadn't worked, the stage was set for the first even-numbered *Star Trek* film, *The Wrath of Khan*. The lessons of the first film were thoughtfully applied, and the second film is still considered to be one of the best. It also cost only $12 million[2] and ended with a domestic gross of $93 million[5]. Two Hollywood rules of thumb to keep in mind are: 1) Studios receive about half the money earned at the box office; 2) A film needs a box-office gross equal to three times its final budget in order to cover the cost of releasing it as well as making it. By any measure of the rules, the second film was a runaway hit.

But with the success of *The Wrath of Khan*, a new factor came into play—money. The actors and other key people responsible for the second movie's success understandably wanted to be paid more for the third. But studios seldom want to spend more money on a sequel because, as a rule, sequels don't match the earnings of the original. So, rather than add all the new salary demands to the overall budget of a sequel, studios generally switch funds from production areas to pay for the increased actor and producer

The *Starship Excelsior* model, designed by Bill George and built by ILM for *Star Trek III: The Search for Spock.* To transform this ship into the *Enterprise*-B for *Generations*, a flare was added to the lower hull, creating a section that could show the damage caused by the Nexus without actually cutting into the original model.

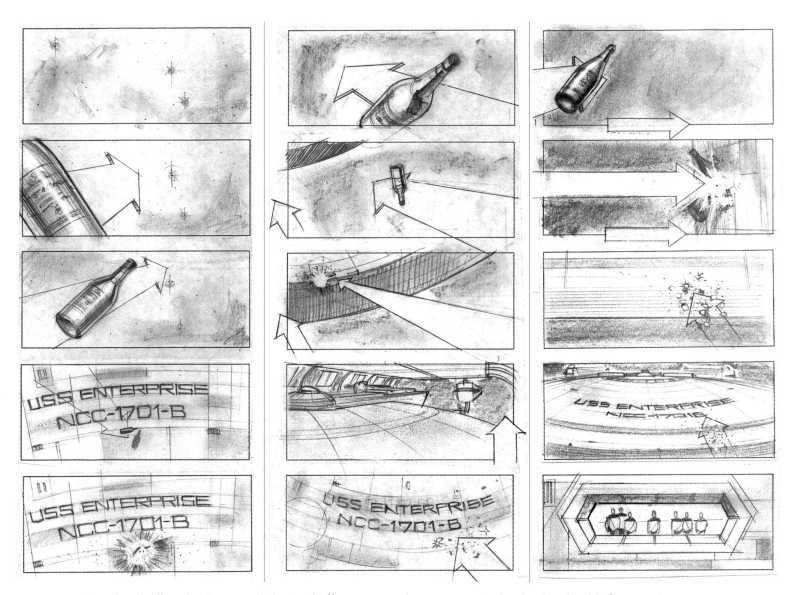

Storyboards allow the director and the visual-effects team to plan a sequence in shot-by-shot detail before exposing a single frame of film. Here are three different versions of the opening sequence of *Star Trek Generations*.
COURTESY OF MARK MOORE, ILM.

fees. In *Star Trek* films, that internal reallocation of the budget invariably has the effect of reducing the number of new sets, starships, and special effects seen in the next film.

Budget changes also affect the creative side of the equation. Writers of sequels not only have to come up with a way to "top" the events of the previous film, they have to do so in a way that doesn't tax the trimmed budget.

With increased salary costs, *Star Trek III: The Search for Spock* ended up costing, in round numbers, $17 million[5], but earned a domestic gross of about $85 million.[5] When the gross is adjusted to allow for inflation and the difference in the cost of movie tickets from 1982 to 1984, *The Search for Spock* didn't do quite as well as *The Wrath of Khan*. The slight decrease meant it was time to go back to the drawing board, to avoid any chance of additional slippage for the fourth film. It also meant that key personnel didn't have quite as much negotiating power to ask for increased salaries. Art could now influence business.

By 1986, this period of creative review had led to the very popular *Star Trek IV: The Voyage Home*, with a cost of approximately $22 million[5], and a domestic gross of more than $100 million[6].

Following the established pattern, in the face of such overwhelming success, cast costs for the next odd-numbered film ballooned, and in a budget-cutting move Paramount made up for part of the

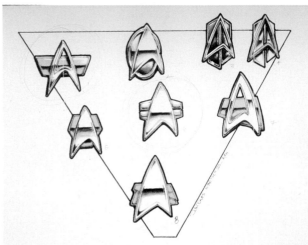

The movie debut of *The Next Generation* gave the design team a chance to bring a new look to several familiar *Star Trek* icons, including the comm badges. ARTWORK COURTESY OF JOHN EAVES.

inevitable cast increases by having *Star Trek V: The Final Frontier* become the first film since *Star Trek II* not to have visual effects created by Industrial Light & Magic.

However, as a cost-cutting move, the decision to drop ILM was, in hindsight, a miscalculation. A Hollywood truism is that blockbuster status is achieved by those films which entice audience members into returning for multiple viewings. But in a science-fiction film, if the visual effects are not convincing or comparable to other recent films, repeat ticket sales are minimal. *The Final Frontier* had the largest opening of any of the *Star Trek* films previously released, but without the multiple viewings that spectacular visual effects can promote, did not last as long as the others. In round numbers, it had cost $32 million[2], but earned only $52 million.[5]

Once again, the odd-numbered film provided a lesson, and for the next, even-numbered film, Paramount returned to what had worked before—the acclaimed director of *Star Trek II*, Nicholas Meyer; the state-of-the-art visual effects of Industrial Light & Magic; and a story based in action, not philosophy.

Star Trek VI: The Undiscovered Country cost approximately $28 million[2], and earned about $75 million[5]. Though all the *Star Trek* films have performed well, especially when foreign box-office earnings and home-video sales are included, the final figures on *VI* indicated what might be a disturbing trend. Going by box-office earnings adjusted for inflation and ticket price increases, the *Star Trek* movie audience had been gradually diminishing even as the cost of including the original cast continued to rise. Once again, business factors were poised to direct art.

As Paramount executives contemplated the next, odd-numbered, *Star Trek* film, number seven, the diminishing audience and increased cast costs for the original crew left little doubt that *Star Trek VI* indeed had been the last outing for Kirk and company. The next film would be the first for the *Next Generation* crew.

But unlike the executives and creative personnel who had overseen the first *Star Trek* movie, now there were six other films to look back on for lessons as to what should and should not be done. Instead of having too little information this time, it could be argued that Paramount had too much.

A look back shows that the development of the seventh *Star Trek* film was less a study in creativity than an example of a film made by a committee—especially a committee of businesspeople. Only the strong team assembled by Rick Berman, with their years of experience on the *Next Generation* television production, enabled the movie to rise above the constraints of its creation and become as good as it turned out to be.

These were just some of the factors that had to be considered at the beginning of the project:

First, Sherry Lansing, John Goldwyn, and Donald Granger—respectively the Chairman of Paramount Pictures' Motion Picture Group, the President of Paramount Motion Pictures, and the Senior Vice President of Production for Paramount's Motion Picture Group—wanted the first *Next Generation* film to be "accessible" to the general movie audience and not just devoted *Star Trek* fans. That meant they wanted the characters and situations in the movie to be fully understandable to someone who had never seen an episode of the series.

Next, Rick Berman was determined that the movie in some way involve the "passing of the torch" from the original crew to *The Next Generation.* Patrick Stewart was equally convinced that the original crew had to share the spotlight with their successors.

Those two requirements alone raised the specter of a movie script with *fourteen* main characters, each of whom would have to be introduced to the audience, along with a story suitable for a feature. Considering that none of the previous six films had ever been able to highlight more than just the three main characters of Kirk, Spock, and McCoy, it seemed that an impossible set of demands had been made before the project had even begun.

From a production standpoint, the movie would also have to be ready to premier over the Thanksgiving holiday weekend—the same timing as *Star Trek IV*—in the year that *The Next Generation* series was to end. That meant that the cast and key technical and production crew would go directly from nine months of television production to a feature-movie shoot, with many of the behind-the-scenes personnel also doing double duty on *Deep Space Nine,* which would then resume production as the movie ended. In addition, several other members of the team were involved in the preproduction work on *Star Trek: Voyager,* slated to premier less than six weeks after the movie. And Rick Berman was overseeing every project.

At first, understanding the pressures that awaited him and the production facilities, Berman commissioned the writing of two different scripts with two different approaches to a "transgenerational" story. One script was written by Maurice Hurley, a seasoned producer from the series' first two seasons; the other by first-time feature writers Ron Moore and Brannon Braga, producers on the final season of the series, and two of the most influential writers of *The Next Generation* episodes. (Michael Piller was also approached, but declined to become involved in a script competition and instead concentrated on *Voyager* and his own original series for the United Paramount Network, *Legend.*)

Both scripts would be based on stories developed by Berman with the writers, and both would involve the original crew with the *Next Generation* crew.

Several times throughout the series, various coverings on Data's head were removed in order to show what lay within. These effects were always designed by makeup supervisor Michael Westmore, whose son, Michael Westmore, Jr., provided the electronic devices that depicted Data's circuitry. Because Paramount executives wanted *The Next Generation* characters to be understandable to people who had never seen the series, a scene showing that Data was an android was one of the script requirements. ILLUSTRATIONS COURTESY OF MICHAEL WESTMORE. PHOTOGRAPHY BY ELLIOTT MARKS.

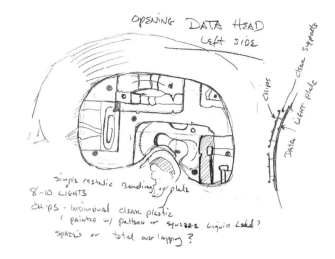

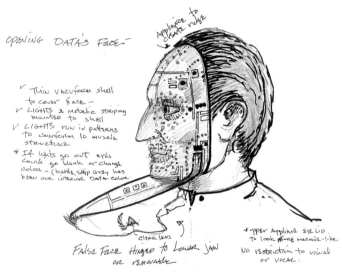

Costume designs for two of the *Original Series* actors appearing in *Generations* included a civilian outfit for Scotty and an orbital reentry suit for Kirk for an opening scene that was filmed but eventually cut from the final film.
ILLUSTRATIONS COURTESY OF ROBERT BLACKMAN. PHOTOGRAPH BY ELLIOTT MARKS.

Berman recalls, "In both scripts, the stories that we developed, at my request, were stories that entailed to different degrees members of *The Original Series* along with *The Next Generation*. First, we went through the story development on both, and both stories were submitted to the studio. We got a lot of notes from the studio, the stories were revised, and then we went to first draft on each. Eventually, it became quite obvious that the studio and I were both leaning toward Ron's and Brannon's script. That's not to say that Maury's script wasn't terrific, it just was far less advanced by the time we really had to make a decision."

As the Moore and Braga script underwent further revisions, it quickly became apparent that both sets of crews could not be handled in the same script. A draft with only Kirk, Spock, and McCoy from the original cast was prepared, and drawing on a lesson from the past, Rick Berman approached Leonard Nimoy to direct the film. Not only had Nimoy brought *The Next Generation* its highest individual episode rating for his appearance as Spock in the fifth season's "Unification," he had also directed the highest-grossing *Star Trek* film, and the blockbuster comedy *Three Men and a Baby*. He was a perfect choice, not only for *Star Trek* continuity, but for directorial expertise.

However, Nimoy's role as Spock was little more than a walk-on—a brief appearance in the first few minutes of the film. As an actor, Nimoy felt that since any of Spock's lines could be said by any of the other characters without changing the nature of the scenes Spock was in, there was no dramatic reason for the character to be there. As a director, Nimoy also wanted to have some input into certain areas of the script.

Unfortunately, with the Thanksgiving release date carved in stone, there was no time to incorporate Nimoy's notes into the script, and Nimoy declined the offer to direct. About the same time, DeForest Kelly also declined his cameo role as McCoy, feeling that he had made a much more effective farewell to the character in *Star Trek VI*.

Fortunately, James Doohan and Walter Koenig agreed to reprise their roles as Scotty and Chekov, providing the sense that the torch was being passed from one crew to another as Berman had wanted.

William Shatner's involvement as Captain Kirk, however, was never in contention. Shatner had been approached about being involved in the movie from the initial story sessions, and had given the project his blessing, a blessing which was, in turn, Kirk's death warrant.

Rick Berman doesn't remember the specific time in the development process in which Kirk's demise was first proposed. "I think we sort of took it for granted," he says, "that if we were going to somehow bring Kirk into the twenty-fourth century, he was going to die. It was something that was *a priori* from Day One because we were facing three choices. One was sending Kirk back after he and Picard had stopped the madman. One was keeping him in *The Next Generation*'s present, alive. And the other one was killing him.

"Keeping him in the present, alive, seemed a little silly. Sending him back didn't really fit well into the story, considering that going back meant returning to an earlier death that's seen in the beginning

Soran's missile and launcher as finally constructed—and eventually reconstructed—on location in Nevada's Valley of Fire. ELLIOTT MARKS.

of the movie. So it seemed appropriate to let him die at the end of the movie, although some are going to accuse us of symbolically having Picard bury Kirk as being some kind of metaphor for *The Next Generation* burying *The Original Series*. That was totally unintentional."

Screenwriter Brannon Braga, however, feels that the emotional power of Kirk's death was never any cause for controversy. "It just felt like the right thing to do," he explains, "kind of passing the baton. And certainly just the image of having Kirk die in Picard's arms and Picard burying him at the end of the movie has an eloquence about it, and will speak to every *Star Trek* fan."

At least, that was the intent.

The reality was that Berman's team came through admirably. Not only did Moore and Braga work as producers throughout the seventh season and write the stellar final episode, they created a feature script that fulfilled all the requirements that had been thrust upon it.

Herman Zimmerman returned to the corridors of the starship whose design he had directed seven years earlier, brought new details to it to make it look even more impressive on the movie screen, and prepared to see it all destroyed in the film's explosive finale.

David Carson, the British director who had made his American television debut with the third-sea-

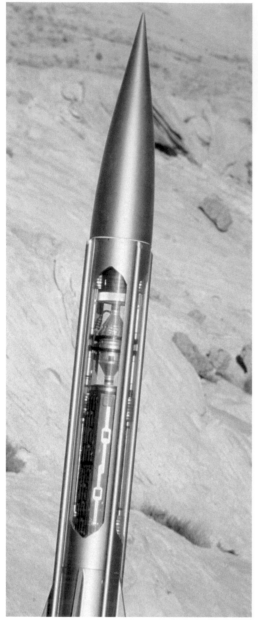

Close-ups of Soran's missile and launcher controls. For the *Star Trek* art department, one of the challenges in designing the control panel was to create a display that the audience would instantly recognize as a countdown timer, but that would still be complex enough to explain why Picard couldn't immediately understand its operation.
ELLIOTT MARKS.

son episode "The Enemy," and who had returned to direct three additional episodes, smoothly made the transition to the big screen.

The film even came in close to its budget of $30 million, an accomplishment that Berman credits to a production team which drew on seven years' worth of television-series expertise to squeeze every last penny out of the budget and put it on screen.

With a touch of pride, Berman says, "I think no one but we could have turned in a movie of this magnitude for this budget, simply because of our expertise with continual penny-pinching. Being television action-adventure people, which is kind of rare today, we know how to do things cost effectively. And that enabled us to do a movie that looks ten million dollars more expensive than it was."

Unfortunately, the cost of making the film was not destined to remain at $30 million. For, after more than a year of being driven by business, scheduling, and budget concerns, the production reached a point at which an impasse was reached between art and commerce.

That point was a preview screening of the movie, still several weeks from its completion.

Such screenings are common undertakings for film studios. Typically, passes for a free screening are given out at movie theaters, inviting a specially selected demographic group of moviegoers to view a work in progress, then rate it on punch cards. Usually, a small group of viewers remains behind after the screening as a focus group, to answer questions about their reaction to the film. Their comments sometimes help guide filmmakers in deciding on the final finishing details of a movie—which jokes to leave in, which dramatic scenes to make tighter, which story points to clarify.

When *Star Trek Generations* was put before a test audience, the message to the filmmakers was one they didn't want to hear, but it was clear nonetheless.

The ending didn't work.

People didn't mind all that much that Captain Kirk would die in this film. But they did dislike the manner of his death—something that harkened back to *The Next Generation*'s first season and Gene Roddenberry's decision to have Tasha Yar die abruptly and senselessly in the line of duty.

For the story climax of *Generations*, Picard entered the timeless fantasy environment of the mysterious Nexus to talk Captain Kirk into leaving to help him stop Dr. Soran from launching a missile that would destroy a sun and kill two hundred million people on the inhabited world of Veridian IV.

As originally filmed, Kirk and Picard leave the Nexus at the same time in the past as the Nexus is approaching Soran's missile-launch complex and as the *Enterprise*'s saucer section is crashing elsewhere on the planet. Picard races to the missile launcher as Kirk faces Soran in and around an open complex of metal stairs, platforms, and catwalks.

During his fight with Kirk, Soran succeeds in knocking Kirk off one of the platforms. Kirk slides off the edge of a rocky cliff, but grasps a rope just in time to slam against the cliff, saving himself. At the same time, Picard fumbles with the missile's controls, accidentally causing the missile and its launcher to cloak.

The weapon that killed James T. Kirk with a shot in the back—but only in the original ending of *Generations*. ELLIOTT MARKS.

Picard now appears to be standing in midair, no longer able to see the invisible controls. He cannot stop the launching of the missile.

Soran sees Picard in midair and prepares to shoot him with his disruptor. But at that very instant, Kirk appears behind Soran on the catwalk, punches him, and knocks him to the rocks a few feet below. Picard calls out to Kirk that Soran has a control padd on his belt, and Kirk retrieves it from the unconscious villain.

Then Kirk returns to the catwalk, presses a few controls on the padd, and drops the cloak from the missile and launcher.

With a smile, Kirk says, "The twenty-fourth century isn't so tough."

And then Soran shoots Kirk in the back!

Certainly, Kirk gave Picard the chance to change the missile's target and when it launches, it streaks toward the horizon instead of the sun, to blow up in the distance. Veridian IV is saved. The Nexus roars by overhead and Soran can't reach it, though he does try a halfhearted jump. Then, when Soran runs at Picard in rage, Picard shoots him.

But none of those story points mattered compared with the disappointment the test audience felt at seeing a hero like Kirk dispatched by a minor villain who simply shot him in the back, especially after Kirk had solved a problem—decloaking the launcher—that Picard, out of character, had caused by accident.

The question facing Paramount was: Should the studio risk releasing a film that was on time and on budget, but which might not please *Star Trek* fans, or should it put the art of *Star Trek* before the commerce of *Star Trek?* Should the studio provide the funds to reshoot the ending, changing it into something that more closely fit what *Star Trek* fans would expect to see?

In the end, story consideration won out over business concerns. On a crash schedule that reunited director David Carson with William Shatner, Patrick Stewart, Malcolm McDowell, and a location crew of about 150 workers in the Valley of Fire outside Las Vegas, a new ending was shot at a cost of between $3 to $5 million.

In the revised ending, Kirk knocks Soran from the cliff, making the villain slide down and catch the rope. Hanging on the side of the cliff, Soran deliberately cloaks the launcher—the action is no longer Picard's mistake. Then Soran slips and the control padd falls onto a bridge. Kirk runs for the control padd, Picard for the cloaked launcher.

Now, when Soran reappears with his disruptor, instead of shooting Kirk, he shoots the bridge, causing it to collapse.

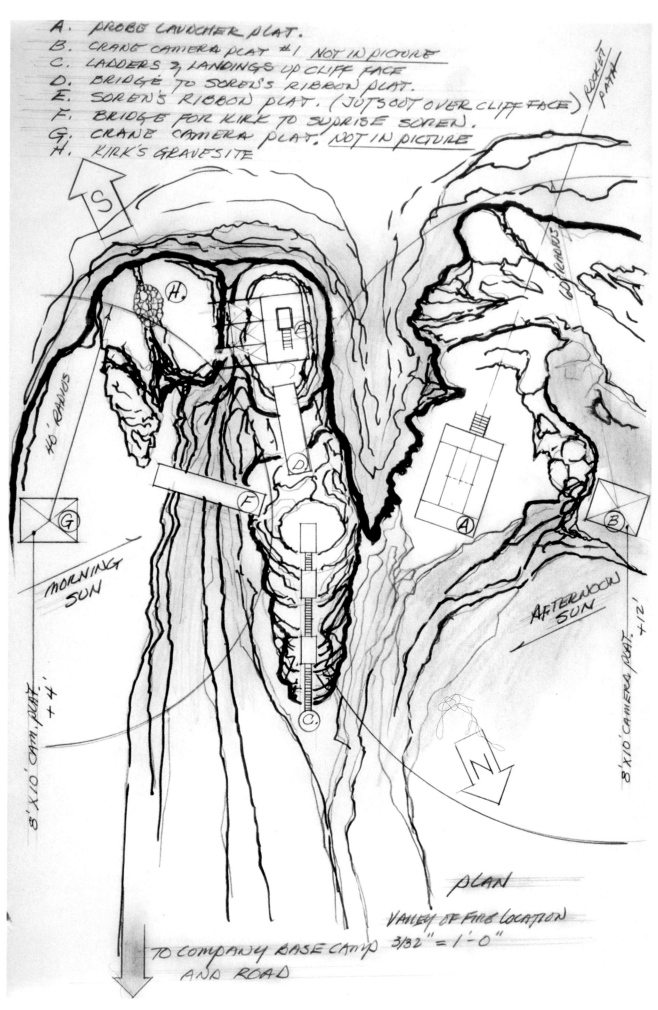

A. PROBE LAUNCHER PLAT.
B. CRANE CAMERA PLAT #1 <u>NOT IN PICTURE</u>
C. LADDERS & LANDINGS UP CLIFF FACE
D. BRIDGE TO SOREN'S RIBBON PLAT.
E. SOREN'S RIBBON PLAT. (JUTS OUT OVER CLIFF FACE)
F. BRIDGE FOR KIRK TO SURPRISE SOREN.
G. CRANE CAMERA PLAT. <u>NOT IN PICTURE</u>
H. KIRK'S GRAVESITE

ROCKET PATH

GO TRCHERS

S

H

E

D

A

F

G

B

40' RADIUS

MORNING SUN

AFTERNOON SUN

8'X10' CAM. PLAT. +4'

8'X10' CAMERA PLAT. +12'

N

PLAN

VALLEY OF FIRE LOCATION
3/32" = 1'-0"

TO COMPANY BASE CAMP
AND ROAD

This planning sketch shows the on-location layout of Soran's launching complex, including key camera positions.
This set had to be re-created when a revised ending for the movie was shot.

The realism of the *Enterprise*'s destruction was achieved in part by actually destroying the *Enterprise* sets that had served *The Next Generation* for all seven seasons. PHOTOGRAPHY BY PENNY JUDAY.

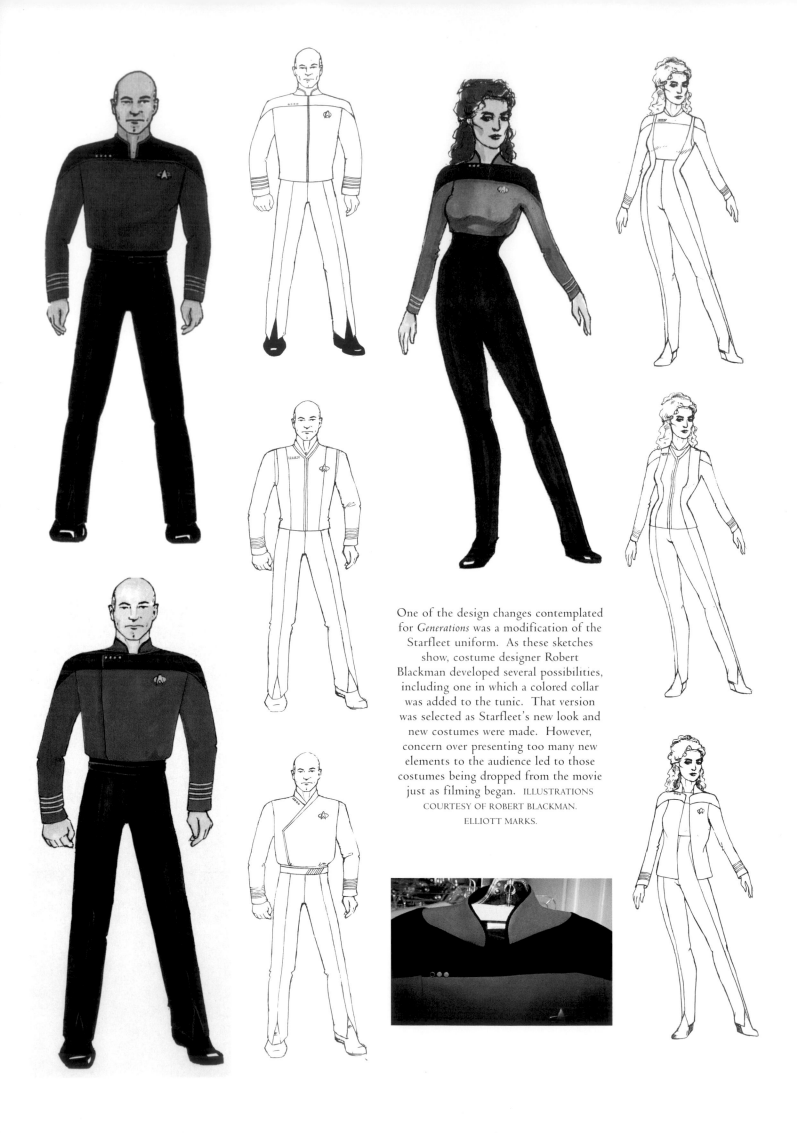

One of the design changes contemplated for *Generations* was a modification of the Starfleet uniform. As these sketches show, costume designer Robert Blackman developed several possibilities, including one in which a colored collar was added to the tunic. That version was selected as Starfleet's new look and new costumes were made. However, concern over presenting too many new elements to the audience led to those costumes being dropped from the movie just as filming began. ILLUSTRATIONS COURTESY OF ROBERT BLACKMAN. ELLIOTT MARKS.

Three designs for the distinctive costumes worn by Guinan in *Generations.*
ILLUSTRATIONS COURTESY OF ROBERT BLACKMAN.

For four years on the *Next Generation* series, television budgets and schedules usually limited groups of aliens to seven individuals, even if the scripts started out asking for twenty-five. But for *Generations,* Robert Blackman was presented with the welcome challenge of designing individual costumes for *thirty* El-Aurian refugees.
ILLUSTRATIONS COURTESY OF ROBERT BLACKMAN.

Two favorite recurring characters from the series appeared in *Generations*—the Duras sisters, Lursa and B'Etor, played by Barbara March and Gwynyth Walsh. ILLUSTRATIONS COURTESY OF ROBERT BLACKMAN. PHOTOGRAPHY BY ELLIOTT MARKS.

The control padd is on the other side. The only way Picard can adjust the launcher's controls is if Kirk makes a death-defying—and heroic—leap from one side of the creaking bridge to the other.

Knowing the danger he's in, Kirk makes the leap, catches the padd, and decloaks the launcher. By then the strain on the bridge is too great and it falls, taking Kirk with it.

This time, instead of dying senselessly, Kirk has willingly and heroically sacrificed himself.

Picard, meanwhile, adjusts the missile's controls so that when Soran reaches the launcher and the missile ignites, its locking clamps are engaged and the missile explodes. In classic storytelling tradition, Dr. Soran is killed by his own creation.

Art having triumphed over commerce, commerce now rewarded art. *Generations* went on to earn a record-setting $23.1 million opening weekend, an eventual $73 million domestic gross, and the highest international earnings of the first seven *Star Trek* films.

Like every other film in the series, *Generations* was a success. But, like all the other odd-numbered films, it had also served as a testbed, leaving its participants inspired with the conviction that with all the lessons they had learned, the next film, even-numbered, would be even better.

Once again, the odd-even pattern held.

They were right.

This section of corridor in the *Enterprise*-D was originally built for the updated original *Enterprise* in *Star Trek: The Motion Picture*. When the sets for *The Next Generation*'s *Enterprise* were being designed, as a cost-cutting move Herman Zimmerman had them laid out to match the established floorplan and already-installed lighting from the movie sets. Additional money was saved by reusing existing branching corridor sections like this one. Today, *Voyager* sets occupy the same stages on the Paramount lot. The mission continues. PHOTOGRAPH BY PENNY JUDAY.

T H E torch had been passed, the lessons learned, and in the words of scriptwriter Ron Moore, it was now time for *The Next Generation* to "kick butt."

Like *The Wrath of Khan,* the eighth *Star Trek* film would be a flat-out action movie. It would have humor like *The Voyage Home.* And most important of all, it would hook *Star Trek* and science-fiction fans by delivering never-before-seen visual effects designed to bring them back into the theaters for multiple viewings. The chief, never-before-seen effect would be the realization of the first new *Starship Enterprise* in nine years, to replace the Andrew Probert –designed television *Enterprise,* which had been destroyed in *Generations.*

With no limits and no studio-mandated requirements for the story, other than it be a good one, Moore

The flash of light on this Borg's chestplate is a *special* effect because it was created live on the set as this scene was filmed. ELLIOTT MARKS.

and Braga attended their first story meeting with Rick Berman with the perfect threat already in mind—*The Next Generation*'s favorite villains: the Borg.

For his part, Rick Berman attended the meeting with the perfect plot complication already formulated: time travel. As Berman explains, "All of the *Star Trek* films and episodes I have been most impressed with—*Star Trek IV: The Voyage Home,* 'Yesterday's *Enterprise,*' 'City on the Edge of Forever,' and I could name half a dozen more—have all been stories that deal with time travel. In a way, *Star Trek Generations* dealt with time travel. Nick Meyer's wonderful movie *Time After Time* dealt with time travel. The paradoxes that occur in writing, as well as in the reality of what the characters are doing and what the consequences are, have always been fascinating to me. I don't think I've ever had as much fun as being involved with 'Yesterday's *Enterprise,*' and having to tackle all the logical, paradoxical problems that we would run into and figure out ways to solve them."

Since a feature-film story required a scope larger than a single television episode, there was no need to choose between the two approaches. A time-travel story involving the Borg was quickly decided upon as the direction to go.

But it wasn't enough to make just a *Star Trek* action film. Michael Piller's influence was inextricably woven into *The Next Generation*'s appeal. There had to be some part of the story that made it personal, that made it revolve around one of the main characters.

Again the answer was simple and direct—always a good sign in developing a strong story.

Five years earlier, Picard had become part of the Borg Collective. To him, the scars of that encounter were permanent. To the Borg, he was the one who got away.

"The Best of Both Worlds" Parts I and II were now simply acts one and two of a bigger story. The new movie, at one point titled, *Star Trek: Resurrection,* would become the final act in Picard's encounter with the Borg. Once again, the storytellers went back to what had worked in the past. Khan had quoted *Moby-Dick* while he had chased Captain Kirk, and that classic tale of obsession would again be invoked to underscore Picard's potentially self-destructive hatred of the Borg.

To make the story even more personal, for the first time the Borg would be given an individual face and voice—the Borg queen. And the time-travel aspect was just as direct—the Borg would go back in time to subvert Earth's development, so that an Earth-led Federation would never be able to develop to resist the Borg in our quadrant of the galaxy.

Another essential component of a *Star Trek* story laid out by Gene Roddenberry is that the *Enterprise* must be considered a character, too. What better way to put a sleek new starship in danger than to have it infiltrated by Borg and face assimilation?

The various parts of the initial story fell into place effortlessly. The imaginative possibilities were literally endless. Berman, Moore, and Braga had only to answer a few key questions to create the spine of their story. To what time would the Borg return? How could Picard stop them this time? What could the movie show that *Star Trek* fans always enjoyed seeing in a *Star Trek* film? And what could the movie show that *Star Trek* fans had never seen before?

The answer to the first two questions would remain to be discovered during the story's further refinement. But the second two questions inspired powerful answers. Fans had increasingly been enamored of *Star Wars*–style space battles, so the new movie would open with one. And there was an aspect of *Star Trek* which had only ever been glimpsed once, in the very first movie—a spacesuit sequence, something which Berman had always resisted during the series because of his concerns that it could not be done believably on a television budget.

But now the time was right for so much that was new about *Star Trek,* and it was time for the venerable franchise to embrace what so many hit science-fiction films had successfully used to insure box-office success.

It was time for a *Star Trek* visual-effects extravaganza.

Visual-effects production is the art and science of bringing to the screen images which cannot be photographed in reality: a starship blazing through space faster than light, an alien world, a hundred million Borg in regeneration cells.

Special-effects production is the creation of live, physical props and actions which can be pho-

Moving actors with cables on set is a *special* effect. *Visual* effects added to the final versions of these scenes include the digital removal of the wires, and, for the sequence on the hull of the *Enterprise,* the addition of a starfield. ELLIOTT MARKS.

tographed in reality, though what they appear to be and what they actually are are two very different things: a starship explodes, but it's really a two-foot-long model; an android opens its head to reveal blinking circuitry, though half of the head is a dummy; a mechanical appendage wriggles from an actor's face, though the appendage and the actor's face are puppets.

Finally, computer-generated images, CGI, are those photorealistically animated effects which are created artificially on the computer screen, often combined with visual effects and special effects to make both blend seamlessly into a real setting.

The new *Next Generation* film would be a cutting-edge combination of all three techniques.

Which was only fitting. For nine years *The Next Generation* had been defining the state of visual

Continuing in a long tradition of actors who can take on many *Star Trek* roles because of extensive makeup, Ethan Phillips made a cameo appearance as the holodeck nightclub manager in *First Contact*. Phillips also played the Ferengi Dr. Farek in the third season's "Ménage à Troi," and, of course, plays Neelix on *Star Trek: Voyager.* .

ROBBIE ROBINSON

JULIE DENNIS

ELLIOTT MARKS

The corridors of the new *Enterprise* thrown into chaos by the double threat of Borg assimilation *and* a film production crew. Note the Borg on the floor. Several mannequins were moved from scene to scene in order to fill the regeneration chambers built throughout the ship. ELLIOTT MARKS.

effects on television, a medium in which the series had had little competition. But now it was time to see if a *Star Trek* film could go up against contemporary, effects-heavy features such as *Independence Day*, *Eraser*, even *Twister*.

The Next Generation had begun its dominance of television visual effects with a potentially risky decision in 1987. Up till that first season of the new series, almost all *Star Trek* effects had been accomplished by photographic and practical means—practical, meaning that physical props and actions were used on set with no photographic trickery. The one exception was the "Genesis effect" sequence from *The Wrath of Khan,* which was one of the first major, computer-generated effects sequences to appear in a feature film.

However, as good as photographic effects had become, they were time-consuming and thus expensive to produce. And two things a television production is always short of are time and money. So as *The Next Generation* moved closer to its start date, Gene Roddenberry and his production team, led in this area by Peter Lauritson, looked for an alternative method.

Lauritson found that method in video compositing—an all-electronic method of combining the different elements of a scene.

For example, to create a shot of the *Enterprise* flying over a planet, the *Enterprise* model could be photographed up to seven times. In the first exposure, the model would be lit by a bright light to simulate a nearby sun. Then that light would be turned off, the model and the camera would be returned to the starting position, and the same movement sequence would be shot again, this time with only the ship's interior window lights turned on.

After that exposure, everything would return to the beginning and another shot would be made of only the blue nacelle lights, then the red nacelle lights, then a backlit exposure intended to create a solid silhouette of the ship. Separate exposures would also be made of the planet.

Director Jonathan Frakes instructs Alfre Woodard in the fine points of phaser marksmanship. ELLIOTT MARKS.

Then, all those different exposures of the ship would be printed onto a separate piece of film. If any one exposure did not line up precisely, chances are they all would have to be reshot. If they did precisely line up, then the final image of the ship would have lost some detail and clarity, owing to the inevitable loss of quality that occurs when a photographic copy is made.

Additional losses of quality would occur when the photography of the ship was combined with the photography of the planet, and then the background starfield. Add a second ship, or a phaser burst or tractor beam, and the complexity of the shot increases again while the quality is further reduced.

With video compositing, however, though every exposure is still shot on film, the process of combining each shot is done electronically. Once the photographic image is converted to a digital one, no further loss of quality occurs, no matter how many exposures are combined. The compositing process is also faster, which means it can be viewed, adjusted, and reviewed several times, an option not available with film compositing under tight television schedules.

However, in 1987, when *The Next Generation* was set to debut on television, the main drawback to electronic compositing was that the final finished shot would exist only on videotape—a medium with much lower image quality than film. When broadcast on television, the lower quality of videotape would not be noticed, because the videotape was still holding an image that was of higher quality than television screens could display. Also at the time, it was usual for studios to take several episodes from a television series and cut them into a movie for release overseas. That reuse of material often brought in millions of dollars of extra earnings.

But if final episodes of *The Next Generation* existed only on videotape, they could never be shown as films.

Based on his analysis of video compositing, Lauritson prepared two budgets for the series—one with film-based visual effects, the other with electronic-based effects.

Though going to video compositing would eliminate any potential foreign box-office revenue the

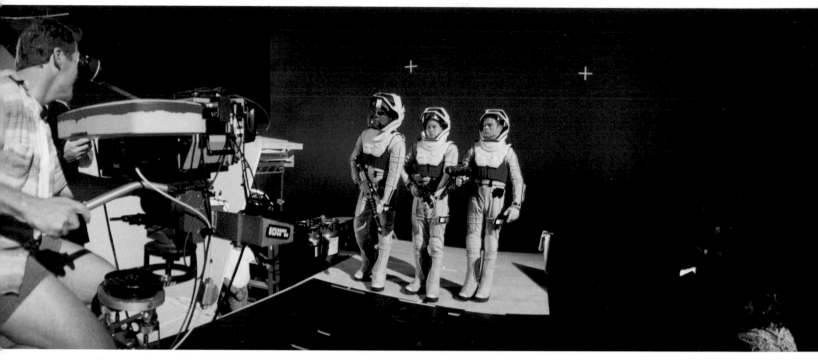

To place Picard, Worf, and Hawk on the outside of the *Enterprise*, live-action footage of the actors was first shot against a blue background. A computer program was later instructed to remove all the blue elements from the scene, and replace them with images of the model starship. Despite the reliance on technology, an artist's eye is still required to match lighting angles and camera moves between the real elements and those that exist only on the screen. ELLIOTT MARKS.

Patrick Stewart and Alfre Woodard on the blue-screen stage used to create the CGI elements that make them appear in the holographic nightclub. The blue shape they're standing behind corresponds to the shape and size of the bar on the nightclub set. ELLIOTT MARKS.

series might earn, it was also less expensive than a film-based approach, and the advantages in scheduling were enormous.

Lauritson says that the studio hesitated before making the decision, but the electronic approach eventually won. Today, virtually every show on television is electronically composited, and with advanced systems using digital-imaging systems capable of producing more resolution than even film can record, even movies, especially effects-heavy ones, have moved to electronic systems.

But though all the intermediate stages, and the final stage, of each episode of *The Next Generation* would be handled electronically, in order to insure the highest quality going into the process, at the beginning all individual elements were shot on film.

In 1987, as far as Paramount was concerned, there was only one supplier for those initial film elements—Industrial Light & Magic. It was there that the new *Enterprise* was built, and it was there that about forty separate, generic shots of the ship were photographed. Though ILM provided no work for the series after the first few episodes, those forty or so shots of the *Enterprise* streaking through space or orbiting a planet were used throughout the entire seven-year run, earning ILM their Special Visual Effects credit on every episode.

ILM returned to the *Next Generation* family with the first *Next Generation* film, *Generations*. For that film, another *Star Trek* milestone was reached—the appearance of the first CGI starship.

On television, other science-fiction series, notably *Babylon 5*, had pioneered the use of totally computer-generated effects. *Star Trek* productions used computers to create energy effects, such as the transporter shimmer and phaser bursts, but Rick Berman had resisted using CGI ships because he had yet to see one that could match the detail of a photographic model. Since *Babylon 5* had started out with CGI ships, there was no transition phase to call attention to their technique, which has improved impressively every season.

However, by the time of *Generations*, ILM's technological prowess had caught up to the demands of Rick Berman's eye for detail and could create computer-generated versions of the *Enterprise* that were almost completely indistinguishable from the photographed version.

The artificial ships were aided in great part by the technique of texture mapping—the process by which real-world detail is added to a computer-generated object. In *Generations*, for example, crisp photographs were taken of the existing model of the *Enterprise*-B, and then those detailed photographs were digitally "painted" onto the computer-generated model.

The scenes in which the *Enterprise*-B encounters the flashing, glowing, twisting Nexus were all realized with a computer-generated ship. The technique made it simple, relatively speaking, for flashes of light from the Nexus to reflect from the hull of the *Enterprise*. Such interactive lighting effects are extremely complex to accomplish when a model must be lit on a stage, to match flashes of light from another element yet to be filmed.

For the second *Next Generation* movie, *First Contact*, ILM enthusiastically took their CGI expertise to the next level, no longer limiting themselves to creating explosions and starships, but creating CGI sets and even, in one scene, helping to create a character.

Digital wizardry made possible the immense pullback from Captain Picard's eye through the vast Borg cube, revealing tens of millions of Borg in their regeneration cells. The same technique placed Picard, Worf, and Hawk on the outside of the *Enterprise* high above the Earth. And in one of the film's most memorable shots, ILM digitally erased the crane arm and blue-fabric-wrapped body of actor Alice Krige as the Borg queen, leaving only her head and a remote-controlled mechanical spine to be lowered into her "body."

As the film moved through production and the key visual-effects shots were developed from storyboards to rough animation to final rendered frames, it became clear that *First Contact* was going to be a worthy competitor among its 1996 science-fiction/action-film peers.

But what Rick Berman never forgot, what Ron Moore and Brannon Braga wove throughout their script, and what first-time feature director Jonathan Frakes highlighted as the heart of the film, was that

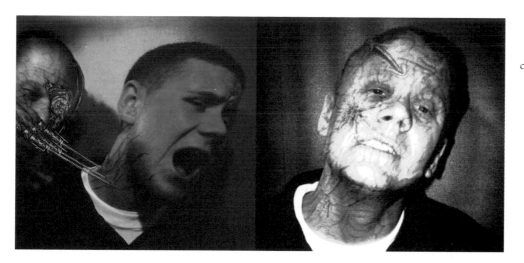

Concept tests of the
assimilation process
conducted by Industrial
Light & Magic.
COURTESY OF ILM.

Practical makeup is combined with
computer-generated imagery in this
sequence showing a crew member
assimilated during a Borg attack.
The growth of the Borg technology
under the crew member's skin was
enhanced by CGI.

ELLIOTT MARKS

Star Trek is not just about starships and big effects—it's about people, in whatever form people take in the twenty-fourth century.

To that end, perhaps one of the most important members of the *Star Trek* team is the artist who puts the unique faces on the people of the *Star Trek* universe, makeup supervisor Michael Westmore.

A winner of nine Emmys and an Academy Award for his artistry, Westmore is the third generation of a Hollywood makeup dynasty. His grandfather, George Westmore, started work in Hollywood features in the 1920s. His father, Monty, ran the makeup department of Selznick International, and his uncles, Perc and Ern, who were twins, ran the same departments at Warner Bros. and 20th Century Fox respectively, with Ern later moving to RKO. Michael Westmore's other uncles included Wally, who ran Paramount's makeup department, Bud, who ran Universal's, and Frank, the youngest, who worked for both Wally and Bud at their respective studios.

Today, Michael Westmore has two brothers in the makeup business, as well as a nephew, a niece, and a cousin. His son, Michael Westmore, Junior, has extended the family legacy by building all the interior electronics revealed whenever portions of Data were opened up on *The Next Generation*, as well as building all the sophisticated flashing devices worn by the Borg in *First Contact*. Viewers fluent in Morse code will have no trouble detecting the "Resistance is futile" message flashed by Data's electronics near the movie's conclusion, and by paying attention, they will be able to read the names of several movie crew members blinked out by the individual Borg units.

In makeup, details count, and Michael Westmore is the master of detail. After ten years of working on *The Next Generation, Deep Space Nine, Voyager,* and the two *Next Generation* features, he has produced more makeup than any other artist in Hollywood. And he shows no sign of slowing down. In fact, if anything, he's speeding up. Westmore's original makeup design for Worf took two and a half hours to apply in the first season of *The Next Generation.* Today, on *Deep Space Nine,* Worf's more sophisticated look can be applied in less than an hour.

Ten years ago, Westmore accepted his first job with *Star Trek* to bring some order to his life. "Until that time," he says, "I was literally living out of a suitcase, traveling around the world. I would spend half the year at home, and the other half in Dubuque, Iowa, or Vancouver, or Budapest, or someplace, doing my laundry on Sunday mornings and looking for the local zoo and museum to hang out in on Sunday afternoons, because I was working six days a week. When the offer to work on *The Next Generation* came along, it gave me the opportunity to stay home and watch my daughter, Mackenzie, grow up."

Westmore's decision to join the series was necessarily quick. He accepted the position at six o'clock on a Thursday evening, and first thing the next Monday he began filming tests of Brent Spiner's Data makeup.

"We tried twenty-one different colors on him," Westmore says, "and then it got interesting when it came down to grey and gold. Gene Roddenberry liked grey, and in talking with Gene, I said, 'You know, we can use grey for dead people and cold aliens and lizards and things, but the metallic gold is a color we really can't use on anybody else.'" Westmore adds with a chuckle, "I had Rick Berman on my side, too, so we went for the gold instead of the grey."

The demands of Westmore's position on *Star Trek* productions have never made him regret leaving the world of feature films. "On the outside," he says, "you'd be lucky to get a movie in which you'd do *one* race of aliens. And then you're going to sit and redesign the thing twelve times while they're looking for the perfect one. Here, we don't have to look for the perfect one, because there'll always be another one we need for next week. It's playing, you know, and it never stops."

Just as *Star Trek* fans admire the elaborate makeup Westmore oversees, they also offer comments from time to time about the various series' reliance on subtle variations of foreheads, noses, and ears. In this case, it's not a lack of creativity that's at fault, it's the familiar television constraints of time and money.

"The more people they throw at us," Westmore explains, "the smaller the makeup piece becomes. Because of the time factor.

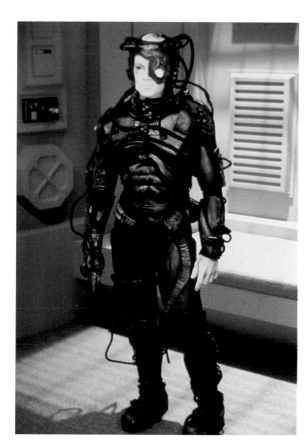

A television Borg—Jonathan del Arco as Hugh, in "I, Borg." ROBBIE ROBINSON.

A feature-film Borg.
ELLIOTT MARKS.

As seen on television, the Borg's biomechanical implants were connected to their bodies beneath their helmets. However, for the movie version, much more elaborate details could be shown.

First Contact Borg concept by Deborah Everton and Gina Flanagan.

For television, it had taken one makeup artist two hours to create a Borg. For First Contact, the more detailed Borg makeup took up to five hours to complete. ELLIOTT MARKS.

SIDE BURN BIBLE

A. HAIR (crepe wool) must match Natural Hair color

  BLENDED HAIR is always better than Single-color.

B. LAY HAIR (wool) in Direction of Natural Growth

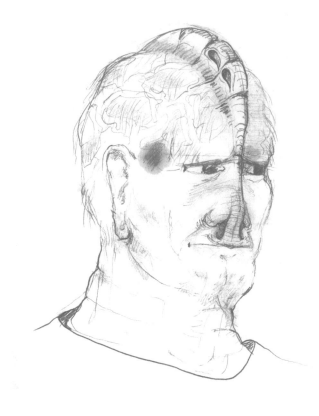

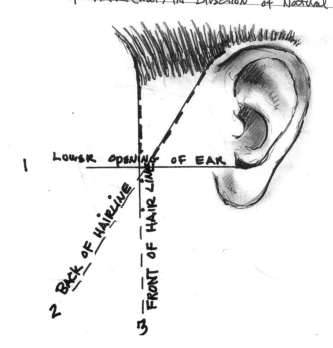

1 — LOWER OPENING OF EAR

2 — BACK OF HAIRLINE

3 — FRONT OF HAIR LINE

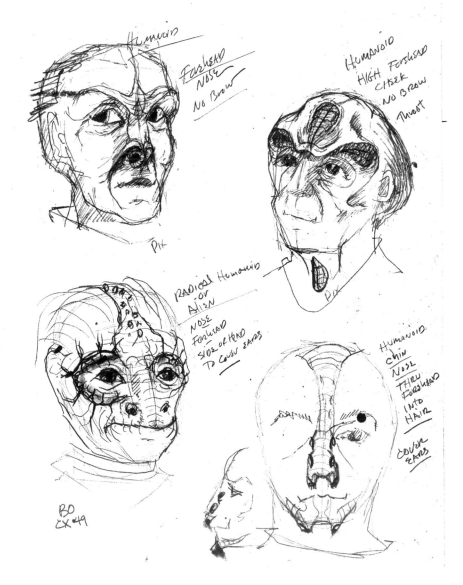

HUMANOID

FORHEAD
NOSE
NO BROW

HUMANOID
HIGH FORHEAD
CHEEK
NO BROW
Throat

Pix

Pix

RADICAL HUMANOID
or
ALIEN
NOSE
FORHEAD
SIDE OF HEAD
TO COVER EARS

HUMANOID:
CHIN
NOSE
THRU
FORSHEAD
INTO
HAIR

COVER
EARS

BD
CX 49

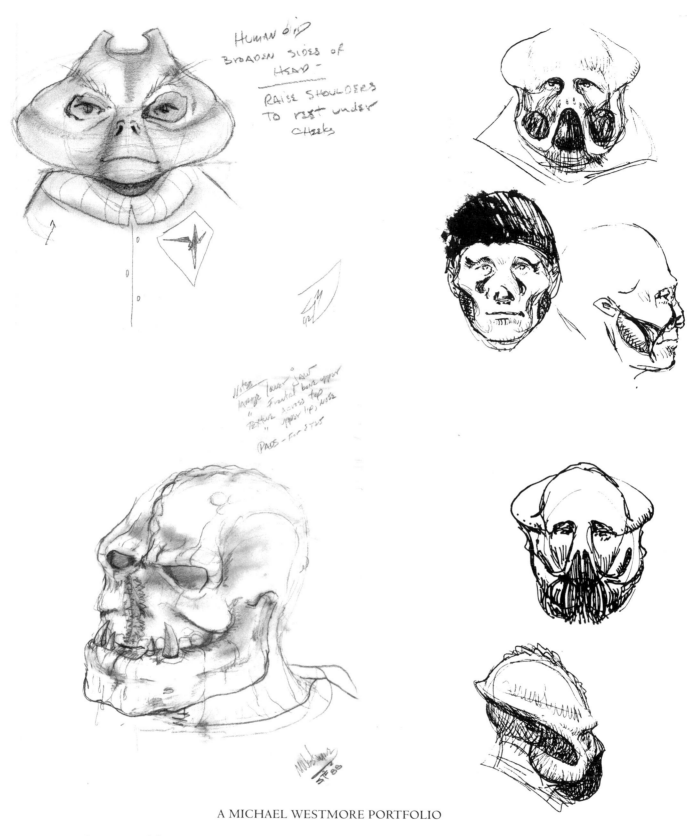

A MICHAEL WESTMORE PORTFOLIO

As the most prolific makeup designer and supervisor in Hollywood, Michael Westmore combines unbridled creativity with incredible speed. As testament, many of these sketches from the run of *The Next Generation* series were completed on the back of script pages, sometimes during production meetings. Whether he's maintaining the details of the pointed sideburns established in *The Original Series*, quickly producing a simple nose or ear modification, or directing the creation of a completely alien head, Michael Westmore is one of the key artists who have helped establish *Star Trek*'s distinctive visual style for more than a decade. ILLUSTRATIONS COURTESY OF MICHAEL WESTMORE.

ELLIOTT MARKS

"You have to figure that each one of those pieces takes a makeup artist to put it on. The actor, if he's going to have a major role in an episode, has to have twelve hours between calls [a Guild rule]. So you can't put him in makeup that's going to take a long time to put on and take off."

Like most other members of *The Next Generation*'s design team, Westmore looked forward to having the opportunity to refine the Borg's overall look in the second movie. Rick Berman, noting the extra development time and money a feature film affords, said, "This is our chance to see the Borg the way we've always wanted to do them."

For Westmore, that meant that what had taken two hours for a makeup artist to create for a television Borg, now took five hours for a motion-picture version. The culprit was, of course, the amount of detail that could be incorporated into the Borg's look.

The first thing that Berman wanted changed was the Borg's helmet. Supposedly, that's where the Borg's biomechanical components make their connection with the Borg's body. But for the film, Berman wanted to see that connection revealed.

"Instead of having an entire helmet," Westmore says, "now we have these individual pieces that are on the head, so you get this bald look. That way the pieces look like they're clamped into the head individually, instead of being a full cap that pulls over the top."

But the most spectacular piece of makeup work in *First Contact,* and one which helped earn Westmore and his team an Academy Award nomination for their work, was one that was totally new—the Borg

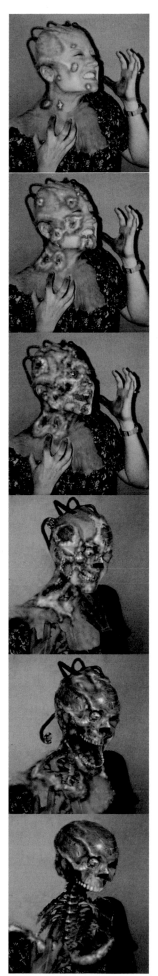

Alice Krige as *Star Trek*'s most threatening—and enticing—alien yet. ELLIOTT MARKS.

A concept test of the Borg queen's disintegration, as visualized by Alex Jaeger at Industrial Light & Magic. A similar sequence in the first-season episode "Conspiracy" created a minor storm of controversy. While not unusual in science-fiction films, such graphic scenes are still rare on television COURTESY OF ILM.

ELLIOTT MARKS

queen. And Berman was committed in his desire to insure that the character look unlike anything else ever seen on film.

"We were given a list of movies we weren't supposed to copy," Westmore says. "*Species, Captain EO,* anything that was in books that had already been published. So we literally got all these pictures and laid them out and said, 'Okay, we can't do *that*. And we can't do *that*. And we can't do *that*.'"

Surprisingly, though, the design process wasn't drawn out. "Right away I had the idea of extending her head," Westmore says. "She's the smartest one of all. We want to give her more brain capacity."

Westmore credits Scott Wheeler with defining the finishing details of the queen. Wheeler sculpted the extended headpiece, and with the clay in front of him and Westmore at his side, began adding the non-human cut-ins and flares that helped transform Alice Krige into *Star Trek*'s most threatening—and enticing—alien yet.

When *Star Trek: First Contact* was shown to a test audience, there was no need for reshoots. Reportedly, the only other movie in Paramount history that received a higher approval rating from a preview audience was *Forrest Gump*. Once again, it seemed the even-odd pattern had worked its magic, and the eighth *Star Trek* film went on to earn the biggest opening-weekend figures of any of the series, and the highest worldwide gross ever.

Some fans hailed the exciting new film as a welcome change of direction for a franchise that was approaching its fourth decade. But Michael Dorn saw the film in a different way, one that is more likely correct.

"I don't think it was a *change* in direction," he says. "I think it was a *return* to the direction that we were comfortable in, which made us popular."

Preparing for a close-up of Picard's final battle with the Borg queen. The ladder is not standard Starfleet-issue. ELLIOTT MARKS.

That popularity was there from the beginning.

It has only grown stronger.

And now, ten years from its debut, with more films like *First Contact* certain to follow, there is little danger of *The Next Generation*'s popularity fading anytime soon.

At the end of *First Contact,* with the launch of Earth's first warp-powered spacecraft, the *Star Trek* saga begins...

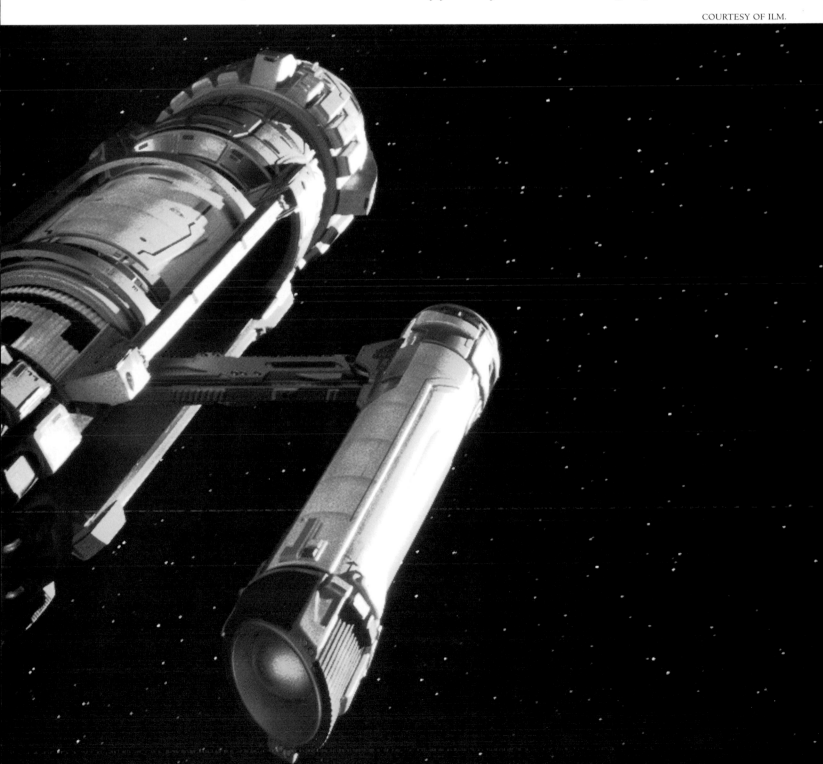

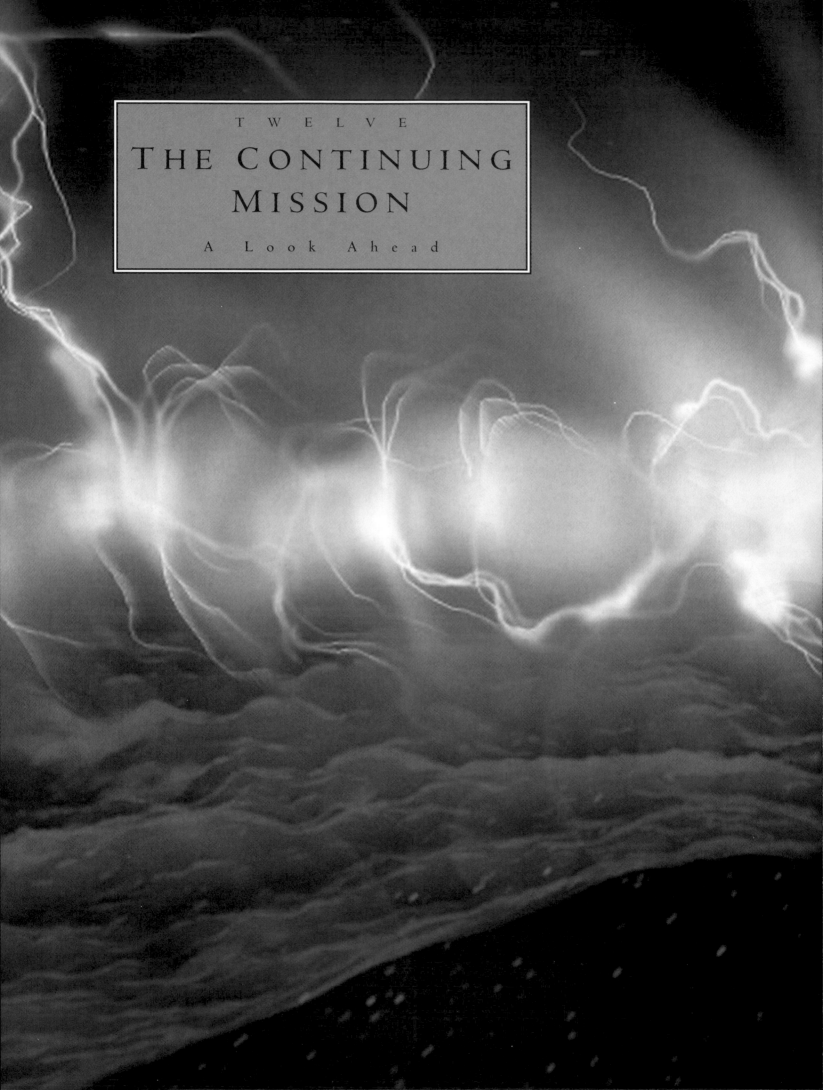

TWELVE

THE CONTINUING MISSION

A Look Ahead

HOW much longer will *Star Trek* last?

It's a question asked as often by executives on the Paramount lot as it is by fans at *Star Trek* conventions.

The answer, for now, is that there's no end in sight. Which is not unusual, even for an entertainment franchise thirty years old, because many classic fictional characters have long had a hold on the public imagination, easily transcending generations, cultures, and years. That's what makes them classics.

For example, as this book goes to press, the nineteenth major James Bond movie is in post-production for release in 1998, thirty-seven years after the first major Bond film, *Dr. No*, hit the screens. In *The Next Generation*'s tenth-anniversary year of 1997, Batman celebrates his fifty-eighth birthday; Superman, his fifty-

One of *Star Trek*'s many future incarnations is depicted in this concept painting for the entrance to
Star Trek: The Experience, at the Las Vegas Hilton Hotel. COURTESY OF PARAMOUNT PARKS.

ninth; Flash Gordon and Dale Arden, their sixty-third; Mickey Mouse, his sixty-ninth; Tarzan of the
Apes, his eighty-third; and Sherlock Holmes, his hundred and tenth. All these characters have been featured in television series in the past, and all have movies in development now, just like the characters
of *The Next Generation.*

Of course, what sets these other classic characters apart from those of *Star Trek* is that their popularity has waxed and waned over the years as they have moved in and out of favor. But *Star Trek*, the
youngest franchise among them, has remained in constant television production for a decade, and in
constant movie production for almost twice that.

Could either of those aspects of *Star Trek* end anytime soon?

Not according to Rick Berman.

"There's always a tendency for people to deep-fry the golden goose," he acknowledges, "for people
to overexploit something. There are a lot of different divisions of Viacom and Paramount, and people
know that there's one franchise they can always make money with. So the question becomes: 'Can you
take too many trips to the well?' And the answer is a resounding: 'Yes, you can.' "

Handpicked by Gene Roddenberry to manage his creation, and now far more than just a steward of
what has gone before, Berman has become an active creative participant in *Star Trek*'s future, as well as
its guardian. Its management and longevity are serious matters to him.

"Can you overexploit a franchise to where people get sick of it?" he asks. "To where people feel that
they are being bombarded with it? To where people begin to lose interest? You sure can," he says emphat-
ically. "I think one of my jobs, in a funny way, has been to remain as vigilant as I can—with Roddenberry
sitting on my shoulder—about fighting against the overexploitation of *Star Trek*. And I do."

In hindsight, Berman believes that *Star Trek* might have come close to the edge of that fine line
between satisfying the audience and overloading it, when *Star Trek: Voyager* began. "I still fear that the

series was put on too early," he says thoughtfully. "I think that it would have been a benefit to both *Voyager* and *Deep Space Nine* if a year or two had gone by after the end of *The Next Generation*. I think what a year or two would have done to *Deep Space Nine* is it would have let *the series* sit as the sole *Star Trek* show for a couple of years, which would have been great for it. Then, I think, *Voyager* would have been far more awaited and embraced. After all, how many hours of *Star Trek* can people devote their time to?"

Berman lists the viewing options that exist today. *The Next Generation* is on five to seven days a week in most markets. *Deep Space Nine* and *Voyager* air new episodes every week, and in many places, *Deep Space Nine* is already being stripped five days a week. Plus, *The Original Series* still airs across the country, and there are the added viewing opportunities provided by home-video copies of all the movies and most episodes.

Berman goes on to point out that when *The Next Generation* began, in 1987, there were no other comparable science-fiction series on the air. "But if you look at things today like *The X-Files* and *Babylon 5* and all the other science-fiction series, combined with the four different *Star Trek* shows that are available during a week, the average viewer doesn't have enough time to devote to everything."

Thus Berman is committed to trying to avoid the overexposure of *Star Trek* wherever possible. He shakes his head as he considers some of the proposals that have crossed his desk. "Believe me, there are a *lot* of *Star Trek*-related things that haven't been done in the last few years as a result of my getting politely crazy about them."

Looking ahead to the future of *Star Trek* in television, Berman says, "Right now, there's no reason to believe we're not going to have two more seasons of *Deep Space Nine,* and probably four more seasons of *Voyager.* But, when *Deep Space Nine* goes off the air and somebody starts saying, 'Let's get another one on—we have all these time slots to fill,' I'll do my very best to try to say no. It won't be fair to *Voyager,* and it won't be fair to the"—for a moment Berman hesitates, as if he were on the brink of revealing a secret before its time, then continues enigmatically—"to any new show that would come along. I don't think we have overexploited *Star Trek,* and I don't think we have made that 'one trip too many to the well.' But I do think over the last two or three years we have come pretty close, and I will continue to do my best to not have that happen."

With *Voyager's* television presence already planned to last until the year 2001, and with a tantalizing hint of at least one new series to follow, it seems certain that *The Next Generation's* fifteenth anniversary will find *Star Trek* still in weekly television production.

But what of *The Next Generation* itself? How long will its movies remain in production?

The blunt Hollywood answer is: Until one of them doesn't make money. But that's not likely to happen in the foreseeable future, because the people who shepherded the series to its greatest successes on television are the same people who are in charge of continuing to bring it to the movie screen.

In April 1997, Paramount Pictures announced that Michael Piller had been signed to write the third *Next Generation* movie, based on a story to be developed with Rick Berman, and slated to be released in late 1998.

As co-creator of *Deep Space Nine* and *Voyager,* Piller has remained involved with *Star Trek* for all the years following *The Next Generation's* last television season. But he is looking forward to returning to the characters with which he began.

For Piller, working on *Star Trek: The Next Generation* "was the greatest job that I ever had as a writer, or as a non-writer. It was really the defining moment of my career to be at that time and place, and

Michael Piller.

Concept paintings of *Star Trek: The Experience.*
COURTESY OF PARAMOUNT PARKS.

to participate in developing *The Next Generation* into the successful franchise that it became."

Even after four years of working on the series, Piller is confident there are more stories to be told. "Gene's influence continues to inspire me and continues to influence me, and I believe that it is his strong convictions about what made this franchise work that will continue to make it work in the future."

Like Berman, Piller considers the competition *The Next Generation* faces after ten years —competition that it helped bring into being. But for movies, Piller feels that the competition for the audience is not centered, as it is in television, on how much time viewers have to spend, but more on the content of the material. In the realm of content, Piller is convinced that *The Next Generation* has no peers.

"The difference between *Star Trek* and the franchises that try to be *Star Trek* is that they think that they're smarter than Gene. They think that they can create a show around a dark future, the armageddon future, the warlike future, and put people in the crises that those kinds of canvases bring. But I've always felt that this franchise is about a positive future, an optimistic outlook, and feeling good. This franchise has a remarkable ability to make people feel good about the future and their potential in the future. And I continue to believe that that is the secret to making this franchise continue to be successful. As long as we stay true to Roddenberry's spirit, we are going to be able to tell the kind of stories that I think touch people in a very intimate and personal way."

As to what the plot for the next film might be, Piller, for now, will only talk about his intentions for the story from his perspective as a writer. "I believe that we must tell a terrific yarn, and it's got to be a wonderful adventure. But at the core of it, I'm going to be most interested in exploring in this next movie—and I know Rick feels the same way—Picard's character, Data's character, and the characters of certain other regulars on our ship, and to find a way to tell a story that really does give us a chance to get inside the skin of those people again.

"That, to me, has always been the most rewarding part of writing. And for *The Next*

Generation, where the sky's the limit as far as subject material goes, and the cast is terrific, and there is the rare pleasure of writing for an actor of Patrick Stewart's abilities, it's such a treat to know that you can do things in this franchise that you can't do in so many others.

"I honestly believe that there is no problem in continuing the philosophies that Gene set forth for a television show into the feature world. I think that his stubbornness in staying true to those ideals really does light the path that we need to follow for the future of this franchise. In movies and in television."

First Contact appeared two years after *Generations* and, combining domestic and international box-office returns, became the highest-grossing *Star Trek* film yet. For now, Paramount has once more tentatively scheduled the next *Star Trek* film to appear only two years after the previous one. Is this a pace that can be continued? Rick Berman hopes not.

"I think that having movies coming out every two years is probably a little too frequent. I would prefer every two and a half, or three years. But it's not really a question of what I feel. It's a question of what the audience feels." Like most things in Hollywood, how the audience responds will set the pace for future film production. But if the two-year cycle holds up, then by 2002 and their sixteenth anniversary, the cast of *The Next Generation* will have equaled the number of films made by the original cast, and by then, the casts of *Deep Space Nine* and *Voyager* might also be available to join them for big-screen adventures.

The near future of *The Next Generation* in films seems to be as secure as the near future of *Star Trek* on television.

But even with Rick Berman's concern over overexploiting *Star Trek,* the next few years will offer some intriguingly new ways to enjoy the franchise—ways as far removed from traditional television and movies as television and movies are removed from radio.

The key to these new presentations of *Star Trek* is that they will be experienced by a carefully targeted and limited number of people, thus avoiding any chance of saturating the market.

One project calls for the production of a 3-D Imax film, about forty minutes long, which will play only in Imax theaters. Though the story is still to be worked out between Rick Berman and screenwriter Hans Tobeason, Berman explains that the film will be different from most other *Star Trek* presentations. "This is a film that will have some kind of educational element to it, simply because Imax locations are very often attached to museums and similar facilities." For now, Berman says, no decision has been made on who, if any, of the characters from the four series might appear. "But it will be *Star Trek* and it will be entertaining."

Perhaps the most eagerly anticipated new *Star Trek* venture is the new *Star Trek Experience* at the Las Vegas Hilton Hotel—a $70 million, 65,000-square-foot entertainment complex that takes visitors into *Star Trek*'s twenty-fourth century, first by beaming them to the bridge of the *Enterprise,* then by taking them on a motion-simulator shuttle ride, and finally bringing them to the Promenade of *Deep Space Nine,* where they'll be able to shop as well as to dine at Quark's bar.

With Rick Berman as Creative Consultant, Herman Zimmerman as Design Consultant, and René Echevarria and Ken Biller as the attraction's writers, every detail of the experience will be as close to *Star Trek*'s reality as twentieth-century technology can make it.

"The *Star Trek Experience* is probably the most fun thing I've done in a long time," Rick Berman says. "And it's going to be an *amazing* experience. We all know that there are a lot of *Star Trek* fans who take it very seriously and would love to experience the world of *Star Trek* as opposed to just watching it, and this is as close as you can come to the process. It's very exciting. It's a lot of fun."

Movies, television, Imax, walk-through re-creations. And what of interactive CD-ROMs, and the thirteen *Star Trek* books sold each minute worldwide?

What about the children with their *Star Trek* action figures, exploring strange new worlds in their backyards, in their imaginations?

The bridge of the *Enterprise*-D is re-created at *Star Trek: The Experience*. COURTESY OF PARAMOUNT PARKS.

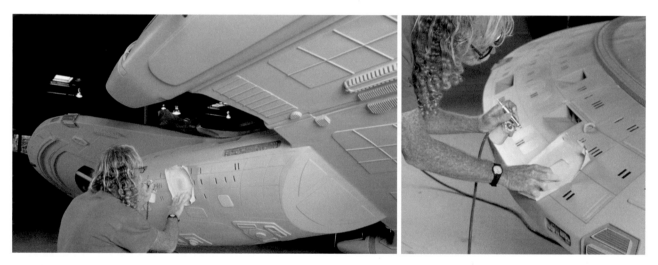

The entrance to *Star Trek: The Experience* features the largest starship models ever built. COURTESY OF PARAMOUNT PARKS.

Ten years ago, the Internet was a small, little-known computer network serving defense contractors, universities, and a few dedicated hobbyists. Today, millions of people around the world can log on, type in the words *Star Trek: The Next Generation,* and discover that there are more than *six million* sites on the Web that refer to it.

In science, there's a concept called critical mass.

It's the amount of fissile material required to permit a chain reaction to become self-sustaining.

More than thirty years ago, with *The Original Series,* Gene Roddenberry triggered a reaction in the hearts and minds of a few million people.

Ten years ago, with the birth of *The Next Generation,* that reaction approached critical mass in millions more. And sometime in the third or fourth season, critical mass was achieved and one person's dream truly became the world's.

So to all of the thousands of people who have worked so hard over the past ten years—as producers, writers, actors, artists, and technical crew—to give life to that dream and insure that the mission truly will continue, on behalf of all the millions who have been and will continue to be moved, inspired, challenged, intrigued, and entertained by your efforts—

Happy Tenth Anniversary.

Now get back to work.

On the eve of *The Next Generation*'s eleventh anniversary, the state of *Star Trek* is stronger than ever. Nowhere is that strength more apparent than in the buzz of excitement surrounding *Star Trek: Insurrection*—the newest feature film chronicling the continuing mission of Captain Picard and his crew.

Looking back over more than three decades of *Star Trek* production, it's quite clear that one of the many secrets of the franchise's success is the way it has changed over that time, continually being reinvented and refined by its creative team to fulfill the changing expectations of its audience. But equally clear is that the most important elements of *Star Trek* have *never* changed. After thirty-two years, the future that *Star Trek* depicts is still full of promise;

In *Insurrection*, Picard must take a stand against an unlikely foe—the Federation. ELLIOTT MARKS.

the inclusive sense of family remains integral to each crew; and though many science-fiction franchises have shown a tendency to veer off into tales of mind-numbing senseless action, *Star Trek* has remained an arena for storytelling in which issues are every bit as important as hardware and special effects.

Star Trek: Insurrection is but the latest example of all that makes the franchise so long-lived—it draws on the best of the past, adds much that is new, and at its heart tells an exciting story that has depth and meaning.

The film's producer, Rick Berman, who once again, for this newest adventure, shares story credit, is well aware of the need to weave together multiple components in a *Star Trek* movie and emphasizes, "We're constantly trying to better ourselves, to stay fresh." Berman's efforts, along with those of his team, have led, this time, to a movie with several different story arcs showcasing the unique essence of the *Star Trek* characters and universe. Berman describes the primary arc as, "Picard taking a very difficult, heroic stand when he feels that an inequity is taking place. He makes a huge sacrifice in order to do what he believes is right."

In the days before the film's release, the details of the events that lead Picard to his heroic actions remain shrouded in secrecy. But Berman is able to say that the ninth *Star Trek* movie "deals with an entire species of people on a planet that is inside a difficult-to-navigate portion of space affectionately called the Briar Patch." Unlike other stories in which Picard has gone against alien villains, "There's some degree of Picard standing up against the Federation as well. In this case, they're turning a blind eye to small group of people—with strange faces and strange-sounding names—who are far away." Berman explains that this conflict between Picard and the Federation is an important element of the movie's theme—one that will resonate with audiences of the twentieth century because, he believes, similar conflicts have greatly affected generations of our society.

However, it's not just meaningful ideas and themes that make a *Star Trek* story—it's how those elements are presented, dramatically and visually. And in both instances, *Insurrection* is a worthy successor to the *Star Trek* adventures that have gone before. "I think the movie definitely has more action than any film that we have made," Berman continues, "and it also has a good deal more romance than any of the films that we have ever made. Simultaneously, we have a little bit of a *Heart of Darkness* story dealing with Data, and we also have a little bit of a Fountain of Youth story in terms of what is the unique quality of this world and why so many people want to get hold of it."

It is this alien planet with its intriguing Fountain of Youth qualities that, in particular, adds a fresh new look to *Star Trek: Insurrection*. As award-winning production designer Herman Zimmerman describes it, "Visually, I think this film's certainly been more challenging than any of the more recent ones. And certainly, it's the most expensive film from the set-design, set-construction point of view since *Star Trek:*

Berman reveals that in *Insurrection* "We have a little bit of a *Heart of Darkness* story with Data." ELLIOTT MARKS.

The Motion Picture. Insurrection had eighteen more sets than we had on *Star Trek: First Contact,* and that picture had thirty-seven sets."

The biggest, most elaborate set of all—perhaps the biggest set ever constructed for a *Star Trek* film—is the Fountain-of-Youth planet's beautiful, and sprawling, Ba'ku village.

Alien villages are nothing new to *Star Trek.* Dozens have been featured on episodes of *The Next Generation, Deep Space Nine,* and *Voyager.* Zimmerman had also led the design team that created the impressive dystopian community of Paradise City in *Star Trek V: The Final Frontier.*

But Zimmerman is quick to point out, "We have never done a village as complete as the Ba'ku village that we created for this film. It's a real place that took up quite a bit of acreage and had a lot of components. It had a farm-irrigation system for the farm, barns for the animals, a farmer's house. We had a whole city square—which we called the 'rotunda'—a circle with market carts and outdoor stalls. And then living quarters, houses, what you might call a big city hall, and a bakery. There was quite a lot to it."

Designing and building such an elaborate set is often not a guarantee that the audience will be able to appreciate the artistry of the production designer and his team. But Zimmerman is pleased with how his work turned out. "You'll see almost all of the village in the opening of the picture. They did an incredible job of editing the opening, and you get a real sense of what this place is—a gorgeous, landscaped piece of architecture that anybody would be delighted to live in."

Part of the challenge of designing the village was creating that sense of enticing comfort while at the same time making it appear like no village on Earth. Zimmerman explains, "The concept of the village was a combination of different Pacific Rim architectures blended together. And one of our criteria was that the people who live there have an ideal climate, so they don't need screens. They don't have

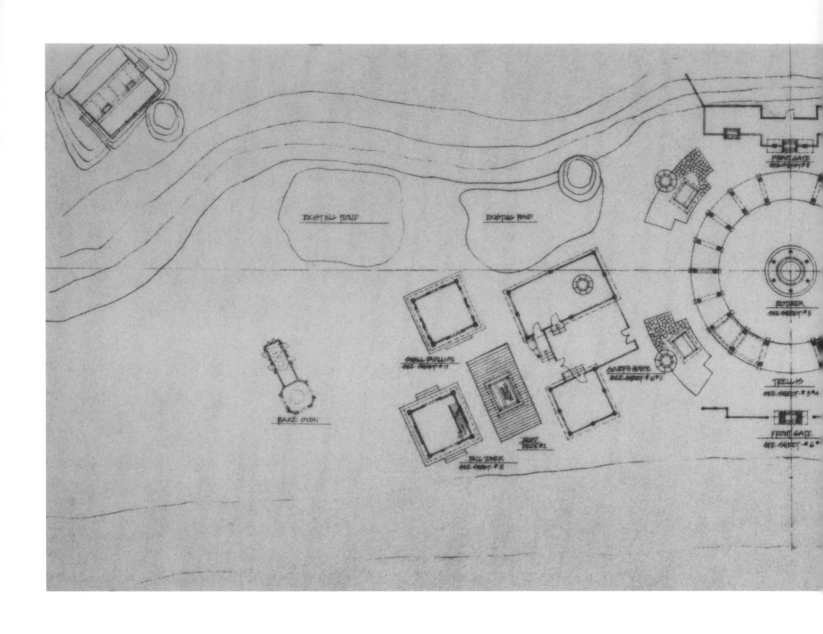

After the initial plans were drawn, the Ba'ku village took shape as a set of architectural models. PENNY JUDAY.

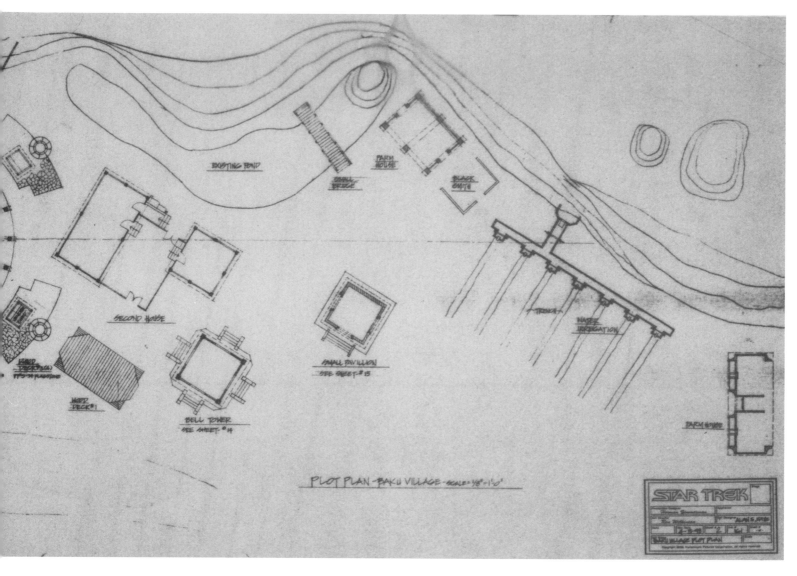

Site plan for one of the largest *Star Trek* sets ever built—the Ba'ku village.

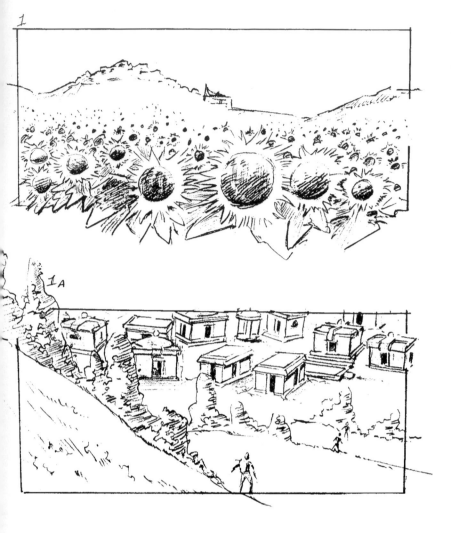

FLY IN.

These storyboard illustrations show part of *Insurrection*'s opening sequence, revealing the apparently idyllic Ba'ku village.

nasty insects. They don't have to put locks on their doors. They don't need glass because they prefer to live both indoors and outdoors. The houses are all fairly open for that reason, and lightweight fabrics are used instead of window treatments. It's a lovely place to exist, by a meandering river, and with all the lush landscape around it, it's Shangri-la."

In fact, the Ba'ku village was such a fully realized creation that it wasn't treated as a manufactured set by the movie crew. It was treated as an actual location, by Jonathan Frakes—reprising his roles as both Commander William Riker and the movie's director.

Zimmerman says only the action sequences featuring optical and visual-effects sequences were storyboarded by an artist to show how the village would be used. "The dialogue, the walk-and-talk, the interplay between the characters, that's all a product of the director's expertise. He sees what he's got and works with it. As you would if you were going into a practical location—downtown Beverly Hills, for instance. You'd look at the streets and the doorways and the park areas, whatever the script was calling for, and you'd design your action to suit."

Rick Berman also credits the Ba'ku village for bringing a distinctive look to *Insurrection.* "One of the things that's different about the movie as a piece of filmmaking is that a huge amount of it was shot on location. Locations near Los Angeles, and locations way up in the High Sierras. With literally hundreds—220 extras—in a whole series of scenes."

Jonathan Frakes agrees that this film won't look like any other *Star Trek* film. "The most obvious difference is that we were out on location for six or seven weeks, so it is an outside movie—an exterior movie. It's wonderful and lush, and," he adds with a laugh, "usually we don't see too many trees in *Star Trek.*"

Star Trek productions, both for the televised series and the feature movies, have always had the reputation of being on the leading edge of film production. Looking back on the past eleven years, Herman Zimmerman recalls, "there are a lot of things that are different. The state-of-the-art optical work on film has progressed geometrically from when I started doing *The Next*

One structure near the Ba'ku village looks nothing like the other rustic buildings. Its purpose is one of the intriguing secrets that brings Picard and the *Enterprise*-E on a mission to this world. ELLIOTT MARKS.

Two hundred twenty extras took part in the filming of *Insurrection*, making the film one of the largest and most complex *Star Trek* productions yet. ELLIOTT MARKS.

In keeping with *Star Trek*'s message of inclusivity for all species, *Insurrection* marks another first as this llama boldly goes where no llama has gone before.
ELLIOTT MARKS.

Generation in 1986-87. We were using backlit graphics, for instance, that either didn't move or moved with a mechanical device called 'polar motion,' which made sequences look like they had some animation in the background. But they were really just repeated animation. They weren't anything that was continuous or that could be used as a story point. We didn't use background television screens in 1987, and it was probably three or four years into *Star Trek: The Next Generation* before, instead of those polar motions, we went to television monitors that could be programmed.

"But by now, eleven years later, we can do computer-generated graphics right on the set with an operator typing in commands and altering images in real time. That certainly wasn't possible when we started out."

The use of new techniques and technologies is not limited to the more technological sets of *Star Trek*, though. In *Insurrection*, even the Ba'ku village benefited from a literally cutting-edge development in CAD-CAM—computer-aided design and manufacturing.

"For instance," Zimmerman explains, "in the Ba'ku village, we made all the columns out of Styrofoam. The drawings went onto a computer disk and were transferred to a master computer on a machine that cut them out to our specifications with a hot-wire knife, making ten-foot-high, eighteen-inch-around, very convoluted shapes which were then hardcoated and made to look like stone. That was actually the basis for most of the buildings that you see in the Ba'ku village. And that's a technique that wasn't available earlier than about five years ago. It's the first time, I think, we've used it on a *Star Trek* picture, and it turned out beautifully."

Even with all the time and effort spent on the Ba'ku village, the *Star Trek* audience doesn't need to worry that other favorite sets were ignored. The *Enterprise*-E is back in *Insurrection*, and looking better than ever with a new piece of equipment on the bridge.

"We tried something in *Star Trek: First Contact* that worked well for that picture but didn't really seem like a good idea on a continuing basis," Zimmerman says. "That was to use a viewscreen that was on only when you asked for it, and otherwise you were looking at a wall. This goes back to Gene Roddenberry's original philosophy of the *Enterprise*, but we've always had a problem letting the viewers know that the viewscreen is a screen and not a window to space.

"If the view is facing forward, we're seeing things in the front of the ship, mostly. It's an obvious conclusion to draw that that's a great big window. In fact, it is not. It's an image that's taken from a forward view or from any other view where there's a camera on an exterior skin of the ship. But we thought we would make a statement on *First Contact* by eliminating the idea of a window even as a possibility, by showing that there's a wall there every time you're not looking at a viewscreen.

"That worked well for *First Contact* because, for the most part, the ship was disabled and they were unable to use those exterior cameras. They were being held captive by the Borg on their own ship. But that didn't work for *Insurrection*."

The end result, Zimmerman says, is that "We now have a viewscreen that is similar to the older-model viewscreens. It's a nice shape that goes with the design of the interior of the *Enterprise*-E, but it's a tried-and-true viewer that everybody's familiar with."

The Ba'ku village under construction. The large columns were manufactured using CAD-CAM techniques that translated the information in the designers' computer drawings directly into commands for the computer-controlled equipment that carved the columns from Styrofoam. For structural strength, each column was supported from within by wooden beams. PENNY JUDAY.

A sneak preview of one small part of a Son'a control room shows that the *Star Trek* Art Department is once again setting the standard for the depiction of alien technology in science-fiction films. ELLIOTT MARKS.

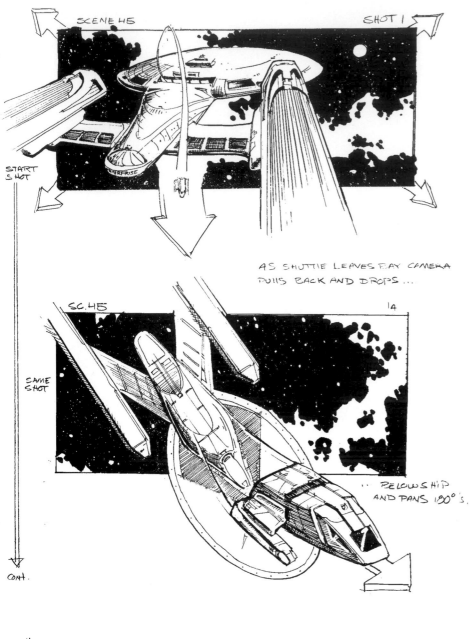

SCENE 45 SHOT 1

START SHOT

AS SHUTTLE LEAVES BAY CAMERA
PULLS BACK AND DROPS...

SC. 45   1A

SAME
SHOT

... FELOWSHIP
AND PANS 180°'s.

CONT.

SC 45   1B

END
SHOT

As this storyboard sequence shows, the *Enterprise*-E returns in Insurrection.
Though this time, she will be realized completely through the use of
computer imagery—a *Star Trek* first.

The *Enterprise* is not the only starship
featured in the film, though, so the stage is
set for some all-new designs as well, both
for Starfleet vessels and those belonging to
a new race of aliens.

The disquieting appearance of the
Son'a is one of the best-kept secrets of
Insurrection, and even the barest hints of their
impressive technology are being carefully
kept under wraps. But it can be revealed that
the Son'a have created a vessel of such
immense proportions that one of the sets
depicting its interior could be achieved only
by a seamless blend of physical construction
and computer-generated imagery. The injec-
tor/collector set, as it is known, rivals the
impressive deflector dish set of *First Contact*
in size, and in the words of Jonathan Frakes,
"It provided the same headaches."

Site of a climactic confrontation
between two of the film's key characters,
the injector/collector set as constructed on
Paramount's Stage 15 represents, in
Herman Zimmerman's words, "probably
one-hundred-thousandth of the size of the
actual ship." On the screen, the characters
who confront each other in this mind-boggling arena will appear to be climbing on
slender supports above a miles-deep
abyss—courtesy of the same computer
visual-effects wizardry that placed Picard
in the middle of tens of millions of Borg in
the opening sequence of *First Contact.*

Though the abyss itself exists only on
film, the physical portion of the set that
was actually built offered dangers enough
of its own. Jonathan Frakes recounts that
"We used a lot of cranes, and a lot of scis-
sor-lifts, and a lot of manpower," to film
the injector/collector sequences. "There
were a lot of guys strapped to cables so
they wouldn't fall off the edge of this set."

The use of computer-generated
imagery—CGI—reaches an important
new *Star Trek* milestone in *Insurrection,* even
more impressive than its traditional uses in
earlier films to create alien vistas and phaser blasts. For the first time in a *Star Trek*
movie, not one shot of a model spacecraft

will be used. Instead, every alien craft, every shuttlecraft, and every Starfleet vessel—*including* the *Starship Enterprise*—will be computer-generated.

CGI starships have appeared in other *Star Trek* films. Many of the Starfleet vessels that engaged the Borg in *First Contact* existed only as mathematical constructs of pixels. In *Generations,* when the *Enterprise*-B encountered the nexus, it was a CGI version that reflected the flickering energy displays.

But in both those films, the majority of shots of both starships were created by photographing large, detailed physical models.

The only trace of a model in *Insurrection* is the surface detail that appears on the *Enterprise*-E. Still photographs of the model used in *First Contact* were digitized, then "texture-mapped" onto the skin of the CGI version of the ship to add realistic detail and shading.

According to Peter Lauritson, the innovative producer who pioneered the use of electronic compositing for visual effects in the first season of *The Next Generation,* in time, the use of totally CGI spacecraft will become the norm, even for the *Star Trek* television series. Though for now in television, where time and money are always in short supply, the use of models still does provide some advantages over computer imagery.

Costumer Designer Robert Blackman sees to some last-minute adjustments on the set. ELLIOTT MARKS.

"There are always certain kinds of shots that models are better for," Lauritson says, "and actually can be more effective and basically quicker and cheaper."

An example of such a shot is what Lauritson calls a "paintscraper." That is, "If you want to get extremely close on any section of a spaceship, a model usually holds up better and is more economical to do that way. If you're creating a structure that you're going to have a camera moving around at various different angles, a lot of times that can be cheaper and easier to deal with as a miniature."

There are several shots like that in *Insurrection,* but with the extra time and money available for a movie, Lauritson, who is both co-producer and second-unit director for the movie, felt, "The CGI approach was a better overall way to work because a majority of the shots were better done that way. So on those few that needed some extra effort and expense, CGI-wise, it was worth doing them that way."

Considering that almost any behind-the-scenes story about movie production inevitably must mention the crew's struggle to stay on a tight schedule and budget, Peter Lauritson's matter-of-fact comment about incurring extra effort and expense might seem unusual. But his words reflect a new dynamic in the ongoing production of *Star Trek* films.

The Next Generation and the *Star Trek* production team have nothing to prove. *Generations* was, in a way, a gamble. It was obvious the movie audience liked the original *Star Trek* characters enough to support six films, but would they be interested in seeing a movie about a crew they had followed on television for seven years? The answer was an encouraging, though not necessarily resounding, yes.

Thus, a little bit of hesitancy still existed among Paramount executives. What if the success of the seventh *Star Trek* film, *Generations,* hinged in some way on the mere novelty of seeing the *Next Generation* crew on the big screen, or on the familiar presence of Kirk, Scott, and Chekov? How would the audience respond to a second film that was pure *Next Generation*?

The eighth *Star Trek* movie, *First Contact,* the highest-grossing *Star Trek* film of all time, answered that question with no room for doubt.

One of *The Next Generation*'s most influential writers, Michael Piller, returns to write the screenplay for *Insurrection*, from a story by Piller and Rick Berman. ELLIOTT MARKS.

With *First Contact*, it was apparent to all that the *Star Trek* juggernaut has smoothly shown its ability to cross the generations, and there is no reason to doubt that its appeal will continue, as long as the same care that has sustained it over the past thirty-two years is maintained. Thus, for *Insurrection*, almost everyone on the ninth feature production team noted that Paramount was more generous in terms of budget and scheduling for this film. With all doubts assuaged, the studio seemed content to let the tried-and-true *Star Trek* team do what they do best—make a great *Star Trek* adventure.

As Herman Zimmerman sees it, "I think the *Star Trek* franchise is getting wider every year. So the studio is well aware of its 'golden-egg' character and I'm sure is, within reason, willing to support it financially because they know it's a winner."

Of course, *Star Trek* is a winner not only because of its imaginative settings and state-of-the-art visual effects. For those aspects of *Star Trek* to have meaning, they must be part of what truly brings *Star Trek* fans back for more, year after year, series after series, and film after film.

In the words of one of *The Next Generation*'s most influential writers, Michael Piller, that all-important ingredient is "a good yarn."

So it's no wonder that for the latest installment of Picard and company's ongoing saga, Rick Berman enlisted Piller's insight and talent to co-write the story for *Star Trek IX*.

Berman's enthusiasm over Piller's return is infectious. "It was a delight working with Michael on this. As much as I love Ron [Moore] and Brannon [Braga], during the course of both of the movies that we wrote together, they were fully employed on television shows, so we were always wrestling to find time to work together. Michael Piller is in development at Paramount and this script became an integral part of his year.

Michael Piller sees Captain Jean-Luc Picard not as "a man of violence, but as a man of principle." ELLIOTT MARKS.

"It was a terrific experience—as enjoyable as when we created *Deep Space Nine* seven years ago. And he wrote an absolutely delightful script."

Piller is equally upbeat about his return to *The Next Generation*. "I got a great deal of pleasure out of coming back and revisiting these characters. And not only that, having the chance to work again with Patrick and Brent and everyone in the cast I'm reminded of how lucky the *Next Generation* writers were to have such talented actors say our words. They just raise the material and light up the screen every time they're on."

Back at the beginning of the writing process, even before the development of the *Insurrection* story was underway, Michael Piller knew what he wanted to bring to it, independent of specific story points and plot twists. "In terms of the actual characters," he recalls, "I had a very strong commitment to bring to this movie a sense of the family that I believe we had come to know and love on the mission of *The Next Generation* which was quite different from the first two movies where they were trying very hard to establish Picard as an action hero and Data as his number-one sidekick."

For this new movie, Piller wanted to show Picard "as the center and a moral leader of a family that would follow him to the ends of the Earth—well, the ends of the universe—to do what's right. I also wanted to rediscover that part of him that showed he was, by definition, a man of principle. To me, his greatest uniqueness as a hero was based on his mind, and the ethical and moral leadership that he provided. He was not a man of violence, but a man of principle. Though I had to deal with the fact that he had evolved in the movies into a man of action."

Like Rick Berman, Michael Piller and Patrick Stewart shared the desire to better their earlier work,

Marina Sirtis and Gates McFadden return as Commander Troi and Doctor Crusher. ELLIOTT MARKS.

and though everyone knew that *Generations* and *First Contact* were successful films of which everyone involved could be proud, a period of analysis and reassessment began. "Patrick was very concerned," Piller recalls. "He felt that the greatest shortcoming of *Generations* was that it was too much like the television show. And he felt that the problems in Picard's character as a movie hero were solved by *First Contact*. So he did not want to go back to the television show, while I wanted to take what I had known and loved about the character on the show and introduce that part of him to the moviegoing audience who, I felt, hadn't really seen the definitive Picard.

"In *Generations*," Piller continues, "he was sort of weeping and second-guessing his choices of a career, which really wasn't fundamental 'Picard.' In *First Contact*, he was on a mission of vengeance, which again is not really typical 'Picard.' And neither one of them is an archetypal-hero role. I felt that to be a hero, he should be acting out of a moral and ethical mindset, and stand for principles that are important to mankind, and certainly to the Federation."

According to all early reports, *Insurrection* entertainingly captures that deeper aspect of Picard's character. "Ultimately," Piller concludes, "we came up with a very original script that is funny and serious, topical, and relevant to themes of our life and existence today. It's a movie *about* something, which I'm very proud of, because that's always the first question I ask a writer when somebody's pitching me: What's it about? So, I think we've got something pretty special."

Piller's passion for *all* the *Next Generation* characters ensured that the movie's concentration on Picard did not result in a slighting of the other cast members. "I think you're going to see some things with the characters you haven't seen the other movies," Piller says. "Some of the most fun things to write and some of the greatest reactions from people at the studio and others who have read the script are genuinely new moments with Geordi, with Troi, and with Riker. It's a unique, original story that

Michael Piller promises his script for *Insurrection* offers some "genuinely new moments" for Troi and Riker. ELLIOTT MARKS.

Worf takes a leave of absence from his duties on Deep Space 9 to once again serve on Picard's crew. ELLIOTT MARKS.

The *Star Trek* Art Department's legendary attention to detail continues to create the illusion that the twenty-fourth century is real. ELLIOTT MARKS.

The good news is that in the twenty-fourth century, the dream of the paperless office finally will have been achieved. The bad news is, offices apparently will still be just as cluttered. ELLIOTT MARKS.

Picard's ready room aboard the *Enterprise*-E. ELLIOTT MARKS.

Look closely, and you might recognize another starship's sickbay beneath the finishing details. ELLIOTT MARKS.

Two-time Tony Award-winning Donna Murphy was one of the first actors to be considered for the part of a Ba'ku woman. ELLIOTT MARKS.

deals with science fiction in a way that *Star Trek* has done only once in a while. A story that is light and fun, and at the same time has a great deal of relevance."

Again, however, Berman's and Piller's story, like the contributions from the technical and design crews, is still only one part of what makes a great *Star Trek* movie. What about the characters themselves—the actors?

That brings us to one of the least understood, and certainly least written-about aspects of *Star Trek's* ongoing production—casting.

Junie Lowry-Johnson is a casting director for *Insurrection,* and has been with *The Next Generation* since casting the crew for the pilot episode, "Encounter at Farpoint," continuing through all seven seasons and three movies, as well being a part of the complete runs to date of *Deep Space Nine* and *Voyager.* She has been honored by her peers with two Emmys® for her casting work on the television series *NYPD Blue.* Yet for all her experience and expertise, she says bluntly, "My mother has no idea what I do. It's too hard to explain."

That sentiment is shared by Lowry-Johnson's fellow casting director, Ron Surma, who has been with *The Next Generation* since the third season and is also a casting director for the latest film.

In simple terms, casting directors work to find the best actor for a role. But casting work is never simple. The reason, Lowry-Johnson and Surma conclude, is that the entire process is a matter of personal taste. "It's a really complex situation," Lowry-Johnson explains, "and nobody can just put their finger on it." The process is further complicated by the fact that, to a certain extent, everyone can recognize a talented actor. "But even among people who can recognize talent," Lowry-Johnson continues, "people have different tastes. So no matter how good you are, it's just subjective. It's just what you like or what you don't like."

However, when it comes to casting actors for a *Star Trek* production, there are some considerations that are not subjective, because of *Star Trek's* very specific needs.

First of all, Ron Surma says, he, Lowry-Johnson, and the *Star Trek* producers tend to look at the résumés of the actors "to see if they've had a lot of classical theater experience. Theatrical experience is wonderful training and, I think, gives an actor more versatility."

Next, he points out one of the most important qualifications for a potential *Star Trek* actor. "We can't use accents. Actors playing aliens should not have an accent that lets you figure out where they're from on Earth. That's the big difference between *Star Trek* and other shows."

The casting directors' job begins long before it's time for actors to come in and audition for a role. The starting point is the script.

"When we get the script," Lowry-Johnson says, "we read it and make our breakdown." In the case of *Insurrection,* "I would have a general meeting with Rick Berman and Jonathan Frakes, and see what they're looking for. And then we would start assembling lists for those particular characters."

Character descriptions at this stage are usually general, not specific. For *Star Trek,* it's not necessary to think of a role as being suitable for a Bruce Willis or a Nicholas Cage. In fact, at the beginning of the casting discussions for *Insurrection,* Lowry-Johnson learned that Paramount had done research and discovered that the addition of prominent movie stars does not add to the appeal of *Star Trek* movies. "If you had Arnold Schwarzenegger in there," she explains, "my feeling is, that's bigger than the picture. It drastically changes the movie and takes you out of it." Thus, one secret to *Star Trek* casting is to find exceptional actors who will be accepted as their characters, and not cultural icons who will constantly remind the audience that it is watching a movie star performing a role.

Sometimes, the producers' and director's instructions to the casting directors can be specific. For *First Contact,* James Cromwell was considered for the part of Zefram Cochrane from the beginning, just as Alfre Woodard was always a front-runner for the part of Lily.

However, for *Insurrection,* Lowry-Johnson says that in the initial meetings, neither the producers nor Jonathan Frakes had anyone in mind for the three key guest-star roles—the Son'a leader, a Starfleet admiral, and the Ba'ku woman who would become Picard's romantic interest.

Thus, the casting process began from scratch, with Lowry-Johnson and Surma beginning their work as they always do, by drawing up a list of literally hundreds of possible actors for each part.

"Ron and I have a philosophy," Lowry-Johnson says, "that you do a huge, massive list for each character, so that when we would have our meeting with Rick and Jonathan, it triggered a lot of thoughts, and a lot of ideas. You veto a tremendous number of peo-

Anthony Zerbe as the admiral who confronts Picard. ELLIOTT MARKS.

Stephanie Niznik as the new Trill stationed at ops on the *Enterprise*-E. ELLIOTT MARKS.

Production Designer Herman Zimmerman confers with Producer
Rick Berman, on location. ELLIOTT MARKS.

ple just in the first meeting, saying no, not right, not this, not that, but it gets people thinking, and it makes you realize how few choices there really are for a part.

"Some people like to do a list with just fifty people on it. But I like to get to that point after we've done the 'kitchen sink' list. Sometimes, at the end of the process, when you haven't cast a part and you're all discouraged, you can go back to that great big list, and names will jump out at you that you missed the first go-around."

After a list of hundreds is winnowed in an initial meeting, a second round of further cutting is generally accomplished after reviewing tapes of the actors under consideration. Even then, the actual number of actors who might come in to audition for a part varies considerably.

For the part of the Ba'ku woman with whom Picard becomes involved, Ron Surma says no more than twenty actors read for the role that was eventually offered to Donna Murphy.

"She's a remarkable actress," Lowry-Johnson says, "with a very prestigious background." Part of that background includes two Tony Awards® for her performances in the Broadway plays, *Passion* and *The King and I.*

Donna Murphy was one of the first actors to be considered for the role, and one of the first to be invited to read for it. After her reading, it was so apparent to the producers and Jonathan Frakes that she was perfect for the part that few others were asked to come in.

Still, some other actors *were* asked, just in case.

Both Lowry-Johnson and Surma have experienced situations in which the very first actor to read for a part was so impressive that it seemed obvious to cast him or her. However, since the casting process is so often a long undertaking, very few people are willing to accept that the first actor to read is the best. Invariably, other actors continue to read, if only to confirm that the first choice is the best one.

"That's exactly how it happens," Lowry-Johnson says. "A lot of the time you come right back to the people you saw the very first day, or your first person sometimes. And sometimes directors say, 'Isn't that interesting?' but as casting people, you do try and bring in your best ideas at the beginning. At least, that's what we've always done.

"Sometimes it doesn't work so well. The producers and directors still want to see the world. But then I realize they also need to do that because you learn a lot during casting. You learn about the part. You learn what continues to interest you. What doesn't interest you. You see things you never dreamed of that you like. Because everyone brings something different. No matter what. Everyone always has a little bit different take on a role. And those differences make the process very interesting."

Some actors, by virtue of their previous work, are not always required to audition for a role. In *Insurrection,* the critical role of the Son'a leader is played by F. Murray Abraham, who in 1984 earned the Best Actor Academy Award® for his performance as Salieri in *Amadeus.* Abraham was offered his part in *Insurrection* without an audition.

In Jonathan Frakes's words, "this movie was even more fun to make than *First Contact*." ELLIOTT MARKS.

Then, in a reversal reminiscent of the way in which Marina Sirtis and Denise Crosby switched roles in the first season of *The Next Generation*, the actor who was initially considered to be the best choice for the role that went to Abraham ended up being offered the equally critical role of the Starfleet admiral who comes into direct conflict with Captain Picard.

The part of the admiral is played by Anthony Zerbe, who, as Jonathan Frakes describes him, "is a legend on the West Coast in theatre."

When Zerbe read for the part of the Son'a leader, he electrified his audience of producers, casting directors, and Jonathan Frakes, by not beginning with the script pages he had been given, but by performing lines from Dante's *Inferno*, then moving into his character's lines as written by Michael Piller.

Frakes recalls that the decision to offer the role of the admiral to Zerbe was unanimous, and, "paid off in spades. He's fabulous in the film. The scene with him and Patrick discussing the Prime Directive has the same weight, I think, as the *Moby Dick* scene with Alfre and Patrick in the last film."

Casting is not just limited to major roles, and, surprisingly, it can sometimes be harder to cast a small role involving only two lines of dialogue, than to cast a major part.

Since *The Next Generation*'s Tenth Anniversary, *Star Trek: The Experience* at the Las Vegas Hilton Hotel has opened to rave reviews and sold-out business. Rick Berman would not be surprised if Paramount decided to open similar attractions in new venues. COURTESY OF PARAMOUNT PARKS.

Ron Surma explains that the smaller roles, "are very hard parts to cast, because for those two lines, you're looking for something very specific. Whether it be a Starfleet officer, or an alien officer on the bridge of one of the other ships, it's very specific and you want to hear it read just the way you want it done."

Lowry-Johnson adds that the search for a perfect reading of the small parts is once again connected to *Star Trek*'s unique requirements for actors. "The two biggest problems that people run into are they cannot do the language—it's very technical, and besides not knowing exactly what it means, it's very matter-of-fact—and some people are just too contemporary in their approach, or their language, or their accent, or their looks. Those two things weed out a lot of people."

Ron Surma notes that the people who have the most success in overcoming those two obstacles are usually those with extensive theatrical experience, which is why such experience is important on an actor's résumé.

One obstacle that faces the *Star Trek* casting directors in their job is not connected to an actor's ability. Some actors, especially in television, don't *want* to be in a *Star Trek* production.

Surma points out that some actors just don't want to wear alien makeup. Lowry-Johnson adds that that decision isn't necessarily based on vanity. Some actors get claustrophobic when their faces are covered by one of Michael Westmore's creations. And there are those actors who just can't handle the challenges of reciting *Star Trek*'s so-called "technobabble." It can be extremely difficult to memorize lines when an actor has no idea what those lines mean.

These concept paintings depict the newest *Star Trek* exhibit, scheduled to open in Düsseldorf, Germany, in late 1998. As *Star Trek*'s popularity continues to grow internationally, more exhibits are being planned for other countries.
CONCEPT ART BY HENRICK TAMM.

The easy-going camaraderie amongst the company of *The Next Generation*... ELLIOTT MARKS.

But resistance to being in a *Star Trek* production is something that is generally limited to the television series. As Lowry-Johnson says, "Actors *always* want to be in a movie! And, I think, *Star Trek* movies are actually considered very prestigious. Probably because of our basic cast of Patrick and Jonathan and Brent. And the fact that for the last two films we've had really exceptional casts, with *First Contact* becoming the most successful of all the *Star Trek* movies there have ever been." Then she adds, "And some people are closet science-fiction fans. People you would never, ever suspect." She declines to name names, however.

If casting is a process difficult to explain, at least the success of every *Star Trek* series and movie that Junie Lowry-Johnson and Ron Surma have been involved with shows they're doing their jobs well.

"Until you've been in on the process," Lowry-Johnson says, "I think it's a very hard experience to explain." But, she continues, describing the appeal of her job, "I think casting is really fun. I think it's really exciting to be in a room and have an actor come in and just make something so real that there is a feeling of excitement—like real life happening right in front of you. People react to it without being able to understand why they're reacting, but sometimes an entire room will get excited. By this little performance that this person did. That's an amazing power. And I think it's a gift to be privy to that."

And, like so many parts of the *Star Trek* production experience, it's a gift that is shared with millions of *Star Trek* fans who are able to enjoy the end result of the casting directors' work.

Dramatically, visually, personally—once again all the compelling threads of a *Star Trek* adventure have been woven together to create a unique entertainment experience. But after eleven years of *The Next Generation*, after thirty-two years of *Star Trek*, that should come as no surprise.

Herman Zimmerman explains why. "This team of department heads who have done *Star Trek* features and/or *Star Trek* television programs for a number of years worked like clockwork. One of the reasons we were able to do such a fine picture even though we started late was the short-hand we all know, being familiar with each other and how the *Star Trek* stories have worked in the past, and what the problems that we solved in the past have been."

Zimmerman doesn't stop there. "Jonathan Frakes is delightful to work with. He's understanding and creative, and makes it a lot of fun at the same time. And Rick Berman and Jonathan are in complete synch with each other. Producers and directors generally have an adversarial association, at least part of the time, during the filming of a picture. That just doesn't happen with those two guys. Rick is a consummate producer, and entirely in control of the story. And he and Michael Piller, who wrote the piece, have worked together for a number of years.

"And we had Mike Okuda and Denise

…is apparent on and off screen. ELLIOT MARKS.

Okuda, and we had Terry Frazee, the effects man who's done several of our pictures. And Matt Leonetti, who photographed *First Contact* so well. I could name almost everybody.

"We had a top-notch crew and they all put their backs to it. I think this film is going to be one of the best."

Zimmerman's enthusiasm and respect for his fellow members of the *Insurrection* crew is shared by everyone, with predictable and much appreciated results.

"If anything," Jonathan Frakes says with satisfaction, "this movie was even more fun to make than *First Contact,* and I was so thrilled to have the family back intact. It wasn't easier, because the movie was hard, and it's a much more complicated and intricate film. But having already done one film with this group, meaning the cast and most of the crew, I think it gave all of us a better opportunity to make a better movie—which this is."

Of course, no matter how good the advance word on *Insurrection,* true *Star Trek* fans are sure to have one overriding question in regard to this ninth movie outing....

Is it good enough to break the curse of the odd-numbered *Star Trek* film?

Jonathan Frakes has the answer to that, having to do with the title the crew affectionately bestowed upon the film during production. "I think just by calling it *Nine of Ten,* we broke the curse."

Without question, on the eve of its eleventh anniversary, the future of *Star Trek: The Next Generation* is as bright as the future it imagines for us all.

The mission continues, with the promise of many more anniversaries to come.

Robert Justman on the set of *Star Trek: First Contact.*
ELLIOTT MARKS. COURTESY OF ROBERT JUSTMAN.

A FTERWORD

"The Missing Year"

by Robert H. Justman

Co-Producer, *Star Trek*
Supervising Producer, *Star Trek: The Next Generation*

H OPEFULLY, THIS POSTSCRIPT will please you. I want to please you, dear reader, because you've pleased me for so many years as one of *Star Trek*'s loyal fans — or, should I say, rather than loyal fans, loyal advocates? For you really are advocates, advocates of an ethical existence and enthusiastic advocates of a television show that postulates that selfsame ethical existence.

Star Trek didn't convert previously unthinking, insensitive people into thinking, sensitive ones. We, the people who made the show, didn't lead our viewers onto a higher plane of human existence. Most of you already had chosen a path, a moral way of life, so your innate beliefs were verified by what we presented every week. You *knew* what was right. *Star Trek* just confirmed your opinion; better than that, it validated beliefs for which you no longer had to feel guilty. There were others just like us, countless others who believed as we did. The future was bright; we *could* make a difference. We were all out there together, lost in the stars, in a vast uncharted universe, little specks of matter residing upon a little larger speck of matter — and perhaps we were not alone.

It has been well over thirty years since the first *Star Trek* episode was televised. I may not want to, but I can accept that fact. Grudgingly. After all, I don't feel nearly as old as I might look. But a new milestone (or is it "millstone"?) has come to weigh me down with the knowledge that *tempus fugit* — and it seems to fugit ever faster as I grow ever older.

Now it seems I must face up to yet another anniversary. Ten years ago, *Star Trek: The Next Generation* debuted before a skeptical audience composed, in part, of eager media critics with an axe to grind, competing television-industry executives predicting instant and utter failure, skeptical "Trekkers" whose passionate loyalty was to the original "classic Trek" (a show they knew they had "saved" from oblivion in syndication hell), and a vast number of bored channel switchers with remote controls seemingly grafted into their free hands. This last contingent owed loyalty to no one other than themselves; all they wanted was to be entertained, preferably by something of substance. I'm proud that, with Gene Roddenberry, Rick Berman, and a talented group of professionals, I helped satisfy some, if not all, of the above groups by producing that first pivotal season of "Son of *Star Trek*"—better known to all as *Star Trek: The Next Generation.*

Yes, ten years have passed since *ST: TNG* first aired, but I can recount some tales about an even earlier "missing" eleventh year when creative ideas were birthed and vital decisions were made. For me, it all began with a party. Paramount studios threw a twenty-year anniversary party at world-famous Chasen's restaurant to celebrate the September 8, 1966, telecast of *The Original Series'* first episode, "Man Trap." And, I was invited.

Why me? I wondered. And, why a party in the first place? Did it foretell something? Surely Paramount, thrifty as ever, wouldn't spring for and publicize an expensive party just to reminisce about old times. Besides, not one of the Paramount executives present that festive evening had even been involved with *The Original Series.* In fact, some of them were still schoolchildren when it was made. Something was in the wind and I had a pretty good idea what it was. So, after hoisting a few with Gene Roddenberry, I went home to wait.

I didn't have to wait very long. In a few weeks I was back at Paramount to rejoin Gene Roddenberry (no, he wasn't coming apart). Surprise, surprise! Paramount had decided to make a new *Star Trek* series. It was a noble and altruistic gesture motivated, no doubt, by the studio's sincere, heartfelt desire to make all the Trekkers in the world happy and, coincidentally, make a billion-trillion-zillion dollars which would, in turn, make Paramount happy too. Make that *incredibly* happy.

So we innocents, overjoyed to be back together again, eagerly went to work creating a whole new *Star Trek* series, and devising ways to make it not only worthy of the original but, we hoped, even better.

Working with Gene again was a joy. And, Ed Milkis, associate producer from the original show and now a highly successful television and movie producer, was there, too, as well as David Gerrold, who wrote the "Trouble with Tribbles" episode. It was like we all went home one night in 1969 and came back to work the following morning in 1986.

The first few weeks were creatively important to what we called "the new *Star Trek.*" (We didn't have a proper name for it yet.) There was much to do and it was important that we not fall into the trap of merely rehashing what we had done twenty years before. Gene encouraged us to submit new ideas to explore during the daily "creative lunches" he hosted in the studio commissary. It began with Gene, Eddie, David, and me, but, as we added staff members, others joined our daily "skull sessions." Dorothy Fontana, who had written for *The Original Series,* knew and understood *Star Trek* as well as any of us, and I convinced Gene to bring her aboard, too.

Excited by the possibilities inherent in a new series, I wrote some memos to Gene which laid out ideas that helped shape the new show's future path. One suggestion, however, drew a strong reaction. I had proposed having a Klingon as one of the ship's crew. But Gene vehemently resisted the idea of having any Klingons at all in the new show, saying, "We're past all that, Bob. You know I don't want to retread anything from before. We don't need Klingons. Period!"

I persisted, "Gene, think what it would mean to have a Klingon as part of our crew, as a friend instead of an enemy." And then he finally saw what I was driving at. It fitted right in with his belief that mankind can and will progress, that we can learn to accommodate other beings' needs as well as our own, and that they, too, can learn to coexist with us. So Worf, the Klingon, was born.

The task of assembling our "team" continued. One day, I noticed several artists' portfolios lying, unopened, in a jumble of unread correspondence on Gene's office couch. I leafed through both of them and, impressed by the evident talent displayed in these "spec" submissions, hired both Andy Probert and Rick Sternbach as our resident designers. Andy, on the new *Enterprise,* and Rick, on new props, made some of the most important and creative contributions to the look of the show and helped take some of the load from the shoulders of Herman Zimmerman, our wonderful art director.

Soon, I received yet another portfolio, from Michael Okuda, a young designer who lived in Honolulu. He wanted to help design for our show and volunteered to fly over and work for nothing. I hired him for what was to be a two-week assignment, designing both the graphics for the ship's modular displays and the lettering styles for our main title and technical credits. Other than an occasional vacation, Michael has never gone back to Hawaii. He even fell in love with a woman who became his wife, Denise, another designer, and he continues to work, as she does, on every *Star Trek* production.

Rick Berman, an executive at Paramount Television, was assigned to monitor the *Star Trek* project as the studio's representative. His intelligence, taste, and energy were clearly evident to Gene, as well as to me. It wasn't long before he became an integral part of our team and, from that time forward, Rick and I were joined at the hip as the show's producers. We were akin creatively, had the same work ethic and liked each other enormously. Since then, Rick has more than fulfilled his early promise, having created and produced *Star Trek: Deep Space Nine*, *Star Trek: Voyager*, and the last two (soon to be three) *Star Trek* movies. He has taken the mantle of leadership from Gene and both nurtures and maintains the *Star Trek* legacy. I'm proud to be his friend...

Whoa! Wait a second. I'm beginning to get serious. Let's have no more of that. That's not why I'm writing this piece. There's still more to reveal about what happened in the year before *ST: TNG* began its broadcast life.

I had pressed Gene to bring back *The Original Series'* costume designer, William Ware Theiss. Bill, seeming daunted by the task, dawdled for many weeks but eventually he came through, creating a whole new look for the people aboard the *Enterprise*. And Gene, ever inventive, inspired him to design a formal uniform for Captain Picard which consisted of a tunic and bias-cut skirt. To my great relief, Patrick Stewart carried it off with great panache.

And now, finally, Patrick Stewart.

One night in October 1986, shortly after I had begun preparing the new series, I attended a course on humor at U.C.L.A. with my wife, Jackie, and my son, Jonathan. Patrick, as guest star, was to "read" from Shakespeare comedies and Noël Coward plays. He began to emote and, within a few seconds, I was thunderstruck. I turned to Jackie and said, "I think I've found our new captain!"

I soon tracked Patrick down and the following week he met with Gene and me at Gene's home. We had a pleasant discussion for perhaps thirty minutes before Patrick had to leave to fly back to London. Gene watched him drive away, closed the door, turned to me, and said, "I won't have him!" When I remonstrated, all Gene would say was "He's not what I have in mind," and he refused any attempts at further discussion. Later, I theorized that, in his mind's eye, Gene had envisioned a "hairy Frenchman, not a bald Englishman."

When Rick Berman "came aboard," he became an avid member of the "Patrick Stewart for captain" support group. And, so did Junie Lowry, our casting director. The three of us campaigned for months to convince Gene that Patrick was the right one to command the *Enterprise*, but to no avail. However, Gene did go so far as to ask his female assistant if our candidate would be attractive to women.

Her response? "Patrick Stewart has no sex appeal."

So, Gene remained adamant. For weeks, we interviewed actor after actor for this most vital role and no one satisfied him, or us. Rick, Junie, and I still wanted to cast Patrick but the more we pushed, the more Gene dug his heels in. Finally, I announced, "That's it! It's over. Forget Patrick! I don't want to hear his name again! We have to find some other captain." And, every time anyone raised Patrick's name, I made the same speech.

But, secretly, I hadn't given up. I suspected that Gene's intransigence was fueled both by his original plan to have a dashing and romantic "French" captain and by feeling that I had backed him into a corner by campaigning so hard for Patrick. I thought he resented being pressured and I hoped that reverse psychology might work, that if I backed off, then Gene might come around after all.

And there was more than a hint of practicality involved, too. We had to cast the role and the start of production was drawing ever closer. The *Enterprise* needed a captain, and soon. Besides, while Rick was surprised by my "defection," I felt he wouldn't give up on Patrick. In fact, I counted on it. Luckily for Patrick and the show—and Gene—Rick never wavered. So, Patrick remained a possibility, a distant one to be sure, but still, a possibility. We continued to look for other "captains."

Meanwhile, we interviewed actors for all the other starring roles. Whoever we finally selected would have to be approved by Paramount's Network Television President, John S. Pike.

Brent Spiner and Eric Menyuk were the two finalists for the role of Data, the android. Brent's portrayal of a Pinocchio-like innocence won out but Rick and I were so taken with Eric that we later cast him as "The Traveller" in the episode "Where No One Has Gone Before," a role that he later reprised.

I asked Junie Lowry to bring in my friend LeVar Burton for the role of Geordi. It wasn't a shoo-in; he had to compete with all the other actors up for the part. He just outclassed them, so perhaps it was a shoo-in after all.

I also suggested Wil Wheaton, whom I had seen in the movie "Stand By Me." It was a unanimous "yes" decision. He had no real competition for the role of Wesley.

Gates McFadden was the first actress to "read" for the role of Dr. Beverly Crusher and she blew us all away. For many days thereafter, we interviewed other actresses on the theory that if the first one was so good, maybe there'd be someone even better. There wasn't.

The longest search, other than the one for captain, was for Worf, the Klingon. Gene wanted Worf to be played by a black actor. There were many candidates, but the role call for physical stature and a *basso profuno* voice, it required someone with perfect diction. Most of the actors we saw suffered from a lack of classical training and they didn't have the range or the flair necessary for such a bravura role. Michael Dorn had it all, in abundance.

We interviewed Denise Crosby for the role of the empathic Counselor Troi and Marina Sirtis for the role of feisty security chief Tasha Yar. It took about fourteen seconds for us to realize that the actresses should be switched, and so we had two more spots locked up.

There were two leading candidates for the role of Commander "Ryker." One, a tall, handsome actor, was marginally favored. We decided to submit him first for studio approval. The other contender was Jonathan Frakes.

Meanwhile, the Patrick Stewart campaign had heated up again due, no doubt, to Rick's persistence. After screening tapes of some Patrick Stewart performances that I previously had obtained, Gene still seemed unimpressed. But, a week later, he scheduled a private meeting in his office with Patrick. Could it be that, finally, he was wavering? (Not leaving anything to chance, I suggested to Patrick that, while he was there, it wouldn't hurt to "charm the pants off" Gene's assistant.) After the meeting concluded, Gene grudgingly admitted that Patrick might well be "an interesting choice." But that was all he said.

A few weeks later, after concluding a final interview with our last viable contender for the role of Picard, we sat there, silent and worried. Even though the actor was excellent and we would submit him for studio approval, we all still had misgivings. But, time was running out and we had exhausted all the other possibilities. Junie Lowry had scoured both the West and East coasts for us. We had even interviewed French actors in an attempt to satisfy Gene. No one really filled the bill for him or us, not even this last very talented performer. No one else had even come close—and it was only a few weeks until we would begin to film our opening two-hour episode, "Encounter at Farpoint."

Gene was lost in thought for a minute. Finally, he sighed, turned to Rick and me, and quietly said, "All right, I'll go with Patrick."

Rick and I were ecstatic; we had our captain—almost. Even though Gene now favored Patrick, the other actor was still in contention. Each one would have to pass muster with the Paramount brass. And Patrick was *bald*!

We decided to play it safe and asked Patrick to send for his toupée, which was still back in London.

On the day he was to meet and, hopefully, be approved by management, the toupée arrived. Patrick put it on. Suddenly, I felt ill. The rumpled hairpiece looked moth-eaten and it didn't fit; it seemed as if he were wearing someone else's hair. Gene came in, took one look and said, "Take it off, Patrick. You're better off being bald."

So Gene, Rick and I went up to present our little-known candidate for the starring role in a very expensive show with a very uncertain future. We needn't have worried; his interview was a piece of cake. Management preferred Patrick to the other actor—even without hair.

And, they were upbeat about all our other selections, except for the role of Riker. Our candidate froze up under the pressure. We asked John Pike to give him another chance. So, a few days later, the guy went back to meet and enchant management. He struck out again.

But, we had a great backup. Jonathan Frakes was now the leading contender for the role. He had to go in, alone, to be interviewed by John Pike and a clutch of studio vice-presidents. Would he wilt too? As Jonathan waited for the signal to enter Pike's office, I caught his eye and gave him a "thumbs up" signal. He grinned, strode confidently into the lion's den and came out a winner. So, we finally had our cast and the rest is history.

The faces before the cameras were different but, for me, the new show was just like the old one because it was still about what matters most to the human race: morality, tolerance, doing unto others—all those so-called Ten Commandments clichés.

Star Trek was "humanistic" and it remains so today in all its incarnations. By that, I don't mean that it's about our species but rather about a state of being which humankind, over the course of its history, has striven to attain. Surely our ideals of fairness and tolerance are not peculiar to this planet alone; such high-minded principles must necessarily develop within other species of intelligent life no matter where they exist in time and space, be it within our own galaxy or universe or even beyond those enormous confines, in other universes too difficult to reach or in yet other unknown dimensions too different to imagine.

And, in that unknown far-off somewhere, there must be others—people, beings, aliens, life-forms, heretofore unknown entities who believe even as you believe, who nurture their very own *Star Treks* and who encourage others like me to do the very best they can for you and all of the countless generations to come.

Thank you, my friends. Thank you everyone, for the past—and for the future, which is, with every new day that dawns, brighter than ever.

During that hectic first season of *Star Trek: The Next Generation*, I stole... I mean, I appropriated a line from C. S. Forester's Captain Horatio Hornblower novels for Patrick Stewart to speak at the end of "The Last Outpost."

One of the bridge crew affirmed that course and speed were locked in and asked his captain for permission to leave orbit. It was time for the *Enterprise* to head out into the unknown for the next great adventure where no one has gone before. Picard sat down, settled back in his command chair, clenched his jaw, and with his eyes (and shiny bald noggin) gleaming, looked forward out into space and responded, "Make it so."

Since what's good enough for Captains Horatio Hornblower, James Tiberius Kirk, and Jean-Luc Picard is good enough for me, I say to you and to Trekkers everywhere: "Live long and prosper" and "Make it so!"

Robert H. Justman
Los Angeles, California

ACKNOWLEDGMENTS

FOUR AND A half years ago, we paid our first "official" visit to the Paramount lot to begin work on what would become a series of four books and assorted articles about the behind-the-scenes production of *Star Trek,* past, present, and future. If there's a bottom line to what we've learned in that time, it's that even the people who make *Star Trek* today don't know exactly how or why it works. Certainly, different people understand different aspects of it, but no one claims to understand the sum of those parts.

We even wonder if Gene Roddenberry completely grasped the phenomenon he had set in motion, or if he just trusted to his instincts and followed his vision, gratified that so many shared it with him.

It wouldn't surprise us. If *Star Trek*'s appeal could be quantified, if it were something that could be written down in black and white, then it wouldn't be unique, would it? There would be a dozen different *Star Trek* clones on television, in theaters, in bookstores. For all that popular culture moves in waves, with networks and movie studios following trend after trend, we find it significant that after thirty years of trying, no one's created another *Star Trek.*

At some basic level, it seems, *Star Trek* can't be described, measured, or quantified, only experienced, and enjoyed: It's the journey itself that counts, not the destination. We feel fortunate to have been invited along for even a small part of that voyage, that continuing mission, and thank all those who made our time behind the scenes so educational, entertaining, challenging, and rewarding.

In terms of this book, more people helped than can be listed here. But the one name that must stand out from all the rest is Rick Berman's. Four and a half years ago, he took a chance, opened the doors for us, and never closed them. His guidance, support, and insights have made all our behind-the-scenes books possible, and we thank him.

Within the *Star Trek* team, we are once again indebted to Herman Zimmerman, who has not only contributed so significantly to the *Star Trek* universe, but who has worked to insure that the contributions of others are properly acknowledged.

For sharing their knowledge, time, and insights into *Star Trek: The Next Generation,* and graciously allowing us to interview them at length, we also thank Robert Blackman, Andre Bormanis, Brannon Braga, LeVar Burton, Dan Curry, Michael Dorn, John de Lancie, Jonathan Frakes, David Gerrold, Richard James, Robert Justman, Peter Lauritson, June Lowry-Johnson, Ron Moore, Denise and Michael Okuda, Andrew Probert, Marina Sirtis, Rick Sternbach, Ron Surma, and Michael Westmore. Both Michael Piller and Jeri Taylor were also invaluable resources for us, and we deeply appreciate their enthusiasm, and generosity of time.

As always, our many friends in the *Star Trek* art departments provided help and support that went beyond merely finding illustrations for this book.

In particular, we thank John Eaves for arranging access to so many fascinating illustrations from Industrial Light & Magic; Greg Jein for once again opening to us his personal photographic archives; and Penny Juday for her onsite photographic contributions of the *Enterprise*'s final hours, and the birth of the Ba'ku Village.

We would also be remiss if we did not thank Dave Rossi, Kristina Kochoff, and Maril Davis, who work with Rick Berman, and Lisa Olin and Ellen Hornstein who work with Jonathan Frakes, for keeping our lines of communication open.

At Pocket Books, words are not enough to describe the appreciation and respect we have for our editor, Margaret Clark. Her creativity, support, expert guidance, and patience are matched only by the superb art direction she has provided this book in helping select many of its illustrations and giving us the best cover we have had to date. Cover designer Joseph Perez and book designer, Richard Oriolo also have outdone themselves, and it is a pleasure to see our work so appealingly presented. Our thanks also go to our first editor, Kevin Ryan, who proposed this book to us five long years ago, and started us on our journey behind the scenes. Also at Pocket, we thank Gina Centrello, Kara Welsh, Donna O'Neill and Donna Ruvituso.

Once again, Paula Block at Viacom Consumer Products has used her expert knowledge to keep us on our toes. Her notes and guidance are always a pleasure to receive, often a challenge, and always make our books better. We appreciate her input and the care she brings to the entire *Star Trek* publishing line.

And finally, for every person we have mentioned, a dozen more gave us a moment of their time, found a file or a photograph for us, showed us a prop, let us read a script, told us a story, and added their musings and recollections to our notes and this book. To all the members of the *Star Trek* team we have met in these past years, on the lot and off, our deepest thanks and gratitude.

It's been a wonderful adventure. We can't wait to find out what happens next.

J&G Reeves-Stevens
Los Angeles
June 1997/August 1998

NOTES

1. Solow, Herbert F.; and Justman, Robert H. *Inside Star Trek.* New York: Pocket Books, 1996.
2. *Variety.* December 2, 1991.
3. *Los Angeles Times.* May 21, 1994.
4. *Entertainment Weekly* Special Star Trek Issue. January 18, 1995.
5. *Hollywood Reporter.* October 4-6, 1996.
6. Nimoy, Leonard. *I Am Spock.* New York: Hyperion, 1995.

"The sky's the limit ..."